# The Spotted Cat and Other Mysteries from Inspector Cockrill's Casebook

CRIPPEN & LANDRU

Lost Classics

# The Spotted Cat and Other Mysteries from Inspector Cockrill's Casebook

## Christianna Brand

### Edited and With an Introduction by Tony Medawar

*Crippen & Landru Publishers*
Norfolk, Virginia
2002

Cover artwork by Gail Cross

"Lost Classics" cover design by Deborah Miller

Crippen & Landru logo by Eric Greene

ISBN (cloth edition):  1-932009-00-0

ISBN (trade edition):  1-932009-01-9


FIRST EDITION


Crippen & Landru Publishers
P.O. Box 9315
Norfolk, VA 23505
USA

www.crippenlandru.com
CrippenL@pilot.infi.net

# Contents

# In and Out of Darkness

The writer best known as Christianna Brand[1] was born in 1907[2] in what was then the British protectorate of Malaya[3]. Among the many who came out to that country from Europe in the hope of making their fortune from rubber and cinchona were two brothers, Alec and Alan Irving. Achieving success quickly they asked their younger sister, Nancy, to join them and act as their housekeeper. She did and it was not long before she met the man she would later marry, Alexander Brand Milne. Some years earlier, Alec Milne and his brother Maitland had left Scotland for Ceylon where they created a flourishing business based on tea. After a time, the brothers had a disagreement and, while Maitland stayed on, Alec travelled to Malaya where, employed as a "visiting agent" by plantation owners to monitor and report on the conditions of their various estates, he met Nancy Irving and, in 1906, they were married — "he in the regulation white suit, complete with monocle, sans glass, which already he affected, and affected was the word; she in white also of course, surrounded by lots of fluffy clematis, very fair and pretty in a lacy dress with her tiny waist enclosed in a belt of Chinese silver."[4]

A year later, on 17 December, Mary Christianna Milne was born. However, there were complications and Nancy underwent a major operation. She was warned that to have another baby would be fatal but the warning was unheeded and, two years later, she died along with the son she was carrying. Nancy's family never forgave Alec Milne nor, it is plain, did Mary — "I didn't hate him or resent him; I simply could not stick the feller".[5] Mary's recorded memories of her early life are few and not always wholly consistent but it would appear that, after his wife died, Alec Milne took his daughter, then only two years of age, to England where he placed her in the care of Nancy's sister Daisy. Daisy already had five children of her own including Ted who would quickly become Mary's favourite among her cousins and who grew up to be Edward Ardizzone, the artist and illustrator.

Mary adored the Ardizzones but, within a few years, she was to return to the Far East with her father and away from her beloved 'family'. Alec Milne was by this time living in India and Mary, still a very young child, was placed in the care of a nanny — "a small, stiff corseted middle-aged woman with a fine greying moustache."[6] These were to be deeply unhappy days — "my bitter childhood"[7] — and Mary was overjoyed when, after a few years, her father informed her that she was to complete her education in

England. Her "blissfully happy"[8] school years were spent at a Franciscan Convent at Taunton, Somerset, which "taught her very little but, with love and compassion, mended her flickering spirit"[9] and she always remembered the nuns and the convent with great affection.[10] Holidays were spent, together with her cousins, at the home of their grandmother in St. Margaret's Bay in Kent — "[Mary] was wonderfully pretty — really lovely to look at — strangely fragile–looking with her very pale skin and fair hair. She was always bursting with energy and vivacity and full of eagerness and enthusiasm ... her sense of fun was infectious. In her company there was always laughter. She charmed everyone. *Particularly* every boy in sight."[11]

Mary could not have been happier, with only the occasional letter from her father, once or twice a year, to remind her of that earlier life she had left behind. However, at seventeen she learned that her father had not been meeting the cost of her education for some time and that he was penniless. Mary therefore left the convent and moved to London where, known by her friends as 'Quif,' she drifted from one job to another — "I can remember how poor I was when I started work. I can remember it taking weeks to save up ... for a hot water bottle. And ever since then my dream of luxury has been a bathroom with a fire and a fitted carpet."[12] One of her earliest jobs, in the late 1920s, was working as nursery governess to the children of Sir Walter Peacock, who himself worked for the heir to the throne, HRH Prince of Wales, later to be Edward VIII. One evening the Prince was to dine privately with Sir Walter and Lady Peacock but he was obliged to withdraw at the last minute. In later years Brand would muse on how the events of the 1930s, in particular the abdication crisis of 1936, might have differed if the future King *had* attended that private dinner and if he had met the enchanting, young governess ...

After she left the Peacocks, Mary became a dance hostess — she was, by all accounts a marvellous dancer — and this doubtless provided the inspiration for what would appear to be her earliest published short story, a light romantic tale entitled, "Dance Hostess"[13] and a number of other stories in similar vein generally featuring a "twist" ending of one kind or another and whose publication details, if any, have in some cases yet to be established. By 1930, Mary was running a club for young girls in the East End of London. Nonetheless, it was her dancing skills that led to her being invited to a party in the West End of London at which she met a young doctor, Roland Swain Lewis, the man she would eventually many. Mary made a huge impression on Lewis and, a few days later, he rang to invite her to join him at a rugby club dinner at the Dorchester Hotel. While, disappointingly, Mary had not the slightest recollection of their previous meeting she readily accepted his invitation as the opportunity to dance at the Dorchester was too good to miss. Their love blossomed and they met regularly on Wednesday evenings and also on Saturdays, when Mary would come to watch Roland play rugby. They married in 1936 and moved into a rented flat in Edgware Road, London, before moving to Portsmouth in 1938 where Roland had secured a job as a specialist in ear, nose and throat surgery.

In 1939, the Second World War broke out and Roland joined the Royal Army Medical Corps, serving as a Major. Within a few months they moved to Blackheath in south London where Roland worked in a military hospital before being posted to Egypt and later the Sudan; he and Mary were to be apart for two and a half years. Mary stayed in London and she soon took up the job that was to change her life.

> "She finished up in a shop, selling large and expensive cookers, and the pots and pans to go with them; and, stupid as ever, she sold far more pots and pans than she did cookers and as she was there to sell the cookers, she naturally was not a great success and she was greatly bullied by a young woman overseer called Agnes Smith. So great was her fear and detestation of this female that murderous thoughts arose in her heart and she finally said to her fellow sellers of cookers and pots and pans 'I could murder her! But as I must not, I shall write a book and murder her in that.'"[14]

Which is precisely what she did, setting the murder not in a showroom selling Aga cookers but in a couturiers where the crime was investigated by a handsome young Scotland Yard detective, Inspector Charlesworth. Much to Mary's amazement and, after being rejected by several firms, the book — *Death in High Heels* — was eventually accepted and published in 1941. Mary was ecstatic — "I began to feel like a millionaire. Probably nothing is a lot more thrilling than to see your first book displayed in a shop, or to see someone reading it in a train or on a bus."[15]   With a realistic and well–defined setting and a clever if fairly linear plot, the book was, to quote Robert Barnard, "a notable debut"[16] though, as Barnard pointed out in a perceptive commentary on her work, the book is not without its flaws: the murder comes too early and the victim is too vaguely defined to arouse much sympathy — this is in direct contrast to the majority of her novels where victims and criminals alike are fully realised and never wholly undeserving of sympathy and understanding.

Some months after publication of *Death in High Heels*, Roland Lewis returned to England and became a consultant ear, nose and throat surgeon at King's Hospital, London. Mary settled down in earnest with the intention of writing for the rest of her life "and bashed away on a huge old typewriter."[17] As well as working on another novel, she extended her range by writing fourth leaders for *The Times*[18] and was employed as a reader by several publishers, producing fair but sharply focused commentaries and editorial advice on dozens of books.[19]   However, London remained under

siege and Brand was frequently forced down into the nearby air–raid
shelters. On one such occasion, the bombing was severe.

> "As I watched, a stretcher was carried carefully down across a pile of crazy
> rubbish, rafters bricks, furniture, the height of a house — and indeed it had
> once been two houses — and laid down on the road. I realise now that, as
> nobody went near it, or attended to the white figure on it, the body must have
> been that of a corpse; it looked ominously short and stumpy. Terrible things
> happen in an explosion."[20]

Miraculously, their home was largely unscathed though "the front door
hung crazily on its hinges; all the windows were black, gaping holes, with
jagged glass around the edges. The rooms were strewn with broken glass,
and most of the furniture was over–turned ... The worst thing is this damn
rocking. The whole earth seems to be shuddering beneath one, heaving
horribly. After all, it's three days now since it happened and I haven't heard
a bomb drop since; but the chair I'm sitting in is doing it as I write."[21]

Mary's second novel escaped damage in the raid.[22] Unlike her first
novel, *Heads You Lose*[23] was accepted for publication on both sides of the
Atlantic, winning the $1,000 Red Badge prize[24] offered by the US publisher,
Dodd, Mead & Co. for the best mystery of the year. The novel came with a
warning attached to a prefatory cast of characters that "among these ten
very ordinary people were found two victims and a murderer."[25] The
detective on this occasion was not Charlesworth, perhaps because of its rural
setting in the village of Pigeonsford in Kent, but a local policeman, Inspector
Cockrill,[26] known to one and all as "Cockie."[27]

> "A little brown man who seemed much older than he actually was, with
> deep–set eyes beneath a fine, broad brow, an aquiline nose and a mop of fluffy
> white hair[28] fringing a magnificent head."

Cockrill, in appearance at least, was based on Brand's father-in-law,
William Lewis, who like his son, was a doctor and had died shortly after
Mary and Roland's wedding in 1936. The book was a huge success with its
blend of comedy and genuine if gruesome thrills[29] — the murderer's victims
are decapitated; and Brand therefore decided to produce a further case for
Cockrill and, for a while, abandon Charlesworth.[30]

Like *Heads You Lose*, this third book — *Green for Danger* — would have
a contemporary setting though the wartime background would not be
incidental, as in *Heads You Lose*, but integral to the plot in which a
sensational murder is committed during an air raid. When the film rights
were sold for £500 just after the war it was for Mary "the greatest thrill of
all time ... London was plastered with huge posters showing a girl under a

green light, lying dead — no title. Except just the name 'Green For Danger.' Everyone was asking what it was, what it could be — a film, a book, some forthcoming event? It was all very cleverly done and can you imagine what I felt looking up at those boards and thinking 'But I know!' "[31]

On the proceeds and despite Roland's protestations, Mary bought a house in 1944. A late Georgian, three-storey house in Maida Vale in very bad repair — "five layers of olive green paint in the lounge, that fanlight all plastered up and a chocolate brown hallway"[32] with a large garden, dominated by a large and beautiful mulberry tree. Mary and her husband were to live there for the rest of their lives, although in later years they spent much of the time at their second home, a cottage in Wales not far from where Roland had been raised.

Her next book, *The Crooked Wreath*,[33] features impossible crimes and is set in 1944 in Kent, in the village of Swanswater two miles out from the Heronsford of *Green for Danger*. Between the book's completion and its publication Mary also produced, at the behest of the Ministry of Health, a "cautionary" novel with a contemporary setting and — daring for its day — dealing with the dangers of syphilis.[34] This novel, *The Single Pilgrim*,[35] was set in part, in Heronsford and, like *The Crooked Wreath*, was published in 1946. It was well received but, while she was already writing on a wide range of subjects and in various genres, Mary's childhood ambition had always been to write detective fiction — "as a girl I became fascinated by the detective story with it's enormous ingenuity and curious element of honesty — its obligation to tell the truth, the whole truth and nothing but the truth, even while it concealed from the reader the significance of that truth."[36]

It was therefore a cause for considerable celebration when, later in 1946, Mary was accorded what for her must have seemed the ultimate accolade, election to the celebrated Detection Club.[37] This mildly eccentric 'dining' club, which still exists, had been created in 1929 by the somewhat less than mildly eccentric Anthony Berkeley who also lived in Maida Vale in the late 1940s and '50s.[38]

> "We used to meet once a month in our funny little club room and then all go off to a restaurant ... everyone was friendly and easy round that dinner table; the members of the Detection Club. There was certainly no jealousy or cattiness or anything but loyalty and helpfulness; and there was no 'showing off.' None of us would have been there if our work hadn't been thoroughly respected by the rest who, after all, had elected us into their midst."[39]

Cockrill featured in Mary's next novel, *Death of Jezebel*, but she decided also to revive Inspector Charlesworth,[40] the detective in her first mystery, *Death in High Heels*. While attending a conference in London, Cockie and Charlesworth solve an impossible crime and a second gruesome murder committed during a pageant staged as part of an "Ideal Homes" Exhibition.

In 1947 Mary wrote a detailed scenario for a film, *Where Is Christine?* which she described as "a modern ghost story because there are, of course, no 'conventional' hauntings in it, no headless bodies and rattling chains and all the rest of it ... the whole is designed to have an air of lightness and charm; only gradually as it moves forward, growing more tense and uneasy and at last more frightening as the unreal world fastens its grip upon the world of reality."[41] While this proposal was not taken up, Mary was however invited to work on *The Mark of Cain*, a film whose plot was to be based on the celebrated Maybrick case. Hired on the basis that she was a 'specialist in Victorian crime', Mary was astonished to learn that she was required to set the plot in the present day. If the concept was bad, the pay was good and she also worked, more or less happily, on several other scripts including *The Secret People* (1951), directed by Lindsay Anderson, before deciding that she had had enough of the vicissitudes and unpredictable behaviour of directors and the film world generally — "Nothing in the world is worse than working on films."[42]

As Mary was unable to have a child of her own, she and Roland adopted a daughter, known as Tora, in 1949. Her next book was *Cat and Mouse*, which she described as "a good old–fashioned melodrama."[43] Despite that description this novel did feature a detective, Inspector Chucky, who also appeared in *A Ring of Roses*, published some years later.

But Cockrill had not been discarded and he returned in her next novel. Although he had not enjoyed the experience of working there in *Death of Jezebel*, this next case found him returning to London, once again to work with "that maddening young, cock–a–hoop chap,"[44] Inspector Charlesworth. Initially, Mary planned to call this new book *Kensington Gore*:

> "Kensington Gore is a street in London and I wrote the whole thing round it, placing the book, naturally in Kensington. Then I discovered that someone else had just done a book with the same title so I had to unravel it all and place it in Maida Vale, and the new title *London Particular*, was one I came to love. A 'London Particular' was a London fog. We don't get them now, not the real fogs, the London Particulars; we're obliged to use only smokeless fuels and it does keep the air a lot more clean. But in those days it really was true that you 'couldn't see your hand before your face'."[45]

*Fog of Doubt*, as the book was titled in America, is not merely set in Maida Vale, where she and Roland lived, it is set in her own home. It is probably Brand's cleverest novel with a beautifully concealed clue that, in the best tradition, is in front of the reader all the time. In her next book, *Tour de Force* it is the turn of Mr. Cecil, the homosexual dress designer from *Death in High Heels*, to make a re–appearance. In what would prove to be the last of Cockrill's novel–length cases to be published, Cockrill solves a murder that takes place on the entirely fictitious island of San Juan El Pirata "some twenty kilometres off the coast of Tuscany" which, if only geographically, is based on Elba. Mary's next novel, *The Three–Cornered Halo*, was also set on San Juan El Pirata and again featured Mr. Cecil and Cockrill's sister, Cousin Hat.

By the late 1950s then, 'Christianna Brand' was at the height of her powers, writing for all sorts of markets and recognised as a leading name in the crime and detective genre. That she suddenly and apparently without any clear reason to do so abandoned writing novels must therefore have come as a terrible disappointment to her readers. It was a decision that circumstances had quite simply forced her to take and one to which she never managed to reconcile herself — "For twenty long years I gave it all up — and it is not hard to imagine the depression and frustration — never mind the financial loss of doing that."[46]   A period romantic mystery, *Starrbelow*, was published in 1959 under the pseudonym 'China Thompson' but, thereafter, Mary did not have another serious novel published until the late 1960s. She did not — indeed, could not — abandon writing altogether. An excellent study of the Victorian murder of Jesse M'lachlan, *Heaven Knows Who*, was published in 1960, a slew of novellas[47] and many short stories, the vast majority of which appeared in *Ellery Queen's Mystery Magazine* then — as now — the pre–eminent magazine for readers of crime and mystery stories. Others appeared in a range of magazines and included a very popular series of "real life" stories for women.[48] But at around this time she was to become famous in a different literary genre, as a writer of a series of comic stories for children featuring the extraordinary Nurse Matilda and based on stories Mary and her cousins had been told as children. In the 1970s she began writing novels, including three mysteries[49] none of which featured Cockrill, and she was much in demand as a speaker, combining sparkling humour with a wealth of anecdotes — sometimes sharp but always amusing — about her own experiences as a writer and those of her contemporaries. But her health became poor and, after a long and painful illness, she died on 11 March 1988.

Fifteen years later, Christianna Brand is, alas, almost forgotten. Few of her books are in print and, if Inspector Cockrill is remembered at all, it is as he was portrayed by Alastair Sim in *Green for Danger*, the film of Brand's best known novel. Yet, strong though that portrayal is, it is not as the author envisaged her detective. And, good though that novel is, it is only one of a series of stories — long and short — in which Cockrill appears and which, together have established him as one of the best loved "official" detectives in the whole of the crime and mystery genre.

This volume is therefore long overdue. It brings together for the first time all of the complete shorter fiction in which Cockrill appears, including two previously unpublished items: a short short story, "Alleybi;" and "The Spotted Cat," a play for the stage. There is also the commentary on Cockrill that Mary produced in response to a request from Otto Penzler and, finally, a checklist of Cockie's cases. This introductory note was put together with the help of the late Roland Lewis and special thanks are also due to Geoff Bradley, John Curran, Harry Keating and Ken Mars Sekiguchi, former editor of the Japanese edition of *Ellery Queen's Mystery Magazine* and most of all to Doug and Sandi Greene for the continuing miracle that is Crippen and Landru.

It is very much hoped that the collection will bring pleasure to Cockrill's many old friends and also that it might encourage those who have not previously encountered him to track down some his novel–length investigations or the other, less well-known work of his creator. The warm and wonderful Christianna Brand has been in the darkness too long; it is time once again for her to come out into the light.

Tony Medawar
Wimbledon, 2002


1. Brand wrote novels under four other pseudonyms. *The Single Pilgrim* (1946) as by 'Mary Roland' is described elsewhere in this preface. *Starrbelow* (1958), a romantic novel, was published as by 'China Thompson' and another romantic novel, *The Radiant Dove* (1974), appeared as by 'Annabel Jones.' Finally, Brand used the pseudonym 'Mary Ann Ashe' for *Alas For Her That Met Me!* (1976), a novel inspired by the life of Madelaine Smith who was tried for the murder of her lover in 1857 which had been serialised weekly in *Woman's Realm* between 3 April and 15 May 1976.

2. Not 1909 as stated in some obituaries.

3. Malaya provides the setting for "Hibiscus Blooms Again," an uncollected novella combining romance and mystery, and "Instinct," an unpublished short story in which the influence of the writings of Somerset Maugham, and Brand's dislike for her father, are evident.

4. Quoted from unpublished notes made by Brand at a time when she was thinking of writing her autobiography.

5. *Ibid.*

6. *Ibid.*

7. *Ibid.*

8. "May I Introduce Myself," *Ellery Queen's Mystery Magazine* (Japanese edition), March 1983.

9. "Autobiography," included in *Cat and Mouse* (International Polygonics Ltd, 1985).

10. Brand drew on her experiences for an unpublished short story, "The Little Nun," in which a novitiate discovers that she has lost her faith, and also for *Cat Among the Pigeons*, an unfinished, unpublished and exceedingly complicated detective mystery set largely in a convent.

11. Quoted from the eulogy delivered by one of Mary's cousins at her funeral in 1988.

12. "Murder in the Showroom," *Evening News*, 16 September 1955.

13. *The Star*, 8 April 1939. This appeared as by 'Mary Brand,' as did two other early short stories, "The Rose" and "Gloria Walked Down Bond Street," which were also published in 1939 in the celebrated London society magazine, *The Tatler* on 18 October and 15 November respectively.

14. "May I Introduce Myself," *Ellery Queen's Mystery Magazine* (Japanese edition), March 1983.

15. *Ibid.*

16. "The Slightly Mad, Mad World of Christianna Brand" *The Armchair Detective*, Vol. 19, No. 3.

17. "May I Introduce Myself," *Ellery Queen's Mystery Magazine* (Japanese edition), March 1983.

18. For example, "Ball or Skein?", *The Times*, 16 February 1944.

19. As examples, she described Leo Bruce's *Case With Four Clowns* as "not the best detective story I have ever read but it is way ahead of most of what I read: original, very well written for style and atmosphere, good in fact very good characterisation ..." while Carol Carnac's *Double for Detection* was damned as "utter rubbish."

20. Unpublished record of the air raid, revised and published as "Spring, 1941" in *Brand X* (London; Michael Joseph. 1974).

21. *Ibid.*

22. In "Spring, 1941" she records that the typescript was destroyed but this is explicitly contradicted in the original version.

23. Her original title was *Dead in a Ditch*.

24. In the words of her British literary agent, "The prize isn't quite as magnificent as we had hoped. The thousand dollars is not an outright award but an advance against royalties." However, as her American agent emphasised, it was never–theless "a really extraordinary advance for a first mystery [sic]." The novel was serialised in *The Saturday Evening Post*, 3 January to 14 February 1942.

25. A 'note' of this kind is featured in almost all of her detective novels.

26. Cockrill later becomes a Chief Inspector and has made the rank of Chief Superintendent by the time of the events described in the unpublished and incomplete short story, "Death on The Day."

27. In common with a number of fictional sleuths, including all of the other policemen created by Christianna Brand, Cockrill's first name is never disclosed. Cockrill's father, also a police inspector and "a small, elderly policeman in plain clothes, distressingly wrinkled and untidy, but with an alert bright eye," was to have been the investigator in "This Credulous Woman," a television play based on the Brides in the Bath murders, which brand mapped out but did not write.

28. In some stories his hair is grey, a fact remarked on by Brand in her profile of Cockrill, included in this volume.

29. Despite the grue, Mary planned to turn the novel into a three act play for the stage but abandoned the idea, perhaps because it would have been difficult to adapt the novel's dramatic ending to meet the requirements of the stage.

30. Charlesworth appeared in the first draft of "Shadowed Sunlight," then entitled "Death Us Do Part," but was replaced by Detective Inspector Dickinson. This novella was serialised in the British magazine *Woman* between 7 July and 11 August 1945.

31. "May I Introduce Myself," *Ellery Queen's Mystery Magazine* (Japanese edition), March 1983.

32. "Murder in the Showroom," *Evening News*, 16 September 1955.

33. Owen B. Howell adapted the novel for the stage but Brand heavily revised his script to produce a final version credited to both writers. However, it does not appear to have been performed.

34. A new edition of *The Single Pilgrim* might be timely since the number of new cases of syphilis in the United Kingdom doubled between 1995 and 2000 and current levels are the highest since immediately after the Second World War.

35. The novel was published as by 'Mary Roland.' Brand's motherless childhood in India, the governess she loathed, her inadequate father, formative years at the "beloved" convent and early career — particularly her experiences as a dance hostess — provide the novel's opening and the background of Stephanie Thorne, its brittle and naive heroine.

36. "The Author Who Has Most Influenced Me." This essay was probably commissioned by the Famous Writers School, for which Mary worked in the 1960s. In it Mary identified Jane Austen who "in her *Emma* produced as ingenious a mystery story as ever was written" and she also paid tribute to Agatha Christie — "the Queen of plot." In "The Detective Story Form," published in *Press & Freelance Writer & Photographer*, August 1950, Mary commented that "A detective story needs at least one central pin, a new or odd motive or method, or some psychological quirk; not just a jumble of clues for the detective to unravel, eliminating suspects as he goes ... starting a detective story is like embarking up on a piece of lace with only the pins to give you the barest outline of what your work is to be. My own laborious method is to work and unpick, work and unpick, and rewind my threads as my pattern develops and changes. As a general rule the outline will be diamond–shaped, or rather kite–shaped — broadening out to about two–thirds of the book when the story is fully developed. After this point there will be no further progress of plot. Only a juggling with what has now been told, and of course such incident as results from what has gone before."

37. No record has been found of the names of her proposer and seconder.

38. Her detailed memories of the Club's early years, albeit at times a little waspish and immodest, were set out in the introduction to a reprint of *The Floating Admiral* (Boston: Gregg Press, 1979) and in *Ellery Queen's Mystery Magazine* (Japanese Edition), May and July 1983.

39. "Famous Writers I've known in the Long–Ago Past," *Ellery Queen's Mystery Magazine* (Japanese edition), July 1983.

40. Charlesworth also appears in the short, short story "Alleybi" and in Brand's final novel, *The Rose in Darkness*. *Death in High Heels* was filmed in 1947 and Brand's visit to the set was probably the inspiration for "The Dead Hold Fast," an unpublished novella in which Charlesworth investigates the death of a camera–man.

41. Elements of film treatment for *Where Is Christine?* appear in the final novel to be published in Mary's lifetime, *The Brides of Aberdar*. She wrote a number of other mysteries in which the supernatural is more or less apparent, including "The Murder Man," "Murder by Dog," "NOFACE," "Inquest," "The Mermaid." Publication details for these stories, if any, have yet to be established but a novella with supernatural overtones, "The Witch," was published in *Woman's Journal*, August 1962.

42. "May I Introduce Myself," *Ellery Queen's Mystery Magazine* (Japanese edition), March 1983.

43. Quoted from the jacket of *Cat and Mouse* (London: Michael Joseph, 1950).

44. Quoted from Chapter 6 of *London Particular*.

45. Introduction to *Fog of Doubt* (Boston: Gregg Press, 1979).

46. "May I Introduce Myself," *Ellery Queen's Mystery Magazine* (Japanese edition), March 1983, in which Brand gave more details.

47. They included three "Bank Holiday" newspaper serials. Two were serialised in five parts in *The Daily Sketch* in August 1958 and August 1959 respectively: "Cyanide in the Sun," which features a ruthless mass–murderer and an ingenious means of dispensing poison; and "Bank Holiday Murder," which was initially entitled "A Shot in the Sun." Publication details of the third, "The Rum Punch," have yet to be established. The serials are set in a seaside resort, Scampton–on–Sea, and feature Inspector Port and Sergeant Troot who, as a Constable, assists Cockrill to solve murders in *Heads You Lose*.

48. The following stories all appeared in the British magazine *Woman's Realm*: "Mother," 17 January 1959; "Grandad," 24 October 1959; "The Right Man for Tilly," 12 May 1960; "Someone to Love," 1 October 1960; "To Remember With Tears," 3 March 1962; and "White Wedding," 19 May 1962.

49. *A Ring of Roses* (1977), published as by 'Mary Ann Ashe' had been adapted from a short story of the same name which was published, as by Christianna Brand, in *The Daily Sketch*, 21 and 22 October 1969; *The Honey Harlot* (1978), set in the late nineteenth century and based on the curious circumstances surrounding the barque *Mary Celeste* which had been discovered in 1872 drifting 500 miles off Gibraltar, without any trace of her crew; and *The Rose in Darkness* (1979), in which Charlesworth made his final appearance.

# Inspector Cockrill

Two thousand words, he says — "or thereabouts." Am I, then, to squeeze this important biography into a mere two thousand words? Is Inspector Cockrill, with all my devotion to him, to be crammed hugger-mugger into so narrow a pint pot?

Well — none better, you may think; for Cockie, it must be admitted, is a little man — unique in being several inches below the minimum height for a British policeman. He came into being in the fine, free, careless days before I became hagridden by the necessity for accuracy in detail. At intervals during his literary career, I have tried to add a bit to his stature, he "looks shorter than he actually is," and so on; but for the most part we find him described as a sparrow, a small, dusty brown sparrow — "soon he was, sparrow-like, hopping and darting this way and that in search of crumbs of information." "What a funny little man!" thinks Louli, in *Tour de Force*, and "A little man, he is," says one of the twins in a short story, "Blood Brothers." He adds, I'm sorry to say: "And near retiring age, he must be. He looks like a grandfather."

For not only is Inspector Cockrill too short to have been in the force; he does also seem to be a bit too old.

True, in *Fog of Doubt* (British title: *London Particular*), his hair is said to be gray, but, were it not so entirely out of character, we might here suspect him of having taken a leaf out of M. Poirot's book. For elsewhere, it is indubitably white: "a little brown man with bright brown, bird-like eyes deep-set beneath a fine broad brow, with an aquiline nose and a mop of fluffy white hair fringing a magnificent head." "Fringing" does not even suggest a touch of baldness but this, I swear, is no more than a thinness on top. He is old enough, at any rate, to be wondering rather anxiously whether he may not be in danger of becoming a dirty old man — dearly loving, as he does, a pretty girl. Nothing could be further from the truth — Venetia and Fran, the loving and confiding sisters, sad, gentle Esther Sanson, enchanting Louli, so comic and so vulnerable, even the bouncy little sexpot Rosie — they were all safe enough with him; and when the dreadful Grace Morland sets her cap at him, "though half-heartedly, for he was not to be considered her equal in education or birth," he thinks of her without rancor merely as a sentimental goat. I mention it only to suggest that he *is* old enough to be already a little in dread of the approach to senility. There is even a terrible moment in *Tour de Force* when the local police chief of the

19

island of San Juan el Pirata refuses to believe he can be in the British police. The tourist guide is forced into apprehensive explanation: "Inspector, he says — he says that you are too old."

"*Too old?*" said Cockie in a voice of doom.

If he is elderly, however, the inspector has made up for it by remaining, like the matinee idols of his youth, at the same age for something like thirty years. Any further comparison would hardly stand up; one could by no means describe his attire as the pink of sartorial perfection. He has a habit of picking up the first hat to hand; "Well, never mind — it's quite a good fit," he will say. Any hat that does not deafen and blind him is quite a good fit to Inspector Cockrill. " 'I must have picked up my sergeant's by mistake,' he said, irritably, pushing the enormous hat up from over his eyes for the fifth time. 'I'm always doing it.' He seemed perfectly indifferent to anything but the discomfort involved by this accident." The hat will be crammed sideways on to his head as though he might at any moment break out into an amateur rendering of Napoleon's Farewell to his Troops. True, on his one visit abroad — Cockie simply hates Abroad! — he does acquire a rather splendid straw, but "contrary to custom, he had bought it, not two sizes too large for him, but considerably too small, and it sat on his splendid head like a paper boat, breasting the fine spray of his greying hair." He wears a rather rumpled gray suit and, far ahead of his time, a disreputable old mac trailing over his shoulder. He smokes incessantly, rolling his own shaggy cigarettes, holding them cupped in the palm of his right hand so that the fingers are so stained with nicotine as to appear to be tipped with mahogany.

But by no means suppose my hero to be a figure of fun. "I hadn't counted on its being Inspector Cockrill," says the young villain in "Blood Brothers," "and to be honest it struck a bit of a chill to the heart of me. His eyes are as bright as a bird's and they seem to look right down into you ..."

He came into being when, having set my first book in London, I wanted a country background — which necessitated a detective from the local force. He is attached, therefore, to the Kent County Police: a tricky job for his author, getting him to London when a crime must be set there — he is obliged to interfere only in an unofficial character, as personal friend of one or another of the suspects. As he disapproves strongly of the innocently brash young Chief Inspector Charlesworth of New Scotland Yard, it makes for some difficulty all round, not to say an occasional unseemly touch of triumph. "*Et, avec un clin d'oeil satisfait, l'Inspecteur Cockrill s'en alla, clopin-clopant dans la nuit,*" says the French translation, rounding off *Death of Jezebel*; and *clopin-clopant* does seem to just about sum it up.

But at home in Heronsford, matters are very different. "Cockie was sitting with his feet up on the mantelpiece — which fortunately was a low one or his short legs would have been practically vertical and his behind in the fire," musing on the horrors of eventual retirement. He'll have to buy a couple of disguises, that's all, and set up as a private detective, to stave off the boredom. But it had better be elsewhere. "Here in Heronsford, no such attempt would be of the smallest use; no density of beard or whisker could long conceal *him* from the sheep, black and white, among whom he had moved, the Terror of Kent, for so long ..."

And indeed he can be pretty fierce. "He was widely advertised as having a heart of gold beneath his irascible exterior but there were those who said bitterly that the heart was so infinitesimal and you had to dig so far down to get at it, that it was hardly worth the effort." Long ago, his wife had died, as had their only child; and with them had died also "all his hope and much of his faith and charity." The heart is there, nevertheless, however deeply buried. He can be very tender and kind, very understanding with all those pretty girls caught up, innocent, in the ugly toils of murder; with the enchanting old grandmother in her room on the top floor of the house in Maida Vale, enlivening her boredom by pretending to be a good deal more dotty than she actually is. And he will have compassion for the guilty, drawn by inner compulsions to the committing of a single crime. On the other hand, he can be forthright and stern. "He thought it unwise and unhealthy that, because she had died for her sins, she should be allowed to grow into a martyr in the family's eyes. He thought they should face the facts. 'She made up her mind to do this thing and she worked it all out thoroughly, and acted quickly and cleverly ...'" There is no false sentiment about Chief Inspector Cockrill, none at all.

The secret of his success? — which, strange to say, is unfailing — well, I wonder. He is not a great one for the physical details of an investigation: "meanwhile his henchmen pursued their ceaseless activities" writes his creator, not too sure herself exactly what those would be; and he is content to leave fingerprint powder and magnifying glass to the experts, using their findings in a process of elimination, to get down to the nitty-gritty from there on. He has acute powers of observation, certainly; a considerable understanding of human nature, a total integrity and commitment, much wisdom; and as we know a perhaps overlong experience of the criminal world. ("And buns in the oven is the net result," says naughty little Rosie, confessing, in *Fog of Doubt* [British title: *London Particular*] to conduct unbecoming a young maiden, on a recent visit to the continent. She adds that now she supposes he will be shocked. "My *dear* child," says Cockie, "you should come to the Heronsford police court some time!")

Above all — he has patience.

And spell it another way, and you have this biography, not only in a pint pot, but reduced right down to a nutshell. For Detective Chief Inspector Cockrill is the dead spittin' image of my father-in-law; and my father-in-law was for over fifty years a medical practitioner in a Welsh mining town about the same size as Heronsford.

Above all, therefore — Cockie's progenitor had patients. And what does a doctor bring to the study of his patients, but those very qualities that we claim for the chief inspector? Observation, understanding, the ability to cleave through the irrelevant to the right and only diagnosis; a keen appreciation of cause and effect, an ever-increasing experience; integrity, wisdom ...

Shrewd and wise he was, my father-in-law, and so is Inspector Cockrill shrewd and wise. Like a good doctor, he inquires into every detail. A young man confesses to the murder of a girl. He has laid upon her breast a brooch in the form of a cross, "to show I was sorry, like."

"You're telling lies," says Cockrill. "The brooch was lying there crooked, with the pin upwards. That doesn't sound much like reverence, does it?" But later, someone discloses that, finding the body, he has picked up the brooch and just dropped it back again. When he had first seen it, it had been the right way up. "I thought it could have been placed there — well, because it was a cross." He added: "Is it important?"

"It depends on what you call important," says Cockie in his acerbic way. "It's going to hang a man."

But in fact he was wrong that time; and often he *is* wrong — till the last hour. He is by no means cocksure — surely the greatest weakness in detective or doctor alike? In *Green for Danger*, out of his depth in the world of anesthetics and operating theaters, he has some bad moments. "Cockrill could not bear to look. His mind, usually so keen and clear, was a dark confusion of terror and self-questioning and a hideous anxiety. He had made an experiment, thinking it all so safe: had taken a terrible gamble with a man's life and suddenly everything was going wrong?" He wipes his damp hands down the sides of the theater gown, fighting off a black panic.

He is sufficiently sure, however, to work without the somewhat inevitable sergeant, a uniformed Dr. Watson to whom he can confide, as he goes along, the workings of his mind — that is, perhaps, why we know so comparatively little of them, until at the end he makes them clear. No doubt some splendid, reliable chap will be at his beck and call in the regular way, to take instructions and see things carried out; but no complacent underling sits at Inspector Cockrill's side, interrupting interrogations with chirpy questions of his own. (I once asked a way-up policeman if a sergeant would really act like this when his superior was present. He replied in a deep voice: "*Not* if he ever hoped for promotion.")

With Mr. Charlesworth, when he becomes involved in cases where that young gentleman is in charge, the inspector maintains an armed neutrality. "Oh, yes!" Charlesworth remarked in his guileless way on their first introduction, "You're the chap that made such a muck of that hospital case down in Kent?" Infiltrating into his cases on behalf of his friends (always with the most generous welcome — Cockie is scrupulous in sharing information and deduction, only very, very slightly obscuring this little point or that — if the silly young fool can't take a hint, too bad!) he pursues his own somewhat Machiavellian way. And Charlesworth is a little inclined to Kindly Pity. He can hardly keep back a grin as he listens to the inspector's great build-up of a highly elaborate case — against the wrong suspect — at the end of the Jezebel affair. A bit past it, poor old boy — these dear old duffers are all the same! Cockie observes the grin and his blood boils; but — *"You're* a clever little man," says the real murderer, inveigled by the fantasy into confession at last.    And with a single look into Mr. Charlesworth's face, off goes the inspector, *clopin-clopant* into the night.

My father-in-law was a small man, white haired already when I knew him.  An old mac trailed over his shoulder as he stumped off on his short legs into the veil of fine rain that hangs incessantly over the valleys of South Wales; visiting twenty or thirty patients in a day, he had a rich choice of hats. But nobody thought of *him* as a figure of fun! His mind was keen, his glance was bright with a sort of mischievous glee. His surgery was an old converted stable; from it he dispensed a little medicine and a great deal of down-to-earth advice, and patients have seriously told me that he could raise the dead. To me, when I write about Inspector Cockrill, it seems that I also for a little while raise the dead, and live again a few hours in the company of one whom I deeply admired and respected and deeply loved. Louli was wrong when she thought of my inspector as a funny little man. "Do you think that the truth really mattered so much?" asks the saddest and best — in the sense of intrinsic goodness — of my murderers; and, "Yes," says Cockie. "It's something sacred. If you're a doctor — you have only one idea, to preserve life. If you're a policeman, ditto — to preserve the truth." Nothing small or funny, it seems to me — about *that*?

Two thousand words, he said. Or thereabouts.

# After the Event

"Yes, I think I may claim," said the Grand Old Man (of Detection) complacently, "that in all my career I never failed to solve a murder case. In the end," he added, hurriedly, having caught Inspector Cockrill's beady eye.

Inspector Cockrill had for the past hour found himself in the position of the small boy at a party who knows how the conjuror does his tricks. He suggested: "The Othello case?" and sat back and twiddled his thumbs.

"As in the Othello case," said the Great Detective, as though he had not been interrupted at all. "Which, as I say, I solved. In the end," he added again, looking defiantly at Inspector Cockrill.

"But too late?" suggested Cockie: regretfully.

The great one bowed. "In as far as certain evidence had, shall we say? — faded — yes: too late. For the rest, I unmasked the murderer: I built up a water-tight case against him: and I duly saw him triumphantly brought to trial. In other words, I think I may fairly say — that I solved the case."

"Only, the jury failed to convict," said Inspector Cockrill.

He waved it aside with magnificence. A detail. "As it happened, yes; they failed to convict."

"And quite right too," said Cockie; he was having a splendid time.

"People round me were remarking, that second time I saw him play Othello," said the Great Detective, "that James Dragon had aged twenty years in as many days. And so he may well have done; for in the past three weeks he had played, night after night, to packed audiences — night after night strangling his new Desdemona, in the knowledge that his own wife had been so strangled but a few days before; and that every man jack in the audience believed it was he who had strangled her — believed he was a murderer."

"Which, however, he was not," said Inspector Cockrill, and his bright elderly eyes shone with malicious glee.

"Which he was — and was not," said the old man heavily. He was something of an actor himself but he had not hitherto encountered the modern craze for audience–participation and he was not enjoying it at all. "If I might now be permitted to continue without interruption ...?"

"Some of you may have seen James Dragon on the stage," said the old man, "though the company all migrated to Hollywood in the end. But none of you will have seen him as Othello — after that season, Dragon Pro–ductions dropped it from their repertoire. They were a great theatrical family — still are, come to that, though James and Leila, his sister, getting very passè, very passè indeed," said the Great Detective pityingly, shaking his senile head.

"But at the time of the murder, he was in his prime: not yet thirty and at the top of his form. And he was splendid. I see him now as I saw him that night, the very night she died — towering over her as she lay on the great stage bed, tricked out in his tremendous costume of black and gold, with the padded chest and shoulders concealing his slenderness and the great padded, jewel–studded sleeves like cantaloupe melons, raised above his head: bringing them down, slowly, slowly, until suddenly he swooped like a hawk and closed his dark–stained hands on her white throat. And I hear again Emilie's heart–break cry in the lovely Dragon family voice: 'Oh, thou has killed the sweetest innocent, That e'er did lift up eye ...' "

But she had not been an innocent — James Dragon's Desdemona, Glenda Croy, who was in fact his wife. She had been a thoroughly nasty piece of work. An aspiring young actress, she had blackmailed him into marriage for the sake of her career; and that had been all of a piece with her conduct throughout. A great theatrical family was extremely sensitive to blackmail even in those more easy–going days of the late nineteen–twenties; and in the first rush of the Dragons' spectacular rise to fame, there had been one or two unfortunate episodes, one of them even culminating in a — very short — prison sentence: which, however, had effectively been hushed up. By the time of the murder, the Dragons were a by–word for a sort of magnificent untouchability. Glenda Croy, without ever unearthing more than a grubby little scandal here and there, could yet be the means of dragging them all back into the mud again.

James Dragon had been, in the classic manner, born — at the turn of the century — backstage of a provincial theatre: had lustily wailed from his property basket while Romeo whispered through the mazes of Julict's ball–dance, "Just before curtain–up. Both doing splendidly. It's a boy!"; had been carried on at the age of three weeks, and at the age of ten formed with his sister such a precious pair of prodigies that the parents gave up their own promising careers to devote themselves to the management of their children's affairs. By the time he married, Dragon Productions had three touring companies always on the road and a regular London Shakespeare season, with James Dragon and Leila, his sister, playing the leads. Till he married a wife.

From the day of his marriage, Glenda took over the leads. They fought against it, all of them, the family, the whole company, James himself: but

Glenda used her blackmail with subtlety, little hints here, little threats there, and they were none of them proof against it — James Dragon was their "draw," with him they all stood or fell. So Leila stepped back and accepted second leads and for the good of them all, Arthur Dragon, the father, who produced for the company as well as being its manager, did his honest best with the new recruit: and so got her through her Juliet (to a frankly mature Romeo), her Lady Macbeth, her Desdemona; and at the time of her death was breaking his heart rehearsing her Rosalind, preparatory to the company's first American tour.

Rosalind was Leila Dragon's pet part. "But, Dad, she's hopeless, we *can't* have her prancing her way across America grinning like a coy hyena: do speak to James again ..."

"James can't do anything, my dear."

"Surely by this time ... It's three years now, we were all so certain it wouldn't last a year."

"She knows where her bread is buttered," said the lady's father–in–law, sourly.

"But now, having played with *us* — she could strike out on her own?"

"Why should she want to? With us, she's safe — and she automatically plays our leads."

"If only she'd fall for some man ..."

"She won't do that; she's far too canny," said Arthur Dragon. "That would be playing into our hands. And she's interested in nothing but getting on, she doesn't bother with men." And oddly enough, after a pass or two, men did not bother with her.

A row blew up over the Rosalind part, which rose to its climax before the curtain went up on "*Venice. A street,*" on the night that Glenda Croy died. It rambled through odd moments off stage and through the intervals, spilled over into hissed asides between Will Shakespeare's lines, culminated in a threat spat out with the venom of a viper as she lay on the bed, with the great arms raised above her, ready to pounce and close hands about her throat. Something about "gaol." Something about "prisoners." Something about the American tour.

It was an angry and a badly frightened man who faced her, twenty minutes later, in her dressing–room. "What did you mean, Glenda, by what you said on–stage? — during the death scene. Gaol–birds, prisoners — what did you mean, what was it you said?"

She had thrown on a dressing–gown at his knock and now sat calmly on the divan, peeling off her stage stockings. "I meant that I am playing Rosalind in America. Or the company is not going to America."

"I don't see the connection," he said.

"You will," said Glenda.

"But, Glenda, be sensible, Rosalind just isn't your part."

"No," said Glenda. "It's dear Leila's part. But I am playing Rosalind — or the company is not going to America."

"Don't *you* want to go to America?"

"I can go any day I like. But you can't. Without me, Dragon Productions stay home."

"I have accepted the American offer," he said steadily. "I am taking the company out. Come if you like — playing Celia."

She took off one stocking and tossed it over her shoulder, bent to slide the other down, over a round white knee. "No one is welcomed into America who has been a gaol–bird," she said.

"Oh — that's it?" he said. "Well, if you mean me ..." But he wavered. "There *was* a bit of nonsense ... rubbish, a bit of bravado, we were all wild and silly in those days before the war ..."

"Explain all that to the Americans," she said.

"I've no doubt I'd be able to," he said, still steadily. "If they even found out, which I doubt they ever would." But his mind swung round on itself. "This is a new — mischief — of yours, Glenda. How did you find out?"

"I came across a newspaper cutting." She gave a sort of involuntary glance back over her shoulder; it told him without words spoken that the paper was here in the room. He caught at her wrist. "Give that cutting to me!"

She did not even struggle to free her hand; just sat looking up at him with her insolent little smile. She was sure of herself. "Help yourself. It's in my handbag. But the information's still at the newspaper office, you know — and here in my head, facts, dates, all the rest of it. Plus any little embellishments I may care to add." He had relaxed his grip and she freed her hand without effort and sat gently massaging the wrist. "It's wonderful," she said, "what lies people will believe, if you base them on a hard core of truth."

He called her a filthy name and, standing there, blind with his mounting disgust and fury, added filth to filth. She struck out at him then like a wild cat, slapping him violently across the face with the flat of her hand. At the sharp sting of the slap, his control gave way. He raised his arms above his head and brought them down — slowly, slowly, with a menace infinitely terrible: and closed his hands about her throat and shook her like a rag doll — and then flung her back on to the bed and started across the room in search of the paper. It was in her handbag as she had said. He took it and stuffed it into his pocket and went back and stood triumphantly over her.

And saw that she was dead.

"I had gone, as it happened, to a restaurant just across the street from the theatre," said the Great Detective; "and they got me there. She was lying on the couch, her arms flung over her head, the backs of her hands with their pointed nails brushing the floor; much as I had seen her, earlier in the evening, lying in a pretence of death. But she no longer wore Desdemona's elaborate robes, she wore only the rather solid undies of those days, cami–knickers and a petticoat, under a silk dressing–gown. She seemed to have put up very little struggle: though there was a red mark round her right wrist and a faint pink stain across the palm of her hand.

"Most of the company and the technicians, I left for the moment to my assistants, and they proved later to have nothing of interest to tell us. The stage door–keeper, however, an ancient retired doctor, testified to having seen 'shadows against her lighted windows. Mr. James was in there with her. They were going through the strangling scene. Then the light went out: that's all I know.'

" 'How did you know it was Mr. Dragon in there?'

" 'Well, they were rehearsing the strangling scene,' the door keeper repeated, reasonably.

" 'Now, however, you realize that she really was being strangled?'

" 'Well, yes.' He looked troubled. The Dragon family in their affluence were good to old theatricals like himself.

" 'Very well. Can you now say that you know it was Mr. Dragon?'

" 'I thought it was. You see, he was speaking the lines.'

" 'You mean, you heard his voice? You heard what he was saying?'

" 'A word here and there. He raised his voice — just as he does on those lines in the production: the death lines, you know ...' He looked hopeful. 'So it *was* just a run–through.'

"They were all sitting in what, I suppose, would be the Green–room: James Dragon himself, his father who, besides producing, played the small part of Othello's servant, the Clown; his mother who was wardrobe mistress, etcetera and had some little walking–on part, Leila Dragon who played Emilia, and three actors (who, for a wonder, weren't members of the family), playing respectively, Iago, Cassio, and Cassio's mistress, Bianca. I think," said the Great Detective, beaming round the circle of eagerly listening faces, "that it will be less muddling to refer to them by their stage names."

"Do you really?" asked Inspector Cockrill: incredulous.

"Do I really what?"

"Thank it will be less muddling?" said Cockie: and twiddled his thumbs again.

The great man ignored him. "They were in stage make–up, still, and in stage costume: and they sat about or stood, in attitudes of horror, grief, dismay or despair, which seemed to me very much like stage attitudes too.

"They gave me their story — I use the expression advisedly as you will see — of the past half–hour.

"The leading lady's dressing–room at the Dragon Theatre juts out from the main building, so angled, as it happens, that the windows can be seen from the Green–room, as they can from the door–keeper's cubby. As I talked, I myself could see my men moving about in there, silhouettes against the drawn blinds.

"They had been gathered, they said, the seven of them, here in the Green–room, for twenty minutes after the curtain came down — Othello, Othello's servant the Clown, Emilia and Mrs. Dragon, (the family) plus Iago, Cassio and a young girl playing Bianca; all discussing — 'something.' During that time, they said, nobody had left the room. Their eyes shifted to James Dragon and shifted away again.

"He seemed to feel the need to say something, anything, to distract attention from that involuntary, shifting glance. He blurted out: 'And if you want to know what we were discussing, we were discussing my wife.'

" 'She had been Carrying On,' said Mrs. Dragon in a voice of theatrical doom.

" 'She had for some time been carrying on a love affair, as my mother says. We were afraid the affair would develop, would get out of hand, that she wouldn't want to come away on our American tour and it would upset our arrangements. We were taking out *As You Like It*. She was to have played Rosalind.'

" 'And then?'

" 'We heard footsteps along the corridor. Someone knocked at her door. We thought nothing of it till one of us glanced up and saw the shadows on her blind. There was a man with her in there. We supposed it was the lover.'

" 'Who was this lover?' I asked. If such a man existed, I had better send out after him, on the off–chance.

"But none of them, they said, knew who he was. 'She was too clever for that,' said Mrs. Dragon in her tragedy voice.

" 'How could he have got into the theatre? The stage door–man didn't see him.'

"They did not know. No doubt there might have been some earlier arrangement between them ...

"And not the only 'arrangement' that had been come to that night. They began a sort of point counterpoint recital which I could have sworn had been rehearsed. *Iago*, (or it may have been Cassio): 'Then we saw that they were quarreling ...' *Emilia*: 'To our great satisfaction!' *Clown*: 'That would have solved all our problems, you see.' *Othello*: 'Not all our problems. It would not have solved mine. *Emilia*, quoting: 'Was this fair paper, this most goodly book, Made to write "whore" upon ...?' *Mrs. Dragon*: Leila, James, be careful, (sotto voce, and glancing at me). *Clown*, hastily as though to cover up: 'And then, sir, he seemed to pounce down upon her as far as, from the distorted shadows, we could see. A moment later he moved across the room and then suddenly the lights went out and we heard the sound of a window violently thrown up. My son, James, came to his senses first. He rushed out and we saw the lights come on again. We followed him. He was bending over her ...'

" 'She was dead,' said James; and struck an attitude against the Green–room mantelpiece, his dark–stained face heavy with grief, resting his forehead on his dark–stained hand. People said later, as I've told you, that he aged twenty years in as many days; I remember thinking at the time that in fact he had aged twenty years in as many minutes: and that that was *not* an act.

"A window had been found swinging open, giving to a narrow lane behind the theatre. I did not need to ask how the lover was supposed to have made his get–away. 'And all this time,' I said, 'none of you left the Green–room?'

" 'No one,' they repeated: and this time were careful not to glance at James.

"You must appreciate," said the Great Detective, pouring himself another glass of port, "that I did not then know all I have explained to you. If I was to believe what I was told, I knew only this: that the door–keeper had seen a man strangling the woman, repeating the words of the Othello death–scene — which, however, amount largely to calling the lady a strumpet; that apparently the lady was a strumpet, in as far as she had been entertaining a lover; and that six people, of whom three were merely members of his company, agreed that they had seen the murder committed while James Dragon was sitting innocently in the room with them. I had to take the story of the lover at its face value: I could not then know, as I knew later, that Glenda Croy had avoided such entanglements. But it raised, nevertheless, certain questions in my mind." It was his custom to pause at this moment, smiling benignly round on his audience, and invite them to guess what those questions had been.

No one seemed very ready with suggestions. He was relaxing com–placently in his chair, as also was his custom for no one ever did offer suggestions, when, having civilly waited for the laymen to speak first, Inspector Cockrill raised his unwelcome voice. "You reflected no doubt that the lover was really rather too good to be true. A 'murderer,' seen by seven highly interested parties and by nobody else: whose existence, however, could never be disproved; and who was so designed as to throw no shadow of guilt on to any real man."

"It is always easy to be wise after the event," said the old man huffily. Even that, however, Inspector Cockrill audibly took leave to doubt. Their host asked somewhat hastily what the great man had done next. The great man replied gloomily that since his fellow guest, Inspector Cockrill, seemed so full of ideas, perhaps he had better say what *he* would have done.

"Sent for the door–keeper and checked the stories together," said Cockie promptly.

This was (to his present chagrin) precisely what the Great Detective had done. The stories, however, had proved to coincide pretty exactly, to the moment when the light had gone out. "Then I heard footsteps from the direction of the Green–room, sir. About twenty minutes later, you arrived. That's the first I knew she was dead."

So: what to do next?

To ask oneself, said Inspector Cockrill, though the question had been clearly rhetorical, why there had been fifteen minutes delay in sending for the police.

"Why should you think there had been fifteen minutes delay?"

"The man said it was twenty minutes before you arrived. But you told us earlier, you were just across the street.'

"No doubt," said the old man, crossly, "as you have guessed my question, you would like to —"

"Answer it," finished Inspector Cockrill. "Yes, certainly. The answer is: because the cast wanted time to change back into stage costume. We know they had changed out of it, or at least begun to change ..."

"*I* knew it: the ladies were not properly laced up, Iago had on an everyday shirt under his doublet — they had all obviously hurriedly redressed and as hurriedly re–made up. But how could you ...?"

"We could deduce it. Glenda Croy had had time to get back into her underclothes. The rest of them said they had been in the Green–room discussing the threat of her 'affair'. But the affair had been going on for some time, it couldn't have been suddenly so pressing that they need discuss it before they even got out of their stage–costume — which is, I take it, by instinct and training the first thing an actor does after curtain–fall. And besides, you *knew* that Othello, at least, had changed: and changed back."

"I knew?"

"You believed it was Othello — that's to say James Dragon — who had been in the room with her. And the doorman had virtually told you that at that time he was not wearing his stage costume."

"I fear then that till this moment," said the Great man, heavily sarcastic, "the doorman's virtual statement to that effect has escaped me."

"Well, but ..." Cockie was astonished. "You asked him how, having seen his silhouette on the window–blinds, he had 'known' it was James Dragon. And he answered, after reflection, that he knew by his voice and by what he was saying. He did not say," said Cockie, sweetly reasonable, "what otherwise, surely he would have said before all else: 'I knew by the shape on the window–blind of the raised arms in those huge, padded, cantaloupe–melon sleeves.' "

There was a horrid little silence. The host started the port on its round again with a positive whizz, the guests pressed walnuts upon one another with abandon (hoarding the nut–crackers, however, to themselves); and, after all, it was a shame to be pulling the white rabbits all at once out of the conjurer's top hat, before he had come to them — if he ever got them! Inspector Cockrill tuned his voice to a winning respect. "So then, do tell us, sir — what next did you do?"

What the great man had done, standing there in the Green–room muttering to himself, had been to conduct a hurried review of the relevant times, in his own mind. "Ten–thirty, the curtain falls. Ten–fifty, having changed from their stage–dress, they do or do not meet in here for a council of war. At any rate, by eleven o'clock the woman is dead: and then there is a council of war indeed ... Ten minutes, perhaps, for frantic discussion, five or ten minutes grace before they must all be in costume again, ready to receive the police ..." But *why*? His eyes roved over them: the silks and velvets, the rounded bosoms thrust up by laced bodices, low cut: the tight–stretched hose, the jewelled doublets, the melon sleeves ...

The sleeves. He remembered the laxly curved hands hanging over the head of the divan, the pointed nails. There had been no evidence of a struggle, but one never knew. He said, slowly: "May I ask now why all of you have replaced your stage dress and make–up?"

Was there, somewhere in the room, a sharp intake of breath? Perhaps: but for the most part they retained their stagey calm. Emilia and Iago, point counterpoint, again explained. They had been half–way, as it were, between stage dress and day dress; it had been somehow simpler to scramble back into costume when the alarm arose ... Apart from the effect of an act rehearsed, it rang with casual truth. "Except that you told me that 'when the alarm rose' you were all here in the Green–room, having a discussion.

"Yes, but only half–changed, changing as we talked," said Cassio, quickly. Stage people, he added, were not frightfully fussy about the conventional modesties.

"Very well. You will, however, oblige me by reverting to day dress now. But before you all do so ..." He put his head out into the corridor and a couple of men moved in unobtrusively and stood just inside the door. "Mr. James Dragon — would you please remove those sleeves and let me see your wrists?"

It was the girl, Bianca, who cried out — on a note of terror: "No!"

"Hush, be quiet," said James Dragon: commandingly but soothingly.

"But James ... But James, he thinks ... It isn't true," she cried out frantically, "it was the other man, we saw him in there, Mr. Dragon was in here with us ..."

"Then Mr. Dragon will have no objection to showing me his arms."

"But why?" she cried out, violently. "How could his arms be... ? He had that costume on, he did have it on, he was wearing it at the very moment he ..." There was a sharp hiss from someone in the room and she stopped, appalled, her hand across her mouth. But she rushed on. "He hasn't changed, he's had on that costume, those sleeves, all the time: nothing could have happened to his wrists. Haven't you, James? — hasn't he, everyone? — we know, we all saw him, he was wearing it when he came back ..."

There was that hiss of thrilled horror again; but Leila Dragon said, quickly, "When he came back from finding the body, she means," and went across and took the girl roughly by the arm. The girl opened her mouth and gave one piercing scream like the whistle of a train; and suddenly, losing control of herself, Leila Dragon slapped her once and once again across the face.

The effect was extraordinary. The scream broke short, petered out into a sort of yelp of terrified astonishment. Mrs. Dragon cried out sharply, "Oh, no!" and James Dragon said, "Leila, you *fool!*" They all stood staring, utterly in dismay. And Leila Dragon blurted out: "I'm sorry. I didn't mean to. It was because she screamed. It was — a sort of reaction, instinctive, a sort of reaction to hysteria ..." She seemed to plead with them. It was curious that she seemed to plead with them, and not with the girl.

James Dragon broke through the ice–well of their dismay. He said uncertainly: "It's just that ... We don't want to make — well, enemies of people," and the girl broke out wildly: "How dare you touch me? How dare you?"

It was as though an act which for a moment had broken down, reducing the cast to gagging, now received a cue from a prompt corner and got going again. Leila Dragon said, "You were hysterical, you were losing control."

"How dare you?" screamed the girl. Her pretty face was waspish with spiteful rage. "All I've done is to try to protect him, like the rest of you ..."

"Be quiet," said Mrs. Dragon, in The Voice.

"Let her say what she has to say," the detective said. She was silent. "Come now. 'He was wearing it when he came back' — the Othello costume. *'When he came back'.* From finding the body, Miss Leila Dragon now says. But he didn't 'come back.' You all followed him to the dressing–room — you said so."

She remained silent, however; and he could deal with her later — time was passing, clues were growing cold. "Very well then, Mr. Dragon, let us get on with it. I want to see your wrists and arms."

"But why me?" said James Dragon, almost petulantly; and once again there was that strange effect of an unreal act being staged for some set purpose: and once again the stark reality of a face grown all in a moment haggard and old beneath the dark stain of the Moor.

"It's not only you. I may come to the rest, in good time."

"But me first?"

"Get on with it please," he said impatiently.

But when at last, fighting every inch of the way, with an ill grace he slowly divested himself of the great sleeves — there was nothing to be seen: nothing but a brown–stained hand whose colour ended abruptly at the wrist, giving place to forearms startlingly white against the brown — but innocent of scratches or marks of any kind.

"Nor did Iago, I may add in passing, nor did Cassio nor the Clown nor anyone else in the room, have marks of any kind on wrists or arms. So there I was — five minutes wasted and nothing to show for it."

"Well, hardly," said Inspector Cockrill, passing walnuts to his neighbour.

"I beg your pardon? Did Mr. Cockrill say something again?"

"I just murmured that there was, after all, something to show for it — for the five minutes wasted."

"?"

"Five minutes wasted," said Inspector Cockrill.

Five minutes wasted. Yes. They had been working for it, they were playing for time. Waiting for something. Or postponing something? "And of course, meanwhile, there had been the scene with the girl," said Cockie. "That wasn't a waste of time. That told you a lot. I mean — losing control and screaming out that he had been wearing Othello's costume 'at the very moment ...' and, 'when he came back.' 'Losing control' — and yet what she screamed out contained at least one careful lie. Because he hadn't been wearing the costume — that we know for certain." And he added inconsequently that they had to remember all the time that these were acting folk.

But that had not been the end of the scene with the girl. As he perfunctorily examined her arms — for surely no women had had any part in the murder — she had whispered to him that she wanted to speak to him: outside. And, darting looks of poison at them, holding her hand to her slapped face, she had gone out with him to the corridor. "I stood with her there while she talked," he said. "Her face, of course, was heavily made up; and yet under the make–up I could see the weal where Leila Dragon had slapped her. She was not hysterical now, she was cool and clear; but she was afraid and for the first time it seemed to be not all an act, she seemed to be genuinely afraid, and afraid at what she was about to say to me. But she said it. It was a — solution: a suggestion of how the crime had been done; though she unsaid nothing that she had already said. I went back into the Green–room. They were all standing about, white–faced, looking at her as she followed me in; and with them, also, there seemed now to be an air of genuine horror, genuine dread, as though the need for histrionics had passed. Leila Dragon was holding the wrist of her right hand in her left. I said to James Dragon: "I think at this stage it would be best if you would come down to the station with me, for further questioning ..."

"I expected an uproar and there was an uproar. More waste of time. But now, you see," said the old man, looking cunningly round the table, "I knew — didn't I? Waiting for something? Or postponing something? Now, you see, I knew."

"At any rate, you took him down to the station?" said Cockie, sickened by all this gratuitous mystificating. "On the strength of what the girl had suggested?"

"What that was is, of course, quite clear to *you*?"

"Well, of course," said Cockie.

"Of course, of course," said the old man angrily. He shrugged. "At any rate — it served as an excuse. It meant that I could take him, and probably hold him there, on a reasonable suspicion: it did him out of the alibi, you see. So off he went, at last, with a couple of my men; and, after a moment, I followed. But before I went, I collected something — something from his dressing–room." Another of his moments had come; but this time he addressed himself only to Inspector Cockrill. "No doubt what that was is also clear to you?"

"Well, a pot of theatrical cleansing cream, I suppose," said Inspector Cockrill; almost apologetically.

The Old Man, as has been said, was something of an actor himself. He affected to give up. "As you know it all so well, Inspector, you had better explain to our audience and save me my breath." He gave to the words "*our audience*" an ironic significance quite shattering in its effect; and hugged to himself a secret white rabbit to be sprung, to the undoing of this tiresome little man, when all seemed over, out of a secret top hat.

Inspector Cockrill in his turn affected surprise, affected diffidence, affected reluctant acceptance. "Oh, well, all right." He embarked upon it in his grumbling voice. "It was the slap across the girl, Bianca's, face. Our friend, no doubt, will tell you that he paid very little attention to whatever it was she said to him in the corridor." (A little more attention, he privately reflected, would have been to advantage; but still ...) "He was looking, instead, at the weal on her face: glancing in through the door, perhaps, to where Leila Dragon sat unconsciously clasping her stinging right hand with her left. He was thinking of another hand he had recently seen, with a pink mark across the palm. He knew now, as he says. He knew why they had been so appalled when, forgetting herself, she had slapped the girls' face: because it might suggest to his mind that there had been another such incident that night. He knew. He knew what they had all been waiting for, why they had been marking time. He knew why they had scrambled back into stage costume, they had done it so that there might be no particularity if James Dragon appeared in the dark makeup of Othello the Moor. They were waiting till under the stain, another stain should fade — the mark of Glenda Croy's hand across the murderer's face." He looked into the Great

Detective's face. "I think that's the way your mind worked?"

The great one bowed. "Very neatly thought out. Very creditable." He shrugged. "Yes, that's how it was. So we took him down to the station and without more delay we cleaned the dark paint off his face. And under the stain — what do you think we found?"

"Nothing," said Inspector Cockrill.

"Exactly," said the old man, crossly.

"You can't have found anything; because, after all, he was free to play Othello for the next three weeks," said Cockie, simply. "You couldn't detain him — there was nothing to detain him on. The girl's story wasn't enough to stand alone, without the mark of the slap: and now, if it had ever been there, it had faded. Their delaying tactics had worked. You had to let him go."

"For the time being," said the old man. The rabbit had poked its ears above the rim of the hat and he poked them down again. "You no doubt will equally recall that at the end of the three weeks, James Dragon was arrested and duly came up for trial?" Hand over hat, keeping the rabbit down, he gave his adversary a jab. "What do you suggest, sir, happened in the meantime? — to bring that change about?"

Inspector Cockrill considered, his splendid head bowed over a couple of walnuts which he was trying to crack together. "I can only suggest that what happened, sir, was that you went to the theatre."

"To the theatre?"

"Well, to The Theatre," said Cockie. "To the Dragon Theatre. And there, for the second time, saw James Dragon play Othello."

"A great performance. A great performance," said the old man, uneasily. The rabbit had poked his whole head over the brim of the hat and was winking at the audience.

"Was it?" said Cockie. "The first time you saw him — yes. But that second time? I mean, you were telling us that people all round you were saying how much he had aged." But he stopped. "I beg your pardon, sir: I keep forgetting that this is your story."

It had been the old man's story — for years it had been his best story, the pet white rabbit out of the conjuror's mystery hat; and now it was spoilt by the horrid little boy who knew how the tricks were done. "That's all there is to it," he said sulkily. "She made this threat about exposing the prison sentence — as we learned later on. They all went back to their dressing–rooms and changed into every day things. James Dragon, as soon as he was dressed, went round to his wife's room. Five minutes later, he assembled his principals in the Green–room; Glenda Croy was dead and he bore across his face the mark where she had hit him, just before she died.

"They were all in it together; with James Dragon, the company stood or fell. They agreed to protect him. They knew that from where he sat the door–keeper might well have seen the shadow–show on her dressing–room blinds, perhaps even the blow across the face. They knew that James Dragon must come under immediate suspicion; they knew that at all costs they must prevent anyone from seeing the mark of the blow. They could not estimate how long it would take for the mark to fade.

"You know what they did. They scrambled back into costume again, they made up their faces — and beneath the thick grease–paint they buried the fatal mark. I arrived. There was nothing for it now but to play for time.

"They played for time. They built up the story of the lover — who, in fact, eventually bore the burden of guilt, for as you know, no one was ever convicted: and he could never be disproved. But still only a few minutes had passed and now I was asking them to change back into day dress. James created a further delay in refusing to have his arms examined. Another few moments gone by. They gave the signal to the girl to go into her pre– arranged act."

He thought back across the long years. "It was a very good act: she's done well since but I don't suppose she ever excelled the act she put on that night. But she was battling against hopeless odds, poor girl. You see — I did know one thing by then; didn't I?"

"You knew they were playing for time," said Inspector Cockrill. "Or why should James Dragon have refused to show you his arms? There was nothing incriminating about his arms."

"Exactly: and so — I was wary of her. But she put up a good performance. It was easier for her, because of course by now she was really afraid: they were all afraid — afraid lest this desperate last step they were taking in their delaying action, should prove to have been a step too far: lest they found their 'solution' was so good that they could not go back on it."

"This solution, however, of course you had already considered and dismissed?"

"Mr. Cockrill, no doubt, will be delighted to tell you all what the solution was."

"If you like," said Mr. Cockrill. "But it *could* be only the one 'solution', couldn't it? especially as you said that she stuck to what she'd earlier said. She'd given him an alibi — they'd all given him an alibi — for the time up to the moment the light went out. She dragged you out into the corridor and she said …"

"She said?"

"Well, nothing new," said Cockie. "She just — repeated, only with a special significance, something that someone else had said."

"The clown, yes."

"When he was describing what they were supposed to have seen against the lighted blinds. He said that they saw the man pounce down upon the woman: that the light went out and they heard the noise of the window being thrown up. That James, his son, rushed out and that when they followed, he was bending over her. I suppose the girl repeated with direful significance: '*He was bending over her*'."

"A ridiculous implication, of course."

"Of course," said Inspector Cockrill, readily. "If, which I suppose was her proposition, the pounce had been a pounce of love, followed by an extinction of the lights, it seemed hardly likely that the gentleman concerned would immediately leave the lady and bound out of the nearest window — since she was reputedly complacent. But supposing that he had, supposing that the infuriated husband, rushing in and finding her thus deserted, had bent over and impulsively strangled her where, disappointed, she reclined — it is even less likely that his own father would have been the first to draw your attention to the fact. Why mention, 'he was bending over her'?"

"Precisely, excellent," said the old man: kindly patronization was the only card left in the conjuror's hand.

"Her story had the desired effect, however?"

"It created further delay, before I demanded that they remove their make–up. It was beyond their dreams that I should create even more, myself, by taking James Dragon to the police station."

"You were justified," said Cockie, indulging in a little kindly patronization on his own account. "Believing what you did. And having received that broad hint — which they certainly had never intended to give you — when Leila Dragon lost her head and slapped Bianca's face ..."

"And then sat unconsciously holding her stinging hand."

"So you'd almost decided to have him charged. But it would be most convenient to do the whole thing tidily down at the station, cleaning him up and all ..."

"We weren't a set of actor–fellers down there," said the old man defensively, though no one had accused him of anything. "We cleaned away the greasepaint enough to see that there was no mark of the blow. But I daresay we left him to do the rest — and I daresay he saw to it that a lot remained about the forehead and eyes ... I remember thinking that he looked old and haggard, but under the circumstances that would not be surprising. And when at last I got back to the theatre, no doubt the same thing went on with 'Arthur' Dragon; perhaps I registered that he looked young for his years — but I have forgotten that." He sighed. "By then of course, anyway, it was too late. The mark was gone." He sighed again. "A man of thirty with a red mark to conceal: and a man of fifty. The family likeness, the famous voice, both actors, both familiar with Othello, since the father had produced it: and both with perhaps the most effective disguises that fate could possibly have designed for them ..."

"The Moor of Venice," said Inspector Cockrill.

"And — a Clown," said the Great Detective. The white rabbit leapt out of the hat and bowed right and left to the audience.

"Whether, as I say, he continued to play his son's part — on the stage as well as off," said the Great Detective, "I shall never know. But I think he did. I think they would hardly dare to change back before my very eyes. I think that, backed up by a loyal company, they played Cox and Box with me. I said to you earlier that while his audiences believed their Othello to be in fact a murderer — he was: and he was not. I think that Othello was a murderer; but I think that the wrong man was playing Othello's part."

"And you," said Inspector Cockrill, in a voice hushed with what doubtless was reverence, "went to see him play?"

"And heard someone say that he seemed to have aged twenty years ... And so," said the Great Detective, "we brought him to trial, as you know. We had a case all right: the business about the prison sentence, of course, came to light; we did much to discredit the existence of any lover; we had the evidence of the stage door–keeper, the evidence of the company was not disinterested. But alas! — the one tangible clue, the mark of that slap, had long since gone: and there we were. I unmasked him; I built up a case against him: I brought him to trial. The jury failed to convict."

"And quite right too," said Inspector Cockrill.

"And quite right too," agreed the great man, graciously. "A British jury is always right. Lack of concrete evidence, lack of unbiased witnesses, lack of demonstrable proof ..."

"Lack of a murderer," said Inspector Cockrill.

"Are you suggesting," said the old man, after a little while, "that Arthur Dragon did not impersonate his son? And if so — will you permit me to ask, my dear fellow, who then impersonated who? Leila Dragon, perhaps, took her brother's place? She had personal grudges against Glenda Croy. And she was tall and well–built, (the perfect Rosalind — a clue, my dear Inspector, after your own heart!) and he was slight, for a man. And of course she had the famous Dragon voice."

"She also had a 'well–rounded bosom'," said Inspector Cockrill, "exposed, as you told us, by laced bodice and low–cut gown. She might have taken her brother's part: he can hardly have taken hers." And he asked, struggling with the two walnuts, why anybody should have impersonated anybody, anyway.

"But they were ... But they all ... But everything they said or did was designed to draw attention to Othello, was designed to gain time while the mark was fading under the makeup of ..."

"Of the Clown," said Inspector Cockrill, " 'a frightened and angry man' who rushed round to her dressing–room that night: after his son had told him of the threat hissed out on the stage. 'Something about gaol ... Something about prisoners ...' " He said to the old man: "You did not make it clear that it was *Arthur* Dragon who had served a prison sentence, all those years ago."

"Didn't I?" said the old man. "Well, it made no difference. James Dragon was their star and their 'draw,' Arthur Dragon was their manager — without either, the company couldn't undertake the tour. But of course it was Arthur: who on earth could have thought otherwise?"

"No one," agreed Cockie. "He said as much to her in the dressing–room. 'If you're referring to me …' and, 'We were all wild and silly in those days before the war …' That was the 1914 war, of course: all this happened thirty years ago. But in the days before the 1914 war, James Dragon would have been a child: he was born at the turn of the century — far too young to be sent to prison, anyway.

"You would keep referring to these people by their stage names," said Cockie. "It was muddling. We came to think of the Clown as the Clown, and not as Arthur Dragon, James Dragon's father — and manager and producer for Dragon Productions. 'I am taking the company to America …' It was not for James Dragon to say that; he was their star, but his father was their manager, it was he who 'took' the company here or there … And, 'You can come if you like — playing Celia.' It was not for James Dragon to say that: it was for Arthur Dragon, their producer, to assign the parts to the company …

"It was the dressing–gown, I think, that started me off on it," said Inspector Cockrill, thoughtfully. "You see — as one of them said, the profession is not fussy about the conventional modesties. Would Glenda Croy's husband really have knocked? — rushing in there, mad with rage and anxiety, would he really have paused to knock politely at his wife's door? And she — would she really have waited to put on a dressing–gown over her ample petticoat, to receive him? For her father–in–law, perhaps, yes: we are speaking of many years ago. But for her husband …? Well, I wouldn't know. But it started me wondering.

"At any rate — he killed her. She could break up their tour, she could throw mud at their great name: and he had everything to lose, an ageing actor who had given up his own career for the company. He killed her; and a devoted family and loyal, and 'not disinterested' company, hatched up a plot to save him from the consequences of what none of them greatly deplored. We made our mistake, I think," said Cockie, handsomely including himself in the mistake, "in supposing that it would be an elaborate plot. It wasn't. These people were actors and not used to writing their own plots: it was in fact an incredibly simple plot. 'Let's all put on our grease paint again and create as much delay as possible while, under the Clown make–up, the red mark fades. And the best way to draw attention from the Clown, will be to draw it towards Othello.' No doubt they will have added civilly, 'James — is that all right with you?'

"And so," said Inspector Cockrill, "we come back again to James Dragon. Within the past hour he had had a somewhat difficult time. Within the past hour his company had been gravely threatened and by the treachery of his own wife; within the past hour his wife had been strangled and his father had become a self–confessed murderer ... And now he was to act, without rehearsal and without lines, a part which might yet bring him to the Old Bailey and under sentence of death. It was no wonder, perhaps, that when the grease paint was wiped away from his face that night, our friend thought he seemed to have aged ..." If, he added their friend really had thought so at the time; and was not now being wise after the event.

He was able to make this addition because their friend had just got up and, with a murmured excuse, had left the room. In search of a white rabbit, perhaps?

# Blood Brothers

"And devoted, I hear," he says. "David and Jonathan?" he says. "In fact you might properly be called," he says, with that glitter in his eye, "blood brothers?"

Well, he can sneer but it's true we was pally enough, Fred and me, till Lydia came along. Shared the same digs in the village — Birdswell's our village, if you know it? — Birdswell, in Kent. Everyone in Birdswell knows us — even if they can't easily tell the difference between us — and used to say how wonderful it was, us two so alike, with our strong legs and big shoulders and curly red hair, like a kid's: and what a beautiful under–standing we had, what a bond of union. People talk a lot of crap about identical twins.

Lydia couldn't tell the difference between us either — seemingly. Was that my fault? Fair enough, she was Fred's girl first — unless you counted her husband, and to some extent you did have to count him: six foot five, he is, and it isn't only because he's the blacksmith that they call him in the village, Black Will. But she switched to me of her own record, didn't she? — even if I wasn't too quick to disillusion her the first time she started with her carryings–on, mistaking me for Fred. "I can't help it if she fancies me more than you, now," I said to Fred.

"You'll regret this, you two–timing, double–crossing bastard," said Fred: he always did have a filthy temper, Fred.

Well, I did regret it: and not so very long after. Fred and me shares a car between us — a heavy old, bashed–up, fourth–hand, "family model," but at least it goes. And one evening, when he'd slouched off, ugly and moody as he was those days, to poach the river down by the Vicarage woods, I picked up Lydia and took her out in it, joy–riding. Not that there was much joy in it. We hadn't been out twenty minutes when, smooching around with Lydia, I suppose, not paying enough attention to the road — well, I didn't see the kid until I'd hit him. Jogging along the grass verge he was, with his little can of blackberries: haring home as fast as his legs would go, a bit scared, I daresay, because the dark was catching up on him. Well — the dark caught him up all right: poor little bastard. I scrambled out and knelt down and turned him over; and got back again, quick. "He's gone," I said to Lydia, "and we'd best be gone too." She made a lot of fuss, woman–like, but what was the point of it? If he wasn't dead now, he would be mighty soon, there wasn't any doubt of it: lying there with the can still clutched in his fat little hand and the blackberries spilt, and scattered all around him. I couldn't do nothing; if I could have, I dare say I'd have waited, but I couldn't. So what was the use of bringing trouble on myself, when the chances were that I could get clear away with it?

And I did get clear away with it. The road was hard and dry, the cars that followed and stopped must have obscured my tyre marks, if there were any. They found half a footprint in the dried mud, where I'd bent over him; but it was just a cheap, common make of shoe, pretty new so it had no particular marks to it; and a largish size, of course, but nothing out of the ordinary. No one knew I'd been on that road — everything Lydia did with us two was done in deep secret, because of Black Will. Will was doing time at the moment, for beating up a keeper who came on him, poaching (we all spent most of our evenings, poaching). But he'd be back some day.

And Fred promised me an alibi, when I told him about it: clutching at his arm, shaking a bit by this time, losing confidence because Lydia was threatening to turn nasty. "I'll say you was in the woods with me," he said. And he did, too. They came to our door, "regulation police enquiries"; but Lydia wouldn't dare to tell, not really, I could see that in the light of day, and they had no other sort of reason to suspect me, especially. And nobody did — it could have been any stranger, speeding along the empty country roads. Fred pretended to be reluctant to alibi me, cagey about saying where we was — because of the poaching. He managed it fine, it sort of threw their interest half way in a different direction. I thought it was decent of Fred, considering about me and Lydia. But brotherly love is a wonderful thing, isn't it?

Or isn't it? Because it hadn't been all for nothing. No sooner was I clear of that lot than he says to me: "Well — has she told you?"

"Told me what?" I says. "Who? Lydia?"

"Lydia," he says. "She's having a baby."

"Well, don't look at me," I said, and quick. "I've only been going with the girl a couple of weeks."

"And her husband hasn't been going with her at all," said Fred. "On account of he's been in prison for the past five months."

"For half killing a man," I said, thoughtfully; and I looked Fred up and down. Fred and me are no weeds, like I said; but Black Will, he's half way to a giant.

"And due out at the end of October," said Fred.

"Well, good luck to the two of you," says I. "It's nothing to do with me. I had her for a couple of weeks, and now even that's over. She reckons I ought to have stopped and seen to the kid: she's given me the bird."

"She'll give you more than the bird," he says, "and me too, when Will comes home. When he knows about the baby, he'll beat the rest out of her, and then God help you and me too."

"The baby could be Jimmy Green's," I said. "Or Bill Bray's. She's been out with them, too."

"That's her tales," he said, "to make you jealous. "They're a sight too scared of Will to let Lydia make up to them. And so ought you and I to have been too, if we'd have any sense." Only where Lydia was concerned, there never seemed to be time to have sense; and six months ago," Fred said, Black Will's return had seemed like an aeon away. "So what are you going to do?" I said.

"What are *you* going to do?" he said. "A hit–and–run driver — you can get a long stretch for that. The kid wasn't dead yet, when they found him."

Good old brotherly love! — Fred worrying about me, when after all I *had* pinched his girl. And him in such trouble himself.

We went out in the car, where no one could hear us: our old landlady's pretty deaf and takes no interest at all in our comings and goings, but Fred wasn't taking no chances ...

Because it was all Fred's idea: that I will say, and stick to it — it was Fred's idea. Dead men tell no tales, said Fred; nor dead girls, neither. "If they find she's in the family way — it's like you said, she was spreading it around she'd been going with half the village. Once she was past talking, Will couldn't pin it on us two: not to be certain."

"Speak for yourself," I said.

"She'd be past talking about the hit–and–run, too," he said. "You say she's sore about that. She won't tell you now, because it means admitting she was joy–riding with you; but once Black Will gets it out of her that she was — and he will — then she'll tell about the accident too; it'll make her feel easier."

"So what do you suggest?" I said. "*I'm* not killing the girl, I can tell you that, flat."

"No," he said. "I'll do that. You've done one killing," he said, not too pleasantly, I thought, "that'll do for you. All I want from you now is an alibi."

"What, me alibi you?" I said. "No one'd believe it for a minute. One twin speaking up for another — the whole village would testify how 'close' we are." (The whole village not knowing anything about us and Lydia.)

But Fred had thought of all that too. If a straight alibi failed, he said, there were other ways of playing it. He had it all worked out — suspiciously well worked out, I ought to have thought; but he gave me no time for thinking. "It won't come to any alibi, our names probably won't even come into it — as you say, the baby could be fathered on half the male population of Birdswell. But if it does — well, you alibi for me, I alibi for you; they'll know it was one of us, but they'll never know which of us; and if they don't know which of us, they'll have to let both of us go."

"And Black Will?" I said. "When we've not only seduced his wife, but murdered her — which one of us will *he* let go?"

"Oh, well," he said, "we'd have to clear out anyway, if it got as far as that: start again somewhere else. But the chances are a hundred to one it'll never come to it. After all, no one suspected you of the hit–and–run affair."

He kept coming back to that: and sort of — nastily. I didn't forget that I'd done him wrong, pinching his girl. But that was his lever, really: while he kept reminding me, he could pretty well force me to go in with him — he was in trouble, but I was in trouble deeper.

So we worked it out: we worked everything, to the last detail. This was Tuesday, we'd do it Thursday night. I'd see nothing more of the girl; but he'd get her to go driving with him on pretense of talking over the baby business. And he'd lead round to the accident, advising her, maybe, to confess to the police it was me; and drive past where it happened. And get her to get out of the car and show him where the boy was lying ... And then — well, then there'd be a second hit–and–run killing on that lonely corner. "*You* got away with it," he kept saying. "Why not another?"

There was a kind of — well, justice, in it, I thought. After all, it was because she was threatening to tell about the hit–and–run that I was letting her be murdered. "But what about clues?" I said. "Even I left a footprint."

He had worked that out too. He and I are the same size, of course, and most of our clothes are the same as one another's. Not for any silly reason of dressing identical, but simply because when he'd go along shopping, I'd go along too, and mostly we'd like the same things; or he'd buy something and it'd be a success, so I'd buy the same, later. We must dress the same on the night, he said, because of the alibi: and we checked our stuff over, shoes, grey flannels, shirts, without jackets — this all happened in September. Our blue poplins were in the wash — we'd worn them clean Sunday, and second–day Monday; so it would have to be the striped wool–and–nylon — a bit warm for this weather, if anyone remarked it, but we'd have to risk that, I said, we daren't ask the old woman to wash out our blue ones special. The last thing we wanted, was to do anything out of the ordinary. That was what the police looked for: the break in routine. That was asking for it.

Our shoes were the same: same size, same make, bought together, a rubber sole with bars across it, but, like I said, new enough not to be worn down, or have any peculiarities . And everything else we'd wear identical: not only for the alibi, but in case of bits caught in the girl's finger–nails or what–not — you've only got to read the papers. Not that he meant to get near enough for that. But she might not — well, she might not kick–in at once, if you see what I mean; he might have to get out of the car and do something about it. And in case of scratches, he said, I'd better be prepared to get some scratches on my own hands too — we could say we'd been blackberry–ing or something.

"Blackberry–ing," I said. "That'd be bloody likely! We both detest blackberries, everybody knows it: or anyway, the old woman knows it, we never touch her blackberry pie." I knew he'd only said it to remind me of the kid: him and his little can of blackberries, spilt all around him ...

"Oh, well," he said, "say we get scratched pushing through the brambles down by the river. Do your poaching down by the bramble patch."

But she didn't scratch him. It was all a bit grim, I think: he couldn't be sure she was properly done–in and he had to get out of the car and have a look and — well, go back and take a second run at her. But she didn't have the strength left to scratch him. All the same, he looked pretty ghastly when finally we met in the moonlight, in the Vicarage woods. He didn't say anything, just stood there, staring at me with a sort of sick, white heaviness. I couldn't exactly say anything either; it was worse than, talking it over, I'd thought it ever would be. I sort of — looked a question at him; and he gave me a weary kind of nod and glanced away towards the river. It was easier to talk about my angle, so I said, at last: "Well, I saw the Vicar."

"But did he see you?" he said. We'd agreed on the Reverend, because he always walked across to the church of a Thursday evening; you'd be sure of passing him, if you want at a certain time.

"Yes," I said. "He saw me. I gave a sort of grunt for 'good evening' and he said, 'Going poaching?' and gave me a bit of a grin. You'd better remember that." He nodded again but he said nothing more; and more to ease the silence than anything else, I said: "Is the car all right? Not marked?"

"What does it matter if it is?" he said. "It's marked all over, no one could say what's old or what's new: you know that, from bashing the boy." As for bits of her clothing and — blood and all that, he'd had the idea of spreading a bit of plastic over the front of the car before he — well, did it. He produced the plastic folded in a bit of brown paper, and we wrapped the whole lot round a stone and sank it, then and there, in the river. There was blood on the plastic all right. It gave me the shudders.

But next thing he said, I really had something to shudder at. He said: "Anyway, *your* number's up, mate. She's shopped you."

"Shopped me?" I said. I stood and stared at him.

"Shopped you." he said. "She'd already sent off an anonymous note to the police. About the hit–and–run."

"How do you know?" I said. I couldn't believe it.

"She told me so," he said. "It was on her conscience."

Her conscience. Lydia's conscience! I started to laugh, a bit hysterical, I suppose, with the strain of it. He put his hand on my wrist and gave me a little shake. "Steady lad," he said. "Don't lose your head. I'm looking after you." It wasn't like him to be so demonstrative, but there you are — it's like the poem says, when times are bad, there isn't no friend like a brother. "It's just a matter of slanting the alibi," he said.

Well, we'd worked that out, too; like I said. There'd always be a risk that they wouldn't accept a brother's alibi, that we two was together. The other time, about the accident, they'd had no special reason to suspect me, they'd accepted that all right; but this might at any moment turn into a murder enquiry.   And a murder enquiry into *us*, now they knew about the hit–and–run.  But as he said — we had the alternative.

I hadn't counted on its being Inspector Cockrill.  When I realised it was him — come all the way over from Heronsford — I knew they meant business.  And to be honest, it struck a bit chill to the heart of me.  A little man he is, for a policeman, and near retiring age, he must be — he looks like a grandfather; but his eyes are as bright as a bird's and they seem to look right into you.  He came into the old woman's best parlour and he had us brought in there, and he looked us up and down.  "Well, well," he said, — "the famous Birdwell twins!  You certainly are identicals, aren't you?"  And he gave us a look of a sort of fiendish glee, or so it seemed to me, and said: "And devoted, I hear?  An almost mystic bond, I hear?  David and Jonathan, Damon and Pythias and all the rest of it?  In face," he said, "you might properly be called — blood brothers?"

We stood in front of him, silent.  He said at last: "Well, which is which? — and no nonsense."

We told him: *and* no nonsense.

"So you're the one that killed the child?" he said to me.  "And drove on, regardless."

"I never was near the child," I said.  "I was in the woods, on Monday evening — poaching."

"Yours is the name stated in the anonymous letter."

"I don't know who wrote the letter," I said.  "But no one can tell us apart, me and my brother."

"Even your fancy girl?" he said.  "It appears it was she who wrote the letter."

"I don't know what you mean," I said, "by my fancy girl."

"Well, everyone else does," he said.  "All the village knows she was playing you off, one against the other.  And grinning behind their hands, waiting for her husband's home–coming."

"But all the village can't tell us two apart," I said.  "I was out poaching."

"That's a damn lie," says Fred, playing it the way we'd agreed upon. "That was me, poaching."

"One of you was poaching?" says Inspector Cockrill, very smooth.  "And one of you was with the lady?  And even the lady couldn't have said which was which?"

He said it sort of — suggestive.  "I dare say she might," I said, "later on in the proceedings.  But there couldn't have been any proceedings that night, there wouldn't have been time:  because the accident happened."

"Why should she say so positively that it was you, than?"

"I daresay she thought it was," I says. "I dare say he told her so. She'd finished with him: it would be the only way he could get her."

"I see," said Inspector Cockrill. "How very ingenious!" I didn't know whether he meant how ingenious of Fred to have thought of it then, or of me to think of it now.

"Don't you listen to him, sir," says Fred. "He's a bloody liar. I wasn't with the girl that night. I tell you — I was poaching."

"All right, you were poaching," said Inspector Cockrill. "Any witnesses?"

"Of course not. You don't go poaching with witnesses. I used to go with him," says Fred, bitterly, gesturing with his head towards me, "but not since he pinched my girl, the bloody so–and–so."

"And last night?" says the Inspector softly. "When the girl was murdered?"

"Last night too, the same," said Fred. "I was in the woods, poaching."

"*You* call *me* a liar!" I said. "It was me in the woods. The Vicar saw me going there."

"It was me the Vicar saw," said Fred. "I told him, Good evening, and he laughed and said, 'Going poaching?' "

"There!" said Inspector Cockrill to me, like a teacher patiently getting the truth from a difficult child. "How could he know *that*? Because the Vicar will surely confirm it?"

"He knows it because I told him," I said. "I told him I'd been poaching and I hoped the Vicar hadn't really realised where I was going."

"Very ingenious," said Inspector Cockrill again. "Very ingenious." It seemed like he couldn't get over it all, sitting there, shaking his head at the wonder of it. But I knew he was playing for time, I knew that we'd foxed him. And Fred knew too. He suggested, reasonably: "Why should you be so sure, sir, that the girl was murdered? Why not just a second hit–and–run?"

"A bit of coincidence?" said Inspector Cockrill, mildly. "Same thing, in the  same place and so very soon after? And when on top of it, we find that the girl was threatening a certain person with exposure, about the *first* hit–and–run ..." He left it in the air. He said to his sergeant: "Have you collected their clobber?"

"Yessir," said the sergeant. "Two pairs of shoes —" and he gave the Inspector a sort of nod, as if to say, Yes, they look as if they'll match very nicely — "and all the week's laundry."

"Including Monday's?" says Cockrill.

"Including Monday evening's, sir. The old woman washes of a Monday morning. Anything they've worn after that — which includes two shirts to each, sir — is in two laundry baskets, one in each bedroom."

"Two baskets?" he says, looking more bright–eyed than ever. "That's a bit of luck. Their laundry's kept separate, is it?"

"Yes, it is," says Fred, though I don't know what call he had to butt in. "His in his room, mine in mine."

"And no chance of its getting mixed up?" said Inspector Cockrill. He fixed Fred with that beady eye of his. "This could be important."

Fred, of course, was maintaining the mutual–accusation arrangement we'd agreed upon. "Not a chance, sir," he said a bit too eagerly.

I wasn't going to be left out, I said: "Not the slightest."

"That's right, sir," says the sergeant. "The old lady confirms it."

"Good," said Cockrill. He gave a few orders and the sergeant went away. People were still bussing about, up in our bedrooms. "I'm coming," called the Inspector, to someone at the head of the stairs. I turned back to us. "All right, Cain and Abel," he said. "I'll leave you to stew in it. But in a day or two, as the song says, 'I'll be seeing you.' And when I do, it'll be at short notice. So stick around, won't you?"

"And if we don't?" I said. "You've got nothing against us, you can't charge us; you've got no call to be giving us orders."

"Who's giving orders?" he said. "Just a little advice. But before you ignore the advice — take a good, hard, long look at yourselves. You won't need any mirrors. And ask yourselves," he said, giving us a good, hard, long look on his own account, from the soles of our feet to the tops of our flaming red heads, "just how far you'd get ..."

So that was that; and for the next two days, we "stewed in it," David and Jonathan, Cain and Abel — like he'd said, blood brothers.

On the third day, he sent for us, to Heronsford police station. They shoved Fred into one little room and me in another. He talked to Fred first, and I waited. All very chummy, fags and cups of tea and offers of bread and butter: but it was the waiting ...

Long after I knew I couldn't stand one more minute of it, he came. I suppose they muttered some formalities, but I don't remember: Fred and I might hate one another, and by this time we did, well and truly, there's no denying it — but it was worse, a thousand times worse, without him there. My head felt as though it were filled with grey cotton–wool, little, stuffy, warm clouds of it. He sat down in front of me. He said: "Well — have you come to your senses? Of course you killed her?"

"If anyone killed her," I said, clinging to our patter, "it must have been him."

"Your brother?" he said. "But why should your brother have killed her?"

"Well," I says, "if the girl was having a baby —"

"A baby?" he says, surprised; and his eyes got that bright, glittering look in them. He said after a minute of steady thinking: "But she wasn't."

"She wasn't?" I said. "She *wasn't*? But she'd told him —"

Or hadn't she told him? Something, like an icicle of light, ice–cold,

piercing, brilliant, thrust itself into the dark places of my cotton–wool mind.
I said: "The bloody, two–timing, double–crossing bastard ..."

"*He* didn't seem," said the Inspector, softly, "to expect her to have been
found pregnant."

So that was it! So *that* was it! So as to get me to agree to the killing, to
get me to assist with it ... I ought to have been more fly — why should Fred,
of all people, be so much afraid of Black Will as to go in for murder? Will's
a dangerous man, but Fred's not exactly a softie ... The icicle turned in my
mind and twisted, probing with its light–ways into the cotton–wooliness.
Revenge! Cold, sullen, implacable revenge upon the two of us — because
Lydia had come to me: because I had taken her. Death for her: and I to be
the accomplice in her undoing — in my own undoing. And for me ... I knew
now who had sent the anonymous note about the hit–and–run accident: so
easily to be "traced" (after she was dead) to Lydia.

But yet — he was as deep in it, still, as I was: deeper, had he but known
it. I said, fighting my way up out of the darkness: "Even if she *had* been
pregnant, it wouldn't have been my fault. I'd only been going a couple of
weeks with the girl."

"That's what you say," he said.

"But all the village —"

"All the village knew there were goings–on; nobody knew just where
they went on, or when. You must, all three, have been remarkably careful."

I tried another tack. "But if she wasn't pregnant — why should I have
killed her?"

"You've just told me yourself that you thought she was," he said.

"Because he told me — my brother told me. Now, look, Inspector," I
said, trying to think it out as I went along, trying to ram it home to him,
"you say she wasn't having a baby? So why should I have thought she was?
*She* wouldn't have told me, if she hadn't been: why should she? It was he
who told me: it was my brother. But you say yourself, he knew it wasn't
true. So why should he have told me?"

He looked at me, cold as ice. He said: "That's easy. He wanted you to
kill her for him."

*He* wanted *me* to kill her! I could have laughed. The thing was getting
fantastic, getting out of hand; and yet at the same time I had a feeling that
the fantasy was a hard, gripping, grim fantasy, that, once it had its hold on
me, would never shake loose. I stammered: "Why should he have wanted
her killed?"

"Because," he said, "she was threatening to tell that it was he who ran
the child down, and left it to die." And he said, cold and bitter: "I have no
wish to trap you. We know that it was your brother who killed the child: we
have proof of it. And we know it was you who killed the girl. We have proof
of that too: there's her blood on your cuff."

On my cuff. Where he had put his hand that night: taking my wrist in his grasp, giving me a brotherly little shake "to steady me". I remembered how I'd thought, even then, that it wasn't like him to be so demonstrative.

Putting his hand on my wrist — fresh from the blood–smeared plastic. Making such a point, later on, about there being no chance of our soiled shirts getting confused, one with the other's ...

So there it is. I wonder if we'll be doing our time in the same prison? — sharing the same cell, maybe? — we two blood brothers ...

Because he'll be doing time all right, as well as me. While I'm doing my time for *his* killing of the girl — he'll be doing his, for my killing of the child.

Well — that's all right with me. He'll be first out, I daresay (is it murder to leave a kid to die, in case, when he gets better, he tells? I suppose not: the actual knocking–down would be accidental, after all). So Fred'll be out first: and Black Will will be there to meet him when he comes. By the time I get out, I daresay Will will be 'in' for what he done to Fred; may even have got over it all by then — it looks like being a very long time away.

But can you beat it? — working it out so far ahead, leading up to it so patiently, so softly, so craftily? Planting the blood on my cuff: and then leading up to it so softly, so craftily ... And all for revenge: revenge on his own twin brother!

After all, what *I* did, was done in self–preservation: there was no venom in it, I wished him no harm. That night after the accident, I mean: when, clutching his arm, begging him to help me — just to be on the safe side, I rubbed his sleeve with the juice of a blackberry.

# The Hornet's Nest

"We've got hornets nesting again in that old elm," said Mr. Caxton, gulping down his last oyster, wiping thick fingers on his table napkin. "Interesting things, hornets." He interrupted himself, producing a large white handkerchief and violently blowing his nose. "Damn these colds of mine!"

"I saw you were treating them," said Inspector Cockrill; referring, however, to the hornets. "There's a tin of that WASP–WAS stuff on your hall table."

Cyrus Caxton ignored him. "Interesting things, I was saying. I've been reading up about them." Baleful and truculent, he looked round at the guests assembled for his wedding feast. "At certain times of the year," he quoted, "there are numerous males, the drones; which have very large eyes and whose only activity is to eat —' he glared round at them again, with special reference to the gentlemen present "— and to participate in the mass flight after the virgin queen." He cast upon his bride a speculative eye. "You are well named, Elizabeth, my dear," he said. "Elizabeth, the Virgin Queen." And added with ugly significance, "I hope."

"But only one of the hornets succeeds in the mating," said Inspector Cockrill into the ensuing outraged silence. "And he dies in the process." He sat back and looked Cyrus Caxton in the face, deliberately; and twiddled his thumbs.

Cyrus Caxton was a horrid old man. He had been horrid to his first wife and now was quite evidently going to be horrid to his second — she had been the late Mrs. Caxton's nurse, quite young still and very pretty in a blue–eyed, broken–hearted sort of way. And he was horrid to his own stout son, Theo, who was only too thankful to live away from papa, playing in an amateurish way with stocks and shares, up in London; and horrid to his step–son, Bill, who, brought into the family by the now departed wife, had immediately been pushed off to relatives in the United States to be out of Mr. Caxton's way. And he was horrid to poor young Dr. Ross who, having devotedly attended his wife in her last illness, now as devotedly attended Mr. Caxton's own soaring blood–pressure and resultant apoplectic fits; and horrid to his few friends and many poor relations, all of whom he kept on tenterhooks with promises of remembrances in his will when one of the choking fits should have carried him off. He would no doubt have been horrid to Inspector Cockrill; but — Mr. Caxton being incapable of keeping peacably to a law designed for other people as well as for himself — Cockie got in first and was horrid to *him*. It must have been Elizabeth, he reflected, who had promoted his invitation to the wedding.

The little nurse had stayed on to help with things after the poor wife died; had gradually drifted into indispensability and so into accepting the pudgy hand of the widower. Not without some heart–searching, however: Inspector Cockrill himself had, in his off–duty moments, lent a shoulder in those days of Mr. Caxton's uninhibited courtship: and she had had a little weep there, and told him of the one great love lost to her, and how she no longer looked for that kind of happiness in marriage; but was sick of work, sick of loneliness, sick of insecurity ... "But a trained nurse like you can get wonderful jobs," Inspector Cockrill had protested. "Travel all over the place, see the world." She *had* seen the world, she said, and it was too big, it scared her; she wanted to stay put, she wanted a home: and a home meant a man. "There are other men?" he had suggested; and she had burst out that there were indeed other men, too many men, all men — it was dreadful, it was frightening, to be the sort of woman that, for some unknown reason, all men looked at, all men gooped at, all men — wanted. "With him, at least I'll be safe; no one will dare to — to drool over me like that when he's around." Inspector Cockrill had somewhat hurriedly disengaged his shoulder. He was a younger man in those days of Mr. Caxton's second marriage and subsequent departure from this life, and taking no chances.

And so the affair had gone forward. The engagement and imminent wedding had been announced and in the same breath the household staff — faithful apparently in death as in life, to the late Mrs. Caxton — had made their own announcement: they had seen it coming and were now sweeping out in a body, preferring, thank you very much, not to continue in service under that Nurse. The bride, unchaperoned, had perforce modestly retired to a London hotel and from thence left most of the wedding arrangements to Son Theo and Step–son Bill — Theo running up and down from London, Bill temporarily accommodated for the occasion beneath the family roof.

Despite the difficulties of its achievement, Mr. Caxton was far from satisfied with the wedding breakfast. "I never did like oysters, Elizabeth, as you must very well know. Why couldn't we have had smoked salmon? And I don't like cold meat, I don't like it in any form. Not in *any* form," he insisted, looking once again at his virgin queen with an ugly leer. Inspector Cockrill surprised upon the faces of all the males present, drones and workers alike, a look of malevolence which really quite shocked him.

She protested, trembling. "But, Cyrus, it's been so difficult with no servants. We got what was easiest."

"Very well, then. Having got it, let us have it." He gestured to the empty oyster shells. "With all these women around — am I to sit in front of a dirty plate for ever?"

The female relations upon this broad hint rose from their places like a flock of sitting pheasants and began scurrying to and fro, clearing used crockery, passing plates of chicken and ham. "Don't over–do it, my dears," said Mr. Caxton, sardonically watching their endeavours. "You're all out of the will now, you know."

It brought them up short: the crudeness, the brutality of it — standing staring back at him, the plates in their shaking hands. Half of them, probably, cared not two pins for five, or five–and–twenty pounds in Cyrus Caxton's will, but they turned, nevertheless, upon the new heiress questioning — reproachful — eyes. "Oh, but Cyrus, that's not true," she cried; and above his jeering protests insisted: "Cyrus has destroyed his old will, yes; but he's made a new one and — well, I mean, no one has been forgotten, I'm sure, who was mentioned before."

The lunch progressed. Intent, perhaps, to show their disinterestedness, the dispossessed scuttled back and forth with the cold meats, potato mayonnaise, sliced cucumber — poured delicious barley water (for Mr. Caxton was a rabid teetotaler) into cut glass tumblers, worthy of better things. The bridegroom munched his way through even the despised cold viands in a manner that boded ill, thought Inspector Cockrill, for the wretched Elizabeth, suddenly coming alive to the horror of what she had taken upon herself. She sat silent and shrinking and made hardly any move to assist with the serving. Son Theo carved and sliced, Step–son Bill handed plates, even young Dr. Ross wandered round with the salad bowl; but the bride sat still and silent and those three, thought Cockie, could hardly drag their eyes from the small white face and the dawning terror there. The meat plates were removed, the peaches lifted one by one from their tall bottles and placed, well soused with syrup, on their flowery plates. Step–son Bill dispensed the silver desert spoons and forks, fanned out ready on the sideboard. The guests sat civilly, spoons poised, ready to begin.

Cyrus Caxton waited for no one. He gave a last loud trumpeting blow to his nose, stuffed away his handkerchief, picked up the spoon beside his plate and somewhat ostentatiously looked to see if it was clean: plunged spoon and fork into the peach, spinning dizzily before him in its syrup and, scooping off a large chunk, slithered it into his mouth: stiffened — stared about him with a wild surmise — gave one gurgling roar of mingled rage and pain, turned first white, then purple, then an even more terrifying dingy, dark red; and pitched forward across the table with his face in his plate. Elizabeth cried out: "He's swallowed the peach stone!"

Dr. Ross was across the room in three strides, grasped the man by the hair and chin and laid him back in his chair. The face looked none the more lovely for being covered in syrup and he wiped it clean with one swipe of a table napkin; and stood for what seemed a long moment, hands on the arms of the chair, gazing down, intent and abstracted, at the spluttering mouth and rolling eyes. Like a terrier, Elizabeth was to say later to Inspector Cockrill, alert and suspicious, snuffing the scent. Then with another of his swift movements, he was hauling Mr. Caxton out of his chair, lowering him to the floor; calling out, "Elizabeth! — my bag. On a chair in the hall." But she seemed struck motionless by the sudden horror of it all and only stammered out, imploring, "Theo?" Stout Theo, nearest the door, bestirred himself to dash out into the hall, appearing a moment later with the bag. Step–son Bill, kneeling with the doctor beside the heaving body, took it from him, opened it out. Elizabeth, shuddering, said again: "He must have swallowed the stone."

The doctor ignored her. He had caught up the fallen table–napkin and was using it to grasp, with his left hand, the man's half–swallowed tongue and pull it forward to free the air–passages; at the same time with his right groping blindly towards the medical bag. "A finger–stall — it's just on top, somewhere ..." Bill found it immediately and handed it to him; he shuffled it on and thrust the middle finger of his right hand down the gagging throat. "Nothing there," he said, straightening up, standing looking down, absently wiping his fingers on the table–napkin, rolling off the finger–stall — and all again with that odd effect of sniffing the air; galvanising into action once more, however, to fall on his knees beside the body. With the heel of his left hand he began a quick, sharp pumping at the sternum, with his right he gestured towards the medical bag. "The hypodermic. Adrenalin ampoules in the left pocket." Bill fumbled, unaccustomed, and he lifted his head for a moment and said, sharply: "For heaven's sake — Elizabeth?" She jumped, startled. "Yes? Yes?" she said, stacatto; and seemed to come suddenly to her senses. "Keep it ready," he said. "Somebody cut away the sleeve." He took both hands to the massage of the heart. "While I do this — can someone give him the kiss of life?"

It was a long time since anyone, his affianced not excluded, had willingly given Mr. Caxton a kiss of any kind and it could not now be said that volunteers came eagerly forward. The doctor said again, "Elizabeth?" but this time on a note of doubt. She looked down, faltering at the gaping mouth, dreadfully dribbling. "Must I?"

"You're a nurse," said Dr. Ross. "And he's dying."

"Yes. Yes, of course I must." She brought out a small handkerchief, scrubbed at her own mouth as though somehow irrationally to cleanse it before a task so horrible; moved to crouch where she would not interfere with the massage of the heart. "Now?"

Mercifully, Cyrus Caxton himself provided the answer — suddenly and unmistakably giving up the ghost. He heaved up into a last great, lunging spasm, screamed briefly and rolled up his eyes. She sat back on her heels, the handkerchief balled against her mouth, gaping. Dr. Ross abandoned the heart massage, thrust her aside, himself began a mouth–to–mouth breathing. But even he soon admitted defeat. "It's no use," he said, straightening up, his hands to his aching back. "He's gone."

Gone: and not one, perhaps, in all that big ugly ornate room but felt a sort of lightening of relief, a sort of little lifting of the heart because with the going of Cyrus Caxton so much of ugliness, crudity, cruelty also had gone. Not one at any rate, even to pretend to grief. Only the widowed bride, still kneeling by the heavy body, lifted her head and looked across with a terrible question into the doctor's eyes; and leapt to her feet and darted out into the hall. She came back and stood in the doorway. "The tin of cyanide," she said. "It's gone."

Dr. Ross picked up the dropped table–napkin and quietly, unobtrusively yet very deliberately, laid it over the half eaten peach.

Inspector Cockrill's underlings dealt with the friends and relations, despatching them to their deep chagrin about their respective businesses, relieved of any further glorious chance of notoriety. The tin had been discovered without much difficulty, hidden in a vase of pampas grass which stood in the centre of the hall table: its lid off and a small quantity of the paste missing, scooped out, apparently, with something so smooth as to show no peculiarities of marking, at any rate to the naked eye. It had been on the table since some time on the day before the wedding. Cockie himself had seen it there, just before the lunch.

He thought it all over, deeply and quietly — for it had been a plot deeply and quietly laid. "I'll see those four for myself," he said to his sergeant. "Mrs. Caxton, of course, the son and the step–son and the doctor." These were the principals and one might as well tease them a little and see what emerged; but for the rest of course — he knew[1]: the how and the when and the why, and therefore the who. Some details to be sorted out, naturally; but for the rest — he knew; a few words recollected, a dozen, no more — and with a little reflection, how clear it all became! Curious, thought Cockie, how two brief sentences, hardly attended to, might so twist themselves about and about as to wind themselves at last into a rope. Into a noose.

He established himself in what had been Cyrus Caxton's study and sent for Elizabeth. "Well, Mrs. Caxton?"

White teeth dug into a trembling lower lip to bite back hysteria. "Oh, Inspector, at least don't call me by that horrible name!"

"It is your name now; and we're emerged upon a murder investigation. There's no time for nonsense."

"You don't really believe —?"

---

[1] And so should the reader

"You know it," said Cockie. "You were the first to know it."

"Dr. Ross was the first," she said. "You saw him yourself, Inspector, leaning over Cyrus as he was lying back in that chair; sort of — snuffing. Like a terrier on the scent. He could smell the cyanide on his breath, I'm sure he could; like bitter almonds they say it is."

It had not needed an analyst to detect the white traces of poison on the peach and in the heavy syrup. "Who bought the food for the luncheon, Mrs. Caxton?"

"Well, we all ... We talked it over, Theo and Bill and I. It was so difficult, you see, with no servants; and me being in London. I ordered most of the stuff to be sent down from Harrod's and Theo brought down — well, one or two things from Fortnum and Mason's ..." Her voice trailed away rather unhappily.

"Which one or two things? The peaches, you mean?"

"Well, yes, the peaches. He brought them down himself, yesterday. He was up and down from London all the time, helping Bill." But, she cried, imploring, why should Theo possibly have done this terrible thing? His own father! For that matter, why should anyone?"

"Ah, as to that!" said Cockie. Had not Cyrus Caxton spoken his own epitaph? *At certain times there are numerous males, the drones, which have very large eyes and whose only activity is to eat and to participate in the mass flight after the virgin queen.* He had seen them himself, stuffing down Mr. Caxton's oysters and cold chicken and ham, their eyes, dilated with devotion, fixed with an astonishing unanimity upon Mr. Caxton's bride. "*Only one of them mates, however,*" he repeated to himself, "*and he dies in the process.*" That also had been seen to be true. "Elizabeth," he said, forgetting for a moment that this was a murder investigation and there was to be no nonsense, "from the hornet's–eye angle, I'm afraid you are indeed a virgin queen."

And Theo, the young drone Theo, stout and lethargic, playing with his stocks and shares in his cosy London flat ... Inspector Cockrill had known him since his boyhood. "You needn't think, Cockie, that *I* wanted my father's money. I'm all right: I got my share of my mother's money when she died."

"Oh, did you?" said Cockrill. "And her other son, Bill?"

"She left it to my father, to pass on if he thought it was right."

"Wasn't that a bit unfair? He wasn't Bill's own father; and it was her money."

"I think she'd probably sort of written him off. I mean, it's easy enough to hop across from America nowadays, isn't it? But he never came to see her. Though I believe the servants let him know, when she was dying; and they did correspond. In secret; my father would never have allowed it, of course."

"Of course!" said Cockie. He dismissed the matter of money. "How well, Theo, did you know your father's new wife?"

"Not at all well. I saw her when I came to visit my mother during her illness, and again at the funeral after she died. But of course ..." But of course, his tone admitted, a man didn't have to know Elizabeth well, to ... There was that something ...

"You never contemplated marrying her yourself?"

But Theo, lazy and self–indulgent, was not for the married state. "All the same, Inspector, it did make me pretty sick to think of it. I mean, my own father ..."

Would Theo, dog in the manger, almost physically revolted by the thought of his adored in the gross arms of his own father — would Theo kill for that? "These bottled peaches, Theo. You served them out, I know; but who actually opened them? I mean, had they been unsealed in advance?"

"No, because they'd have lost the bouquet of the Kirsch. Right up to the last minute, they were sealed."

"Can you prove that?"

"Elizabeth can bear me out. We nipped in here on the way to the wedding — I drove her down from London — for me to go to the loo in case I should start hopping in church. And she took a quick dekko just to see that everything looked all right. She'll tell you the bottles were still sealed up then; you can ask her."

"How quick a dekko? Tell me about this visit."

"Oh, good heavens, Inspector! — the whole thing took three minutes, we were late and you know what the old man was. We rushed in, I dashed into the cloakroom, when I came out she was standing in the dining–room door, looking in, and she said, "It all looks wonderful," and what a good job Bill and I had done. Then *she* went into the cloakroom and we both got into the car and went off again."

"Was the tin of cyanide on the hall table then?"

"Yes, because she said thank goodness Bill seemed to have got it for her and saved her more trouble with Father."

"No one else was in the house at this time?"

"No, Bill had gone on to the church with my father."

"O.K. Well, send this Bill to me, will you, Theo? And tell him to bring his passport with him."

He was ten years older than his step–brother; well into his thirties: blond headed, incisive, tough, an ugly customer probably on a dirty night; but rather an engaging sort of chap for all that. Cockie turned over the pages of the passport. "You haven't been in this country since you were a boy?"

"No, they shipped me out as a kid; my new papa didn't want me and my mother doesn't seem to have put up too much of a fight for me. So I wasn't all that crazy to come rushing home on visits."

"Not even when she died?"

"At that time I was — prevented," he said briefly.

"By what, if I may ask?"

"By four stone walls," said Step–son Bill, ruefully. "Which in my case, Inspector, did a prison make. In other words, I was doing time, sir. I got into a fight with a guy and did six months for him. I only got out a few weeks ago."

"A fight about what?"

"About my wife, if you have to know," he said sullenly. "I was bumming around, I admit it, and I guess he got her on the rebound. Well, bum or not, I took and chucked her out and that was the end of her. And I took and pulled him in, and that was the end of *him* — in the role of seducer, anyway."

"You divorced your wife?"

"Yeh, I divorced her." He looked at Inspector Cockrill, and the hard, bright eyes had suddenly a look almost of despair. "I think now I made some pretty bad mistakes," he said.

"At any rate, having got out, you learned that your step–father was marrying the nurse; that your mother's money was in jeopardy, perhaps? So you came across the hot foot, to look the lady over?"

And having looked her over ... Another drone, drawn, willy–nilly — the more so for having been for long months starved of the company of women, for having been deprived of the wife whom he still loved — into the mass flight after the virgin queen. "It was you, I believe, who brought the poison into the house?"

"Yes, I did. The old man was furious with Elizabeth because she hadn't ordered it. How could she, poor girl, when she wasn't here half the time? So I went down and fetched it, just to save her more trouble, and put it on the hall table so he'd think she'd got it."

"But she was in London: how could she?"

"Oh, heck, he couldn't care: if it wasn't there, she was responsible."

"And after all this alleged fuss and urgency, it never got used?"

"Didn't I tell you? — it was only to make more trouble for Elizabeth. He was a man that just loved to find fault."

"I see. Well, we agree it was you who introduced the cyanide. Was it not also you who handed a plate of cold meat to your step–father?"

"Was it I who —? For heaven's sakes, Inspector! Those old ladies were running around like a lot of decapitated hens, snatching plates out of our hands, dumping them down in front of just anyone who'd accept them."

"You might, however, have said specifically to one of them, 'This plate is especially for Mr. Caxton.'"

"I might at that," said Bill, cheerfully. "Why don't you ask around and find her: she'll tell you." He shrugged. "Anyway, what does it matter? The poison wasn't on the meat, was it? It had been put on the peach."

"If it had," said Cockie, "it had been put there by someone very clever." He dwelt on it. "How could it have been placed there so that the whole dose — to all intents and purposes — was on the one mouthful that he happened to take? The first mouthful."

And he sent Step–son Bill away and summoned Dr. Ross. "Well, doctor — so we have it. *Only one mates; and he dies in the process.*"

"You're referring to the thing about the hornets?" said Dr. Ross rather stiffly.

"That's right: to the thing about the hornets. But nobody could call *you* a drone, doctor. So busy with that little bag of yours that you had it with you out in the hall, all ready to hand."

"At intervals of about one week," said Dr. Ross, "policemen like yourself exhort us not to leave our medical bags in unattended cars." He fixed Inspector Cockrill with a dark and very angry eye. "Are you suggesting that it was I who murdered my own patient?"

"Will you declare yourself outside the mass flight, Dr. Ross? You must have seen a good deal of our little queen in the sickroom of the late Mrs. Caxton."

"I happen to have a little queen of my own, Inspector. Not to mention several little drones, not yet ready for flighting."

"I know," said Cockie. "It must have been hell for you." He said it very kindly. He added: "I accuse you of nothing."

Disarmed, he capitulated, immediately, wretchedly. "I've never so much as touched her hand, Inspector. But it's true — there's something about her ... And to think of that filthy old brute ..."

"Well, he's gone," said Cockie. "Murdered under your nose — and mine. And talking of noses —"

"I smelt it on his breath. Oh, gosh, the faintest whiff — but there was something. I thought it must be just the Kirsch — the Kirsch on the peaches."

"Such a curious meal!" said Inspector Cockrill, brooding over it. "He was the bridegroom: you'd think everybody would be falling over themselves to please him. But no: he didn't like oysters, but he has to have oysters, he hated cold meat but all there is, is cold meat, he was violently teetotal but he's given peaches with liqueur on 'em." He sat with his chin on his hand, his bright bird eyes gazing away into nothingness. "There has been a plan here, doctor: no simple matter of a lick of poison scraped out of a fortuitous tin, smeared on to a fortuitous peach–in–liqueur; but a very elaborate, deep laid, long–thought–out, absolutely sure–fire plan. But who planned it, who carried it out and with what ultimate motive ... He broke off. He said at last, slowly: "Of course whatever's in the will, as the law goes now she will still be a rich widow; more agreeable to her, presumably, than being a rich wife."

"You don't honestly think that Elizabeth —?"

"Elizabeth had nothing to do with the preparation of the food; she hasn't been in the house for the past three days, except for that brief interlude when she and Theo came in on their way to the church. Each of them was alone for a period of a minute or two — Elizabeth probably for less. Not nearly enough time to have chanced prising open the tin, scooping out the stuff, doctoring the peaches (which anyway were still in sealed bottles) or the cold meat or oysters. On the other hand — Elizabeth is a trained nurse." He mused over it. "He had a bad cold. Could she have persuaded him to take some drug or other? On the way back from the church, for example."

"He was a man who wouldn't touch medicines. He got these colds, the place was stiff with pills and potions I'd prescribed for him, but he'd never even try them. Besides," he insisted, as Bill had before him, "the stuff was on the peach?" And it was that fat slob Theo who had been responsible for the peach. Not that he wanted to suggest, he added rather hurriedly, that Theo would have murdered his own father. But ... "You needn't think I haven't seen him gooping at her."

"You needn't think I haven't seen you all gooping at her."

"I've made up my mind," said the doctor, quietly and humbly, "if I can get out of this business with my family still safe and sound, never so long as I can help it, to see Elizabeth again."

"You are a worker," said Cockie. "Not a true drone. It will be easier for you. Bill is a drone; he admits it — only *he* calls it a bum."

And so was fat Theo a drone. Bill, Theo, the doctor ...

But the doctor had a family of his own, whom he had had no intention, ever, of deserting for Elizabeth the Virgin Queen. And for that matter, so had Bill a wife of his own, whom, even now, even knowing Elizabeth, he cared for. And Theo was sufficient unto himself and would go no further than a little yearning, a little mooning, an occasional sentimental somersaulting of the fatty heart. *Only one of the mates* ... Of the four, mass flighting after the queen, only one in fact had been a potential mate; and sure enough had died.

Of the three remaining — which might be capable of murder, only to prevent that mating?

Investigation, interrogation — the message to Harrod's, to Fortnum's, to the chemist's shop in the village; the telephone calls to Mr. Caxton's lawyers, to Step–son Bill's few contacts in America, to the departed domestic staff ... The afternoon passed and the light summer evening came; and he stood with the four of them, out on the terrace of the big, ugly, anything–but–desirable residence which must now be Elizabeth's own. "Elizabeth — Mrs. Caxton — and you three gentlemen ... In this business there is only one conceivable motive. Money doesn't come into it. The new will had been signed, Mr. Caxton's death now or later made no differences to its contents. None of you appears to have been in any urgent financial need. So there's only one motive, and therefore only one question: who would commit murder to prevent Cyrus Caxton from ever holding Elizabeth in his arms?"

Stout Theo? — who might yet have keen enough feelings, whose sick revulsion might be the more poignant because his own father had been involved. Or Step–son Bill? — who for this same unendurable thought of the beloved in the arms of another, could half–kill a man and cast off for ever the woman he still loved. Or the doctor? — who, of them all, had most closely known Elizabeth; who, as Cyrus Caxton's medical adviser, knew only too intimately the gross body and crude appetites of the conquering male ...

Theo, Bill, Dr. Ross. Out of these three ... Softly, softly catchee monkey, said Inspector Cockrill to himself. Aloud he said: "This murder was a planned murder; nothing would have been left to chance. So why, I go on asking myself, should his first mouthful of peach have been the fatal one? And I answer myself: 'Think about that spoon!' "

"You mean the spoon Theo was using to dish out the peaches?" said Elizabeth quickly. "But no, because Theo didn't hand the plate to his father. He couldn't know which peach he'd get."

"Unless he directed a special plate to his father?" suggested Bill, casting a quizzical glance at Inspector Cockrill. He reassured a suddenly quacking Theo. "O.K. pal, take it easy. We've already worked through that one."

"In any event, it wouldn't account for the first mouthful being the poisoned one. And Elizabeth," said Inspector Cockrill severely, "please don't go trying to put me off! That was a red–herring — to draw my attention away from the other spoon: the spoon handed directly to your husband by Master Bill here."

She began to cry, drearily, helplessly, biting on the little white screwed–up ball of her handkerchief. "Inspector, Cyrus is dead, all this won't bring him back. Couldn't you —? Couldn't we —?" And she burst out that if it was all because of her, it was so dreadful for people to be in all this trouble ...

"But your husband has been murdered: what do you expect me to do, let it go at that, just because his murderer had a sentimental crush on you?" He came back to the spoon. "If that spoon had been smeared with poison —"

She stopped crying at once, raised her head triumphantly. "It couldn't have been. Cyrus looked at it to see that it was polished clean; he always did after the servants left, he said that I ..." The lower lip began to wobble again. "I know he's dead; but he wasn't very kind," she said.

Not Theo then: who could not have known that the poisoned peach would reach his father. Not Bill, who could not have poisoned the peach at all. "And so," said Dr. Ross, "you come to me?"

It was very quiet out there on the terrace; the sun had gone down now and soon the stars would be out, almost invisible in the pale evening sky. They stood, still and quiet also, and for a little while all were silent. Elizabeth said at slowly: "Inspector — Dr. Ross has a wife of his own; and children."

"He still might not care for the vision of you in the arms of 'that filthy old brute' as he called him."

"That went for us all," said the doctor.

"But it was you that went for Mr. Caxton, doctor — wasn't it? Or *to* him, if you prefer. Went to him and put down his throat a finger protected by a rubber finger–stall."

A finger–stall — thrust down the throat of a man having an every–day choking fit. A finger–stall dabbled in advance in a tin of poison.

"You don't believe this?" said Dr. Ross, staring aghast. "You can't believe it? Murder my own patient!" Elizabeth caught at his arm, crying out, "Oh course he doesn't mean it!" but he ignored her. "And murder him in such a way! And anyway, how could I have known he would have a choking fit?"

"He was always having choking fits," said Cockie.

"But Dr. Ross couldn't have *got* the poison," said Elizabeth. "It wasn't he who fetched the bag from the hall." She broke off. "Oh, Theo, I didn't intend —"

"I got the bag," said Theo. "But that doesn't mean anything."

"It could mean it was you who dabbled the finger–stall in poison."

Theo's round face lost colour. "Me, Inspector? How could I have? How could I know anything about it? *I* don't know what they use finger–stalls for and what they don't."

"Anyway, he wouldn't have had time," said Elizabeth. "Not to think it all out, undo the poison tin, find the finger–stall in the bag. Finger–stalls are kept in a side pocket, not floating about at the top of a medical bag."

But in fact that was just where it had been: floating about at the top of the medical bag. Bill, crouching beside the doctor over the heaving body, had located it immediately and handed it to him. "I had used it on a patient just before I came to the church," said Dr. Ross patiently. "You can check if you like. I threw it into boiling water, dried it and chucked it back into the bag. I was in a hurry to come to the wedding."

In a hurry — to come to Elizabeth's wedding. "So the finger–stall was in the fore–front of your mind then, doctor? — when you brought in your medical bag and put it down on the chair and your eye fell on that tin of poison. Everyone is milling about, just back from the ceremony, not thinking of anyone except the bride and bridegroom. You take a little scoop of the poison, using the finger–stall — just in case occasion arises. And occasion does arise. What a bit of luck!"

"Inspector Cockrill," said Elizabeth steadily, "this is all nonsense. Dr. Ross smelt the stuff on Cyrus's breath, long before he put the finger–stall down his throat. You saw him yourself, like I said sort of — snuffing ..."

"Sort of snuffing at nothing," said Cockie. "There was nothing to snuff at, was there, doctor? — not yet. But it placed the poison, you see, in advance of the true poisoning with the finger–stall. The man chokes, the doctor leans over him, pretends to be suspicious. *Then* the finger–stall down the throat; and this time there *is* something to snuff at. And when the finger–stall is later examined, the fact of its having been down the man's throat will account for traces of cyanide on it. Now all that remains is to pin–point the earlier sources of the poison. Well, that's easy: he wipes off the finger–stall on the napkin; and then, so innocently! — places the napkin over the peach." His bright eyes, bird–like, looked triumphantly round upon them.

The all stood rigid, staring at the doctor: horrified, questioning. Elizabeth cried out: "Oh, it isn't true!" but on a note of doubt.

"I don't think so, no," said Cockie. "This isn't a crime where anything was left to chance. And this is based on the chance that the old man might have a choking fit."

She went over to the doctor, put her two little hands on his arm, laid her forehead for a moment against his shoulder in a gesture devoid of coquetry. "Oh, thank God! He frightened me."

"He didn't frighten me," said Dr. Ross stoutly; but he looked all the same exceedingly pale. To Cockrill he said: "He got these choking fits, yes: but — once or twice in a year. You couldn't risk all that on the chance of his having one."

"So that brings us back to you, Theo," said Inspector Cockrill, blandly. "Who gave him peaches in Kirsch and *made* him have one."

Theo looked as likely as his father had ever done, to have a choking fit. "*I* made him have one?"

"My dear Theo! A man is a rabid teetotaler. You provide him with a peach in a thick syrup of Kirsch — observing that he has a heavy cold and won't smell the liqueur in advance. He takes a great gulp of it and realises that he's been tricked into taking alcohol. You knew your father: he would go off into one of his spluttering rages and if he didn't choke on the peach, he'd choke on his own spluttering. And it isn't true, is it? that you didn't know about choking fits, and how the air–passages may be freed with a finger, covered with a finger–stall. You must have seen your father in these attacks at least once or twice; he'd been having them for years."

He began to splutter himself. "I couldn't have done it. Gone out into the hall, you mean, to get the bag, and put the stuff on the finger–stall then?

Elizabeth showed that earlier; I wouldn't have had time."

"We were all preoccupied, getting your father out of his chair and lowered on to the floor. The seconds pass quickly."

But she couldn't bear it for Theo, either. "Don't listen to him, Theo, don't be frightened! This is no more true than the other theory. He's — he's sort of teasing us; needling us, trying to make us say something. If Theo did it, Inspector, what about Dr. Ross? Why should he have sniffed at Cyrus's breath, when he was lying back in the chair. There would have been nothing to smell, yet. You say he was pretending; but if it was Theo who put the poison on the finger–stall — why should the doctor have pretended? Unless ..." She broke off, clapped her hand to her mouth; took it away immediately, began to fiddle unconcernedly with the handkerchief. Inspector Cockrill said: "Yes, Elizabeth? Unless —?"

"Nothing," said Elizabeth. "I just mean that the doctor wouldn't have put on an act if it had been Theo who'd done it."

Unless ... He thought about it and his eyes were brilliant as stars. "Unless, Elizabeth, you were going to say — unless they were in it together." And he looked round at the three of them and smiled with the smile of a tiger. "Unless they were all three in it together."

Three men — united: united in loving the same woman, united in not wishing actually to possess her; united in determination, however, that a fourth man should not.

The first casual exchange of thought, of feeling, of their common disgust and dread; the first casual discussion of some sort of action, some sort of rescue; the vague threats hardening into determination, into hard fact, into realistic plotting. But — murder! Even backed up by the rest — which one of them would positively commit murder? And, none accepting — dividing the deed, then, amongst them: as in an execution, where a dozen men fire the bullets, no one man kills.

Bill's task to acquire the poison, see that it remains available in the hall. Theo's task to ensure, as far as possible, that a chance arises to use the poisoned finger–stall. The doctor, of course, actually to employ it. But lest that seem too heavy a share of the guilt for any one partner to carry, let Theo be the one to go out into the hall and poison the finger–stall; let Bill take the bag from him, hand the poisoned thing to the doctor. Executioners: does he who administers the poison, kill more than he who procures it? — does he who presents the victim to the murder, kill the less because he does not do the actual slaying? All for one and one for all! And all for the purity of Elizabeth, the Virgin Queen.

Elizabeth stood with him, weeping, in the hall, while a sergeant herded the three men into the huge, hideous drawing–room and kept them there till the police car should come. "I don't believe it: I utterly don't believe it, Inspector. Those three? A plot —"

He had said it long ago: from the very beginning. "A very deep–laid, elaborate, absolutely sure–fire plan."

"Between the doctor and Theo then, if you must. But Bill — why drag Bill into it?"

"Ah, Bill," he said. "But without Bill ...? You have been very loyal; but I think we must now come into the open about Bill?"

And he was back with her, so many weeks ago now, when Cyrus Caxton's proposed new marriage had first become an open secret. "With your job, Elizabeth, you could travel, you could see the world." "I *have* seen the world," she had answered. "All right," she admitted now, in a small voice. "Yes. I did go to America, with a private patient. I did get married there. Cyrus knew that I'd been married and divorced. I didn't tell other people because he didn't like anyone knowing that I was — well, he called it second–hand."

Married; and divorced. Married to one who "bumming around" had heard through the devoted family servants that his mother's illness would be her last. "Inspector, we were desperate. He wouldn't work, he gambled like a maniac, my nursing wouldn't keep the two of us. And yet I couldn't leave him. I told you that I had had a lost love; well, that was true in its own way. My love he was — and yet not lost really after all: my love he is still and to my ruin ever shall be. I supposed some women are like that."

"And some men," said Cockie; thinking of that suddenly desolate look with which he had said, "I think now that I made some pretty big mistakes."

"I've been so ashamed, Inspector," she said, weeping again. "Not only of what we were doing; but of all the lies, all the acting."

"Yet you went through with it."

"You don't know Bill," she said. "But yes — it's true. He wrote to his mother secretly, through the servants. He said a girl would get in touch with her, a wonderful nurse, who would soon be coming over to England. He told her to say nothing to the old man but to try to get this girl engaged to look after her; of course the girl was me, Inspector. The idea at first was simply to look after his interests, to try to get his mother's money ensured to him, before she died. But then he got this other idea. The old man would soon be a widower; and he thought of him as a *very* old man, old and, he knew, in bad health. He hadn't seen his step–father for years, to an adolescent, all adults seem far more aged than they are. He imagined an old crock far more in need of a nurse than of a wife. So — the first thing was a divorce. He beat up a man whom he accused of having an affair with me; he over–did that a bit and landed himself in prison; but even that he didn't mind, it helped in speeding up the divorce because of the reason for the assault."

"Without a divorce, you couldn't have inherited, of course. The marriage with the old man had to be water–tight."

"Inspector," she said, in anguish, "don't believe for one moment that this began as a murder plot. It started from small beginnings, as I've said; and then in that gambler's mind of his, it just grew and grew. Here was this golden chance. He knew that I had this — this power over men; something that I just have, I can't help it, you've seen for yourself how, without any effort on my part, it worked. With such an asset — how could he bear not to exploit it? A sick old man, recently widowed, a pretty little nurse already installed: how could it fail?"

"And he was prepared to wait?"

"He saw the thing in terms of a year or two, no longer. Meanwhile he would remain in England, we could see one another — after all, he was a member of the family. And I would provide him with money, I suppose; and he would gamble."

"But before this happy condition of things, you must nurse the dying mother; and then get to work succeeding in her place with the widower."

She turned away her head. "I know you think it sounds terrible; put that way, it seems terrible to me too — and it always has done. But — well, of course I had only Bill's picture of the situation, the picture of an ailing old man who would want a — a nurse rather than a wife … And when I found out differently — well, once again, you don't know Bill. What Bill says, you have to do. And I did nurse her: she was dying, I couldn't make any difference to that, but I did nurse her and care for her — almost her last words were of gratitude to me. When she died, I could hardly bear it. I rang up Bill in America and told him I couldn't go through with it. But … Well, he just said —"

"He said you *must* go through with it: and came over here himself, to make sure that you did?"

"To make sure of that — and of something else?" she said, faintly.

"Yes," he said, thinking it over. "Of something else too. Because he's still in love with you, Elizabeth, in his own way. And he might drive you to the altar with a horrible old man; but he would never let you get as far as the old man's bed."

And in that determination, he had found unexpected allies. "I suppose, Inspector, he may have meant to do it himself — God knows, he never to me breathed a word of such a thing. As I say, back in the States, he was visualising this old–man–and–nurse relationship. But anyway, he's a gambler, here was this chance and nothing must stand in the way of it. Then he came over here and saw me again: and saw me with his step–father … And then, perhaps, finding how the other two felt about it, I suppose he roped them in. Another gambler's chance: so typical of Bill. Only this one will come off for a change, because in this way the law can't do anything to them?"

"How do you mean? — can't do anything?"

"Well, but — who has committed any crime?  Bill has bought a tin of stuff for killing wasps:  there's nothing wrong in that?  Theo has bought a bottle of peaches — nothing wrong in that either?  The doctor — well, I suppose he did put a finger–stall down Cyrus's throat.  But *he* didn't poison it.  None of them has actually done one wrong action.  They can't even be put in prison?"

"Only for a very short time," acknowledged Cockie.

"For a short time?" she said, startled.

"Till they're taken out and hanged," said Inspector Cockrill.

"You don't truly mean that?  All three of them could be — executed?"

"All three," said Cockie.  "For being concerned in a murder:  that's the law.  The flight of the queen, Elizabeth — *at certain times of the year the drones sit around eating* — well, we saw them do that — *and gazing with huge eyes upon the virgin queen* — well, we saw them do that too.  And then, *the mass flight after the queen*:  and that also we've seen.  But here something goes wrong with the comparison; because only one succeeds in the mating; and therefore — only one dies."

"You mean that these three —?"

"I mean that these three are not going to die.  It would be too inartistic an ending to the metaphor."

"What can save them?" said Elizabeth, beginning to tremble.

"Words can save them:  and will save them."

"Words?"

"A dozen words:  carelessly spoken, hardly listened to, attended to not at all.  Except by me when later I remembered them.  Your husband saying, 'Why couldn't I have had smoked salmon?' and you replying, 'We got what was easiest.'  A plain–clothes man who had all this time sat quietly on a chair by the front door, got up, as quietly, and came forward; and Inspector Cockrill shot out a hand and circled with steely hard fingers, her narrow wrist.  "Why should oysters have been easier than smoked salmon, Elizabeth?" he said.

A very elaborate, long–thought–out, deep–laid, absolutely sure–fire plan ...

The ugly collusion between husband and wife, to implant in the household of the dying mother, a new bride for the rich widower soon to be.  On the husband's part, probably nothing more — nothing worse intended than an impatient waiting from then on, for the end of a life whose expectations had been somewhat underestimated.  On hers — ah! she had been on the spot to recognise in advance the long years she might yet have to serve with a man who at the least sign of rebellion would pare down her inheritance to the limit the law allowed.  Had she really confessed to Cyrus

Caxton an earlier marriage? Not likely! "You are well named Elizabeth —
the virgin queen," he had said; and added, "I hope." Of them all, the one
who had had most cause to dread Mr. Caxton's marriage bed, had been
Elizabeth herself.

The plot then, laid: but in one mind alone. Use the ex–husband,
expendable now, as red–herring number one; ensnare with enchantments
long proved irresistible. Such other poor fools as might serve to confuse the
issue. With gentle persistence, no injury pin–pointable, alienate servants
too long faithful and now in the way. Add, the scene set, sit, sweet and
smiling, little hands fluttering, soft eyes mistily blue — and in the back of
one's scheming mind, think and think and plan and plan …

"You can't know," she said, spitting it out at him, as they drove away
from the house, the three men left sick and bewildered, utterly confounded,
watching her go: sitting between himself and his sergeant in the smooth
black police car, ceaselessly, restlessly struggling against their grip on her
wrists. "You don't know. It's all a trick, trying to lead me up the garden path."

"No," said Cockrill. "Not any more. We've been up enough garden
paths: with you leading *me*." His arm gave slackly against the tug and pull
of her hand, but his fingers never left their firm hold. "How well you did it!
— poking the clues under my nose, snatching each of them back when you
saw it wasn't going to work — and all with such a touching air of protecting
your poor dear admirers, fallen into this terrible trap, for love of you. But
I matched you," he said with quiet satisfaction, "trick for trick."

"You can't know," she repeated again.

"I knew from the first moment," he said. "From the first moment I
remember his asking why he couldn't have had smoked salmon. *You*
ordered the meal: accuse who you will — whatever you had said about the
meal, that would have been decided. So why give him oysters; which would
only make him angry? If one thought about it — taking all the other factors
into consideration — the answer had to be there."

"But the tin! You saw it yourself when we came into the dining–room
— how could I have hidden it in the vase?"

"You hid it when you went out to 'look'; it wouldn't take half a second
and you had your little hankie in your hand, didn't you? — all ready to
muffle your finger–prints." And with his free hand he smote his knee. "By
gum! — you'd thought this thing out, hadn't you? — right down to the last
little shred of a handkerchief."

She struggled, sitting there between them, ceaselessly wrenching to ease
their grip on her wrists. "Let me go, you brutes! You're hurting me."

"Cyrus Caxton didn't have too comfortable a time, a–dying."

"That old hog!" she said, viciously. "Who cares how such an animal dies?"

"As long as he dies."

"You'll never prove that I killed him, Inspector. How for example," she said, triumphantly, subsiding a little in her restless jerking to give her whole mind to it, "how could I have taken the poison from the tin?"

"You could have taken it while you were in the house with Theo, on the way to the church. Theo went off to the downstairs cloakroom —"

"For half a minute. How long does a man take, nipping into the loo? To get the stuff out of the tin, do all the rest of it —"

"Ah, but I don't say you did 'do all the rest of it' — not then. 'All the rest of it' had been prepared in advance. We'll find — if we look long enough; and we will — some chemist in London where you bought a second tin of cyanide. The tin here was a blind; there was time enough even during Theo's half–minute, to take a quick scoop out of it (no doubt you'd arranged to have it left on the hall table) — just as a blind. That lot, I suppose, you disposed of in the cloak–room when you went there, after Theo."

"You know it all, don't you," she said, sarcastically; but she was growing weary, helpless, she had ceased to struggle, sitting limply between them now, slumped against the seatback.

A very deep–laid, elaborate, absolutely sure–fire plot: and all to be conceived in the mind of one little woman — a woman consumed, destroyed, by the dangerous knowledge of her own invincibility in the hearts of men. But the cleverness, thought Cockie; the patience! The long preparation, the building–up, piece by piece, of the 'book' itself, the stage–props, the make–up, the scenery: as a producer will work long months ahead on a projected production. Then — the stage set at last, the puppet actors chosen: curtain up! The 'exposition' — "Bill, for goodness sake collect the things from the chemist for me, the old man will slay me if I don't get his wretched wasp stuff. Just leave it on the hall table, let him think I got it ..." And, "Theo, I've ordered the stuff from Harrod's, but I never thought about a desert. You couldn't hop across to Fortnum's and get some of those peaches–in–Kirsch? — I've seen them there and they look so delicious. Teetotal? — oh, lord, so he is! But still, why should everyone else suffer? — perhaps this will make up to them for having no champagne. And he's got his usual fearful cold, may be he won't even notice." In the excitement and confusion, who would remember accurately, who would carry in their heads, all the commands and counter–commands, all the myriad unimportant small decisions, and who had made them? Who, for that matter, of her three cavaliers, would shelter behind her skirts to cry out, "It was Elizabeth who told me to." So Bill introduces the poison into the house, and Theo the peach which is to be found guilty of conveying the poison; and if the doctor does not bring in his medical bag, then busy little Elizabeth, ex–nurse, will be there to remind him of police exhortations. The stage set; the cast assembled; the puppet actors (Inspector Cockrill himself included to do the observing) — moved this way and that at the twitch of a thread, held in a small hand already dyed red with the victim's blood.

For even as he swallowed his last oyster, munched his way resentfully through his cold meat, began on his peach — already Cyrus Caxton had been a dying man: had not the doctor smelt the cyanide upon his breath? "Why couldn't you have got smoked salmon?" he had asked angrily: and, after all, smoked salmon could have been sent down from Harrod's as easily as oysters. But "We got what was easiest," she had replied; and even then, Inspector Cockrill had asked himself — why? Why should oysters, which require cut lemon, a little red pepper and perhaps some brown bread and butter, have been easier than smoked salmon which requires just the same?

Answer: because you cannot conceal a capsule of poison as easily in a plate of smoked salmon, as you can in a dozen of oysters.

A man who likes oysters will retain them in his mouth, will chumble them a little, gently, savouring their peculiar delight for him. A man who does not care for oysters — and Mr. Caxton was not one to make concessions — will swallow them down whole and be done with it.

Cyrus Caxton had had a heavy cold, he was always having colds and the house was full of specifics against the colds, though he would not touch any of them. Among the specifics would certainly be found bottles of small capsules of slow–dissolving gelatine, filled with various compounds of drugs. A capsule emptied out might be filled with just so much of the preparation of cyanide as would kill a man. An oyster, slit open with a sharp knife, might form just such a pocket as would accommodate the capsule and close over it again.

No time of course, as she had truly said, to have achieved it all in the brief moment available when she and Theo had visited the house. But an oyster bar would be found in London, if Cockie searched long enough — and he would search long enough — where a little, blue–eyed woman had yesterday treated herself to a dozen oysters: and left behind her, if anyone had trouble to count them, only eleven shells. A small plastic bag, damp with liquor from the oyster, would no doubt also have been got rid of in the downstairs cloakroom. For the rest — it wouldn't have taken a moment to duck into the dining–room (Theo having been sent off like a small boy to the loo "in case he started hopping in church") and replace one oyster with another, on Cyrus Caxton's plate.

Ten minutes later Elizabeth, the Virgin Queen, had given her hand to a man who within that hour and by that same hand, to her certain knowledge would no longer be alive; and had promised before God to love, cherish and keep him till death did them part.

Well, if there was an after–life, reflected Inspector Cockrill coming away from the Old Bailey a couple of months later, at least they would be soon reunited.

Meanwhile, he must remember to look up hornets; and see whether the queens, also, have a sting.

# Poison in the Cup

The girl must have been leaning with her full weight against the door, for when Stella opened it, she almost fell into the hall. She said: "I've taken an overdose of morphia."

Panic rose in Stella's breast. What did one do? What were the proper steps to take? A doctor's wife for fifteen years, and still she didn't know. She had closed her mind to it, she loathed it all so much, the dreary people with their sicknesses and miseries, trailing up her garden path, taking up the two best rooms on the ground floor. She dragged the girl into surgery, heaved her into the one armchair. "My husband's out." But she could ring Frederick. "I'll get hold of his partner," she said.

The girl lay with closed eyes in the big chair: a small, ginger–haired creature with leaden eyelids and a slack, pink mouth. Her legs, sprawled before her, were exquisitely shapely and yet unattractively large for her small body. The tiny, rather grubby little hands lay laxly in her lap. Was she already sliding into coma? Ought one to be wasting time on telephone calls, ought one not to be administering emetics, antidotes …?

Frederick was not in. She crashed back the receiver in despair. The hospital! — she ought first to have thought of ringing the hospital direct. Only for heaven's sake, what was the damn number? And she thought again, groping blindly for the telephone directory, I don't even know the number of my husband's own hospital …

And so observed the small hand, surreptitiously moving, surreptitiously hoicking up a stocking, pulled askew by her stumbling passage through the hall, no doubt, and now cutting uncomfortably across her plump white thigh. And all of a sudden, Stella knew. She said: "You're that girl, Kelly, from the hospital!"

The girl opened her eyes and gave her a small, sweet, sly smile. She said: "I suppose you're his wife?" Her voice was a little, dying–away murmur.

Stella left the telephone and came and stood over her. "And you haven't taken morphia at all — have you? This is all just a laid–on drama. You've come merely to make a scene."

The girl smiled again, that sly little, faintly mocking, secret smile. She said nothing.

Stella caught at her arm, jerking the lolling figure upright. "There's no

72

use giving *me* enigmatic glances, my dear. I'm not a man, I'm not impressed. You haven't taken morphia or anything else and you can now get up and trot ignominiously back to the hospital." She gave the soft, slack arm another jerk. "Come on — get out!"

The girl dragged her arm free and lay back in the chair again, looking up at her spitefully from under her pale, reddish eyebrows. She said: "What will Richard say?" and added her silly, faint dying–away voice: "You know he and I are in love?"

"I know you've been pursuing him round the hospital ever since you came there," said Stella. "But all doctors get that kind of thing and I'm sorry if I disillusion you, but you've been nothing to Ricky but a bloody bore. All these ringings–up in phoney voices, all these sloppy little notes ... My dear girl, my husband is fifteen years older than you are — he's married, he's a very busy man — he hardly even knows you exist."

The girl had been leaning back in the chair quietly listening. Now she opened her eyes. She said: "Of course you'd be the last to know, wouldn't you?" and closed her eyes again.

It was all no use: just a silly, obstinate, hysterical little bitch, trying to make herself interesting. Stella lost all patience. "All right, have it your own way, but now I'm bored with you, as bored as Richard is. Will you kindly get up and get out of my house."

The girl said in her dying–away voice which yet was half–mockingly triumphant: "But I'm going to have a baby," and pulled aside the cheap little, tarty little coat for a moment, and softly folded it again over her body.

Stella sat down on the edge of the examination couch for a moment and gave herself over to a sick despair. For what a muddle, what a sordid, endless, desperately damaging muddle might not this dreadful little creature land them all in, to satisfy her craving for notice. A doctor ... And the wretched girl had been, in some sort, his patient; he had attended her for a couple of days up at the hospital for a poisoned finger — that was, in fact, how all this nonsense had begun. But if she'd been his patient — then that meant the attentive interest of the General Medical Council ... And the girl was undeniably pregnant. A physical nausea rose up in her at the thought of the gossip to come. The leering eyes and the whispering tongues, the goggling excitement of the hospital staff, the no–smoke–without–fire routing; the ceaseless threat from the girl herself to scenes and dramas and collapses and recurrent phoney suicides. Marriage to Ricky had been dull enough in all conscience; but now how precious it began to seem in its monotonous security. For what if patients began to fall off, if poverty and struggle came to be added again, as in the old days of their building up of the practice, to the dreary round of surgeries and night calls and cancelled parties and always–arriving–late ... I couldn't face it, she thought; I couldn't go back to the scraping and saving, the petty economies, the cheeky tradesmen, the little, niggling, mounting debts ... But if this girl persisted in this charge of hers ...

There was a step in the hall of Frederick Graham, Ricky's partner, came into the surgery.

Ricky would have stood for a moment, rather helpless, hesitant, diffident; but Frederick, the debonair, just lifted a devil's eyebrow and said with his easy smile that he was sorry, he hadn't realised there was anyone here ...

If this stupid little bitch had had to fasten upon one or other of them, why couldn't it have been Frederick? — who, after all, was ten times more glamorous, surely, than poor, self–effacing, quiet Richard. Frederick was a bachelor and consequently far less susceptible to this kind of blackmail. And yet ... After all, he *was* a bachelor; and in that case ... Like a sick thrust into her heart came the knowledge that she couldn't have borne that: the thought of Frederick in the arms of this creamy–soft, sleechy–soft little creature. For many months now, when the hum–drum of life with Richard had become too much to bear, she had titillated herself by pretending that she and Frederick ... The truth is, she thought, that I'm no better than this miserable little strumpet here. But at least she had made no scenes, played out no dramas — Frederick had no more idea of her day–dreams than had Ricky himself.

The girl in the chair opened her eyes and gazed up starrily at Frederick. "I know you! You're Mr. Graham, the surgeon." She added in a silly, baby voice: "I'm Ann."

Frederick drew his brows together in one of his quick black frowns. "It's Nurse Kelly from the hospital, isn't it? What's she doing here?" But the truth began to dawn. He said: "Not still chasing after Ricky?"

"She and he are going to have a darling little baby —" said Stella.

"Oh, for heavens' sake —!"

"— and she's taken an overdose of morphia: can you imagine?"

He flicked the girl over with a sharp, professional eye. "Morphia? How long ago?"

"Before I left the hospital," said Ann Kelly, defiantly.

"She's been here fifteen minutes or so," said Stella. "In such a state of coma when she arrived that I had to half carry her in. So I suppose that would tally." She added with triumphant sarcasm that under the circumstances her present state of liveliness was interesting, wasn't it?

"Liveliness is a symptom in the initial stages," said the girl, temporarily coming–to to defend herself.

"Not by the hour, my dear: even I know that. And you've forgotten to be dry and thirsty."

"*And* to have pin–point pupils," said Frederick, bending forward over her and lifting an eyelid before she could prevent him. He straightened himself.

"Now then — what's all this nonsense about?"

The girl slowly opened her coat again and again folded it about her. "Richard Harrison's the father," she said. She rolled her head towards Stella. "Naturally, *she* won't believe it."

"Neither will anyone else," said Frederick; but, the threat about the drug allayed, he had time to consider. Stella saw the quick frown, the tiny shock, the immediate acceptance of all that this might yet mean to them — to herself and Richard, to himself, to the practice.

"I shall have to try to convince them, shan't I?" said the soft little voice.

And then Ricky was there: standing in the doorway with his doubtful look, his self–deprecating air, that air of quietness and simplicity ... "What on earth —? Good Lord! What's she doing here?"

"Oh, Richard," sighed Ann Kelly, and toppled forward out of the chair and lay huddled at his feet.

Stella lost her temper. "Oh, my God! — the play–acting little bitch!" As the two men stopped to raise the girl, she thrust them aside. "Leave her alone! There's nothing on earth wrong with her, last time she did this I could see her surreptitiously hoicking up her stocking; she's no more fainted than I have." And she said, viciously, shrilly that if only the silly bitch knew how awful she looked, with her skirt all rucked up and her legs at silly angles, she'd get up now of her own accord and not continue to present to her dear Richard so unlovely a display of not very clean under clothes. As the girl, sure enough, began to try to struggle back to the chair, she explained: "She's come here with some drama about having taken a lethal dose of morphia; and you are the father of her chee–ild."

"Oh, my God!" said Ricky as if he could stand not one moment more of it.

"Never mind, my dear, it's all a damn bore but it's no worse than that. She's got herself into a jam and the only way out is to make herself into an interesting little martyr. Just take no notice and nobody else will."

"We'll see about that," said the girl.

Ricky stood looking down at her miserably. "Surely you don't want to ruin me?"

"If I'm dragged through the mud," said the girl, "I want to know you're there with me."

"There'll be no mud, if only you won't be foolish."

"But I want mud," said the girl. "I revel in mud. I want to see you wallowing in it, because you've been so cold and unkind, and thrown aside my love as though it meant nothing. And her too — she's been very clever and managing this evening, seeing through all my poor little defences, so sure of herself, sneering at me, mocking me — but I have the whip hand, and I'll use it, I'll pay her back for every sneer and every taunt, you see if I don't." Exhausted with spite she leaned back in the chair again and closed her eyes; and on her lips was that sly little, evil, sweet smile.

Ricky disregarded this outburst. He stood looking down at her dispassionately: or, thought Stella, irritated, almost with pity. He said: "You haven't really taken morphia, *have* you?"

"I have — enough to kill me."

"How long ago, then?"

"Just before I left the hospital. I took it from the poison cupboard on B. Ward. You can ring up and ask them, if you like, I left a note saying I'd stolen it."

"And telling them why?" said Frederick: all casual.

"Of course not. I wouldn't let you down," she said to Ricky, fluttering her eyelids. "No one knows." But she added with an evil look at Stella: "Not yet."

Ricky leaned forward, as Frederick had done, put a hand to her wrist, lifted her lip with a thumb to observe the moist gums and tongue, pulled down an eyelid. She wriggled and smirked beneath his touch but he might have been a veterinary surgeon examining a doubtful sheep or cow. "Well — you definitely have not taken anything." To Stella, he said: "I must go. I only dropped in for ten minutes smoke and a cup of tea between my patient's labour pains. She'd better just be got back to the hospital; but give her something first — a cup of something hot, coffee would be best, strong and black and plenty of sugar." He hesitated. "Freddie — would you mind seeing her back?"

"No, of course. I think someone should make sure that she gets up to no tricks ..."

Frederick seeing her back to the hospital ... Leading her in, the heroine, pathetic or triumphant as best suited her; staging collapses, noisy outbursts about cruel Mrs. Harrison, yelling her bitchy little head off about Richard getting her into trouble, giving her a baby ... Angrily boiling up the kettle in the kitchen, Stella thought with black despair that peace of mind was gone for ever: nothing, nothing would stop this girl. If one act failed, another would take its place; they would find her hanging about their door, besieging the houses of patients or friends, following Ricky about the hospital, making scenes in the wards ... Matron would bundle her off no doubt, at last; but the damage would be done by then. No use to plead, to appeal, to threaten, to command — the girl was lost to shame, beyond control; having nothing to lose, was in the strongest position of all. I wish to God she *had* taken morphia, thought Stella, pouring boiling water over the heaped coffee in the jug. Much *I'd* have done to bring her back to life! For two pins, I'd give her the damn dose myself! And straight upon the idle thought — formulate, positive, determination born complete and mature from the womb of necessity, it came — the knowledge of what she must do. Her heart reeled, her hands were clammy and cold, but without hesitation or remorse she recognised what was to be. Ann Kelly had told all the world that she had taken an overdose of morphia, that she wanted to die. Well, so she should.

A curtain descended between two distinct halves of her mind: the half that felt and the half that acted. All so easy, all so safe, so obvious. The note to the hospital authorities would be produced at the inquest; if morphia proved not to be missing from the hospital cupboard, it would be assumed that she had got it in some other way. The girl was hysterical, unbalanced, an exhibitionist; and in the family way. One more suicide by one more little psychopath; and no one, she has said, had been told the story about Richard Harrison being the father of the child ...

Cool, decisive, without further reflection, she walked through to the surgery. "Ricky, I think you'd better take her through to the drawing room. We don't want anyone to come in and find her here." She gave the two men no time to argue, hustled them, half dragging the girl, through to the other room. "Sit her down on the sofa. The coffee won't be half a minute." She closed the drawing–room door behind her and swiftly unlocking the cupboard in the surgery, took out the bottle of morphine tablets.

How many? She emptied half a dozen of the tiny pills into her hand, replaced the bottle, locked the cupboard, replaced the key. Back in the kitchen, she gave herself not a moment to reconsider: dropped the tablets into the cup, poured on the coffee, hot and strong, stirred in abundant sugar — walked through to the drawing room and thrust it under the girl's nose. "Come on — drink this!"

The girl pushed it aside. "I don't want it!"

"*Drink* it!" said Stella. The men looked up uneasily half shocked by the vicious determination in her voice. The girl took the cup and drank, sipping it slowly, till all but a spoonful of dregs remained. Stella took the cup from her and went back with it into the kitchen; once there, she rinsed it out with scalding water, carefully preserving, however, the lipstick on the rim and the girl's finger–prints and her own on the outside: stirred the coffee in the pot, poured out just enough of the muddy deposit, left the cup on the draining–board of the sink and went back into the drawing–room. The whole thing had taken not half a minute. She said, taking care to preserve the irritable scorn of her manner, "I trust you're now better?" and could stand aside and wonder at her own grim determination; the subservience of her feeling self to the dictates of that remorseless, curtained–off other half of her mind.

They all stood looking down at the girl, Frederick impatient, Ricky on the hop because he ought long ago to have gone back to his case, Stella ice–cold and yet with a fluttering at her innermost heart. For now the other side of her mind had begun to work again, to admit the possibility of danger, the necessity to plan, to calculate. If the girl went back to the hospital now, they would soon enough see that she had indeed taken morphia and would deal with her accordingly. And to have her life saved now would make matters worse a hundredfold than they had been before, for the girl, conscious of no genuine attempt to administer poison to herself, would become aware that someone else had done it for her. And then — what a story would she not indeed have to relate? — confirmed by the fact that no morphia in fact would be found missing from the hospital. Or if she kept silent it would appear all a genuine attempt at suicide — since in view of her condition the dose would be diagnosed as a lethal one — and far more credence would be given to any story she chose to tell. No: the first step had been taken and from that there could be no going back. I am a murderess, thought Stella: a murderess — and from the very first step of my murder I am committed. I can't turn back.

She took another sudden resolution: drew the two men away and into the dining–room end. "Do you think we're wise, after all, to let her go straight back to the hospital? Would it be better to keep her here for the night? I could ring up and make it all right with Matron: tell her some terradiddle. In the morning the girl will be more rational, we can talk sense to her. Don't you think that for her to arrive back, late at night, in triumph, having made a lovely scene at Dr. Harrison's house, would be a mistake? Yank her back in the cold, clear light of morning and let Matron have her on the carpet. Meanwhile, I'll make up the bed in the spare room and we can let her sleep off the whole affair."

"I believe you may be right," said Frederick. "Only in that case it's a pity we gave her the black coffee." He glanced over towards the sofa. "She seems to be considerably woken–up already." (This must be the first signs, the restless, voluble symptoms before the coma set in. Time was growing very short.)

Ricky glanced for the hundredth time at his watch. "I simply must go. Yes, I think this is best, Stella. Everything looks clearer by daylight and I'll go to Matron myself and sort it out with her. She's a good soul!" He turned back to the lolling figure on the sofa. "Look here, my wife thinks you'd better stay here for the night and then we can talk things over in the morning, more calmly. It's a pity you had the coffee but I'll give you something to counteract that and you can have a good sleep; then you'll feel better." He gave her no time to argue but went through to the surgery and returned with half a dozen small white pills. "Give her these, Stella, with a drop of warm milk." He rolled them out of his cupped hand on to the high mantelpiece.

"Six?" said Frederick, looking at them a bit doubtfully.

"It's only that Restuwell stuff; they're quite mild and she's had all that coffee. Now I must rush." He gave not a backward glance at the girl but hurried off out of the door. They heard the car engine purr into life outside.

"They'll think it very peculiar, won't they —?" said the cool, sweet voice from the sofa, "— you keeping me here for the night. I suppose they'll think Mrs. Harrison didn't want it to come out about my trying to commit suicide because I was having a baby by her husband: and they gave me antidotes and things and kept me here till I was all right again."

"An impression you would do nothing to correct, would you?" said Frederick, savagely sardonic.

"Of course not," said Ann Kelly: smiling her little smile.

Stella's self-control fell away from her, suddenly, as though her clothes had ripped apart and fallen, leaving her naked. "You utter little bitch! You vile, filthy, lying, black-mailing utter little bitch!" She stood over the girl, dreadfully shaking, one hand clenched as though she would hit out at her. Frederick caught her shoulder and pulled her away and she collapsed against him, lying convulsed with great, shuddering sobs, against his breast. "Oh, Frederick! Oh, God, Frederick, it's all so vile, so terrifying, so horrible ..." Vile and terrifying and horrible to have this cool, smiling, taunting little face lifted to hers like an evil white flower: to know that soon it would smile its sneering little smile no more ... To be unmoved by that knowledge; to know oneself suddenly not human any longer, not capable of ordinary human pity or remorse ...

Frederick held her close, strong, reassuring, kind. "Hush, my dear, hush, don't upset yourself, don't let it get you down. You've been marvellous, love, you've handled the whole thing perfectly, and you'll see, it'll all be all right in the morning." He held her away from him, pulled out a handkerchief, dabbed at her livid, tear-stained face. "Come on, dry up those lovely blue eyes of yours; it isn't as bad as all that.

She leaned her head for a moment, just for a moment, against that firm, kind shoulder; revelling uncontrollably in her first physical contact with him, drowned for a moment in the first revelation of his tenderness. "Oh, Frederick —!"

"Oh, Frederick ...!" mimicked the soft little, sneering voice.

They moved apart sharply, as though a sword had been cleft between them. Stella cast one venomous glance at the sofa and went out of the room. "I'll ring Matron."

Matron seemed only mildly surprised to learn that Nurse Kelly was at Dr. Harrison's house. "Has there been any drama at the hospital, Matron? She says she left a note saying she'd taken some morphia —"

"Yes, there was some rubbish of that sort," said Matron. "But the poisons are all accounted for and I'm getting a bit used to the young lady's tricks — not to say fed up with them. Why did she come to *you*?"

"Well, you know she's supposed to have a crush on my poor husband?" (Better to be casually frank ...)

"They all do this kind of thing," said Matron, comfortably. "It hasn't prevented her going around with one of the housemen."

"You know she's going to have a baby?"

"Oh," said Matron rather flatly. She added: "Are you sure?"

"When she really shows you —"

"I supposed I ought to have spotted it," said Matron. "Well, tomorrow I shall send the young lady packing. Him too, if I had anything to do with it but I don't."

"Him?"

"Well, young Bates is obviously the father. They've been very thick, and there's been nobody else."

Obviously the father ...! All for nothing — a murderess and all for nothing: the whole ugly threat dissipated into gossamer. In this new light, Stella saw that any suggestion against Ricky would have been brushed aside: Matron, sturdy and outspoken, would have stamped a scornful foot upon the first whisper of scandal, despatched the girl before she's had time to make further trouble, probably extorted from the young man an admission of responsibility. All safe: all harmless and clear and un-sensational. And now ...

Too late. If she made any move now to save the girl, Ann Kelly would be abroad with the dangerous knowledge that in this house an attempt had been made upon her life. Very well: by her own folly and malice she had signed her death warrant and execution must be carried out. She had declared, and in writing, her intention of destroying herself by this means, and nurses must have opportunities of obtaining drugs and covering over the traces of their depredations. If she were not alive to deny it, the police would accept her as a suicide. With the threat of scandal gone, there was nothing to connect her death with anyone in the Harrison household.

Matron thought it a good idea if the girl could be kept for the night; in the morning she might be less hysterical and could be dealt with. They rang off in mutual trust and friendliness. Once released, Stella flew to the poisons book in the surgery. A ball point pen was kept in the book, always handy.

Not daring to put on a light, she picked it up and, turning back the pages at random, here and there altered a figure.

Ann Kelly was making a small play for handsome Dr. Graham, gazing up at him with increasingly bright eyes; her hands, thought Stella, looked like plump claws, waving as she chattered. Frederick was looking at her a little curiously. "She seems very over–excited," he said, aside, to Stella. "Better get her upstairs, I think." He took the six tablets from the mantelpiece. "Don't forget these."

"I don't want them," said the girl, looking at Stella like an obstinate child, the coy glance reserved for Frederick.

"Mrs. Harrison will bring you a nice hot drink —"

"I don't want any more of Mrs. Harrison's nice hot drinks. She'll probably put arsenic in it if she hasn't already." But she saw the gathering frown, the coming together of the slanted black eyebrows. "Well, all right — for *you*, Dr. Graham," she said.

He dropped the pills into her hand and she swallowed them dry, one at a time, tossing back her head with each swallow. She looks like a hen, drinking, thought Stella, revolted.

Frederick took her up the stairs, a hand under her elbow, but she would have no more assistance. "I don't want her fussing around me," she said, tossing her head towards Stella who was hurriedly making up the bed. "If you'll leave me alone, I'll go to bed quietly, honestly I will. I'm — a bit exhausted." She clutched at a last moment of drama. "It's been rather a strain."

"Well, the bathroom's there," said Stella. She fished a clean towel out of the linen cupboard and ushered the girl in. When she returned to the bedroom, Frederick was going hastily through the scruffy handbag, dipping a hand into coat pockets. "We can't take any chances." But there was nothing there; and when she returned from her very brief ablutions, they left her. The point of no return, thought Stella. But the point of return had been passed half an hour ago.

He took her down and she flopped wearily on to the disordered sofa and let him bring her a drink and sit there quietly with her, while the whisky did its reviving work. Once he went upstairs and poked his head into the darkened bedroom. "A bit restless, but sound asleep and rather un–beautifully snoring," he said, grinning, coming down again; and when Ricky returned he said the same thing to him. Asleep ... Rather restless ... Like a doomed ship, thought Stella, rolling, wallowing, settling down at last into the waters of death. "You don't think we'd better ...?" But better — what? There was nothing now to be done.

The sound of the stertorous breathing reached them again and she and Ricky made their way up to bed. She sent him on ahead, and made a pretense of going into the room to see that all was well. "She's quite quiet now; only snoring a bit," she said rejoining him. "I dare say she was pretty worn out, silly girl," he said. "She'll be better in the morning." And he added, humbly and gratefully, "Thank you, darling. You were splendid," and kissed her. She turned away her head.

And in the morning, the girl was dead. Ann Kelly would smile her sweet, sneering, malicious little smile no more; and Stella Harrison was a murderer.

Suddenly the house was full of policemen, large, slow, kindly–spoken men, led by a small, quick, snapping little man called, apparently, Chief Inspector Cockrill. "Sorry about this, Mrs. Harrison. Very unpleasant for you. And you say the girl was hardly known to you, to you or Dr. Harrison either ...?"

Up at the hospital Matron told her story: evidently they had all underestimated the lengths to which the girl herself had over–estimated the dose which it would be safe to play with ... At the house, they went through the anticipated routine. The coffee cup proved all that it had promised: the Chief Inspector dipped in a tentative little–finger tip and sucked it — "No, nothing there — just black coffee," — and gave instruction for a few drops to be poured off and the rest sent to the laboratories. "We'll get a quick analysis done here, Sergeant: I dare say the doctor has some re–agents about the place. We shan't find anything but it'll be nice to know for certain. Can't be too careful, Mrs. Harrison, for your sake and the doctor's. She might just possibly have smuggled something into it."

"Just as well I didn't wash it up," said Stella. "But with all the fuss ..."

It was a Sunday. Ricky and Frederick sat wretchedly side by side on the sofa. "I'd have sworn she'd taken nothing."

"So would I," said Frederick.

"You examined her carefully?"

"Well — we were both prepared, you see, to believe she'd taken nothing. I know the type," said Ricky, "and they never have taken anything; and Stella had seen her pulling up her stocking when she was pretending to be half unconscious. And if she had taken the stuff — well, it must have been getting on for an hour before we saw her, and she'd have been showing symptoms long before that."

"I quite agree," said Frederick. He added slowly: "Of course, Ricky, we were basing the whole thing on the assumption that if she'd taken anything it would have been before she left the hospital — which is what she said. But — suppose she'd taken it just before she walked in here? She'd have been at such an early stage that we'd have been justified in missing any signs."

"I'd have thought there'd be something, even so," said Ricky. (Silly blind fool! thought Stella — can't he ever leave well alone ...?)

"I must confess," said Frederick, looking back, "that when she went up to bed I did think she seemed over–excited. I said so to you Stella, didn't I? — and flushed and not flopping about as she had been. But ... Well, I suppose it was the stocking episode — I was so convinced that it was all an act ..." He broke off wretchedly, conscious of a failure and of the dire consequence of that failure to a human life.

When Ricky was uncertain and floundering, Stella could feel only irritation and a sort of contempt. Now, with Frederick so unwontedly at a loss, she was filled with a sense of protectiveness. She pointed out: "I'd just given her strong black coffee for that very purpose — to wake her up."

"You let her put herself to bed, Mrs. Harrison?"

"She wouldn't let me help her; we just left her to it."

"She said she was — exhausted was the word," said Frederick, thoughtfully. "And that she'd been through a strain. So — once again, you see: one accepted it as natural. But I suppose it was in fact symptomatic — flushed, excited ..."

"And she was breathing very heavily," said Ricky. "I ought to have gone in ..." These men! They seemed bent upon making themselves look inept fools and worse. "*I* went in," said Stella. "She was snoring, yes; but she just seemed heavily asleep."

And so on, and so on — question and answer, but quiet, amicable, just talking it over ... Times, places, words said, words unspoken. The story of the call to Matron, a passing reference to the "crush" of the young lady on the doctor. "No doubt you get lots of that kind of thing?"

"Doctors do," said Ricky, briefly.

"And there was a boy friend in the case anyway?"

All unsuspicious, friendly — safe. Uniforms roaming about the house, meanwhile, yes: but what was there to find? Chief Inspector Cockrill closed the notebook in which he had been making what appeared to be random scratchings of an indecipherable nature and rose to his feet. "Perhaps Mrs. Harrison would show me the house and let me get my bearings." And on the way upstairs he said, toiling after her, "All this must have been unpleasant for you?"

"Horrible. But I'd never seen the girl before and I can't say I fell in love with her. I don't pretend to be personally all that upset." (Play it carefully!)

"At least she won't be able to make scenes about the doctor any more. I hear she was always creating, up at the hospital."

She shrugged. "Everyone knew it was really the boy friend who was responsible for the child."

He seemed to pause for a moment. He said quickly: "There was never any other suggestion, I suppose?"

She could have cut out her tongue; but anyway Ricky was sure to have come blurting out with it some time. She took the bull by the horns. "I dare say she was all for pretending my husband was the father; but of course she had no hope of being believed."

They had come to the landing. He stood there, facing her, small for a policeman, elderly, a crest of grey hair crowning a splendid head. "All the same, you must have been worried? Mud sticks. If she'd gone round saying this kind of thing —"

"She couldn't go round saying it if she was dead."

"Just what I was thinking," said Chief Inspector Cockrill.

She lost a little of her poise. "Anyway we all know it was this young man at the hospital."

"Oh, you knew that, did you?"

"Matron told me when I rang her up."

"But that would be quite towards the end of the evening? By that time," he said, his bright, dark eyes on hers, "you'd have had time to get pretty worked up about it all?"

And suddenly it wasn't so easy and friendly after all and, showing him the room where the girl had died, the bathroom she had briefly visited, she knew that it hadn't been really, any of the time. Hysteria rose in her, his hand on the banister as he followed her back down the stairs seemed like a great spider, hairless and horrible, creeping down after her to fasten itself upon her very life. She crushed down the panic, forced herself to quietness; but her head seemed stuffed with warm cotton–wool, nothing was clear, she could not remember, could not correlate, could not calculate ...

And in the hall Ricky came up to her, drawing her out of earshot. "Stella — I'm sure there's some morphia gone from the surgery."

"Nonsense!" she said sharply. "There can't be." They would be asking this question soon; he must, he must, give calm, reassuring answers.

"Suppose she helped herself while she was alone in the room?"

"She never was alone in the room, Ricky. I didn't leave her, not for a second; and then you and Frederick were there. Besides the key —"

"A nurse would know whereabouts to look for the key. We all have some convenient hidey–hole."

"But I tell you, Ricky, she wasn't left alone. Do stop muttering or they'll get suspicious. Later if you like we'll add up the book if that'll make you happier —"

But not Ricky! Ricky must go forward painfully to the Inspector and say that as he's just been saying to his wife, he has a wretched feeling that there ought to be more morphia ... "You see, Stella," he said over their heads to her, "whatever she'd taken must be accounted for somehow. If she got it from here, we mustn't let the blame fall somewhere else."

There was an altercation at the surgery door. Someone was insisting that the child had been knocked down by a car, she wasn't going to carry him round to any other doctor's, not if she knew it ... "You go ahead," said Cockrill, seeing Ricky's stricken face as the mother seemed about to be turned from the door by the policeman posted there. "I'll just take your poisons book and be skimming through it." And he sat down with it on his knee, turning the pages earnestly like a child with a picture book. Frederick, comfortably sure that all was well with it, went out to help with the screaming child. After a while, the Inspector looked up. "Both partners would have access to this book, Mrs. Harrison."

"Of course," said Stella.

"I see they use a ball point pen."

"We keep one marking the page in the book."

"M'm. Useful things," he said, "except that one never has a refill when one wants one. I see in this case they've changed to blue. Up to a week ago, it was black."

So that was it! In the dim light, last night, she had not been able to see what in daylight was perfectly evident: that the two, rather smudgy, grey–blue colours in fact were different. Figures, on pages chosen at random, two months back, three months, six months back — standing out clearly as having been altered in a different coloured ink ...

She began to talk rapidly and feverishly. "Do you mean that there's been an alteration in the figures?"

"What gives you that idea?" he said.

"Well, I mean ... You're suggesting that they've been altered in the new blue ink. But ... Well, that shows," she said, desperately, "that my husband wouldn't have done such a thing, none of us would: I mean, we'd know about the change of colour, wouldn't we? So it must have been the girl. She must have taken the dose from the poison cupboard and altered the figures in the book —"

"Why?" said Inspector Cockrill.

"Why? Why alter the figures, you mean? Well, she wouldn't want to get my husband into trouble, I suppose. She was in love with him, after all."

"I thought you didn't believe she was in love with him?"

"Well, I seem to have been wrong, don't I? Because, after all, we didn't think she would really commit suicide, but she has, hasn't she? I mean, a nurse would know — poison cupboards aren't really all that inaccessible, Inspector, not in everyday life. It's only the patients who'd have a job knowing where to find the little key —"

"You don't give your husband a reassuring reputation, Mrs. Harrison. Would the book be close to the cupboard?"

"Yes, and with the pen marking the place. At least that's where it was —"

"Last night?" said the Inspector.

"That's where it would have been last night; because you see obviously the girl noticed it, and just picked up the book and altered the figures, far back where they wouldn't be noticed —"

"How do you know it was far back?"

"Well, you were looking far back," she said, desperately. But the cotton wool was clearing away a little. "I only mean that the girl had common sense; and she was nursing this phoney romance about my husband, her mind would work in this way. And she'd said, she'd left a note saying, she was going to take morphia —"

"The note said that she *had* taken morphia."

"But we know that she can't have, or they'd have seen the symptoms. And there was none missing from the hospital so she *must* have taken it from surgery."

"Under your very nose, Mrs. Harrison?" She was silent, defeated. He insisted: "You did tell me earlier, didn't you, that you'd never left her alone in there for a moment."

"I mean … I meant … Not alone in that sense; of course I was in and out …"

But Ricky would let her down. Ricky would blurt out, in that idiotic honesty of his, that she had assured him, when he closely questioned her, that the girl could not possibly have taken the stuff. She thought with dark anger of the harm he had already done: of the dangerous corners, skillfully turned, only to be blocked by his exasperating, innocent candour. And, damn it all, whose fault was all this in the first place? It was his book, after all, his poisons cupboard, his diagnosis, his love affair …"

His love affair.

For in fact who knew, who could be so certain, that Ricky was exquisitely innocent? No smoke without fire — surely he must have given the bitch some encouragement, to make her so hot after him? And if so — if so, didn't he deserve everything that was coming to him? — for deceiving her like this, deceiving her with this cheap little, grubby little tart … And if Ricky were out of the way … The memory of Frederick's arms around her, rose up like an incense, hot and heady. He loves me, she thought. All this time, he's been loving me too and both of us just too — well, just too good, that's all, to let Ricky down. She remembered the hard, strong arms, his voice when he had called her marvellous … What had he said about her "lovely blue eyes …"? He was horrified to see me caught up in this sordid little drama, seeing me humbled by this dreadful girl — and all through Ricky, all because Ricky can't keep his hands off the nurses, never caring how much he lets me down …

She knew what she must do. She knew that now the truth was out — that murder stalked with unveiled face through their little house and that she must act. What she had done, she had done to save Richard: done for his sake entirely, she insisted to herself, to save him from the consequences of his own sickening sins. Very well then, if anyone was going to have to pay the price, it surely should not be herself? Innocent or guilty, it was he who had brought about this horrible tragedy: innocent or guilty, then, let him pay. She raised her blue eyes to Inspector Cockrill's bright brown ones. She said: "Inspector — who do you suspect?"

He looked back at her with a sort of glitter. "It's my duty to enquire into things, Madam."

She bowed her head. "What am I to say? Well — no, of course it isn't true that I never left the girl alone. I was just trying to …" And she said, blurting it out, raising miserable blue eyes again: "One must protect those one — loves."

"You are referring to your husband, Mrs. Harrison?"

"My husband?" she said, startled. "Yes, of course. But, Inspector —

don't think for one moment that I believe my husband was really the father of this girl's child ..."

"Oh, I don't, Madam," he said, with the faintest possible mocking imitation of her tone.

"Of course it was upsetting. She threatened to make disgusting scenes at the hospital; as you said, it wasn't till much later that we knew, when I talked to Matron, that there was nothing really to worry about." She added with apparent inconsequence that her husband had gone back to his patient by then.

"Leaving the sedative tablets for the young lady to take?"

She permitted herself one terrified, upward glance; then lowered her eyes. "Six small white tablets. I wondered perhaps if such a large dose could have contributed to her death: quite innocently, of course, naturally — only, if it were administered on top of whatever quantity of morphia it was that she gave herself —"

"Very ingenious, Madam. But that wouldn't account for the alterations in the book: would it?"

"I wish you wouldn't start calling me Madam," said Stella, fluttering. "Why suddenly so stiff? You don't suspect *me* of being a murderer, I suppose?"

"How could I?" he said. "You had no opportunity, had you?"

"I gave the girl that coffee ..."

He shook his head. "Nothing there; we've already done a rough check."

She breathed more freely. "Well, but I was alone with her for some time, earlier on."

"Only for a few minutes, really. No time for any other teas or coffees, and if you'd given her any pills or powder undisguised, I think she'd have mentioned it. And later one or both of the gentlemen was with her all the time. You didn't even see her to bed; you came straight down with Mr. Graham."

"I did go into her room for a moment," said Stella, "on our way up to bed." She let it hover in the air for a moment. "But of course Mr. Graham had seen the first symptoms before that — hadn't he?"

It had caught him on the hop: he gave her his bright, appraising glance. "Of course," said Stella, "she might have smuggled something up to bed with her; and that's why she wouldn't let me stay."

"But as you've just said — Mr. Graham had already seen the symptoms. And it still doesn't account for the book."

The last hope gone; and she was glad. With Ricky out of the way ... She said: "Inspector — frankly: do you suspect someone?"

He gave her a wouldn't–you–like–to–know smile, turning back the pages of his notebook, narrowing his eyes, underlining half a dozen words. What they were, she could not see; but might not one hazard a guess? — "He placed six tablets on the mantel–piece ...?" Frederick had said: "Rather a large dose?" and Ricky had accounted for it, glibly. "These Restuwell things are very mild." But if they had *not* been Restuwell ...

The two men came in from surgery, their hands moist and pink from washing, after their ministrations to the child. Inspector Cockrill rose. "Doctor, a word with you, if you wouldn't mind?" Ricky acquiesced, unsuspiciously and they went off together to the surgery. Stella was left alone with Frederick. He said compassionately: "You look all in."

But she was all right again now: only still sick and dizzy with relief, after the traps and tensions of the past horrible half hour. She went up close to him, collapsed against him, butting her forehead into his shoulder: leaning there. He put one arm around her and gave her a little shake. "Bear up, love! Nothing more to worry about now. He just wants to check the book with Ricky, I suppose; and then they'll all clear off and everything will be as–was."

She did not move. She said, faintly, (and could not damp down the little, stabbing thought, half grim, half humorous, that she was behaving not at all unlike the departed Miss Kelly, after all) — "After last night, Frederick, nothing can ever again be quite 'as–was'."

He released himself, taking her by the shoulders, holding her away from him, looking down, smiling, into her eyes. "My dear, don't take it so desperately! The poor girl's dead but there's nothing we can do about it. It —"

She interrupted him. "I mean — you and me."

"You and me, Stella?"

And she knew: already, at the very sound of his voice as he said it, puzzled, "You and me, Stella?" — she knew: it was all for nothing, he did not love her, it was madness to go on. But she went on, she was driven on, she could not help herself. "Now that we've — found each other, Frederick, don't let's go on keeping up this terrible pretense. After all I've gone through, honestly I couldn't bear any more." She felt the withdrawal, the repudiation, the shock: "When you held me in your arms last night, when you said I was marvellous —"

"So you were marvellous," he said, trying to wrench the whole thing back to normality before it was too late, trying to save her from her own shame. "You behaved like an angel —"

She thrust herself against him, clinging to his arm. "Don't hold me off, Frederick, don't let's pretend any more ..." And her nervous volubility got the better of her, and she began to gabble again, pouring out with bitter spite her apologia, the ugly defamation of Ricky, Ricky supposed to be so honourable and upright and all the time betraying her with a dirty little strumpet like that ... Her gorge rose as she saw the girl before her, lolling in the chair, the author of all the terror and trouble of the past horrible hours and she poured out her loathing, sicking up from the depths of her soul all the loves and hates and passions and eroticisms of the long, unloving, unlovely years. "Why should he stand in our way, what do we owe to him any longer — deceiving me, betraying me, messing about with a trollop like that, getting her into the family way and then when she promises trouble — murdering her, murdering her, honestly I wouldn't put it past him, to shut her mouth ..." As he tore himself free from her grip, she clutched at him again, yearning up into his face, blind to all but the knowledge that this scene must continue, must go on, go on and never end; because when it was ended, there would be nothing left of hope. "Oh, Frederick! At least you and I are free of it all, we do belong to each other ..." She was beyond control, shaking, shuddering, her hands clawing at his arms.

He gave one mighty heave, thrusting her away from him and lifted his hand and hit her across her ashen face; and slammed out of the room.

She fell back on to the sofa, where only last night that hateful, smiling, evil little creature had lolled and taunted and brought the ruin into all their lives. Now indeed she was defeated. She had murdered — and all for nothing. She had betrayed an innocent man, her husband, kindest and best of men, as well, in her heart, she knew. If last night she had dreaded poverty, with him — what would it be like now, without him, without him the bread–winner; what would it be like with a husband in prison "for life" for a sordid murder ... Divorce? But of what use was a divorce when the dream was gone? — that dream which she now recognized with instant, bitter disillusion as nothing but the figment of her own sick, greedy imagination. She put her hand to her cheek and rising stood staring into the looking–glass over the mantelpiece ...

Six little tablets had lain there: six white tablets upon whose innocence she herself had cast the first shadow of doubt — the shadow which now stretched out so dark and dangerous over the life of the only person in the world who cared for her. "Oh, God — Ricky!" She whispered to that white face staring back at her from the mirror. "What have I done to him?"

But ... She began to see that all might not yet be lost: that she might at one swoop save Ricky and repay that blow across the face. She heard the slam of the door as Frederick burst out of the house, the angry altercation with the policeman stationed outside. She began frantically to tidy her disordered hair, straighten her dress, steady her shaking hands. She went out into the hall. "Inspector — could I see you one minute, in here?"

Ricky was standing in the hall. He gave her a look that frightened and puzzled her: a look of incredulous, heart–broken, bitter reproach. Well — she must explain it all away later; she could always manage Ricky. Meanwhile ... "Sit down, Inspector. I've got to — tell you something." She perched herself, knees nervously locked together, on the edge of the sofa.

"This is horrible for me, absolutely horrible. May I ask you first — am I right in thinking that you suspect my husband? I mean — the book being altered —"

He was eyeing her curiously. "As to that, it's fair to tell you that your husband says he simply can't understand it. He has no other answer."

"And then those tablets. Six little tablets that were supposed to be Restuwell — but could have been morphine?"

He continued to watch her, silent.

She was calm again now; but she said on a rising note: "— and which my husband never administered to that girl."

He jerked up his head. "Didn't give them to the girl?"

"Don't you remember the evidence, Inspector? He put them on the mantelpiece and — then he left the house. I went into another room, to telephone Matron. When I came back there were still six tablets in their little row on the mantelpiece. It was Mr. Graham who actually handed them to the girl and made her swallow them." She sat up very straight. "Inspector, my husband is in danger; and he's my husband. Who is to say that those tablets were the same ones he handed to Mr. Graham?"

Inspector Cockrill sat for a moment very still. When he spoke it was equably. "You mean that Mr. Graham might have slipped across to the surgery when you were on the telephone, helped himself to morphia tablets, picked up the pen and altered the book — and exchanged the tablets without the girl realising what was happening?"

It was beautifully neat. "You'd already worked out the possibility?"

"One has to think of all sides," said the Inspector, tolerantly.

"Nothing was said as to whether he left the room while I was 'phoning'."

"But what could be his motive in doing such a thing?"

"The girl could have destroyed the practice, you know, with all the vicious scandal." She saw his deprecatory glance. "But of course, Inspector, that was not the motive." And she straightened her shoulders, again, clasping her hands on her knee till the knuckles were gleaming knobs of ivory against the dull white flesh. She said again: "This is horrible for me: but I must protect my husband. You see, Inspector — Mr. Graham was in love with me."

That brought him up, startled. "In love with you?"

"I think it had been going on for years," she said. "He never said anything. I never knew and God knows, Ricky never knew. But last night — well, it started with his just being kind and comforting and then — he just lost his head, I suppose; he put his arms round me, he called me wonderful and marvellous, he raved about my blue eyes, all that sort of thing, you know. I — was utterly taken aback. What my husband would say if he knew ...!"

The Inspector was silent again. He said at last: "Hardly account for the murder of the girl though, would it?"

Stella grew excited. "Do you understand *any*thing about that girl, Inspector? She was vicious; vicious and hysterical and a mischief–maker. She hated me because she fancied herself in love with my husband — she'd have done anything to blacken my name. And she — saw all this, you see. I suppose he thought she was half dopey, anyway, as I saw he simply lost his head, he didn't care whether she was there or not. But then ... She could have destroyed us all. Bad enough running round saying that she was having a baby by my husband; but if she could add to it that his wife was having an affair with his partner! And all so easy! — people knew about the other thing, but nobody in the world knew about this, he was the very last person to be suspected. And she was so utterly worthless; and after all she wanted to die ..." It was strange how clear her mind was, taking into consideration every point, every twist and turn; and yet how limited — for somewhere in her consciousness she knew that this was not all. Yet what could one do but meet each blow as it came; and before it came ... "This morning when I — I realised you suspected my husband — well, Inspector there are only three people involved and I knew that my husband was no more guilty than I was. I — well, engineered him out of the room, I knew you'd ask him to show you the poisons book. You see I — well, I wanted to make a test. I spoke to Dr. Graham, I went up close to him, I let him think that what he'd said last night had been — well, not unwelcome to me. He responded at once. He put his arms round me, he called me his angel; and I played up, I said things against my husband, I pretended to believe that he'd deceived me with that girl. I said — I drew back from him and looked into his face, Inspector, and I said that if my husband were convicted of her murder — then he and I would be free. He knew at once; he knew by the look on my face when I said that, that I'd realised the truth — that that was what he had been thinking, that he'd killed the girl himself, knowing Ricky would get the blame. And once again, he lost his head; he pushed me violently aside, knocking his hand against my face — you can see the mark, here — and rushed out of the house. God knows where! To think up his version, I suppose — no doubt *I* made up to *him*, no doubt it was *I* who wanted my husband accused! But you'll be ready for that now, Inspector. You'll be ready for anything that comes."

"Yes," he said. "I'm ready for anything that comes."

She was exhausted; her mind twisting through the terrible underground warren of her doubts and fears; but she forced herself to a sort of outward calmness, sitting down quietly, hiding her shaking hands in her lap; very pale, head bent, eyes cast down. "It's — not a pretty story," she said.

He sat down beside her and a little to her astonishment, leaned over and put his fingers to her wrist. He said: "Now, do you know, Mrs. Harrison, I think that's rather where you and I disagree. I do think it's a pretty story;

as pretty a story as ever I listened to — even prettier than the one you told me before."

Terror rose in her, a wild, upward surge. "What do you mean? What story?"

"The story about your husband," he said. He left his thin, hard hand across her wrist, like the hand of a mother, absently quietening her child while her mind is elsewhere. "You've been very clever, Mrs. Harrison. You've stuck so closely to the truth and that's what most people fail to do. The conversation with Dr. Graham just now — I daresay my sergeant, outside in the hall, will confirm almost every word that passed between you; just a matter of the interpretation. Which of course it might be; everything may be, when one comes to look closely at it. Don't you agree?" And he dropped his note of sardonic banter and said sharply; "For instance — that coffee?"

"The coffee?" she faltered. But surely — surely she was safe enough there. Surely she had made no mistake; the lipstick on the rim, the finger–prints, hers as well as the girl's, just as they would have been, no silly nonsense about wiping away all the prints — she'd been rather proud of that. "I gave her some coffee, yes. My husband told me to."

"That's right. He told you to. You left the two men in the surgery with the girl, and went through to the kitchen. That gave you a little time to think, I suppose. Suddenly you came back and packed them all off to the drawing–room. That's true isn't it? It's in your own statement."

"Yes, it's true. Why not? I thought it would be more comfortable for them in the drawing–room. There's only one decent chair in the surgery."

"You said earlier that the reason was that you might be interrupted by an emergency patient."

"That too. All sorts of little considerations."

"One little consideration would be that it left the surgery free?"

"I suppose you mean for me to go through and get the morphia tablets —?"

"Thank you," he said, and again he had that glitter in his eye. "Morphia tablets — stirred into the coffee: hot, strong black coffee with lots of sugar in it so that she would not taste anything else. You came back into the drawing–room and handed the cup to her —"

— and screamed at her to drink it! — *drink* it! Would Frederick now come hurrying forward with little damaging, dangerous recollections like these? The cotton–wool was closing down upon her once more, stifling her brain with its clouds of unreason, inability to co–ordinate. She clawed her way though it feebly, up to the surface. "And may I ask — when did I alter the book?"

"Any time," he said. "Then or later. I don't think that matters. You'd given her the coffee: and in the words of the poet there was 'poison i' the cup'."

She rallied her whole fighting spirit. "A literary policeman — how engaging!"

He gave her a small, sardonic bow. Let the poor mouse take what cheap comfort it may, the bow seemed to say, before the cat gobbles it up.

And yet, after all ... What can he prove? she thought. He's just trying to bluff me. He knows, yes: but if I admit nothing, his knowledge is of no use to him, none at all. All right, so I could have taken the morphia, I could have altered the book; but when could I have administered the dose? Not when I was alone with the girl, or she'd have said so — when she said, for example, that I'd probably put arsenic in the next hot drink I gave her. And for the rest of the time, I was never alone with her, or anyway not till after she'd begun showing symptoms. There's only the cup of coffee: and he may guess about that but he can't know — the cup is safe. All I have to do is stand firm and not let myself be drawn ... And in the blessed relief of it, she asked, taunting him, the mouse growing suddenly large and mocking, insolently menacing, not a mouse any longer but a rat with bared white fangs, match for any stupid great cat: "And do let me ask you, Inspector — did you, 'in the words of the poet' — *find* any poison in the cup?"

"No," he said. "You'd been careful to rinse that out."

"But it still had dregs in it."

"From the dregs in the coffee pot, no doubt."

"Goodness," she said, all sarcasm. "How neat!"

"Yes, it was," he said. "Very neat. Nobody else, by the way, could have handled the cup? Your own story does confirm that?"

"Certainly," she said. "I'm not afraid of the cup, not in the least. I take full responsibility — nobody went into the kitchen after I left the cup there, on the draining board. With some dregs of coffee in it and nothing else — you said so yourself, Inspector, you dipped your finger in and sucked it and you said —"

"I said there was nothing there but black coffee," he said. "And that was true." And his fingers on her wrist grew suddenly from a light, restraining touch to a ring of steel. "You'd forgotten to put any sugar in the dregs," he said.

# The Telephone Call

It was midnight. The Chief Inspector delivered the usual caution. He exchanged glances with Detective Inspector Cockrill and added, "But there's no hurry. You can do it in the morning if you'd rather." They didn't want Counsel claiming later that they'd browbeaten the boy into making a statement when he was hysterical and worn out.

But there was no fight left in him. "Give me the pen," he said. "I'll write it down. I'd rather. I'm used to writing things." He headed it: "One short story of mine that *will* get published. Only, posthumously, I suppose." In those days there was still the death penalty.

But in fact it would appear before sentence was carried out: why else *should* sentence be carried out?

I wanted to marry Pam (the statement read). I had no money, Pam said, by way of a joke, "You'll have to murder your rich Aunt Ellen." I said, "Yes, and let Cousin Peter swing for it — if he did, I'd scoop the lot." We went on discussing it. We pretended it was a joke long after it had ceased to be one.

Pam was in it with me, but she didn't murder my aunt. She was miles away at the time. All she did was to say what I'd told her to, over the telephone.

My cousin Peter and I had adjoining flats — bed–sitts they are, really, but they're called service flats. The walls are a thin as paper. I could hear Peter's typewriter pecking away from dawn to dusk. He hasn't done much better with his writing than I have, but God knows it hasn't been for his want of working: peck, peck, peck with two fingers on that damn typewriter — it used to send me mad. But at least when the day came, it meant that any time up to six o'clock he would be there in his flat, without an alibi.

I had asked Aunt Ellen to ring me up at four and being Aunt Ellen she rang at exactly four. So our Mrs. Jones, who does for Peter and me, was there to hear me say that I'd go round to Aunt Ellen's house for tea at five thirty. "Would you mind if I make it just a bit later, Aunt Nell? I'm working on a short story for the *Black Tulip* magazine. I promised I'd get it done today. If I could have another clear hour at it, I could finish it and drop it off on my way to you."

The story had been finished three days ago, actually, the last paragraphs cooked up to look a bit careless as though I'd dashed them off in an increasing hurry before I rushed off to my tea date. I motioned to Mrs. Jones standing hatted and coated, to wait for her money and as soon as Aunt Ellen stopped talking, I put the receiver down, unobtrusively, on the table instead of hanging up, and fished for the three half crowns. "Thanks awfully, Mrs. Jones. See you next week then?"

If I didn't get the chance to put the receiver back before the police came milling around, there'd be Mrs. Jones to testify that at the time of Aunt Ellen's call I'd had my attention diverted and might well have failed to replace it properly. It was a little thing but I'd thought of even that.

So, now nobody could telephone me while I was out of the flat. I wasn't afraid of people calling in person; both Peter and I have trained our friends, and each other, not to interrupt us during the day — we refuse to answer our doorbells between nine and six. But anyone might phone and I couldn't have someone giving evidence that, through the thin walls, he'd heard my phone ringing and ringing and had not heard me answering it.

Mrs. Jones had brought back our shoes from the cobbler's. I knew she would put Peter's in the locker outside his door, without disturbing him; we had Mrs. Jones well trained, too. I nipped out and got them and put them on. They were a bit tight, but wearable. I put a pair of my own shoes in the pockets of my macintosh — I musn't be found wearing Peter's.

I would chuck his shoes in the river as I came away; but prints would be found on the scene of the crime of a recently mended sole and with luck the cobbler would recognize his work, and Peter wouldn't be able to produce his shoes. Not that I relied that much on the prints. I used Peter's shoes because I couldn't risk leaving prints of my own. The real proof against him was to come from the ashtray clue.

Some time ago Aunt Ellen suddenly announced that both of us must give up smoking — a nasty, dangerous habit and one she was quite sure neither of us should risk. I had no intention of giving up smoking for her or anyone, but of course I gave her my word. Not so, honest Peter. "It's no go, Aunt Nell," he said; "I could promise till I was blue in the face but I know I'd never stick to it — the minute your back was turned I'd be puffing away like a chimney, I know I would."

For a moment I thought he'd gone too far. She looked at him and she looked at me. She looked at me for a long time as though she expected me to say something, but to this day I don't know what — I'd given my solemn promise, what more was there to say? She waited and I waited. And then, suddenly, one of her right–about turns and she was laughing and saying that, well, that's candid anyway, and no doubt she was just a tiresome old lady full of crinks and cranks that nobody takes any notice of; and from then on, the place was covered with horrid little ashtrays, whenever we go to see her, and jokes about ashes being good for the carpets, till I could almost scream.

But that's Peter for you! Out he comes, blurting refusals and denials and confessions, with his air of innocence and downrightness, and he gets away with it time after time. I remember thinking so then. I remember thinking, He could get away with murder! It gave me a sort of savage pleasure that he was going to have to try. Not that I had anything against him — he's a sweet chap, really, would do anything for anybody; though all his damned honesty does get on one's nerves a bit.

The next time we were there together, I brought away one of the ashtrays. There were so many of them that one wouldn't be missed — or if it was, Aunt Ellen wouldn't be alive to tell the tale. I wrapped it up in a handkerchief, complete with Peter's cigarette ashes and Peter's cigarette ends and Peter's fingerprints. Of course there would be no ashtray used by *me*; I didn't smoke any more — not at Aunt Ellen's house anyway.

A quarter past four. I got out the ashtray; but the stuff in it smelled a bit stale and who knows what the police can find out in their scientific tests these days? So I filled it with today's stubs from a couple he'd smoked in my room at lunchtime and some fresh ashes. The fingerprints, of course, I cherished carefully, wrapping it all up in the handkerchief again and stowing it away in the pocket of my mac. I put on the mac and a soft hat and a pair of gloves; it was cold enough outside to warrant them. I patted the pockets to see that I had my own shoes. Then I sat deliberately down in a chair and thought it all over, detail by detail.

Peter or me. That was all it boiled down to — Peter or me. Same motive — the need for money. Same testimony — he working in his flat, I in mine. Neither of us with proof — he with no telephone, I with mine (accidentally) cut off. Neither of us answering the doorbell. Same lack of alibi — no one to prove that either of us had positively not been out.

Peter and me — two young men of about the same height and build, possessing hats and macs much the same in color and shape — just in case I should be noticed near that lonely house on that misty evening. I'd bought a special mac, unidentifiable, in case it should get bloodstained; if that happened I should have to get rid of it.

Peter and me — nothing to choose between us as suspects for the murder of our rich Aunt Ellen. But footprints found in the garden might be identified as his and fingerprints found on a newly used ashtray most certainly would be identified as his. *And* my alibi for the actual time of the murder.

Aunt Ellen was surprised that I got there so early — twenty to five. I said that I hadn't stopped to deliver the story after all, that I still had it in an envelope under my arm. She went on into the drawing room. I excused myself and ran upstairs, still with my gloves on. I got dear departed Uncle George's old revolver — she'd kept it on the landing, ready–loaded against burglars, since she lived there alone — she was gutsy old girl. I then went back to the drawing room and, giving myself no time to think, I shot her between the eyes.

She looked more surprised than ever and it seemed a long time before she died, but I daresay it wasn't really. My head went a bit muzzy. I dropped the gun down beside her and I remember making a sort of brushing movement down the front of my macintosh and being pleased that there was no blood on it, after all.

But then my head cleared. I got out the ashtray, put it on the table, and arranged in it the butts from Peter's cigarettes, stubbed out the way he stubs out cigarettes — after all, he'd smoked them himself. I took the receiver off the telephone and left it dangling. I arranged a nice footprint, not too obvious, in the rose bed outside the window, as I left. I went down to the river and changed into my own shoes and weighted Peter's with stones and threw them in.

I checked again for blood but there was none on me. I checked my hat, my coat, the buttons on my coat, my handkerchief — all the things that other murderers seem to strew so liberally about them. All present and correct. I set fire to the ashy handkerchief and ground the remnants into the mud. I settled the envelope under my arm and not risking a bus I walked quickly to the offices of the *Black Tulip*.

The fiction editor looked rather less than delighted when I produced the short story. "*Did* you promise me one?"

"Well, I like that," I said. "I've sweated blood getting it done by your deadline and made myself late for tea with my Aunt Ellen to boot." I picked up the telephone from his desk. "I'll give her a buzz, if you don't mind. It's worth my inheritance for me to just turn up with, 'Sorry I'm late, old girl'."

"Okay," he said, going back to his work. "Help yourself."

I dialed Pam's number — you can't trace numbers on our dial system. She gave me the signal that it was all right at her end and to go into the act. "Aunt Ellen?" I said. She duly went into the act and I must say she did me proud. She knew by then that I must have done it, and I think she was frightened, so she sounded a bit hysterical and that helped. I kept saying, "What? What? *What?*" and after a bit I said to the editor, "Hey, listen to this."

"What is it?" he said.

"I can't quite make it out," I said. "It's my Aunt Ellen. Something about — someone coming downstairs or something. Something about a — *gun?*" I held the receiver so that he could listen, too. At the other end, on the word "gun," Pam threw a book on the floor with a bang and gave a sort of chopped–off scream, very effective. I'd told her to wait half a minute and then put the receiver back. We didn't want the editor's office staff getting too nosey; I think you can trace a call if the receiver is off.

He'd gone a bit white. "It sounds as if —"

"I'm going over there," I said. I started to leg it out of the door. "The address — what is the address?" he called after me; "I'll ring the police." I yelled back the address as I pelted off the stairs.

The police arrived before me but that was all right, too. I hung around while they argued over the time of death but they never can be certain within half an hour or so — and they spotted the footprints and the ground out cigarettes and the fingerprints. I went back with them to Peter's flat and stayed with him, all solicitous. They hauled him off to the station "for further questioning." They "thought he might be able to help them." So did I.

It's fascinating to lay things on and then sit back and watch people behaving just as you'd planned for them to do. Even the police — they seemed almost helpless, as though they simply must move to the clockwork pattern set for them. Sending for Mrs. Jones, asking about Peter's shoes, getting in touch with the cobbler; checking which brand of cigarettes Peter smoked, how far down he smoked them, whether he ground them out in the ashtray in any special way. I'd meant them to do all the things they did, and they proceeded to do them. It made me feel a little like God.

And then moving through into my place. It was Inspector Cockrill who stayed behind for that. My newly mended shoes were safely on my feet — no mud from Aunt Ellen's flowerbeds on them. And my clothes all present and correct and my lovely watertight alibi. After all, I'd been standing there in the editor's office while Aunt Ellen practically described her last moments, blow by blow.

Inspector Cockrill noticed my telephone receiver not properly on its hook. Mrs. Jones went into her clockwork act also, bearing out all I had said.

"I see," said Inspector Cockrill. "The young gentleman was speaking to his aunt about coming to tea with her and he more or less interrupted the conversation to speak to you. Right? And then he forgot to replace the receiver. Right?"

"Unless he rang somebody afterwards," said Mrs. Jones.

"Well, no, I didn't," I said. "I must have failed to notice that I hadn't put it back properly."

"I see," the Inspector said again.

And then the clockwork began to break down.

He sent Mrs. Jones away and made a come–hither sign to his sergeant, and his sergeant came hither, which is to say unpleasantly close to me.

"The fact is then," said Inspector Cockrill, "that the phone call you made from the *Black Tulip* office was a fake."

So now it's midnight and Peter's gone home and it's me that's at the station "for further questioning." I fought for a bit but now they've got Pam talking and, anyway, I'm sick of it all.

So here's my last short story and if it gets published you'll know what's happened to me. I want to ask Inspector Cockrill just one question and then I'll sign the statement and be done.

The young man put down the pen and lifted his haggard face. Inspector Cockrill, unsmiling, gathered together the sheets, bunched them tidily, and handed them to the Chief Inspector. Standing like two choir boys together, they quietly and unhurriedly read the statement through.

"Okay," said Cockrill.

He answered the question and then handed the pages back to the young man who read them through once. The young man initialed each page. At the end he added, "I see. It couldn't have been Aunt Ellen's house I was speaking to from the magazine office. I'd been through to her earlier and failed to put my receiver back. If you're through to a number and don't replace your own receiver, then nobody else can get through to that number until you do replace your receiver. I hadn't known that."

The young man then signed his name at the end of the statement.

# The Kissing Cousin

Outside the hospital the horn of a car tooted twice. "There's your pick–up," observed Bill, who could see the gates from his bed. His sister grimaced. "Just because he once happened to be passing and gave me a lift —"

"And by now extraordinary coincidence keeps on happening to be passing and giving you lifts —"

"Well, Alan's here this morning by respectable arrangement," said Franca. She leaned out of the window and then gave a thumbs–up sign to the little grey car at the hospital gates. "So that I may duly go back and wash down Aunt Adela's kitchen walls."

"You should utterly refuse," said Bill, indignantly.

"What — and lose my inheritance?"

"Old wretch! It's all blackmail, she'll never really leave us a penny."

"Speak for yourself," said Franca, waving her arms as she struggled into her overcoat. "You're already cut right out for having fought against me white–washing her larder."

"Which I then did myself, fell off the ladder and bust this ruddy leg. There's justice for you!"

"Well, I'll divvy up with you, fifty–fifty," promised Franca. "*When* I get it." She patted his plaster tenderly. "Now then, be good, eat up your nice rice pudding and don't flirt with the nurses. Remember you're Maureen's bhoyo now." Maureen was Bill's latest light of love, splendidly red–headed, and with the deepest of Irish brogues. "G'bye, love!"

Franca ran off down the ward, a delicious snowball in the white wooly coat, pale hair bobbing above its high collar — scattering farewell waves among the rest of the patients, who responded fervently with such limbs as were not in splints or plaster. The swing doors shushed to behind her.

"I trust all your temperatures will now return to normal," said Sister severely — but even she was smiling.

The car waited, with a tall, slim young man hopping somewhat impatiently beside it, his tweed fishing hat pushed back on his blond head at an angle Franca had come to know — an angle that made her heart do a little skip at the sight of it. But as she approached, Maureen walked through the hospital gates and came up on the other side of the car.

"Well, hallo there! Have you been visiting my bhoyo?"

"You and your bhoyos!" said Alan.

100

"And aren't you the bhoyo yourself, with those blue eyes of yours! It's like looking up into heaven," said Maureen, winking broadly. She suggested to Franca: "What with me own tethered up in there like a goat —"

"You lay off!" said Franca, laughing. "I need this one to transport me to my Great Aunt Adela's kitchen walls."

"See you later then," said Maureen. Cozened into it by Bill, she had left her own digs to come out and share the lonely cottage with Franca, for the time he must spend in the hospital.

Alan lifted the tweed fishing hat and replaced it on the back of his head, standing watching Maureen run off up to the hospital. "O.K. Frank — jump in!"

She scrambled into the passenger seat. "But *don't* call me Frank."

"Well, what a silly old name — Franca! You're not an Italian girl."

"Never mind that, remember I am still a girl."

They drove along the High Street, dodging the Saturday traffic, amiably arguing, turned at last into the long lane that led to The Hall.

"Must you really spend the whole afternoon washing down these miserable walls?" Alan said.

"It's only fair to help my poor old aunt. She sent for us when my father died; and she let us have the cottage free. I must say," admitted Franca ruefully, "she certainly gets her money worth in other ways."

"I'll come in and give you a hand then, shall I? How about it?"

"Good heavens, she wouldn't let you near the place! I've told you, she won't see anyone. She's a bit crackers, really."

"She must be, living all alone in that great house."

"She's got Keeper." Keeper was the huge black mastiff. "Not that he's any use: he won't go near anyone or let anyone come near *him*. So the only living creature she trusts is no good to her."

"She trusts you and your brother. You say you even have a key."

"Oh, well, us. After all, we're her family. She's known us, on and off, all our lives."

"And could hardly suspect either of you of stealing what you'll inherit anyway?"

"What *I'll* inherit," said Franca, with mock pride. "Bill's argued himself out of it."

"Goodness!" he said. "You'd be quite a rich girl, wouldn't you?" And a look came into the blue eyes, a strange look, as though a dark cloud had passed across the sky.

She said, quickly: "But it won't really happen. There's still the famous next–of–kin she's always threatening us with."

"Ah — you mean the kissing cousin!" he said.

"Kissing cousin! What's that?"

"Don't you say that in England? Perhaps it's just an expression we use down under."

"In Australia?"

"New Zealand," he corrected patiently. "When will you ever learn? New Zealand is hundreds of miles from Australia."

"Well, you seem to get around so much —"

"Footloose and fancy–free," he said. "That's me. And not a penny to bless myself with, accordingly. But as to a kissing cousin — that's one who's outside the old laws, when you weren't allowed to marry close relatives. A cousin far enough removed for you to kiss him without its being incestuous." He smiled down into her face. "Lucky cousin!"

"Well, my cousin Robert's not within kissing distance in the geographical sense. His grandfather was Great Aunt Adela's brother — a remittance man, she says, packed off in his youth to be out of the family's way."

"Whose descendants, however, would be closer than you?"

"So she reminds us when we jib at doing anything." She laughed, shrugging. "It's all nonsense, anyway; there's no will really, hidden under the carpet or anywhere else."

They had come to The Hall with its tiny lodge cottage. "Well, a million thanks for the lift." She climbed out and ran off up the short drive to the main house. He began to turn the car in the narrow lane.

The drive lay dankly under its carpet of fallen autumn leaves, the moisture dripping down pat, pat, pat, from the trees. At the far end, the old house was shuttered and silent. She put her key in the door. The great black dog thrust his way past her, in a hurry.

She called: "Aunt Adela? It's me!" and pushed open a door and saw the thing that lay beyond it.

And then she was flying, flying down the avenue, yanking open the gates, screaming after the departing car: "Alan, stop! Come back! Come back!"

He glanced over his shoulder, reversed to where she stood, leapt out and caught her in his arms. "What's happened?"

She leaned against him in an ecstasy of thankfulness. "Oh, Alan, thank God you hadn't gone! The whole place — it's been turned upside down. And she's — she's ..." She stood for a moment, motionless, pressing her palms hard against her eyes as though to blot out the memory of it. "She's lying all huddled up in a corner, and — oh, Alan, it's too awful — I do believe she's been murdered!"

The police arrived; Chief Inspector Cockrill in charge — small, alert, with bright brown bird–like eyes. Experts milled about behind closed doors. Franca sat wretchedly with Alan in the big old kitchen, Keeper curled up in his corner. Inspector Cockrill came in, drew out a chair and sat down with them at the scrubbed white wooden table.

He said, without preamble: "Well, it's murder. A blow on the head and she fell back against that oak chest and that was the end." He spoke directly to Franca. "Someone came in via the front door — no other entry has been tampered with — and silenced her and then ransacked the house. Nothing's been taken. It was a search. Now, you have the key to that door?"

"Yes," she said innocently. "The only one. She was very eccentric, you know, she trusted no one else. She sealed up all the outer doors and destroyed every key except this one." She fished down her front and produced a latch key on a stout silver chain. "She made me swear to wear it always, and I always did. I don't think I've had it off in the past year or more. I even sleep with the wretched thing."

"M'm." He said abruptly, "You inherit the lot, is that right?"

"I don't think so, really. It was all a sort of blackmail. She used to pretend she was changing her will. I suppose," said Franca, half ironically, "you're hardly suspecting *me* of killing my poor old aunt for the money she might leave me?"

"You inherit," he said briefly. "And you hold the only key to the door. I really have to consider the possibility."

"But, for heaven's sake —!" She began to grow a little frightened.

And Alan protested. "What — *this girl?*"

"Her aunt was a very frail old woman."

The both sat staring back at him incredulous.

Franca said at last: "But someone's been searching the house. What could *I* possibly have been searching for?"

"To see if there really was a will?" He looked at her keenly. "Or did you, perhaps, lend the key to anyone? It needn't have been recently — they might well have had it copied."

"No, of course not," said Franca. "Who would I have lent it to?"

"I wonder," he said, and looked down his nose and twiddled his thumbs. In the silence of the big room, the movement made a loud, rasping sound.

Fear grew up in her heart. Surely they can't really entangle me in this horrible thing! And yet somebody — somebody ... She started when he suddenly spoke to her again.

"But when did you last see your aunt?"

"Yesterday, tea time. But I rang her up last night, about half–past nine. I always did. She was all right then. She said she'd soon be going to bed."

"Have you any witness to all this?"

"Well, no, but —"

"You see," he said, "she never did go up to bed. She was still in her day clothes." He thought it over. "Would she have opened the door to anyone at that time of night?"

"Not at night, or any other time. She just didn't like people, she wouldn't see *anyone*."

"She saw you."

"I was her niece," said Franca briefly. "And useful to her."

"And, after all, probably her heir?"

"Oh, for heaven's sake!" she said again, exasperated.

At her side, Alan suggested coolly: "Do you not think that the time has come to introduce the little matter of the kissing cousin?"

The Chief Inspector's bright eyes grew brighter. He was like a bird, head cocked to one side, alert and listening. "What cousin is this?"

"My cousin Robert, her next–of–kin," said Franca, triumphantly. "Who really would inherit, and who's at least more likely than I am to have killed the poor old woman."

"Why would he, if he's the next–of–kin?"

"Perhaps like you, Inspector, he believed in a will in my favour." And she thought suddenly of the ransacked house. "That could be what he was searching for."

"She'd have opened the door to him all right — being a relation," Mr. Cockrill said.

Here might have been an escape route, but she told the truth doggedly. "No, she wouldn't. She'd never set eyes on him. None of us has. His father — grandfather — was a remittance man, sent off to be out of the family's way." To her utter horror, her voice began to falter. "Sent away to ... Well, sent to ..." But she forced herself to be calm. "Sent off to Australia." she said.

"Where the New Zealanders come from," said Alan lightly, but for the second time that day, she saw the look that passed like a dark cloud across the bright blue of his eyes.

She had no further opportunity to talk to him. The police took her with them to interview Bill in his hospital bed.

"I'll get hold of your aunt's solicitor," said the Chief Inspector as he left, "weekend or no weekend, and find out about any will. There's none hidden in the house now, that's for certain. My men would have found it."

"So you *see!*" said Franca, obviously triumphant.

"I said there's none now," said Mr. Cockrill, departing.


Bill was anxious about her returning to the cottage that night. "Suppose the chap came back?" he asked.

"There's nothing for him to come back for," Franca replied.

"Well, I really don't like it. Two girls alone out there."

"I've got to go, Bill. Keeper's shut up all by himself in that tiny place, not even his own old home."

"You could go and fetch him."

"And stay with him where? I can just see anyone taking me in with that monster."

And Maureen, arriving for the evening visit to her bhoyo, agreed with her. "Sure we'll be all right, the two of us and Keeper. I'll protect Keeper to the death," she promised Bill, laughing.

No little grey car awaited them outside, no young man impatiently hopping, hat pushed back on his yellow head. Where is he now? Franca wondered; and remembered that strange look that would pass across his face, and closed her mind to the memory.

They hired a car instead and had themselves driven out to the cottage. From within came the banshee wail of Keeper's hysterical howling. It added to the eeriness: a night dark after heavy rain; the little lodge huddled at the gates of the grim old mansion, shuttered and silent now, where last night a poor old woman had been savagely done to death. They paid off the driver and crept to the cottage door.

Keeper shoved his way past them and dashed out, joyfully barking, then came back in again out of the rain, bringing a strong smell of wet dog. They turned on all the lights, banked up the kitchen fire, then sat with an effort at enthusiasm over a hot supper, hashed up by Maureen out of tins.

"Ah, now, Franca, all we need is a couple of nice, comfortable bhoyos!" She was somewhat put out by the defection of Franca's Alan. "But wouldn't you know he'd desert you just when you had need of him? He's a lightweight, that one. You should put no reliance on him."

"I don't," said Franca, rather crossly. "I hardly know the chap."

"Ah, come off it!" said Maureen with her ready laughter. "All those lifts home with a little bit of lunch or supper on the way. But all the same ..." She then broke off suddenly, shot out a hand and caught Franca by the wrist. "What's that, outside?"

Absolute silence. They stared at each other, petrified. The rain had stopped, no wind rustled, and laurels with their heavy, wet leaves, pressed too close about the tiny cottage. And yet —

Maureen whispered: "There's someone there!"

"It's rain dripping down from the trees." But Franca's heart thudded in her breast. "Who could it be?"

"The police guarding us?"

"They'd have said."

"Then ... Oh, God," said Maureen, "that I let Bill blarney me into this! If it's the murderer? If it's the kissing cousin."

"He wouldn't harm *you*, Maureen. It's — it's *me*."

"What harm could he possibly wish to you?"

"If there really is a will in my favour ... We were away all day working — she could have got her solicitor out here, she'd have trusted him, he could have brought witnesses with him."

"Your cousin — Robert, is it? — couldn't have known all that now."

Franca shuddered. "He's killed one person, Maureen. Perhaps he — just wouldn't take any chances. In case the will did turn up some place."

"Because if you were dead —" said Maureen, very white.

If she were dead, the kissing cousin would be safe to inherit. And somebody was outside the house, out there in the dark — creeping, pressing close against the curtained window, watching, listening.

Franca sat with her hands clasped tightly, pressed against her throat. "Maureen — I'm terrified!"

And she thought about it, wildly leapt to her feet and rushed to the window, would have pulled aside the curtains but for the sudden sick terror of seeing the white face pressed close against the glass.

"I don't want the money," she cried out. "If there's a will I'll tear it up, I swear I will, I'll disclaim it. I won't touch a penny. But there isn't, I know there isn't. If — if you're the kissing cousin — I promise you, I'm sure there isn't a will, I'm sure you're the heir."

The silence that followed was most frightening of all, the blank wall of silence following upon the hysterical crying out of her own voice.

She crept back to Maureen. "Oh, Maureen, thank God you're here! What would I have done without you? I'm sorry, I'm sorry you're let in for this, but I couldn't have borne it alone."

"Ah, now, don't you worry about me," said Maureen robustly, but her voice was shaking.

Silence fell again. And into the silence, suddenly shrilling, the telephone bell. "Franca, we've been mad!" Maureen cried. "Why didn't we ring up? Whoever it is — tell them. Say to send the police. Meanwhile ..." She yanked open a drawer and took out the largest of kitchen knives. "Just till they come," she said.

Till they came. And that couldn't be much less than half an hour. Franca gave the knife one shuddering glance and ran out across the little hall and into the sitting-room. It was the Chief Inspector on the phone.

He said: "Well, there *is* a will; but the old woman kept it herself."

"Oh, Inspector, never mind that! Please come out here quick. There's someone outside the house — creeping about."

"We're on our way," he said, and slammed down the receiver and was gone.

At her end, she replaced the receiver slowly and crept back through the hall towards the kitchen, and stopped.

Close up against the glass panel of the front door — a shadow. A shadow, the shape of a man's head. A man's head, wearing a hat pushed back at an angle she too well knew.

Maureen was standing in the kitchen, the knife still held in her hand. She looked terribly pale. She gestured wordlessly towards the back door. A knife had been thrust through from outside, between the lock and the jamb.

She said: "I just managed to shoot the bolt this side."

Franca looked wildly about her. "Where's Keeper?"

"He got out. The door — began to open. And you know what Keeper is; he squeezed through and dashed out. I grabbed at his collar but of course I couldn't hold him. But — Franca! — I know now where the will is hidden."

Out of the whirl of her terror–stricken thoughts, Franca stammered: "The will?"

"That great collar of his, it's stitched between the layers of leather. I could feel the bulge. No wonder he was called Keeper!"

"Call out," said Franca urgently. "We'll call out and say that's where it is."

"He'll never get near Keeper," said Maureen. "We must get Keeper back. We must open the door and get Keeper in again and then get hold of the will and — pass it out."

"He's out there," said Franca, almost sobbing. "I saw his shadow." She grasped at a new hope. "The police are coming."

"We could both be dead by the time they got here. Me too, now that I know." She went to the kitchen door. She called out, her voice wavering: "Let the dog back in. The will is hidden in his collar. But you'll never get near him. Let him in and we'll get it and give it out to you." She was silent, listening against the door. "Oh, my God, Franca — yes, he's there! He's — I think he's moving away."

"Maureen, don't open that door!"

"It's our only chance," said Maureen, and lifted her hand, pulled back the bolt, released the door. Keeper thrust his way in, opening it just wide enough for his bulk, and she slammed it to again. "Quick — get his collar off!"

Trembling, half–stupefied, Franca knelt by the great dog and fumblingly undid the collar.

Maureen snatched it from her, ripped at the stitches with the kitchen knife. "Yes. It's here."

She stood with her head bent, feverishly cutting at the leather. But behind her ...

"Maureen! You forgot to bolt the door again."

"Never mind, never mind," said Maureen, red head bent, intent on her work. She flung down the collar, triumphantly held aloft a folded piece of paper.

Franca screamed: "The door — the door!"

"There's no one there," said Maureen.

And with one swift movement she tossed the paper into the heart of the glowing coals and, knife raised in her right hand, took one pace forward.

One pace forward — towards Franca.

Frozen in fear, Franca crouched beside the great black dog, cowering at her side away from the advance, and cried out, screamed out, almost blinded by the light of horrified recognition: "Maureen! You! *You* are the kissing cousin!"

Maureen was white as death, the hand that held the knife shook uncontrollably. But she forced an evil grin.

"The killing cousin, more like," she said, and now there was no rich Irish brogue to disguise the strong Australian *timbre* in her voice.

They stared at each other — two girls. One girl crouched, terrified, on the cold kitchen flagstones: the other girl advanced white–faced, with a knife clutched in her shuddering hand.

Franca stammered out in a sort of stunned astonishment: "You're — frightened."

"Of course," said Maureen. "Do you think I spend my life going about killing people? But my father thought the old woman might come across with a fat cheque if she thought he'd given the family a male heir — so he named me Roberta and told her it was Robert. All the same, I was her heir. And do you think I was going to let you come in and scoop the lot?"

"If you kill me, Maureen, it's my next–of–kin who'll inherit now, not you."

"That's why I had to find the will and destroy it. And now it's destroyed. But meanwhile, Franca, you know too much." She moved a step closer, but her face looked sick with dread.

Franca cried out: "Maureen, you're being watched. Alan's outside, I saw him."

"A shadow," said Maureen. "The power of suggestion — I put it all into your mind. It was me."

Hope died; revived a little. "The police —"

Maureen glanced at the clock. "Yes. So I must get it over with — and meet them, as I go fleeing down the lane with the hideous news: the door forced open (*I* did that of course, while you were on the phone); the masked figure entering with the knife ..." And she lifted it again. She said: "I — must!" and with a sort of choking scream, lunged forward.

And behind her the door burst open and he was there — Alan, blue eyes blazing, lithe body hurling itself forward, grasping the raised hand, forcing it down — down — twisting the arm behind her back. Clenched fingers relaxed their frantic grasp; the knife fell with a clatter to the stone floor. And there came the sound of heavy boots thudding across the sodden grass.

The Chief Inspector had gone with his prisoner, promising to send a policewoman to watch over Franca for the rest of the night. Alan led her into the sitting–room, lit the gas–fire and sat down, a little aloof, in the chair opposite. She curled up, tense and nervous, Keeper pressed close against her.

"Now, come on Frankie, you can relax! It's all well and truly over."

"Oh, Alan, thank you for being there!"

"I had no intention of heroics, I assure you, I just thought I'd run round and see how you were, when the police let me go."

"The police? Did they think it was you?"

"You thought so yourself at one stage," he reminded her. "But *I* knew that it wasn't me; and driving out here I got to thinking: Well , then, *who*? And I thought about that silly old name of yours, Franca, and how you didn't like being called Frank, and suddenly wondered whether there might not be a young woman who, for special reasons, *did* like being called Robert. We'd all assumed a man cousin, but if there was some girl around ..."

"We didn't really know Maureen. She was just Bill's latest!"

"And I remembered you'd told the police you had no witness when you ran across to The Hall. So Maureen hadn't been with you at the time your aunt was killed."

"How could she have got in?" said Franca. "Aunt Adela would never have opened the door to her."

"I dare say the Inspector's asking her that at this very moment."

"Poor Maureen," said Franca. "She was so sick and terrified; it was horrible to see it. And all for nothing. Of course Aunt Adela had never changed her will; Maureen would still have been her heir."

"You will be now. She can't benefit by a crime."

"There are other heirs before me. If there wasn't a will in my favour ..." She looked in astonishment at his suddenly radiant face. "You are horrid! Are you glad I'm not going to be a millionairess?"

"Footloose," he said, quoting himself, "and not a penny to bless myself with. So how could I have told an heiress that I was no longer fancy free?"

She shot up straight in her chair, so that Keeper, disturbed, gave a couple of warning growls. "Alan, are you saying ...?"

"If you'd only get rid of your chaperone for a minute, I'd be able to tell you, wouldn't I?"

There was one swift way of doing that. "It's time he went out."

She ran into the hall, Keeper lolloping beside her, and opened the door to let him out. A policewoman stood there, her hand lifted to knock. She lowered it and stepped inside.

"I've been sent by Chief Inspector Cockrill ..." And suddenly her plain round face went pink with excitement. "That's how it was done! She never did open the door and let somebody in! After all, if you keep a large dog, the last thing you do at night is to open the door and let him *out*. And the murderer would be waiting there, you see, just as I happened to be just now." He voice trailed off. "Oh, well," she said, shrugging and went away quietly into the kitchen.

What was the use of talking to two people who just stood wrapped in an embrace and didn't seem to know you were even there?

# The Rocking-Chair

The crowd grew restless as the visiting vicar droned on. All they really wanted was a proper good look at her ladyship's hat. "It's never that old straw with a couple of flowers from the garden pinned on in front?"

The Duchess sat waiting her turn, oblivious of it all. Her mind was a million miles away, conning over what her visitor had told her about the three dead ladies ...

Fifteen years ago. She recalled the case but only very vaguely. A house by the lakeside on the island — St. Martha's Island, that was, off the Cornish coast — and sitting room, three women lying dead, spread out like a trefoil clover–leaf, their poor heads forming the centre point. Shot at very close range, three shots fired, no more — almost certainly by one or other of themselves; but the weapon so splashed with blood that no finger–prints could be lifted from it. Two quiet, pleasant, harmless sisters, known to everyone on the island; and a younger woman known to nobody anywhere. To this day, it had never been established who in the world she could have been.

But her visitor knew: and all these years later had come to consult the Duchess as to what should be done about it. The visitor was a not entirely lovable old party called Miss Maud Trumble, rich and famous author of dozens of really quite terrible books — though why anybody who could have changed her name to Dawn Cloud or something, should go on calling herself Maud Trumble, was beyond the Duchess's imagining.

"— and will therefore ask her Grace to declare the bazaar — OPEN," concluded the vicar, raising his voice to a light bellow to alert her ladyship, who appeared to be three–quarters asleep. The Duchess came–to with a start and said in her clear, carrying, bazaar–opening voice, "Oh, Gosh! — is it me?"

The Hat had been well worth waiting for. She shed a few peony petals as, bowing her thanks to right and left, she scrambled arthritically down from the platform and forced her guest on a round of the produce stalls. "I'll have some of that jam, it looks quite delicious!"

"It's the rhubarb lot that cook sent down from the Castle, m'lady —"

"Oh, my goodness, then I certainly won't! Thank you, Peggy, for the warning." She bent a searching gaze upon the stall–holder. "You *are* Peggy, aren't you? Peggy-with-the-glasses-on, that our dear chauffeur Bill married?"

"No, your grace, I'm Peggy–a–bit–deaf that he ought to have married. Her, he had to," said Peggy with a pious sniff. "Which is different."

"Oh, yes, it is, *isn't* it?" said the Duchess, vaguely effusive, and hurried Miss Trumble away. "That'll teach me to show off to you," she said ruefully, "the Aristocracy being gracious with the Peasantry." But she had spotted a friend in the crowd. "There's Chief Inspector Cockrill, just the person we want! He'll help us."

"After the debacle of our Three Dead Ladies," said Miss Trumble stiffly, "we, on the island have little faith in the mainland police. However, by all means bring the gentleman in. I shall have much pleasure in putting him through his paces."

"Oh, dear!" said the Duchess. "Perhaps —"

"No, no, I insist. He looks hardly up to my metal," said the lady, and indeed Inspector Cockrill, small, elderly, hot and rather cross, a battered straw hat breasting the fine spray of his graying hair, was hardly an awe–inspiring figure. Miss Trumble approached him, nevertheless with a rapid résumé of the situation. Her Grace intervened with hasty introductions. "So do come home, Cockie, the car's here and we could have a little booze– up."

"What, at three o'clock on a boiling hot afternoon?" said the Inspector; but he capitulated and, half an hour later, sinking back into a chair in her big, untidy private sitting–room up at the Castle, with a cup of tea in his hand, prompted: "Well, tell me about the ladies."

" 'The Ladies'?" said the Duchess, startled. "I was only there for an hour or so, I didn't have to go."

"The ladies, the *ladies!* Perhaps, Miss Trumble," said the Inspector, whose time was not unlimited, "you would care to outline the case for me? I remember very little about it."

"Then I will inform you," said Miss Trumble, "of what the police had at the time to work upon." She plonked down the facts before him like a small dollop of cold porridge. "Two sisters. Mrs. Cray, Rosemary, aged fifty seven, Miss Rosalie Twining five years younger. Quiet, harmless, charming. Mrs. Cray extremely religious, from her convent days. Devoted to one another," said Miss Trumble, relaxing the chill a little, "and loved by all. In our tiny community, loved by all."

"And then this young woman?"

"Aged thirty two or thereabouts. Very neat and tidy, exceptionally so," said Miss Trumble, looking coldly upon the Inspector whose appearance certainly did not enter into this category. "Health had been good — well, up to then. No informative dental work. Clothes very ordinary —"

"What exactly was she wearing?"

"I'll tell you what she *was* wearing," said Miss Trumble. "She was wearing a pendant, imitation scarab set in gold." She added off–handedly that the two ladies were wearing identical pendants and again deflected attention by bringing it sharply to the most important point of all, the dead girl's face. The bullet that had killed her had gone rather high. Nothing too dreadful, said Miss Trumble with a shudder, but — unrecognisable.

"And no one ever did recognise her? There must have been world–wide publicity. But then, of course, no photograph would have helped. And on the island?"

"Nobody. Not even in the shops and yet there'd been a breakfast — coffee and rolls."

"But how long had she been there?"

"Two nights at least. The last ferry had been at half past five on the Monday evening, and they died on the Wednesday morning."

"Ferry tickets?"

"No dice there. And there's no other way for her to have got to the island, and you can take that from me flat," said Miss Trumble, perhaps guiltily aware that very few other facts were being given to them absolutely flat.

"You didn't see her yourself, Miss Trumble? Even after ... all the commotion at the house —"

"You can't see their house from mine," said Miss Trumble. "It's round the bend of the lake, between me and the harbour. You can't see any houses from mine." That was what was so wonderful, she said, the remoteness, and yet less than half a mile from the dear harbour and the comic little old fashioned little shops ...

"Where can she have concealed herself?" interrupted the Inspector. Miss Trumble was known to rabbit on more than somewhat in her works, about the marvels of St. Martha's Island.

"No one ever discovered. And yet, we all know one another in our tiny community, any stranger stands out a mile. We don't encourage visitors, Inspector; we are content among ourselves, all so loving, so generous, so — carefree ..." Miss Trumble had taken the invitation to a booze–up literally and now took a decidedly carefree draught of her vodka tonic. "My sweet house, down by the water's edge — the mornings, dew–pearled — for all the world, I would not miss a single one of those awakenings to a summer morn ..."

"And you live there all the year round?" said Cockie, interrupting again. And yet, thought the Duchess, should he not be just a trifle more attentive? Somewhere under all this guff, she had a feeling that Miss Trumble was testing him, daring him. Her own police had failed in the investigation. Even after all these years, she did not want a mainland policeman to do better.

"Except for my Roamings." Maud Trumble was noted for an almost obsessive research into the more exotic regions of the world for "colour" for her highly exotic novels. She expatiated upon the Roamings with a wealth of detail which soon had the Inspector longing for a return to the Duchess's verbal hedge–hoppings. "But — back to St. Martha's! Summer tourists, you will exclaim: the girl lost among a clamour of summer tourists. But no — a tiny hotel catering only for the Regulars, occasionally a house let to carefully vetted tenants." Nor was camping permitted. "We want no week–end fornication in our beautiful woodlands."

"Goodness!" said the Duchess. Maud Trumble's works were full of practically nothing else *but*, though her tents were pitched mostly in far Tibet or on the sands of Araby ... "And no signs of her having slept out of doors, or of course you'd have told us?"

"Of course," said Miss Trumble, heartily.

So — back to the two sisters. "Visitors for some years, always took the same house, quite accepted by us all. The General and Mrs. Cray — her sister seldom came, in those days, she was in America. Only a girl she was when Mrs. Cray was married, came over from finishing school in Switzerland for the wedding and then within a week or so was off to the United States, I've no idea why. Some quite prestigious jobs there and then when war broke out she got herself sent home and had a post in the American Embassy in Grosvenor Square. Stuck it out when the bombing came, but Mrs. Cray — she was always so high–strung and nervous ... They'd decided to buy the house anyway and retire to the island when the General left the army; so she settled down and made a home for him there till the time came."

"And the sister?"

"Bombed out in '43 or whenever it was — V.1. you know; the doodle bugs we used to call them," said Miss Trumble with the easy familiarity of one who, safe on her island, had never seen a bomb fall in her life. "And they released her from her job and she salvaged what she could and came and settled down with her sister. And the General came home at last and there they all were shuch a happy little threeshome — threesome," corrected Miss Trumble, slightly taken aback.

All the same, mildly squiffy she might be, but Miss Trumble was playing a game with them. It was like a detective story, thought the Duchess, where the clues are placed not so much squarely before the reader as slightly obliquely, so that they come out as not quite what in fact they are. She suggested: "Mrs. Cray had no children? Was she very much devoted to her husband?"

"Doted," said Miss Trumble.

"And the sister?"

"Doted. We all doted upon him, so handsome, so charming!"

"She didn't perhaps dote just a smidgeon too much?"

"Rubbish! Had a young man of her own in America. Couldn't get married because his wife was crippled or something, couldn't ask for a divorce. She didn't talk much about it; Mrs. Cray of course didn't approve. But anyway, he was killed in the war — sent over with the American army to the Middle East and his ship sunk off Salerno."

"And the General?"

"Staff job in Cairo, the last two or three years, then invalided out — his heart. And three years later, they came back from shopping and found him. Lying back in the old rocking–chair. Mumbled out a few words, "Happiest hours ... Honeysuckle Rose ..." The place was called Honeysuckle House, and of course her name was Rosemary. But it was strange," said Miss Trumble, "that he should die in that old rocking–chair."

"Why strange?"

"It was a double rocking–chair, interesting old piece, Victorian. Bit battered, you know, but he loved it: never would let anyone sit in it, it was tucked away in a corner. They kept it in their shrine — Mrs. Cray built a sort of shrine around his memory, right there in the sitting room: the rocking–chair with a piece of ribbon tied across it like they do in museums, and his uniform, medals, cap, gloves, riding boots, old photographs —"

"I see," said Inspector Cockrill.

"You see what?" said Miss Trumble, rather sharply.

"Where the weapon came from. His old army automatic, which, by the way, he should have handed in. But — loaded?"

"Two women in that lonely house in the woods — that's why he had it there in the first place."

"Not sharing your faith in the island community?" said the Duchess, a mite nastily. "But anyway, the girl doesn't sound like a ma ... like a marauder." It had seemed only civil to join her guest in the booze–up and marauder seemed suddenly rather a tricky old word to say. "They hadn't been expecting her?"

"No, no, mid–morning and they were still in their negligees. They'd never have done that if they'd been expecting a visitor; they were terribly proper. Shall I be a little generous," said Miss Trumble, "and tell you something which I know now, but the police never knew. The ladies had never in their lives set eyes on the young woman."

It was certainly all very odd. Mr. Cockrill got up and went over to the window, staring down unseeingly at the huge stretch of parkland beneath the castle, the broad terraces, the high–walled gardens with their orderly rows of vegetables and flowers. "Were there no papers? Didn't she carry a handbag?"

"A plastic thing. Nothing in it but toilet tissues, a little money, very ordinary cosmetics. All very neatly stowed into their compartments," said Miss Trumble, again in the oddly challenging way.

The Inspector was silent. "Miss Trumble," said the Duchess, "I take it that you know who she was? When they died — did you know then?"

"Absolutely not," said Miss Trumble.  She made a visible effort to pull herself together.  "Absolutely not."

"I mean — you weren't harbouring her, were you?  You were all so free on the island and generous —"

"I never set eyes on the girl in my life," said Miss Trumble.  "Never spoke two words to her in my life."

Very odd.  All very, very odd.  Two harmless women known to everybody, and a stranger known to nobody.  The bodies had been discovered, Miss Trumble revealed, in the late afternoon.  By the time the mainland experts arrived, what havoc might not have been wrought by the tiny and inexperienced police force that so blameless an island would warrant?  No prints on the gun, no indication of the order in which the three women had died.  There were suggestions that they had sat down in conversation for at least a little while — Mrs. Cray's chair hitched a little closer to the central chair so that her "good ear" might be towards the visitor, Miss Twining's spectacles on a table close to hand ... Why Miss Trumble should suddenly burst into slightly tipsy giggles was perhaps explained by her suddenly remarking that when they first met, the three ladies appeared to have been wearing gloves.  Red, white and blue gloves.  "Not Union Jack, gloves.  Nothing so loyal as that.  Blue gloves and white gloves and red gloves ..."

"Red, white and blue —?  Oh, my goodness!" said the Duchess, blinded by a sudden revelation.  "That does explain a lot."

If Inspector Cockrill was similarly comforted, he did not betray it.  "What about the ladies' wills?"

"A few small bequests.  All the rest for the benefit of the island.  Nothing interesting there."

Impasse.  The Inspector turned back from the window.  "Miss Trumble — why should you have come to the Duchess with this problem?  Why to *her*?"

"I explained that to her.  I had to come to London so I thought I'd just run down and see her.  The young woman was in some remote way related to her."

"Everyone is in some way related to me," said the Duchess.  "With so old and fecund a family, if that's the right word, they more or less have to be."  It was like Adam and Eve, she added vaguely.

"But how did Miss Trumble know about it?"

"If anyone is related to a Duchess," said Miss Trumble, somewhat scathingly, "pretty soon *everyone* knows about it.  They show off."

"I never can think why," said the Duchess.  "I don't think I show off, and I *am* one."

"But, Miss Trumble —?"

"A question hangs over it all," said Miss Trumble, "and I should not die without someone knowing at least as much as I do.  So — just go on guessing," she invited the Inspector.

Chief Inspector Cockrill did not entirely care for the word guessing, but was obliged to guess anyway. "It can only have been a case of blackmail. And, considering the three scarab pendants, something to do with the General."

"The General's life in Cairo was an open book," said Miss Trumble. "A man devoted to his wife — I've seen his letters home, she would proudly show them round — so loving and caring, longing only to be back on the island; and his love for ever and ever to his Honeysuckle Rose. But happy enough in Cairo, made friends with a British couple with a charming small girl, verging on teen–age.

If not the General, then one or the other of the sisters? But — blackmail? Mrs. Cray had been a model of piety, married at twenty three to a man upon whom she had doted, as Miss Trumble would have said, to the end of his life and after. And enquiries appeared to have elicited not a breath of scandal against the sister, pursuing her prestigious jobs in Washington, D.C., and at outbreak of war, very properly dashing home to offer her (non–combatant) services to King and County ...

Or the visitor had done the shooting? The gun, being kept as a means of defence as well as a relic, would have been readily to hand. But the girl had been eleven or twelve when the General had known her in Cairo. True, little pitchers had long ears ... But, again, those letters had sounded very genuine, to his Honeysuckle Rose.

"Why *now*?" said the Inspector. "Why didn't you tell the police then, what you knew? Or at least contact her relatives?"

"I knew nothing about her relatives. If she'd been in Egypt, she wasn't there now; and no one ever came forward. As for the police — you, yourself, now know as much as the police ever discovered. You seem no nearer to suggesting a solution. The red, white and blue gloves, for instance — what do you make of that?"

The Duchess opened her mouth to reply, but Cockie was already saying, calmly: "Well, that when you so subtly led us into believing that this all happened in the summer, you were deceiving us. The sisters were doing their housework when the girl arrived, red rubber gloves for washing up, white cotton for dusting. That leaves the girl with blue ones and she wasn't wearing dainty net gloves for a walk through the woods along the lake: she was wearing woolly blue ones — to keep her hands warm — wasn't she? And if it was winter, there need be no mystery about her coming to the island undetected. At half past five in the evening it would be dark. She simply stepped off the ferry and, carrying her light case, or even just a rucksack, walked off along the path —"

"Less than half a mile — *to your house*, Miss Trumble," said the Duchess reproachfully.

"I tell you, I never set eyes —"

"You were off on your Roamings — otherwise, you must have. You told us you never missed a summer's day on your island — those dawn awakenings ... She was there in the winter."

"Are you suggesting," said Miss Trumble, stiffly, "that she broke into my empty house?"

"No, no, of course not," said the Duchess. "You'd told her she could use it — you'd told her the way to it along the path and where she'd find the key. She wrote to you, I suppose, one of your innumerable fans, and the letter reached you, forwarded on, when you were just about to set off for Peru or wherever it was —"

"Outer Mongolia," said Miss Trumble haughtily. Peru, indeed! Why not Grand Central Station and be done with it? "I do not journey to ordinary places."

"— and you dashed off this kind note to her. She was an aspiring writer, perhaps, and you thought she should have a chance to work without having to worry about rent and things. Her letter would show that she was an acceptable sort of person, she could quote my name as an earnest of respectability — though when I think of some of my ancestors," said the Duchess, "that's always a bit of a joke."

"And she'd refer to the island," said the Inspector, "and mention having known General Cray when she was a child, and heard all about it. So —"

"Do you suppose that after the killings, every house on the island wasn't thoroughly searched?"

"You kept a tiny bit emphasising how neat she was," said her Grace. "You were needling Inspector Cockrill, to see whether or not he'd get the significance. The significance was that she kept your house like a new pin —" She looked encouragingly at Mr. Cockrill and he did not fail her. "She'd stack away her bit of luggage wherever you kept yours — all sorts of cases for your different travels. She used a sleeping–bag, probably, to save laundry problems and so on, and that also would be rolled away tidily. Her few clothes were very ordinary, you said; and, hung up at the end of one of your closets, they'd excite no attention. She'd automatically wash up and put away what little crockery she used. Probably you'd told her to help herself from your deep freeze till she got around to some shopping —"

"Had I also invited her to use my credit cards?" said Miss Trumble, acidly. "None were found, nor any cheque book."

"Do you think a girl as hard up as that would have a bank account?" suggested her Grace. "Thousands don't. She'd have hoarded up her pennies and the police wouldn't think anything of a few five pound notes stashed away somewhere. You wouldn't need British currency where you were going, and you had complete faith in the islanders. Like the key — you'd just have tucked the key into some hiding place near the front door and told her where she'd find it. She wouldn't risk carrying it around in the plastic handbag — if she lost it, she couldn't get another. Oh, and of course, like a good girl, she'd cover up your typewriter when she wasn't using it; and any bits of work she'd done, would be taken as something of yours."

Miss Trumble looked not over–pleased at the idea of amateur efforts being mistaken for her own, but only asked, coldly: "And all this I kept to myself when the news broke?"

"But it never did break, did it?" said the Inspector. "Not in Outer Mongolia. And by the time you got home, except on the island the furore would have died down. You'd heard nothing of it by the time you got back to your house —"

"There was a note there from the police," said Miss Trumble. "In case I got home and found signs of their intrusion. They told me briefly what had happened — ten weeks ago by that time — but said there was no sign of any intruder."

"And of course no lights would have been seen," said Cockie. "Your house wasn't in view of any other. But didn't they check for the girl's finger–prints? — all over your place."

"They were perfectly satisfied that no one had been there." She shrugged. "I told you I had a low opinion of the mainland police."

The Duchess did not remark that it would probably have been the island police who did the house–combing. She said only, "So you kept quiet?"

"Well — yes. I had time to think it all out before I need reveal that I was back at home. After all, it didn't really matter where the girl had stayed."

"Not to the police," said the Inspector.

She looked at him shrewdly: "What are you hinting at?" and added suddenly: "All this has been told to you quite privately. You will respect my confidence?"

"So far, Miss Trumble," said Cockrill rather grimly, "I think we have in fact had very little *of* your confidence."

"I'd have told it all to the Duchess, but she suddenly rushed me off to this wretched bazaar of hers. You were brought in and it has amused me to challenge you. So I ask you again — what are you hinting at?"

"It might not matter to the police where the girl had stayed," said Inspector Cockrill. "But it mattered very much to you, Miss Trumble — didn't it? This precious island, no one admitted who wasn't approved and accepted all round: and you, without even a word of warning, had intro–duced a stranger of whom you knew nothing — who in the event proved to have been in all likelihood a blackmailer and who certainly had brought about the dreadful deaths of two much–loved members of your little community ..."

Miss Trumble's face had gone a rather pasty white, beneath its cu–stomary crocodile tan. "I recognised at once what I had done. But ... Her letter had been forwarded to me at Ulan Bator, my last outpost before I set off on my trip — I was distraught with preparations; on an impulse I just dashed off a note to her. If I hadn't ..." She asked rather pathetically: "Do you really think she had it all planned? A blackmailer for sordid money?"

"Perhaps not that," said the Duchess, kindly. "It could have been for something much more innocent ..."

"Such as — for acceptance?" said the Inspector. "She comes to the house, she draws attention to the scarab pendant she's wearing, identical with their own. She says — she says that the donor had told her that if she ever needed to, she should bring it to Honeysuckle House on the island of St. Martha and show it, as proof of identity to —"

"To her mother," said Miss Trumble.

To her mother! "Oh, Miss Trumble!" said the Duchess reproachfully again, "you told us that neither of the sisters had ever even seen the girl."

"Well ... When babies are to be adopted," said Miss Trumble, "they are often taken away at birth so that the mother need feel less pang in parting with them. And a sister of Mrs. Cray would certainly have been obliged to part with an illegitimate child. Remember, this all happened many years ago. Things were not nearly so easy as they are these days. And Mrs. Cray was so rigidly pious and upright; to the end I think Rosalie was a little in awe of her."

"But would she really have been so obsessed with her sister's morality as to snatch up the gun —?"

"She was a little deaf," said the Duchess. "If she misheard, if she got things wrong, if she thought that the General —"

"The love of her life," cried Miss Trumble, inspired. "Faithless! That highly strung creature, all her aggressions crushed down by the long years of self–enforced discipline! Who knows what nameless suspicions might not have been harboured all this time, in that secret heart?" The great novelist was clearly getting into her stride, not un–assisted by vodka tonics. "The beloved husband — false! The sister a traitor to their life–long devotion! The storm blows up, overwhelms her at last — the gun is to hand, she seizes it up and in one mad moment blots out all the pain ..."

"A moment's reflection might have saved them all a lot of trouble," said Cockie, discouragingly. "The General had known her sister only for a few days — at the time of his own marriage. He then saw her rarely on her holidays home from the States. But to be the age she was at the time of the killings, the girl must have been conceived long before that."

"Before she even left Switzerland?" suggested the Duchess. "Hence the hurried departure to America were she would be unrecognised. A Swiss lover —"

"What would a nice pacifist Swiss be doing in Cairo during the war?" said Cockie. "Surely so much more likely —"

"The American boy–friend!" said her Grace. "Couldn't get a divorce because the poor crippled wife went on not dying. So the child was adopted. Then the war and Miss Twining came home, and the lover was eventually packed off with the U.S. army to the Middle East and later to Italy where he died. But meanwhile, she have written to him to try to get in touch with the adoptive parents, now in Cairo, and to send her news of the child; and told him about the scarab pendants. Perhaps it was even she who'd arranged that if her daughter ever wanted to find her —"

"So, Miss Trumble, you see," said the Inspector with none of his habitual acerbity, "if the deaf woman gets things wrong, becomes hysterical and starts shooting around — that's really no fault of yours."

"It was my fault that she ever went there," said Miss Trumble. "And wherever the wrong may have lain — it was through her going there that it was exposed. I knew as much as you do now: I should have worked out the truth, as you've done — I should not have let her go. And before I die, I wanted to get it off my conscience, at least not to have it all hoarded up within me. I could hardly have told anybody on the island; but the Duchess … I've heard about your Grace," she said. "You have a reputation for being clever about this kind of thing — elucidating things — and for being kind. It's true that I've been playing games with the Inspector, challenging him. But to you I'd have told it all, simply and outright. It would have been like going to confession."

"*Absolvo te!*" said the Duchess, in the words of the absolution and like the priest in the confessional sketched a sign of the cross in the air. "Dear Miss Trumble — in fact there is nothing to be forgiven. There was no blackmail, no relationships, no illegitimate child, no nothing: we've just been working through the possibilities: perhaps trying to prove to you that our police aren't quite so dumb after all. But of course there was no reality in any of it. It's much, much more simple than that; isn't it Cockie?"

"You did a kind and generous thing, Miss Trumble," said the Inspector. "You did no wrong at all."

"In fact nobody in all this business has done anything wrong," said the Duchess. "Unless you could count that poor woman, not responsible for what she was doing —"

"No court would have condemned her," said Inspector Cockrill. " 'While the balance of her mind was disturbed' — that's the official phrase."

"The girl dropped in at the house," said the Duchess, "with only the kindest intentions. She happened by chance to be on the island, and she wanted to tell the General's widow how, as a little girl, she had known him in Cairo, and how often he had talked to her about his home and his love and longing to be back there … And she'd catch sight of the rocking–chair, perhaps, and say how often he'd described it to her, that battered old Victorian relic, the double rocking–chair — and told her how the happiest hours of his life had been spent in that old chair, gently rocking to and fro with his arms about his one true love —"

"— and the poor wife leapt to her feet," said Cockie, "and cried out, 'But it's *her* chair! I never in my life sat rocking in that chair with him!' The chair, bomb–battered that her sister had salvaged from those days when she — and he — had been alone together in London. Where he'd crawled in to die as a last message to the true love of his life — mumbling out his dying words — to *her*."

"No wonder you laughed, Miss Trumble," said the Duchess, "when you told us that Miss Twining wore spectacles and Mrs. Cray was rather hard of hearing. It was like my two Peggies, wasn't it? — Peggy–with–the–glasses–on, as they call her in the village, and Peggy–a–bit–deaf. He must have known it from the moment he set eyes on the little sister — come over to London for the wedding. It was like our dear chauffeur, Bill — he was marrying the wrong girl."

"And you tell me that there was no wrong in that?" said Miss Trumble.

"They couldn't help falling in love; and it really was love, if it lasted all those years, spent mostly apart. For the rest — he kept to his promise, he went through with the marriage. She went abroad, they kept out of temptation's way. When they were thrown together by the war, they two in London with the wife safely tucked away on the island — well, if at the end they could say that their happiest hours had been spent in a rocking–chair," said the Duchess, "I do think that that was most honourably sticking at least to the letter of fidelity. The only small deception was in those letters — over the head of their recipient, sending all his true love to his Honeysuckle Rose. Well, her name was Rose too, wasn't it? Rosalie."

"But all this the poor wife couldn't know," said the Inspector. "And Miss Trumble has most graphically described what could have been the state of her mind. The gun was there and she just simply picked it up ... Many, many murders have arisen in the same sort of way." He cast about for his disreputable old straw hat and, holding it across his chest, made a not ungraceful obeisance to his late enemy. "I agree with her Grace, Miss Trumble. You did only what was generous and kind and there's no need to blame yourself at all." To his hostess he said: "Don't bother to ring. I can find my own way to the portcullis."

"Fool!" said the Duchess, and went out with him at least to the head of the stairway. "Poor old trout! I think she really feels guilty and upset. But I suppose she'll get over it?"

"One way or another," said the Chief Inspector, "I dare say she will."

Miss Trumble hadn't taken too long. She was standing at the little side table when the Duchess returned, pouring out for herself a sufficiently reviving vodka tonic. "My *dear*!" she said, "I've got it all worked out already! Have to fiddle the scene, of course and disguise the characters ... I thought perhaps — Pocahontas: that would please my dear American public. Marries the man Rolfe, you know, but has never got over her passion for John Smith or whatever his name was, that she rescued from whoever it was, I can look all that up —"

"She being twelve years old at the time?" murmured the Duchess but the great author swept on, "— and there in the noble hall of her home stands the splendid gilt couch that had seen the consummation of all their love —"

"But it was a rocking–chair," protested her Grace, "and the whole point is, that nothing happened there."

"Oh, I don't think my readers would like that at *all*," said Miss Trumble.

# The Man on the Roof

Sergeant Crum who, with the assistance of only a fledgling constable, runs the tiny police station in the village of Hawksmere, rang up Chief Inspector Cockrill in Heronsford. "It's the Duke, sir. Phoned to the station and says he's going to shoot himself."

"The Duke? What Duke? Your Duke, up at the Castle?"

Sergeant Crum took a leisurely moment to reflect that in his own small neck of the woods they were hardly so rich in the gilded aristocracy, as to necessitate discrimination. Inspector Cockrill, however, had not stayed for an answer. "What have you done about it?"

"Tried to get my constable, sir. Gets his dinner in the village, he does, being his home is there; the Sardine Tin they call it, these days, since the old people —"

"Yes, well, never mind the constable's domestic arrangements —"

"— and they told me he'd suddenly rushed off," continued Crum, placidly. "Said he'd heard a shot or something of that. They hadn't heard nothing, but the old people are getting a bit —"

"Well, get after him fast, for goodness sake! I'll be there in half an hour at latest ..."

The sergeant pursued his unhurried way and at the North Gate leaned out of his car to question the lodge keeper; and learning that His Grace had gone down a two–three hours ago towards South Lodge, cursed himself mildly for not having thought of that, and started on the long haul round the Castle walls to what had once been the opposite entrance. South Lodge, of course! Fisher couldn't have heard a shot fired up at the Castle.

The constable met him at the little wooden gate of the gravelled path that led up to the lodge, clinging as though for support to his bicycle. Over his large rather handsome young face was spread a strange pall of grey. He said, "He's dead, Sarge."

"Dead? He's done it?"

"Seems like it. Lying on the floor in the parlour. Lot of blood around."

"You're sure. You didn't make certain?"

"Door's locked, sir. I looked in at the window but it's too small to get through. And anyway ..."

"I was held up. Went out of my way. You came here direct?"

"Yessir. I heard the shot, I guessed what it might be. And I knew he'd

123

be here; I saw him this morning, turning in at the gate. So I got on me bike and came over."

The lodge was in fact a lodge no longer. In the not too distant past, its magnificent wrought iron gates had been removed and the gap bricked up except for a small postern door; and the high wall ringing the castle and its grounds, rebuilt in a curve that now left the little house standing outside on its own, in an expanse, something under an acre, of dull, flat land — at present covered in a blanket of Christmas snow, about two inches deep. A hedge completed a sort of high ring around the building, with a break in it to admit of a small wooden gate leading up to the tiny porch over the front door. The redundant lodge–keeper had been allowed to remain in residence until the accession of the present duke about three years ago, when he had been evicted with his poor old wife, so that His Grace, whose single bleak passion was the collection and destruction of butterflies, might convert the place into a sort of playroom for himself and his hobby. Considering that there must be, up at the castle, at least seventy rooms which might equally have served his purpose, the dispossessed might be forgiven for suggesting resentfully — but not to the Duke — that a nook could have been created for him there.

Now, in the light snow, two narrow lines, clearly the marks of the constable's bicycle tyres, led up and away from the front door; the return journey having apparently been decidedly wobbly. There was no other mark in the snow. "No sign of his footsteps!"

"No, well, it hadn't started snowing when I saw him going in through the gate." For whatever reason, the constable had lost colour. "That was about couple of hours ago."

"Oh, well …" Sergeant Crum abandoned a secret hope that by delaying his errand until the Inspector should come, he might shift onto other shoulders the onus of the whole alarming affair; for sudden death is not a commonplace in quiet little Hawksmere, nestling under the calm shadow of the castle up the hill. He started off through the light flurry of swirling snow, some vague instinct suggesting that it might be well to avoid the tracks of the bicycle tyres. You could see where the constable had propped his machine against the wall of the house and gone up the two or three steps. Snow was shuffled as his footprints came down, and appeared to move round to the right. "I ran round to the side window," said Fisher, following his glance. He indicated a small window to their left. "You can't see in so well from there."

"Yeah, well, you'd know, wouldn't you?" said Sergeant Crum.

The door was secured by a Yale lock, the sort that clicks shut of itself; to be opened, when the door is closed, only by its own particular key. "M'm," said the sergeant. He tramped round in the constable's footsteps leading round the house, and returned with his rugged countryman's visage the same curious shade of grey. "Certainly *looks* very dead," he said uncomfortably and lifted up his heart in a wordless prayer.

The prayer was answered. There came the throbbing of a car in the snow–bound stillness and Chief Inspector Cockrill stood at the little gate. For once his shabby macintosh was not trailing over one shoulder but was worn with his arms in the sleeves; and pushed back upon his noble head with its spray of fine grey hair, was the inevitable ill–fitting hat: Inspector Cockrill is known to pick up any hat that happens to be at hand, to the considerable inconvenience of the true owner. Anything that does not actually deafen and blind him is perfectly acceptable to the Terror of Kent.

He remained for a long time intently surveying the scene: the little house in its flat white circle of snow, ringed in by the wall and the hedge so as to be almost invisible to anyone not looking in over the gate. Nice setting for a locked–room mystery, he thought: which God forbid! Fortunately, it appeared to have been a good, straight–forward suicide, heralded in advance by the gentleman himself. And from what he had heard, there would be few to mourn the passing of the sixth Duke of Hawksmere — very few indeed.

A pretty little building, almost fairy–like in its present aspect, its highly ornamental pseudo–Gothic facade a–glitter with its dusting of snow. An octagonal room, flat–roofed, with a small side window where the lodge–keeper might sit watching out for the first signs of approaching vehicles, all ready to leap out and open the gates. Into this room, the door opened directly. There was an opposite door leading to the back of the house, two or three small rooms and the household offices: only the front had been designed to be seen, the rest was cut off and hidden away behind it, considerably less decorative in appearance. The room was furnished only with a desk and a trestle table, upon which were distributed the tools of the Duke's preoccupation; with a typewriter, a chair, and sheaves of paper work. There was no other furniture in the house.

Inspector Cockrill stood quietly, taking it all in. The door leading to the other rooms was locked and bolted on this side: there could be nobody else in the house unless they had entered by a back door or window: and in fact there was nobody there. The body lay across the front door, so that, upon entering, one saw nothing but the head and shoulders (turned away from the door) and an outflung hand and arm. The shot had gone through the right temple and out through the other side of the head, somewhat higher up; a bullet was lodged much where one would have expected it to be, high up on the post of the opposite door. An open thermos jug stood on the desk with a puddle of cooling coffee left inside, and there was a piece of foil that had evidently been wrapped round a packet of sandwiches. The time was still early afternoon.

It was almost an hour before, having set in motion the wheels of investigative law, Mr. Cockrill decided: "Well, I'd better go up to the Castle and see them there." But before he went, he summoned the constable to stand before him — very pale, hands hanging faintly twitching, at his sides. "So, boy. Fish your name is, is it?"

"Fisher, sir," said the constable, hardly daring to contradict.

Inspector Cockrill conceded the point. "Well, now, once again — you heard this shot?"

"Having me dinner, I was, sir at home with me gran and grandad and Mum and Dad and all. And I heard this shot and I thought, the old bastard has done it at last, I mean," said the constable in a terrible hurry, "His–Grace–has–done–himself–in–at–last, sir."

"You knew of this habit of the Duke's, of constantly threatening suicide?"

"Being as he often rang up the Station — which he did today, sir."

"M'm. Who else heard the shot?"

"Well, no one, Mr. Cockrill, sir. Gran and Grandad, they're a bit deaf and me mum and dad was arguing and the kids all quarreling, kicking up a row as usual. Besides —"

"Besides?"

"They'd've only said good riddance, and to leave things be."

"Oh," said Cockie, coldly. "Why would they have said that?"

"Well, account of ... I mean, nobody liked the old b— I mean nobody liked the Duke, sir, did they?"

"You, however, stifled your feelings and dashed off to his assistance."

"Only me duty, sir," said Constable Fisher rather smugly.

"How did you know he'd be here?"

"Well, I saw him arriving. And he always did spend most of the day here, brought down his sangwidges and coffee and that."

"And seems to have consumed them. Does that strike you as rather odd?"

"What, like 'the prisoner ate a hearty breakfast'?"

The Inspector bent upon him an appreciative eye. "Exactly. Who eats up his lunch before he sets about killing himself?"

"If a gentleman had — well, like moods, sir ... And it was a while ago: the coffee's gone quite cold."

"Yes, well ... Now once again, Constable. You were at this door within six or seven minutes of your hearing the shot? The door was locked? You went round to the window and looked through. The window round at the side of the room, not to this one next to the door, which is nearest."

"You couldn't see the whole room from the little window, sir. Even from the other one, I wouldn't see much. But I could see a good bit of him. I — well, I got a bit rattled, sir, seeing him lying there like that, sort of dead like."

"Very dead like," said Cockie, sardonically. "You didn't think of going in and trying to resuscitate him?"

"But he was dead, sir. His head —" He puffed out his cheeks and put a hand over his mouth.

"You'll get used to it," said the Inspector, more kindly. "It shakes one, the first time. So, you got on your bike and rode back to the gate? A bit wobbly, those tyre marks, the returning ones."

"Yes, well I was a bit ... Well I didn't know what to do, sir, till the sergeant came."

"In other words, you lost your head."

To Sergeant Crum he said, grumbling: "A wretched young rookie! The Duke of Hawksmere, no less, announces his forthcoming suicide and who's on the spot? — this great, green baby of a rookie constable, not yet dry behind the ears." He glanced up at the Castle frowning down, formidable, upon them from the hill top. "God knows what on earth the Duchess is going to say ..."

What the Duchess in fact said was, comfortably, "Oh, well, he was always threatening suicide, *wasn't* he? His farewell notes simply litter the place. If the police had always had someone important at the ready, no other work would have got done at all." But that poor boy, she added, must have been scared stiff, all on his own, having to cope. "And you say it's not really quite so simple?"

Not simple at all. But for the moment he dodged it. He said, gratefully: "Your Grace takes it very calmly."

They sat in her private room with its charming pieces of period furniture, made cozy by large, comfortable armchairs. The Duchess had always seemed to him, in many ways, like a comfortable armchair herself: warm and well cushioned and to all the world holding out welcoming arms. "Well, yes — I can't pretend to be heartbroken, he was only a fairly remote cousin, you know, and such a misery, poor man!" Her son, the young Duke, had died in an accident up at his University three years ago and his cousin succeeded to the title.

"I stayed on here at the castle with him, though. I longed to retire to the Dower House and be on my own. But he was a mean man, he cared nothing for the estate and the people — he was doing a lot of harm all over the place. Now his brother will succeed him and he's a very different kettle of fish. He loves it, and Rupert, his boy, and darling little Becca, they really do care about it, too. And what a change for them! Poor as church mice they all were till Cousin Hamnet inherited. Everyone thinks that if you belong to a great old family like ours, you must naturally be rich, but of course, apart from the title, that needn't be so at all. And they certainly weren't." It was on account of this, she believed, that Hamnet had never got married; though now, as a matter of fact, there were murmurs about his doing so.

"So Hamnet was pretty happy to succeed?"

"Well — not happy as we've seen. He was not a happy man. A depressive, I suppose the psychiatrists would say and he certainly got no joy out of being Duke of Hawksmere. But there *is* a joy, you know, in being at the centre of it all and caring about the land — running it properly, looking after people, one's own people. It sounds condescending, referring to them as 'our people' but they do become like one's own, so many have been for generations with the family. One gets very protective towards them, and I'm thankful to say that Will, the new duke, and darling Rupert and Becca have the feeling very strongly. I must confess," said the Duchess, "that I've loved it all. Even the bazaar–opening I've secretly rather enjoyed."

"Nobody opens a bazaar like Your Grace," said Cockie, handsomely.

"Well a new Grace will be opening them now and they're all so happy to be here, now and for ever. The children were here a lot in their school hols, inseparable friends with the family down at South Lodge. Poor Dave, a bad attack of calf–love, it was rather touching, all great hands and feet and blushing like a peony every time she came near him ..."

Inspector Cockrill, unfamiliar with any South Lodge family and ignorant of whoever Dave might be, preferred to probe a little further into the family of the new Duke. "They're all staying here at the moment, I understand?"

"Yes, for Christmas. I'm so happy to have the kids here."

"A handsome pair, I believe? Tall, are they? Take after their father?"

"Oh, my dear, no — *ants!* I mean, compared with my own beautiful son, they seem so dark and little."

"Pretty light–weight, are they?"

"Both of them ..." She broke off, looked at him warily. "Why should you ask? You've got something up your sleeve, you old devil! You've been holding out on me."

"No, no," said the Inspector. "I just wanted to get the facts from you, unprejudiced. And so I have; and in return I'll offer Your Grace a fact, which I wouldn't do for most people, so please keep it absolutely to yourself alone." But he could hardly bring himself to speak it aloud. "Have you ever heard, Duchess, of a 'locked room mystery'?"

"You mean like detective stories? Doors bolted, windows barred, wastes of untrodden —" She broke off, incredulous. "You don't mean it? The lodge down there in the middle of all that snow —?"

"The constable rode up to the front door on his bike. He walked a little way round to a side window and back. He rode back down to the gate. He and his sergeant then walked up to the house. *I* walked up to the house. Apart from those footsteps coming and going and the two lines coming and going of the bicycle tyres — there isn't a break in the whiteness all round that place. Ringed round by the wall and the hedge, the lodge sitting like a cherry in the middle of an iced cake. Not a single sign."

"Oh, well," said the Duchess, "what's really so odd about that? Naturally he'd have let the door close when he went into the lodge — the Duke, I mean; and in this weather he'd keep the windows shut. He went down before the snow began. Had this gun with him — presumably in case he came on suicidal at any time, which he was always doing; and he did come on suicidal. He rang up the police station as usual, sat down and composed yet another note and this time, for a change, poor old Ham, he really did shoot himself. I mean, you say he was just lying there —?"

"Almost right across the doorway," said Cockie. "Right hand flung out, fingers curled as thought the gun had just fallen from them. The first thing you saw as you pushed open the door — his hand with his fingers half–curled. Death instantaneous, shot at very close range; and no question of one of these medical freaks when a man moves about a bit; even walks a little distance, after death. He died at once and lay where he had fallen."

"And in fact the constable even heard the shot. So where's the mystery?" said the Duchess, reasonably. "Where's your locked room?"

"The locked room is the lodge," said Cockie, "locked in, as it were in all that untrodden snow. A man dead in the lodge, very recently dead, death instantaneous, from a gun–shot wound at close range. And the mystery is very easy to state and not at all easy to answer. The mystery is — where is the gun —?"

"Where —?"

"— because it isn't lying there close to his right hand where it ought to be, and it isn't anywhere else in the lodge and it isn't anywhere outside in all the snow." The cigarette held in his cupped hand sent its pale smoke spiraling up between his fingers: and he flung the butt suddenly with an almost violent movement, into the heart of the flickering fire. "So damn the blasted thing," he said. "Where the hell *is* it?" And apologised immediately, "I beg your ladyship's pardon!"

"Oh no, don't apologise," said the Duchess. "I do see. It's dreadful for you." Well, and dreadful for all of them, she added with growing recognition of what it must mean.

For if the Duke of Hawksmere hadn't shot himself at last — who had done it for him?

"And how did that person get away —?"

"And what did he do with the gun —?"

They sat for a long time in silence, thinking it over. The Chief Inspector said at last, reluctantly: "There seems to be only the one possible solution?"

"M'm," said the Duchess. She looked at him rather unhappily. "Are you thinking what I'm thinking?"

"Just a question of what on earth could have been the motive," said the Inspector, shrugging.

"Motive? Oh!" She looked quite horrified. "You're not thinking what I'm thinking after all, Cockie." And what he *was* thinking was absolutely, absolutely, said the Duchess earnestly, "*absolutely wrong.*"

The handful of men at the disposal of the police had been supplemented by carefully selected village helpers and at South Lodge there was much pushing and thrusting and beating about hedges and ditches in search of the missing weapon. Result: exactly nil. By now, in the magical way that such things happen, the local press at least had got wind of the affair and their reporters had come swarming over in a fever of excitement from the neighboring small towns: doubtless Fleet Street would be soon upon them. Already they were creating a dangerous nuisance, slouching about in the inevitable filthy old macintoshes, humped under the weight of swinging cameras, trampling all over the sacred ground. "Couldn't do much about it," said the Inspector's own sergeant, Charlie Thomas, from Heronsford. "What with the search and all, there aren't enough men to keep them back; it's like a blob of mercury, you think you've got them all under your thumb and suddenly they're scattering into little blobs all over the place again. But anyway, with fresh snow falling we couldn't do much more in the way of investigation, Chief. All the tracks are disappearing and we'd sorted out every last detail of what might have been a clue."

The Inspector stood for a long, long time looking about him — looking outward to the ring of wall and hedge surrounding the flat expanse of white: tramped round through the churned up snow to the window through which Constable Fisher had peered, trembling, for his first sight of the Duke's dead body. Later Fisher had been hoisted up by way of the same window frame, to look over the many–spired parapet for any sign of the revolver's having been tossed up there. "No, Sarge, nothing up here!" From no other vantage point could it have been thrown there.

And no gun anywhere else in the house. Not in the room where the Duke had died nor in the empty rooms out at the back: the connecting door had been locked and bolted from this side, all the windows and back door had been similarly fastened, boarded up in most cases — it was as though someone, having made all safe from within, had come out into the octagonal room, and locked the intervening door behind him. Nor was there any sign of anyone having been in the back of the house for many long months. Inspector Cockrill gave vent to a satisfied sigh. He liked things to be exact.

It was late evening when, having left in charge trusted henchmen of his own, he collected his sergeant and drove with him back to Heronsford. The night was dark but star–lit, all a–glitter where the headlamps picked out the leafless twigs of the hedges, frost–laden. He sat in the passenger seat, the cigarette smoke curling up through his nicotined fingers. "Well, then, Charlie — what do you make of it?"

"Not a lot," said the sergeant, eyes on the unrolling white ribbon of the road.

" 'Sealed room.' No marks in the snow that aren't accounted for."

"Time of death?" prompted the sergeant.

"The doc says very recent. Works out at about the time young Fish says he heard the shot."

"Fisher," said Charlie.

"I don't know why I keep thinking that it's Fish. Well — so?"

"Well, so. So there are questions to be asked," said the sergeant. "No acrobatic leaps possible or trapeze acts or any of that stuff: the distance between the lodge and anything else are much too great. So number One would be: Could anyone have been hiding in the lodge? Answer — we searched it thoroughly, even the roof outside, and positively there was not. Well, we were looking for the gun, but if a man had been there we'd hardly have missed him. Question two — and this one I know you're a bit fond of: Why were the returning bicycle marks so wobbly? Answer — the wretched lad was scared out of his wits, having been first on the scene and found the Duke dead — his hands were probably shaking like jellies, on the handlebars, and even Crum observed that he was pale and distressed. Question Three, then: did he really hear the sound of the shot? — no one else did. Answer — sure enough, we have only his word for it. Question Four then is: was it really the Duke who telephoned the Station? and the answer to that is that Sergeant Crum who took the message is so thick that he would never think to question it. Number Five: why did Crum bat off up to the Castle when the constable was supposed to have heard the shot from his home, which he couldn't possibly have done if it had been fired up at the Castle? — and that's the same answer, the man is as thick as two planks. Question Six — did the Duke really write the suicide note which was propped up on the desk? Answer — yes, probably, but it could have been written under coercion. Finally — and this is the sixty million dollar one — how did the murderer get away, taking the gun with him? Answer —"

"Or answers ..."

"Pretty obvious, Mr. Cockrill, don't you think? Only one way, really. Different versions of the same, depending upon who the murderer *was*."

"Except in the case of the one I think of as Number Four."

"Four?" said the sergeant, almost as though they were playing a word–game. "I've only got three."

Inspector Cockrill ran over them, ascribing to each a motive or motives. "I've only just now decided to add in this fourth one. In that case, the motive could be anything: his late Grace was a deeply unlovable man." They sat silent a little while, musing over it all, while the little car crept across the light carpet of snow — in this narrow, little–used byroad hardly disturbed at all. The Sergeant said at last: "It's odd that with the first three, the motive does in each case seem to be vicarious — if by that I mean, on behalf of other people."

"Well, I'd hardly say that: other people would benefit, certainly. In the first, it would certainly seem so vicarious, as you call it, as to be very hard to believe." He added rather gloomily that they mustn't forget that the Duchess appeared to have a candidate of her own and one without even a motive. "And that makes five."

The sergeant was hardly impressed. "Oh, well, sir — the Duchess!"

The Inspector had sat all this time nursing the enormous hat on his boney knees. Now, as they reached his gate, he scrambled out, clapping it back on to his head. "Yes, well — 'the Duchess' you say, my lad. But the Dowager Duchess of Hawksmere, let me tell you, is an exceedingly shrewd old bird. And I'm a bit scared of her: there's nothing she'd stop at to protect 'our people,' let alone her own family." He slammed–to the car of the door and stood hunting through the pockets of the disreputable old mac in search of his keys. "Oh, thank goodness, here are the damn things! I'm in need of a hot drink and bed. So goodnight, Charlie. Go off home now and sleep well. Tomorrow is another day."

Another day. For all but the late Duke of Hawksmere, lying so quiet and stiff in his metal cold–box, split like a herring to reveal his body's secrets: with nothing to disclose, however, but the recent consumption of a sandwich meal, and a gunshot wound in the head.

The new day was less than gladdened for Inspector Cockrill by the arrival of the Chief Constable of the county. A choleric, ex–military man, he huffed and puffed a good deal, unable to face the grotesquerie of a "locked room mystery" right there in their midst, and for comfort settled on the solid facts relating to the missing weapon. Well, yes, said Inspector Cockrill, a common enough type of weapon left over from the last war; impossible to say how many ex–officers might, for one reason or another, have failed to hand back their revolvers at the conclusion of hostilities. The passage through bone, explained the experts, would make it difficult to ascribe the bullet to any one particular gun. ("Very helpful," said the Inspector, sardonically.)

"Was the late Duke known to have possessed such a revolver?"

"If you recall, Sir George, you, yourself, undertook to question him on the subject."

"Yes, well, so I did question him. Called on him and asked him. But delicately, you know, stepping very delicately. He hardly seemed to know what I was talking about. But he certainly didn't deny that he had such a weapon."

"*Very* helpful," reflected Cockie again, but did not say it aloud.

"Well, you can't march in with a sniffer–dog and search a place like the Castle," said the Chief Constable, huffily. Besides, he added, these people who were always threatening suicide, never really did it.

"Nosir," said Cockie, in the authentic accents of Police Constable Fisher at his most wooden. He explained the probable difficulties in ascribing the bullet to the late Duke's — or indeed to any — revolver.

"Which anyway you've lost," the Chief Constable reminded him sourly.

"Oh, yessir, so we have," said the Inspector, more in the Sergeant Crum line this time. Sort of thing that could happen to anyone the voice suggested.

At first light, the search for the missing gun had begun again — village people tremendously eager and helpful, said Cockie. Although, he added limply, none of them had liked the Duke, most of them having understandable grudges against him. To tenants so long accustomed to the cherishing rule of the Duke of Hawksmere, with the family arms around "our people," he had seemed a mean, to them a dangerous man.

The Chief Constable was as appalled as the Inspector could have wished. "Good God, man, they'll all be on the side of the killer! You don't know *who* may have found the thing and be harbouring it somewhere. They must be taken off at once, search them, search their homes, search every house in the village ..." He stumped off angrily to wreak further havoc from the comfortable ambiance of the Heronsford Police Station, and Chief Inspector Cockrill was able to give out, with a lightened heart, that these arbitrary orders came not from himself — as if he would! — but from the Chief Constable in his un–wisdom. He must, however have considerably over–rated his superior's enthusiasm; Sir George would never have contemplated an intrusion into the Castle itself.

The search there was more easily concluded than might have been expected — by anyone but the Inspector himself. "Under some papers in a drawer of the late Duke's desk," he explained to the Dowager Duchess. "Surprise, surprise!" he added, sardonically.

"*Not* a surprise?" said the Duchess. She suggested: "After all, it may not be the one that was used? I hear the bullet may not prove to be traceable. Perhaps he didn't have this one with him. He presumably didn't always lug one around with him."

"So how did he propose to shoot himself down at the lodge? He rang up the Station and said that he was about to do so."

"Well, *some*one rang up the Station. Would Sergeant Crum necessarily have questioned the voice? And there'd be suicide notes all over the place. Whoever it was could just have used one of those."

"Your Grace ought to be in my job," said the Chief Inspector, respectfully.

"Do you know, Cockie," said the Duchess on a note of not very sincere apology, "in this particular case, I really believe I should."

Mr. Cockrill felt in duty bound to report to his Chief Constable though by no means to unravel matters clearly for him. "Her Grace put the gun there herself, of course, as I knew she would."

"The *Duchess?*"

"The Dowager. It was in a package sent up with her letters this morning — well, of course her post has been prodigious. Posted last night here in Hawksmere — well, everyone's been in and out of the village, in and out of Heronsford, up and down to London like yo–yos, lawyers and so forth: a duke doesn't die like ordinary men, let alone get himself murdered. Mind you, the postage alone may tell us something," suggested Cockie. "Don't you think?"

It patently told the Chief Constable nothing whatsoever. He huffed and puffed and went off at a tangent. "Why in God's name should the Duchess do such a thing?"

"Protecting the family?"

"For heaven's sake — the family! You're not suspecting the new Duke of Hawksmere in a business like this?"

"He had everything to gain. But, well, no — he's a big man, heavy, unlike his children. Ants, the Dowager calls them. 'So dark and little'."

"Well, then young Rupert. You wouldn't —"

"His father succeeds to the title the sixth Duke. Rupert is now heir to the title. And he loves the place deeply and the people on the estate — the family owns half the county. He was horrified by the way the late Duke was treating them. And the Duke, in the intervals of suicide notes, was threatening to marry and get an heir for himself. We have to consider young Rupert —"

"Good heavens, Cockrill, I shall never live this down!"

"— or there's the girl," continued Cockie, remorselessly. "She felt the same about it all. And of course their parents now become duke and duchess instead of being just hard–up nobodies ..."

Sir George looked as though spontaneous combustion were just around the corner. The daughter of the Duke! Or the heir to the dukedom! But comfort was at hand. He demanded triumphantly, "Just explain to me how either of them could have got away from the building? The tyre marks, the footmarks, are all accounted for, and there are no others. So how could either of those young people have got away from the place?"

Oh, well, as to that, said Cockie, tremendously off–hand, one could think of three or four explanations in each case; surely Sir George must have worked them out for himself? And he suddenly caught sight of Charlie Thomas and must rush off and join his sergeant, if Sir George would excuse him ... To Charlie, he said: "I can't resist pulling the old buffer's leg."

"You'll get yourself into trouble one of these days, Boss," said the sergeant laughing. But what on earth, he wondered, was going to happen next?

"What will happen next," said Cockie prophetically, "is that a letter will arrive suggesting a new and totally unexpected suspect and a new and totally unexpected method of getting away from the lodge — snowy surroundings, bike marks, footprints and all."

And duly the letter arrived and was handed over to them by the Duchess herself. "In this morning's post. Addressed to me. The postmark? — but Cockie dear, you've no notion what the mails have been like — with the Duke's death you know, all the business letters and the sympathetics — poor loves, so tricky for them to know just what to say! I mean, 'so sorry to hear that your cousin has been murdered. Whatever will you do about the funeral? Yours affectionately, Aunt Maude.' The children are reading through them in fits of giggles, they are so naughty! But as to the post-marks, I'm afraid we just slit all the envelopes open and threw them away: it's not like the Americans who put their addresses on the back, I never get used to it. But out they've gone and with this sort of cheap writing paper, there wouldn't be a matching envelope, we'd never trace which belonged to which."

Nor had the typewriter proved traceable to anyone in or around Hawksmere, probably done in a pretense of testing a demonstration model somewhere in London, Cockie thought. A very old trick. Style, predictably illiterate.

"Dear Dutchess," ran the letter, "I am well away now and soon will be abrord so to save truoble for others I confes to the murder of the duke of Hawksmear he was a relaton of yors but he was a dead rotter and he deserved to die. I went doun befor the sno began he let mne in I told him he mite as well comit suiside but he siad he would not now as he was hopeing to het marrid he did not seam to have a gun but I bruoght one along with me in case. I cuold not make him write a suiside note but there was one rihgt there on the desk just lying about.

"By now it was snoing and I pushed the gun in his back and mad him ring up the police station and say he was going to shoot hisself then I put tghe gun near his head and shot him. When I opend the door it was quite I haerd a bycicle bell and I went back and closed the door when I hared the person go away I cam out and I saw footsteps in the snow going round the house and I followed them and there was a window. I climbed up by the window on to the roof and when the jurnalists cam crowding round I showed myself and a policeman came and hauled me down so I said I only wanted to get a shot of the snow with the footmarks, as if I was a jurnalist and they quit beleived me. I better say I saw the policeman was being hoisted up to see if tghe gun was on the roof, so I lay up against the parapet where he would be leaning over to look and unles he bent right over he wuld not see me and he did not he only calld out no gun here. That is all. There was a lot of peeple hated tghe duke long before he was a duke and I was one of them. Yuo need not look any further."

"Well, well, well," said Cockie, handling over this effusion to his sergeant. "What did I tell you?" He went on down to the lodge and summoned the constable. "Well, now, Fish —"

"Fisher, sir," said the constable a trifle desperately.

"All right, never mind that. You were the man sent up to see if the gun had been thrown onto the flat roof of this room. Why did you choose to climb up via the side window?"

"It couldn't have been thrown from any other point, sir. There's a porch over the front steps and there weren't any other marks in the snow."

"The gun could have slithered back and come to rest just under the parapet. You didn't think to hook yourself right over the edge and look downwards and inwards?"

"The gun wouldn't have done that, Mr. Cockrill, sir." He made a chucking movement with his hand. "It would slither away, sir, not backwards; but anyway, with the snow it would probably just stay where it fell. So it would be about in the middle of the roof. And it wasn't."

"So if a man were hiding close up under the parapet where you looked over —?"

"I could well have missed seeing him. I wasn't looking there." And come to think of it, a man *had* tried to climb up on the roof, two or three in fact, but each time been hauled back before he got there. "Them journalists, sir. If anyone got far enough, he would have seen if a gun had been thrown up there."

In fact, several of the culprits had been traced but none admitted having got up as far as the roof, and the consensus of opinion had been that this was true. Still, it might be well to scan the newspapers for press photographs of the snowy ground, taken from a high angle ...

He came back to Constable Fisher. "The late Duke had a good many enemies? You yourself hardly loved him, I daresay?"

The constable's air of ease gave way to pallor and tensed–up fingers. "I never hardly set eyes on him, sir. Him being the Duke and all."

"Till the day before yesterday?"

"And by then he was dead, sir."

"Yes, so he was. It must have been a shock, peering in at that close–shut window? Now, tell me again — why that particular window?"

"You can't see right into the room from the nearer one, sir. Not into the whole of the room."

"No you can't, can you? But how did *you* know that?"

"Well, sir, being as my gran and grandad used to live here —"

"They *lived* here?" said Cockrill, and glanced with a sort of gleam towards his sergeant. "They *lived* here? And were chucked out by the Duke, I suppose? — and had to squash in with the rest of your big family, all in one little cottage? — the old folks cranky and carping, I daresay — as old people are when they see too much of the young, your parents resentful and answering back, all those noisy brothers and sisters worse than ever, and everyone miserable. In other words — the Sardine Tin!"

"Except I think it must be more peaceful, sir, in a sardine tin."

No wonder, reflected the Inspector, that I kept thinking of him as Fish. "Never mind your constable's domestic arrangements," he had said, choking off Sergeant Crum's ill–timed explanations; and all that time ... "All right for the moment, then, Fisher." But to Charlie he said: "Well, Sarge — the simplest explanation after all? It was only that, being more or less strangers to these parts, we had no idea that such a motive existed? But now —"

A shot that nobody else had heard. Down to the lodge on one's bicycle and up to the front door. The Duke, placidly consuming sandwiches, is easily persuaded to admit the uniformed figure of the local rozzer. Some excuse — the police require the handing over of the revolver which His Grace is understood to have in his possession. Gun in hand, force the telephone call to the police station — with any luck Sergeant Crum will go batting off up to the Castle, thus giving one more time. Force the production of the suicide note and then — one shot and it's done.

It's done: but all of a sudden it's — horrible. Back away to the open front door, gun in hand, having forgotten in one's panic, to throw it down beside the outflung hand. Stand there, shaking, trying to wipe off tell–tale fingerprints and, horror, horror! — the door is blown shut by the whirl of the wind that is sending the snowflakes a–flurry, and one is locked out on the step, with the gun in one's hand. Round to the window in hopes it may open sufficiently to throw the gun into the room: but it is closed and barred. And at any moment, Sergeant Crum may arrive.

Down to the gate then, a–wobble with nervousness, on one's bike, and when the hue and cry goes forth, join eagerly in. For who will think of looking in the pocket of the heroic discoverer of the crime, for the weapon which brought it about?

Nervous? Yes, of course he would be nervous. But so what? A man is dead whom all the world detested, Gran and Grandad can come back to the cosy little home, Mum and Dad will be free and happy again and the pack of younger brothers and sisters will be safe from the ceaseless censure of the older generation, and settle down happily once more. And Her Grace can move out to the dear little Dower House and the new duke is a kind and generous man, and Rupert, friend of one's childhood will be heir to the dukedom; and long–loved Becca will be rich and happy, and always down here at Hawksmere to be adored from afar. And how grateful, could they have known, would everyone for miles around have been, to the begetter of all this happiness ...

But first — the gun. One cannot carry it around in a uniform pocket, and where to hide it in the narrow confines of the village to which one is now restricted? Post it off to the Castle, then, with a message to the Duchess, "Please put this back where it belongs, for all our sakes." Her Grace must recognise that the thing has been done by someone here on the ducal estates, by one of "our people." Her Grace won't make trouble for anyone who will throw themselves upon her mercy; and Her Grace knows very well how to protect herself ...

The sergeant had been mulling it over, muttering at intervals into the recital, "M'mm, m'mm ..." Now he said: "And the letter?"

"Ah!" said Cockie, for the first time losing confidence a little. "The letter!"

"Very interesting, that letter. Not in fact the work of an illiterate? The mistakes are deliberate: a writer who spells 'brought' as 'bruoght' knows what letters there are in that difficult word. A true illiterate would write 'brort' or something. *And* this isn't an accomplished typist. It's easy to hit a *g* when you intended an *h* and he keeps putting 'tghe.' But Fisher types very well and I don't think he's bright enough to have thought all this up. So that would bring us to —"

"The new heir," said Cockie, none too happily. "Young Rupert."

"It's one thing for a lad like young Fisher, to want to help his grand–parents to get back their old home," said Charlie. "But Rupert's dad becomes a Duke, they're all in the money and what's probably the most important point, 'our people' will be safe from the tyrant — who was threatening to marry and spawn a breed of mini–tyrants for ever."

"So, how do you suggest he got away, leaving no trace in the snow? You don't suggest that Rupert was the man on the roof?"

"There never was any Man on the Roof, sir, *was* there? Just some damn journalist, trying to be cleverer than the rest; and *he* was hauled down and after all, he wasn't Rupert, whoever he many have been. But we've both thought of ways in which someone other than Fisher, could have got away from the lodge ..."

And there was the sound of hooves chiff–chuffing across the grass and a light voice exhorted: "Now, darlings, be good horses and just stay there!" and, with a thump at the door, the two young people came into the room. "The ants," said Cockie, sotto voce to the sergeant, and "Look here, Inspector, you're *not* accusing poor Dave of murdering Cousin Ham?" demanded Lady Rebecca on a note of scorn.

An ant she might be, but a very pretty ant, the cloud of dark, soft hair crowned by a shabby little riding bowler. The brother was as dark and scarcely taller, very slender and no less shabbily fitted out. Poor as church mice, the Duchess had said, and clearly their late cousin had not been generous with hand–outs despite his sudden acquisition of title and great wealth. Inspector Cockrill said, mildly: "Are you referring to Police Constable Fisher?"

"Yes, we are, we've just met him in the lane, and he's petrified."

"If he did kill the Duke, that would be fairly natural?"

"Of course he no more killed the Duke than I did!"

"In fact, my boy, we were just discussing that very possibility. That you *did*."

"Who, me? What a lot of rubbish! Why on earth should I want to kill rotten old Cousin Hamnet?"

"Just because he *was* rotten Cousin Hamnet."

They were leaning back negligently against the edge of the table, feet crossed in their well–worn riding boots. "Good lord," said Rebecca, "you're not going to suggest that he was the Man on the Roof, beloved of our Aunt Daisy — the Duchess Daisy," she elaborated. "And if not, how did he get away from the lodge without leaving great humping footprints in the snow?"

"Well ... We had an idea," said the Inspector easily, "that he might have used a bicycle."

"Oh, that's great!" said Rupert. "I haven't even got a bicycle."

"But your dear friend Dave Fisher — he had a bicycle."

It rocked them a little, but the boy said nonchalantly enough, "Don't tell me, let me guess. I borrowed Dave's bicycle?"

"At gun-point," suggested Becca, mocking, her pretty little nose in the air.

"Or by cajolement. He would be very much on your side."

"You seem to have a simple faith in the trustworthiness of your force," said Rupert.

"Well, but — to such a good friend. And it does all seem to fit?"

"It doesn't fit at all," said Rebecca. "We were together the whole afternoon, out riding." She saw as she spoke the weakness of this double alibi and added, "My Aunt Daisy saw us from the window. She'll tell you so."

"I'm sure she will," said the Inspector drily.

Rebecca slid down from her perch on the table edge. "So we'll be going home now because I can assure you that Dave didn't do it and neither did Rupert, so just *don't* be silly about it."

"No, indeed, since you put up so convincing a case. On the other hand," suggested Cockie, "you leave yourself undefended."

"Who — me?" said Becca as her brother had said before her.

"You had exactly the same possible motives as your brother. One or the other of you came down here before the snow fell —"

"Why one or other? — why not both of us?"

"Because only one person could have ridden away on that bicycle, with or without Constable Fisher." The sergeant opened his mouth to speak but Mr. Cockrill quelled him. "You came down here before the snow fell, one or other of you. You started a long argument with your cousin, about the running of the estate; about his possible marriage, perhaps. But it was all no good — you lost your temper, the gun was lying around as usual, ready for use if the fancy took him and you picked it up. By that time the snow had fallen but while you stood panicking on the doorstep, there appears the gallant Saint Dave to the rescue on his trusty bicycle; no need in your case, Lady Rebecca, for any gun–pointing or even cajolement: up you scramble and, wobbling a bit with the extra weight and general insecurity, you'd duly arrive at the gate. Off you scarper and the friend of your childhood is left, rather scared, but glowing with the knowledge that he has saved — well, I'll still say one or other of those he loves."

"Not bad," said Rupert with a determined air of superiority but looking, all the same, a little pale. "But surely there must be other candidates, not just Becca and me?"

"There aren't, you know. Your father — but he's too big and heavy to have shared a bike with Fisher, who's a big chap too — I've tried an experiment and the bicycle broke down; and what's more he has an alibi rather more convincing than that of a brother and sister out riding, watched by Her Grace, your cousin Daisy. Someone from round about? — well, the police aren't entirely idiots, you know, whatever you may believe to the contrary on this occasion; and we've made very thorough investigations — you can count them all out."

"So you seriously think you have a case against us — against one of us?"

"Or Constable Fisher," said Cockie placidly.

Rupert slid down and stood beside his sister. "Well, we'll be going now, if you'll excuse us. You can bring the hand–cuffs up to the Castle any time — be my guest! Come on, love," he said to his sister, "we'll go and lay this mouse at the feet of our 'ever present help in times of trouble' and see what *she* has to say to Mr. Cockrill about it."

The Inspector waited until the shuffle of hooves had trotted off into silence. Then he stretched himself. "Well, Charlie, at least we've got that off our chests!" And perhaps another time, he added laughing, his sergeant would refrain from breaking out into expostulation when his superior officer dropped a clanger.

"It was you saying that only one person could have ridden away on the bike — with or without Fisher. Of course anyone who had ridden the bike up to the lodge could just have ridden it back again; and any bike, for that matter, it needn't be Fisher's. The tyre marks were snowed over before we really got at them."

"Well, it doesn't matter either way. The tracks were made by the constable: he'd seen into the room, he described it to Sergeant Crum. The tyre marks were made by him, riding his own bike — quite possibly giving a lift back to the gate to someone of fairly small physique. And we've eliminated everyone except that precious pair." He heaved himself up and shrugged on his dreadful old mac, thrust the hat on to his head and gave it a thump which brought it down over his eyes. "Damn the thing, it never used to be as big as this," he said, irritably shoving it up to his forehead. "I'll get on to the Castle now and, in my turn, place my poor mouse at the feet of her ladyship. Who, however, is their cousin and not their aunt."

"Does it matter?" said Charlie, surprised.

"Not a bit," said the Inspector and folded himself, mac and hat and all, into his little police car. "See you, Sarge!"

"In one piece, I hope," said Charlie, rather doubtfully.

The Duchess of Hawksmere met him in the vast hall where she stood surrounded by his trio of suspects. "Oh, Cockie — how nice to see you! Now you, my loves," she said to the young ones — apparently, without affection on either side, including among her loves the village constable — "go off and get some coffee and buns or something and don't make any more fuss." One freckled hand on the bannisters, she began to haul herself up the stairs. "Sorry to be so slow, Inspector, but my arthritis is giving me hell today ..." At the door of her sitting room, she ushered him in. "Find a chair for yourself; but first pour me a drop of vodka, like an angel, and help yourself to whatever you like. And no nonsense about being on duty and all that — we're both going to need it I promise you!"

The Chief Inspector thought that upon his side, at any rate, this would certainly prove only too true. He cast the mac and hat upon a chair and sat down with her before the agreeably flickering fire. "Well, Duchess?"

"Well, Cockie! I was sure you'd come up after the kids, with all their dramas, and here you are, and we can settle down and have a real good yat."

Only the Duchess of Hawksmere, reflected the Inspector, would refer to a serious discussion of a murder in the family, as a good old yat. "I have to walk circumspectly, my lady!"

"Oh, not with me. I mean nobody ever does: it's because I'm so dread–fully un–circumspect myself. So I thought," she suggested with her own particular brand of authority and humility, "would it be possible for you to outline for me the cases you have against all these young people? Because I really do think I can help you, you know."

He thought it over; it was all highly unconventional but he, no more than

Her Grace, had never been, would never be, a slave to that sort of thing. Moreover, he was curious about her own so far undisclosed candidate. "If it honestly will go no further —?"

"Cross my heart and wish to die," said the Duchess, making a sign upon her well–upholstered bosom.

"Well, then ..." Somewhat gingerly and with many ifs and ands, he outlined one by one his suspicions of the young heir, Rupert, and of his sister, the Lady Rebecca. "And then as to Fish —"

"Fisher," said the Duchess. "I do think its so hurtful to get people's names wrong. I do it all the time, myself, but I'm old so it doesn't count. Besides, I call everyone darling, such an actressy habit, I simply hate it: but at least they don't realise that half the time it's because I can't think who on earth they are!"

"Duchess, you are trying to charm me," said Cockie, severely.

"Am I? Well, perhaps I am — I never know I'm doing it. But we need a little gaiety in all this awfulness, don't we? So, well that's those three and then that brings us to the Man of the Roof. The letter."

Chief Inspector Cockrill expatiated at length upon the letter. Don't let's be silly about that, was the unexpressed burden of his reflections. Aloud he said: "We know that that was just a diversion."

"But a very potent diversion, Chief Inspector, wouldn't you say? I mean — hardly to be denied outright, at least with any certainty. No possible proof. For or against. Is there?" She fixed him with a quizzical look which told him that he might as well be a bazaar that Her Grace was about to open. He knew he was at her mercy; and would love every minute of it. "But first, Cockie dear — another drink?"

"Not another drop, Duchess, thank you."

"Oh, but you must, or I can't. And you know that I can't get weaving till I'm vodka up to the ankles. I get so tired," said the Duchess, looking as wan as every evidence of robust health would allow, "and when I'm tired, my mind simply won't work, I'm helpless."

It seemed to Inspector Cockrill highly desirable from his own point of view, that Her Grace should remain without reviving vodka, but she had him in thrall. He reluctantly poured out two small rations, ("Oh, Cockie, for goodness sake!") and more generously topped them up. "So now, my dear, what are we to do? Because you know perfectly well that my two young ones couldn't possibly have killed the man, and neither could poor, dear Dave Fisher. So we come back to the letter. Who wrote the letter?"

"You wrote the letter yourself, Duchess, and posted it on one of your necessary expeditions up to London. Or didn't post it at all — just 'found it' among your letters."

"Well, what a thing to suggest! But really very perspicacious of you, Cockie. Yes, of course. I thought it might come in nicely for covering every eventuality: because if you could just settle for that, (only keeping it to yourself, of course) and never be able to find a trace of the murderer — well, who could say a word against you?"

"My Chief Constable for one, could say a word against me and would, most vociferously."

"Oh, that pompous old fool! Nobody will listen to a word he says; you just leave him to me. All you need do is cast about like mad, dragging in Scotland Yard and Interpol and all that lot, trying to trace the letter, trying to ferret out all Hamnet's old enemies, which after all would take you back twenty or thirty years: and finally give up and say the case is closed or whatever the expression is."

"No case is ever closed," said Cockie.

"Well, keep it a bit open but just never solve it. Because what the letter says is true, millions of people simply hated poor old Ham, long before he was ever a duke; he was a misery to himself, always saying he wanted to die, never having the courage to get around to doing it. And now the lovely Man on the Roof has done it for him and everyone will simply love him for it and no one would want him to be caught at all."

"Except me," said the Chief Inspector, somberly.

"Well, I do call that rather lacking in appreciation of my efforts to help you!"

"You don't suppose that *I'd* be content with some cooked–up nonsense, no one ever knowing the truth?"

"Well, but someone does know the truth, don't they Cockie? I mean, I've told you all along, haven't I? *I* do."

"Your Grace has never had the goodness to divulge it to *me*."

"Oh, Cockie, how cross and sarcastic! Well, I'll divulge it now. But only," said the Duchess, downing the last of her second vodka tonic, "if you promise, promise, promise never to do anything about it."

"Are you asking me to let a criminal go free?"

"No, I'm not. I don't think there is any criminal — except the Man on the Roof. I think Hamnet did at last really go ahead and commit suicide. Ate his lunch, thought things over — he was always a bit dyspeptic after meals — rang up to the police station, and reached for the gun. And then ..." she put out her pudgy hand with its carefully tended, varnished nails and touched his own nicotined fingers. "Trust me! You'll be grateful to me, honestly you will. I'm not practising any deceit upon you — and it will solve everything."

You are old, he thought, and stout and arthritic and nowadays no beauty, but damn you ...! "Well, all right," he said at last, grudgingly. "So —?"

"So — that boy, Cockie! You kept on saying it yourself — to be first on the scene of the bloody death of the Earl of Hawksmere, no less — a baby, a great, raw green rookie of a baby policeman, not yet dry behind the ears. In a total panic — wouldn't he be? What he said was the truth, my dear — he heard the shot, leapt on his bike and pedalled like a lunatic down to the lodge and up through the snow to the front door. And the door was open. Hamnet always left an escape route, didn't he? — rang up in advance so that if ever he did take the plunge, someone could get there in time to haul him back to life. The door was open — how would anyone have heard the shot if it had been fired from behind sealed–up windows and doors? He looked inside and the first thing he saw was the Duke's head, dreadfully wounded, and the revolver lying there, fallen from the dead hand. So — what would any of us do? — he panicked and, in an automatic impulse, bent down and picked up the gun."

"Oh, my *God*!" said the Inspector.

"Yes, it was a bit Oh–My–God, wasn't it? — since the Number One lesson a policeman is taught, is never ever to touch anything at the scene of the crime. He would have thrown it down at once, I daresay, but another lesson came into his mind as he began to calm down — watch out for fingerprints! He got out his hankie or whatever, and started wiping his own off the gun and — horror of horrors! — there comes a flurry of wind, and the door blows shut."

"Leaving him locked out, with the gun still in his hands. Nips round to the side window to see if he can throw it back in, but the window's tight shut. So he shoves the thing into his pocket and, very nervous, wobbles back to the gate and when Sergeant Crum arrives — not the most observant of men — goes into his act. The door was closed, he could only see the body by looking in through the window ..."

"Well, there you are, Cockie — and there *he* was, poor wretched boy, and just think of his state of mind. Marching about all evening pretending to be searching for the weapon when all the time it was in his uniform pocket. And now, for days, he'll be kept on duty in the village — and where in little Hawksmere can such a thing remain hidden for any length of time, with everyone searching for it? So what does he do? — he posts it off to me. Of course he can't be sure that I've guessed the truth, but people have got into a sort of habit of thinking I'll cope. And that's all, really, except for the lovely, convenient Man on the Roof, made up for you by me."

He sat almost paralysed in the deep armchair, looking at her smiling face. "Constable Fisher — lost his head and just picked up the gun ... Is this what you really believe?"

"It's the simple truth, my dear. And simple is the word."

"He's admitted it?"

"I haven't asked him. It was so obvious."

Not to assembled forces of the law, it hadn't been. "But to prefer to be suspected of murder —?"

"He could always tell the truth in the end."

"Why not have told it from the beginning?"

"My *dear*," said the Duchess, "you'd have had his guts for garters!"

He leapt to his feet. "Well, one thing's for certain — I'll have them now."

"Yes, well — the only thing is, if this story gets out you'll look a bit a fool, old love, won't you?"

Chief Inspector Cockrill, the Terror of Kent — a bit of a fool, right here on his own patch. "Hey, now, Duchess, if you *don't* mind —"

"Oh, but I do mind," she said. "I don't like to think of you looking foolish." And she pleaded, "Let the boy go! He's been through a bad time, you can be pretty sure of that; he won't do it again. There's nothing against Rupert and Becca, there's been no crime; this is what actually happened and that's the end of it. But the Man on the Roof — there he is, all worked out so nicely for you and it all hangs together perfectly, now doesn't it? Someone out of the past caught up with the Wicked Duke and you never had a hope in hell of catching up with the someone from the past. Gradually the whole affair will fade and Chief Inspector Cockrill, for a miracle, has failed to Get his Man; but for the rest, everyone is happy." And one couldn't help thinking, said the Duchess, confiding it to the fireplace, that it is less humiliating to fail to solve a very difficult case, than to have failed to solve such a very simple one as a young officer losing his head ...

"No one must every know," said the Inspector; and it was capitulation.

"Good heavens, no! I'll talk to Dave Fisher and tell him what I've guessed and that, to save his skin, I've played a naughty game all round; and just to pipe down and never get it into his head to confess, because he'd get me into trouble. I could even suggest that you rather suspect that this might have happened, but you have to investigate every possibility ..."

"Except the right one," said Chief Inspector Cockrill, rather stiffly. He collected his droopy macintosh from the back of the chair, clapped the hat on his head and hastily removed it, in the presence of her ladyship. "And honestly — not one word of this to anyone?"

"Oh, not a word," vowed the Duchess, even now casting about in her mind for someone one could safely confide in. For really it had been rather a bit of fun! "But I *told* you!"

"You told me —?"

"That in this case, I really should have been in your job," said the Duchess. She too rose. "I say, Inspector — what about one more little one? I really think we could do with it; do join me!"

Inspector Cockrill paused a moment and then cast down his hat and coat again, upon the chair. "Do you know Duchess — I think I will," he said.

# Alleybi

"Oh, Samivel, Samivel," said Inspector Cockrill, pushing their two glasses across the counter for the same again. "Vy wornt there a alleybi?"

Detective Inspector Charlesworth looked at him with pity and exasperation; poor old boy, breaking up at last! He explained with a patient kindness, not lost at all upon Inspector Cockrill, that what he had been trying to tell him all this time was that there *was* an alibi — an alibi that so far appeared impregnable. And yet it must have been this fellow, Perkins — there simply wasn't anyone else that could have killed the woman. "You can see the whole picture: just settled in the village, butcher's shop getting nicely started, invited to be in the church choir, a riot at the Boy Scouts' concert last week; nice little home above the business and a jealous wife with the hell of a temper! — and then this floozie turns up out of the past and begins to blackmail him."

"Which he admits?" said Cockie.

"Oh, yes, he told us so frankly. She didn't ask for anything the first time — just, didn't he love her any more and wasn't there something they could do about it? But this afternoon, she appeared again and turned on the heat. He says that he gave her five pounds out of the till and let her out by the back door of the shop, which is invisible to the neighbours; and went back to his radio. He's a violent soccer fan, and the second half of the big game was just starting; it was half past three."

"And you say the wife confirms some of this?"

"Yes, she does; she was lying on her bed resting, and she says she heard him come up about then and switch on the set. She furthermore says, and it's true, that the door of the sitting–room squeaks so badly that no one could go in or out without being heard."

"Unless of course the only other person in the house happened to have fallen asleep," said Cockie.

"She says she was awake and reading all the time."

"— or happened to be your everloving wife."

Charlesworth drowned half his beer at a gulp. "Well, of course we aren't only going by what *she* says. The point is this. The woman's body was found at half past four in a lonely lane a mile away from the house; she'd been dead about half an hour, that's to say she must have been killed at four o'clock. But during the second half of the soccer game, Arsenal scored four times — and each time they scored, Perkins appeared at the window of his sitting–room and waved a signal to a friend of his, across the way — a bedridden old man who hasn't got a wireless set. What's more, the moment the game was over, he trotted in to see the old man and gave him a move–by–move account of the game; he'd even made notes."

"Which covered the whole of the second half?"

"Every minute; and if you're thinking of collusion, several people saw the notes. It was a regular practice between them, apparently; they were both devoted adherents of Arsenal, and it meant that the old boy didn't have to wait for the morning papers. I must say, Perkins does seem to be a very kind little man."

"Kind little man don't usually go about hitting people on the head with meat hatchets."

"No," said Charlesworth. "And yet — well, it's his meat hatchet, him being the butcher; and anyway — who else? No one in the village had ever set eyes on the woman; she came from Liverpool or somewhere, miles away." He finished his beer. "Well, I must get back on the job; but it's a bit of a facer, isn't it? What would *you* say?"

"I'd say, 'Vy wornt there a alleybi?' " said Cockie. "But *I'd* say it to the jealous, hot–tempered wife."

# The Spotted Cat

*A play in three acts*

*Cast*:

*Graham Frere* — a barrister, something over forty.

*Tina Frere* — his wife. A young thirty–six, very attractive, probably dark and small.

*Leonard Burge* — rather less than forty, attractive, intelligent, a foil to Graham. A physician, specialising in kidney disease and having recently, through a scholarship to America, opened up a new field of research in nephritis, thus in a short time greatly improving his status, financial and reputational.

*Julie Crowle* — Tina's daughter by an earlier marriage. Necessarily only about eighteen.

*Bunny Babbitt* — older than Julie and a complete foil to her. A niece of the departed first husband. Goes through life with the ghost of a hockey stick in her hand and the word 'honour' on her lips. Perhaps has a slight stutter or other physical drawback.

*Fritz Harte* — a young doctor of middle–European extraction and cosmopolitan upbringing.

*Inspector Cockrill* — a dried up little elderly policeman, in plain clothes.

*Two or three attendant policemen*

*Scene*:

The drawing room at the home of Graham and Tina Frere.

— First on an evening in November.

148 .

— Secondly an evening in the summer.

— Thirdly, the following morning.

It is, in fact, in Kent:  this need not be specified but must not be impossible — to account for the presence of Inspector Cockrill who is well–known (to the author at any rate) to be in the Kent Police.  To use a small town outside London has further advantages, in the rapidity with which clues etc. can later be checked:  for example, there are only two or three chemists.

The room is furnished with taste and charm but by no means very expensively — probably with 'finds' from the local antique shops.  There would be one or two items bought in the days of Graham's short–lived prosperity.

The front door is so placed that we can see people arriving in the hall: there are, perhaps, two large glass dividing doors, of which only one half is actually used.  There are bookshelves and a sofa and to the right of the door as you enter, there is a chair, and also a large–ish table from which drinks are habitually dispensed.

It is a creaky old house, and people moving about it can be heard from the drawing room.  This is arranged so as to avoid deflection of the interest of the audience when scenes are taking place in the drawing room which would otherwise be subject to possible interruption.

Somewhere off–stage there is a kitchen to which people now and again repair; and the principle bedroom is over the drawing room.


# Act 1

*Scene:  The drawing room in Graham and Tina's house.*

*Time:   Early evening.*

*When the curtain goes up, the stage is in darkness, except for the hall, beyond the big central glass doors. Here a dim light switch is burning. The door to the drawing room is abruptly opened. Graham Frere stands there, slightly swaying, fumbling for the light switch of the drawing room. Two figures are silhouetted against the dim light of the hall, in a close embrace. The audience cannot see who they are; and Graham, with his back to the light, could see still less.*

GRAHAM:     (*with slightly drunken dignity*) Oh — beg your pardon!

*Exit Graham, closing the door behind him. His heavy footsteps mount the stairs. Immediately the two break up: there is a murmur of a voice, which need be only half heard.*

MALE VOICE:        He's gone —
FEMALE VOICE:      Quick — the window ...
MALE VOICE:        Can you manage ...?
FEMALE VOICE:      Come back later ...

*It is important the audience, even when they later see these two, cannot be sure who was there in the dark. The whole thing is over in a very brief time.*

*Exit Male, by the french window.*

*Exit Female, into the hall.*

After quite a pause the front door opens and a second light is switched on, brightening the hall, now seen through the glass and also through the drawing room door which Tina has left open.

*Enter, into the hall, in an only half–heard babble of conversation, Julie, Bunny and Fritz. Julie runs off upstairs, Fritz goes toward the kitchen, Bunny enters the drawing room, still in outdoor hat and coat.*

BUNNY:     Well, thanks awfully —
JULIE:     I'll whizz up and change —
FRITZ:     I take the ice cream —
JULIE:     Shove it in the fridge: kitchen's down there ...

*Bunny carries a paper cone of flowers. She puts them on a table and goes over to re–arrange the curtains which have somehow got pulled aside.*

*Enter Tina.*

TINA:     (*all charm*) You got some? Oh — kind Bun!
BUNNY:     I couldn't get the roses —

*Tina unwraps an untidy bunch of chrysanthemums and the charm abruptly fades.*

TINA:     (*exasperated*) Oh, *Bunny!*

| | |
|---|---|
| BUNNY: | — the roses were five and six. |
| TINA: | But these are half dead. |
| BUNNY: | I'm half dead myself, matter of fact, I had to go right down to the High Street ... |
| TINA: | You've only been gone twenty minutes. |
| BUNNY: | I met Julie and Fritz and they gave me a lift. I say, Auntie, he *is* a smasher. |
| TINA: | Bunny — how many times have I told you not to call me 'Auntie'? |
| BUNNY: | Sorry — Aunt Tina: I always forget. Oh, and I got you an ice cream block. |
| TINA: | What on earth for? |
| BUNNY: | Haven't you seen your iced soufflé? |
| TINA: | Oh, my god — no.? |
| BUNNY: | Flat as a pancake; and all the cherries at the bottom. |
| TINA: | Well couldn't you have done something? |
| BUNNY: | You sent me to buy the flowers. |
| TINA: | Really, I don't know what I keep you for, you get more useless every day. |
| BUNNY: | When Uncle George was alive, we did have a char. |
| TINA: | (*relenting a bit*) Two when I first married Graham. |
| BUNNY: | Poor Auntie. |
| TINA: | He swore if I married him he'd never touch a drop again. And while he didn't, the briefs came rolling in ... |
| BUNNY: | Of course you did marry him rather *soon* after. And him being a barrister ... |
| TINA: | (*laughing*) Am I so disreputable? |
| BUNNY: | You were charged with murder. |
| TINA: | But let off with a caution! |
| BUNNY: | (*earnestly*) Oh, of course you were innocent, darling, we all know that, as if you'd have murdered poor Uncle George. But Graham was your counsel and people do say things in a place like this. |
| TINA: | It doesn't matter what they say — his work's in London. Well — never mind. Is Fritzie just the same? |
| BUNNY: | Just the same. And a gorgeous car — only painted bright yellow. |
| TINA: | He's very well off. |
| BUNNY: | Yes, and he was *kind*, wasn't he ...? |
| TINA: | He's wasted no time looking Julie up! |
| BUNNY: | And he went on coming to see us after Uncle died, not like Dr. Burge. |
| TINA: | Why should Dr. Burge go on coming? He was the doctor — the |

patient was dead.

BUNNY:      Fritz was the doctor too.

TINA:       Fritz was a half–cooked medical student, running errands for
            Dr. Burge.

BUNNY:      Well, there's no patient in the house *now*, Auntie — Aunt
            Tina: and Dr. Burge comes now.

TINA:       What do you mean?

BUNNY:      Honestly, I believe … Well, I mean, I think you ought to be
            careful, Auntie, *I* believe Dr. Burge is falling in love with you.

*Enter Julie and Fritz.*

TINA:       Fritzie, how nice! After all this time!

FRITZ:      Madame, you are wonderful! You have grown backwards.

JULIE:      (*contemptuous of this Gallic flattery*) D'you mean her bottom
            sticks out?

*Bunny bursts out laughing but Tina is not amused. There is an air of friction
constantly between mother and daughter. Bunny hastily changes the subject.*

TINA:       Don't be silly, Julie.

BUNNY:      Did you put the ice–cream —?

FRITZ:      Top of the refrigerator.

JULIE:      We got a tin of crushed pineapple.

TINA:       Yes, well we had ice–cream and hot pineapple *last* time
            Leonard came.

BUNNY:      If he didn't come so often —

TINA:       Bunny, please!

JULIE:      Dash it all, Bun — his evidence saved her life.

BUNNY:      If he'd saved Uncle George's life, which is what he was there
            for — he wouldn't have had to.

FRITZ:      But Dr. Burge — he is a great doctor.

BUNNY:      That's not what we found.

TINA:       Bunny, will you please go and get on with the dinner and mind
            your own business.

*Bunny shrugs like a schoolgirl and goes sulkily off.*

TINA:       Oh, dear — that child!

FRITZ:      She does not love Dr. Burge?

TINA:       Just jealous.

JULIE:      She has a crush on Mama — poor old Bun!

FRITZ:      You still have her with you? You are so good!

| | |
|---|---|
| TINA: | Oh, well — she tries to make herself useful. |
| JULIE: | *And* doesn't have to be paid. |
| TINA: | Considering that I keep her ... body and soul |
| JULIE: | Oh, all right, Mama, skip it. Fritz, have a drink? |
| TINA: | Yes, Fritz — how awful of us! |
| FRITZ: | Really, we should not. We are on our way to a party. |
| JULIE: | Wait and see my Step. Where is he, Mama? |
| TINA: | (*glancing upwards to the bedroom overhead*) Upstairs, changing. This house! — you can hear everything. Listen to Bunny — clop, clop, clop — in a minute the kitchen door ... there it goes! |

*Julie and Fritz are pouring drinks for themselves*

| | |
|---|---|
| JULIE: | Hey! — not that glass. That's the Step's special — with the spotted cat. |
| FRITZ: | Oh — pardon! But, was not the spotted cat ...? |
| TINA: | (*laughing*) Ye–ers: it was! |
| JULIE: | It's all right, you needn't put on a face. She was acquitted. |
| TINA: | I was not acquitted; I was 'discharged with no case to go before a jury;' which was much more grand. |
| FRITZ: | But, where I gave evidence ... was this not a trial? |
| JULIE: | (*remembering back*) Did *you* give evidence? |
| FRITZ: | But I? I was the big hero. I said two times, 'I don't know' and three times 'I can't remember'. And this was not a trial? |
| TINA: | No, because I wasn't what they call 'put in peril'. I wasn't being tried for my life, I was being tried — before a magistrate, not a judge — to see if there was anything to try me *on*. And there wasn't. So that was that. |
| FRITZ: | But by your British law — you cannot be tried again? |
| TINA: | Oh, yes, because I never was tried — not before a judge and jury. |
| JULIE: | Thanks to your dear Dr. Burge: who Bunny now thinks it's practically immoral to have to dinner (*imitating Bunny*) 'Honestly, Auntie Tina ...' |
| FRITZ: | What a — brouhaha — at the hospital! DR. LEONARD BURGE IN THE WITNESS BOX. BEAUTIFUL WIDOW CHARGED WITH MURDER ... |
| JULIE: | Not a word about beautiful daughter. |
| FRITZ: | Not a word about brilliant young foreign doctor, saying two times 'I don't know' and three times 'I can't remember' ... |
| JULIE: | The spotted cat pinched all our publicity. |
| TINA: | But for the spotted cat, there'd have been none. |

| | |
|---|---|
| FRITZ: | Of course if a doctor is a little careless, there is always publicity. |
| TINA: | It was I who was careless. |
| FRITZ: | It was — a misunderstanding. Dr. Burge said he would increase the strength of the dose. You thought he meant that you should give more pills. With any other patient, nothing would have happened. But the heart was very weak. And so — the end. |
| JULIE: | Except for the spotted cat. |
| FRITZ: | But why — I could not understand why — should Inspector Cockrill ever have suspected) |
| TINA: | (*bitterly*) Oh, but didn't you know? My husband informed upon me, before he died. He wrote in and said I was going to murder him. |
| JULIE: | He only said you might. |
| TINA: | I beg his pardon — he only said I might. |
| FRITZ: | Because he found the note? |
| TINA: | A scrap of paper with half a dozen words, and a meaningless doodle of a spotted cat. We were always leaving each other notes — weren't we Julie? |
| JULIE: | Well, the note did say he was being difficult. |
| TINA: | He was *always* being difficult — he was ill. But he promptly decides that I must have a lover. Me — a lover! I was nursing *him* day and night. |
| JULIE: | He was ill: he couldn't help imagining things. |
| TINA: | He wasn't too ill to write in to old Cockie and say that if he died there must be a post mortem. |
| FRITZ: | It was very — unpleasant — for you. |
| TINA: | It was certainly was. Because he did die, and there was a post mortem — and there was this overdose of barbiturate, this Morphon. |
| JULIE: | So he *was sort* of justified. |
| TINA: | In leaving me to be treated like a murderess? |
| FRITZ: | But — not seriously. |
| TINA: | Only thanks to Graham. You see, Graham fell in love with me from the first moment — |
| FRITZ: | We all do. |
| TINA: | He did it to some purpose! He worked like a demon for me, he got hold of Leonard Burge and they worked out what must have happened — and of course after that, the whole thing fizzled out. |
| JULIE: | So she married Graham: which Bunny also thinks is hardly decent. |

| | |
|---|---|
| FRITZ: | And Dr. Burge went off to his triumphs in America. |
| TINA: | And it's all forgotten and done with. |
| FRITZ: | (*raising his glass*) Except for a cocktail glass — with a spotted cat. |
| JULIE: | That's my step–papa. He looks on the spotted cat as his mascot now: because it introduced him to Mama. |
| TINA: | Which also shocks Bunny to the core. |
| JULIE: | 'Honestly, Auntie Tina ...' |
| FRITZ: | 'Honestly Auntie Tina,' we are late for our party ... |
| JULIE: | Yes, we must go. Oh — here he is, coming down now. |
| FRITZ: | We are late, Julie. Madame — *mes adieuz* ... |
| JULIE: | All right, come on, skip the foreign speeches. G'bye, Mama. |
| TINA: | Goodbye, Fritz. Have a nice time, darlings ... |

*Exit Julie and Fritz, from the drawing room: they can be seen in the hall, looking up to where Graham is coming down the stairs.*

| | |
|---|---|
| JULIE: | Hello, step. We've got to rush off ... |
| FRITZ: | Good evening, sir. |
| GRAHAM: | (*off stage*) Who's this? |
| JULIE: | Fritz Hart. You know Fritz. |
| GRAHAM: | Oh — do I? |
| JULIE: | We did wait. We wanted to see you. |
| GRAHAM: | I saw *you* all right, my girl! |
| JULIE: | What do you mean — saw *me*? |
| FRITZ: | Julie! |
| JULIE: | All right, all right, sorry, coming ... |

*Exit Julie and Fritz through the front door.*

*Enter Graham. He looks tired and haggard and is still a little tight.*

| | |
|---|---|
| GRAHAM: | Caught them necking in here. Most tactless! — |
| TINA: | Oh, hallo, darling. |
| GRAHAM: | — Where's my glass? |
| TINA: | There, in front of you. |
| GRAHAM: | My glass with the spotted — Oh, yes, here it is. |

*He takes up his glass, pours some sherry into it, spills a little and mops it up with his handkerchief.*

| | |
|---|---|
| TINA: | They were in *here*? When was that? |
| GRAHAM: | About six. The case packed up. I caught the early train. |

TINA:      But at six o'clock ... Oh, well, perhaps I'm wrong.

GRAHAM:    Wrong? What about?

TINA:      Nothing, never mind — I wasn't thinking. You lost, did you?

GRAHAM:    Yes, we lost. At least I suppose so. I left the boy to finish.

TINA:      Oh, Graham — why didn't you stay?

GRAHAM:    What for? I'd done my piece: unfortunately for them.

TINA:      If I'd paid to have my case defended — I'd expect counsel to finish it himself.

GRAHAM:    In your case — counsel did.

TINA:      But Graham — I mean, what was the hurry?

GRAHAM:    I wanted to get home to my charming wife.

TINA:      You wanted to get out to the nearest pub.

GRAHAM:    The pubs were closed — worse luck.

TINA:      Then you've had one at the station; when you picked up the car.

GRAHAM:    I've had half a dozen. We should have won hands down, Tina. The truth is, my dear — I've lost my touch.

TINA:      Yes. Because you're drinking again.

GRAHAM:    It isn't the drink, Tina: You know that.

TINA:      Now, don't start all that other nonsense, Graham. You know that's just imagination. Leonard told you ...

GRAHAM:    Well — please God he's right.

TINA:      Just strain and over–work —

GRAHAM:    Over–work! That's rich! Poor Tina — I meant to make things so wonderful for you ...

*He comes over and embraces her. She resists at first.*

GRAHAM:    ... I meant to give you everything in the world. Oh, Tina — do you hate me now, because ...?

TINA:      Graham! — of course not ...

*His embrace grows more passionate, she resists but finally succumbs to the purely physical side of it: she is a woman who will always respond to physical love–making, whether or not her emotions are engaged.*

*The front door bell rings.*

TINA:      Quick — Graham! That's Leonard!

GRAHAM:    Blast Leonard!

*Bunny's voice at the front door. She opens the drawing–room door and ushers Leonard in, in a sulky schoolgirl voice, exits.*

| BUNNY: | Dr. Burge. |
|---|---|
| TINA: | Leonard! Hallo, come in … |
| LEO: | I hope I'm not late? |
| GRAHAM: | In the nick of time. My wife was giving me a lecture on the evils of drink. |
| LEO: | (*coldly*) It seems to have made her hair very untidy. |
| TINA: | Really, Graham! He's like a great schoolboy, Leonard. Graham — give Leonard a drink. |

*Graham goes to the table and begins pouring drinks for all three.*

| LEO: | Why — have you taken to the bottle, Graham? |
|---|---|
| GRAHAM: | Tina thinks so. Sherry? Or gin or something? |
| LEO: | What are you drinking?· |
| GRAHAM: | Dry sherry. |
| LEO: | That'll do me fine. |
| TINA: | I only say he nips out for nips and he nips out too often, and it's doing him no good. |
| GRAHAM: | It's doing my practice no good either. That's the end of the Tio Pepe. |
| TINA: | There's another bottle somewhere. Ask Bunny. |
| LEO: | Then why do it? |
| GRAHAM: | Why do what? |
| LEONARD: | Why nip out for nips? |
| GRAHAM: | I like it. It jollies things up — you've no idea! — to have counsel come rolling into court half an hour late … |

*Bunny at the door*

| GRAHAM: | … Oh, Bun — is there some sherry somewhere? |
|---|---|
| BUNNY: | I'll get it. |
| GRAHAM: | No, no, I'll get it if you tell me where it is. |
| BUNNY: | I don't mind a *bit* … |

*Exit Bunny.*

| TINA: | Let her be a martyr. |
|---|---|
| GRAHAM: | What was I —? Oh, yes: Counsel coming back from lunch, '… 'pologise Lordship 'n court, humbly submit may't please good old Lordship, all adjourn glorious, glorious pubs for a quick one …' |
| TINA: | (*impatiently*) Oh, Graham! |
| GRAHAM: | Well, then, darling, don't fuss! |

*Enter Bunny with new bottle of Tio Pepe: she unwraps the paper and starts searching about in the background.*

GRAHAM:     Sorry, Leonard, we're boring you. Tell us *your* news.
TINA:       We saw you in the papers — very grand! 'Famed scientist greets U.S. ree–search workers ...'
LEO:        Birdsmere doctor, you mean, remotely heard of in connection with work on the kidneys ...
BUNNY:      I can't see the corkscrew.
TINA:       Julie had it. Fritz Hart's just been in, Leonard.
GRAHAM:     I thought he'd gone back to wherever–it–was for good?
LEO:        No, I pulled a few strings for him at the hospital. Don't know what the attraction is in England.
TINA:       One of the attractions is out with him now, on a party.
GRAHAM:     They were having a *neck*ing party when *I* got in.
TINA:       (*with exaggerated off–handedness*) Never mind about that now, Graham.
BUNNY:      I don't see when that was.
TINA:       All right, Bunny.
BUNNY:      Well, Julie wasn't necking, as you call it.
GRAHAM:     Necking, pecking, canoodling, what does it matter? When I arrived home they were *in — here — necking*. What's wrong with that?
BUNNY:      When you arrived home they were down in the High Street, with me ...
GRAHAM:     What do you mean, Bunny?
BUNNY:      ... because when we got back, your car was already in the garage.
TINA:       Bunny — please go and get on with dinner.
GRAHAM:     My car was here ...?
BUNNY:      Yes, so you couldn't've —
GRAHAM:     And the kids were with you?
TINA:       Bunny!
BUNNY:      Well, he's just been imagining things, again that's all.
TINA:       All right, Bunny, please go.
BUNNY:      Well, I don't see why Julie should suffer because he makes things up.
GRAHAM:     (*suddenly shouting*) All *right*, Bunny!

*Exit Bunny, scuttling.*

GRAHAM:     (*half to himself*) I came in here. I saw two people in here, in the dark. But there was nobody, Tina! If there was nobody ...

TINA: Now, Graham, darling ...

GRAHAM: She's right, isn't she? There was nobody here. It's happened again. Hasn't it, Tina? It's happened again?

LEO: Nothing's happened. (*Suggesting*) You'd had a couple, Graham ...

GRAHAM: No, no: it's not the drinking. Well — never mind. Skip it. Have a drink yourself, old boy.

LEO: Don't get het up about it, Graham. You're a bit worn out, you're nervously exhausted ...

GRAHAM: Nervously exhausted! For God's sake — let's face the thing, don't call it bloody silly names! I'm going off my head, that's the truth of the thing, I'm going off my head, I'm going mad.

LEO: You're not 'going mad.' You get a bit mixed up ...

GRAHAM: Oh, for God's sake, Leonard! I see things. I don't get 'mixed up' — I see things that aren't there to see, I think things happen and they didn't happen, I think I did things and I did other things ... Not once, not twice, a dozen times — a dozen times in the past three months, more than a dozen times ...

LEO: You get your time–factors mixed ...

GRAHAM: When did I see those two kids in here — tomorrow?

LEO: And then this business of the nips in pubs.

GRAHAM: It's nothing to do with pubs, Leonard.

LEO: What form do they take?

GRAHAM: I've told you. It began with the woman in the garden ... No, it began before that, but that first put it into my head that I was going mad.

LEO: You'd been asleep, you were still dreaming.

GRAHAM: Was I dreaming when I bought red roses for Tina and lo and behold! — they turned into yellow carnations? Was I dreaming when I made that phone call to you the other night, saying God knows what? Was I dreaming when ... Ah! — you haven't heard the latest, Leonard, this one's really charming ...

TINA: Oh, Graham — need you?

GRAHAM: Friday, it was, last Friday. I sat up late working, I finished the work, I stowed all my stuff away in my brief case, and off I went to bed, as pleased as Punch. Next morning ... Oh, my God, it makes me sick ...

TINA: Next morning, Bunny came in here ... She found he'd — well, he hadn't put his stuff in the brief case, he'd torn it up. That's all it is.

GRAHAM: That's all it is. Except that I'd propped my brief case up on a chair; here, this chair: and I'd got hold of my driving gloves

|  |  |
|---|---|
|  | and stuffed them out with paper into the shape of hands — stuffed them full of pornographic pictures — |
| TINA: | They weren't pornographic. |
| GRAHAM: | They were the best I could do — a pin up girl, all bottom and bosoms, a dirty joke written on a bit of paper, the notes of one or two of my prettier cases, a Sodomite vicar, you know, two or three nice rapes ... And these — hands — these gloves, were sticking up out of the brief case and they were holding — they were holding ... |
| TINA: | A pair of black lace panties, Leonard, that was all. |
| GRAHAM: | A pair of your knickers, Tina, call things by their names. |
| LEO: | (*who has not heard this before, really shocked and upset*) No — I hadn't heard that one. Well, Graham — it's — significant perhaps. But it's not very dreadful really ... |
| GRAHAM: | It may not be to you. It is to me. And if the 'significance' is that I'm wallowing in frustrated sex, I can assure you that my wife and I give one another full physical satisfaction — don't we, Tina? |
| TINA: | Really, Graham ... |
| GRAHAM: | Well, don't we? This is a chat with the doctor, dear, not a tea–fight with the Vicar's wife. |
| TINA: | Yes, but still — |

*Enter Bunny.*

|  |  |
|---|---|
| TINA: | — Dinner, Bunny? |
| BUNNY: | Well, the soup's a bit queer. Ought it to have all those black bits? |
| TINA: | I shouldn't think so. (*To the others*) We'd better come back to this later. Poor Leonard — coming to dinner and getting all our troubles: not to mention black bits in the soup! |
| GRAHAM: | *And* nothing to drink. |
| TINA: | Help yourself to some sherry and bring it through — to have with the black bits. |
| GRAHAM: | Yes, good idea. Go ahead, I think I will too. |
| TINA: | Should you, Graham? |
| GRAHAM: | Now, don't let's start on the Curse of the Drink again. |

*He is sitting in his armchair and begins to feel about for the glass which he believes he has put down on the floor beside the chair.*

|  |  |
|---|---|
| TINA: | I only meant — sherry on top of gin. |
| GRAHAM: | I wasn't drinking gin. |

TINA:       Yes, you were — gin and Dubonnet.

GRAHAM:     I was not — I had sherry. Where'd I put the damn glass?

TINA:       Well, all right, darling, never mind, leave it: I daresay you did
            have sherry.

GRAHAM:     What do you mean, Tina? I tell you *I — had — sherry.*

LEO:        (*exchanging a significant glance with Tina which Graham can
            intercept*) Well, skip it now, Graham come on in to dinner.

GRAHAM:     I — had — sherry! I've been drinking sherry the whole bloody
            evening, I had —

TINA:       Leave it, Graham!

GRAHAM:     Where is the bloody glass? — I tell you I had sherry, you're
            wrong, I know it was sherry, I *know* it was sherry ...

*He finds the glass and lifts it: it has the dregs of a dark red fluid —
Dubonnet. He stares at it, pitches the contents into the fireplace and crashes
the glass down upon the mantelpiece; and blunders out of the room.*

*Bunny goes after him.*

*Tina waits till the door closes and their dimly seen figures in the hall,
disappear: their steps mount the stairs. Then with an air of quiet triumph,
she picks up a duplicate glass from behind her own chair and places it with
a little clonk, on the mantelpiece beside the other.*

TINA:       It worked!

LEO:        Yes. It always does now. He's 'conditioned', he's expecting it.

TINA:       (*brightly*) Did you have to buy the whole set?

LEO:        Yes. I've got the rest at home. One black cat, one white cat,
            one ginger cat, one tabby cat, one striped cat — one spotted
            cat. The lot.

TINA:       What a bore! Thirty bob!

LEO:        What a bore, as you say. Thirty bob. Thirty pieces of silver ...

TINA:       Oh, *darling!*

LEO:        ... For sending a man to be crucified.

TINA:       Don't be so dramatic!

LEO:        The last man who did that went out and hanged himself.
            Sometimes, I know how he felt.

TINA:       If you get sentimental at this stage — you won't *have* to hang
            yourself: the law will do it for you.

LEO:        We must think of some other way out.

TINA:       There's only one other way out — and we've used that before
            dear. (*No reply from Leo*) All right. If you want to risk it,
            we'll give it up. You can confine yourself to disease of the

|        |                                                                                     |
|--------|-------------------------------------------------------------------------------------|
|        | kidneys — and I'll go on giving dear Graham 'full physical satisfaction.'            |
| LEO:   | Yes, Tina: what did he mean by that?                                                |
| TINA:  | After all, my dear — I *am* married to him.                                         |
| LEO:   | You swore to me ... But I know you, Tina: anything in pants —                       |
| TINA:  | So you see you can't just give up, Leo: can you? (*She is afraid she has gone too far*) Darling — you know I loathe it — |
| LEO:   | He was mauling you about when I came in here —                                      |
| TINA:  | *You* were mauling me about when *he* came in here! — a little earlier.            |
| LEO:   | — *And* you were letting him.                                                       |
| TINA:  | For our sake, darling. I was being sweet and understanding about his troubles. 'I'm afraid, Graham dear, you really do drink too much!' |
| LEO:   | It's my belief half *that's* because of you.                                       |
| TINA:  | Because of me?                                                                       |
| LEO:   | You'd wear out any man in a month.                                                   |
| TINA:  | I'd wear you out, my sweet! Only give me the chance!                                 |

*She kisses him passionately but he pushes her off.*

|        |                                                                                     |
|--------|-------------------------------------------------------------------------------------|
| LEO:   | Be careful. If he came in again ...                                                 |
| TINA:  | He won't — not this time.                                                            |
| LEO:   | He never suspected?                                                                  |
| TINA:  | You saw — he thought it was Julie and the boy–friend. So I cashed in on it. Another 'delusion'. |
| LEO:   | We take too many risks.                                                             |
| TINA:  | I thought it was safe: but he got an early train. And I'd got rid of Bunny, but the kids gave her a lift. Blast the lot of them. |

*A sound outside.*

|        |                                                                                     |
|--------|-------------------------------------------------------------------------------------|
| LEO:   | She's coming back.                                                                   |
| TINA:  | No, no, we'll hear her. There — listen! He's lain down on the bed, she's fussing round, 'Let me get you some warm milk, we always had warm milk when we got concussion playing hockey ...' That girl drives me up the wall! |
| LEO:   | Our old way was best. Absolutely no risks. Tina — I don't think we can go on with this. |
| TINA:  | You mean — Graham?                                                                   |
| LEO:   | If I didn't have to *see* him.                                                      |
| TINA:  | But — it would mean everything. Giving up altogether.                               |

| | |
|---|---|
| LEO: | I'll be moving to London. It'll be easier ... |
| TINA: | And leaving me here? In — this! (*Her gesture suggests the dullness, the increasing poverty of her present life. What Leo really represents for her, is a change from it all*) |
| LEO: | To set out — in cold blood — to drive a man mad. I can't, Tina. I can't. |
| TINA: | (*deliberately*) He's been talking again about the spotted cat. |
| LEO: | He hasn't? |
| TINA: | Just now. Just before you came. It was like those old days after the trial. Sort of — hinting. |
| LEO: | Oh, my God. |
| TINA: | We'll never be free of it, Leo. |
| LEO: | No. We'll never be free. Together or apart ... |
| TINA: | Not while he's — sane. If I could just leave him ... |
| LEO: | You can't just leave him. Why did you *do* it, Tina. Why marry him? We'd got rid of the one ... |
| TINA: | I've told you, I was terrified, I couldn't believe he hadn't seen the truth. |
| LEO: | And the spotted cat? |
| TINA: | You name's Leo like a leo–pard: a leopard, a leo–pard. What's a spotted cat but a leopard? So the note must have been meant for *you*. |
| LEO: | Other people didn't see it. |
| TINA: | But he was the barrister, working on the case. And he seemed so keen and so clever. |
| LEO: | It's only you that call me Leo. And anyway, in those days it was supposed to be Dr. Burge. |
| TINA: | I couldn't think straight, everything was so terrifying; you'd gone off to the States and left me ... |
| LEO: | I *had* to go. |
| TINA: | And he was in love with me, he was besotted, I thought — and I still think, Leo — that he was blinding himself. I thought, underneath, he knew. |
| LEO: | But knew! Knew what? That the drawing of the spotted cat was a pun on my name, that therefore we were lovers; that therefore, between us, we'd killed your husband. And he used it to blackmail you — into marrying *him*? |
| TINA: | Well, but — |
| LEO: | The truth is Tina — you married him because you wanted to. He was full of money in those days, was dear Graham. |
| TINA: | He was drinking like a fish. |
| LEO: | Ah, but he gave up drinking — all for your sake, Tina; and when Graham keep sober there's nothing he can't do. I was |

one better than your poor old crock of a husband; but Graham came along and he was better still.

TINA: As if I ever cared two pins for money.

LEO: You! — you care for nothing else, you need money, Tina, you ought to have money, you're wasted without it. And in those days, Graham looked like having more money than I did. Now it's me that going up: and so ...

TINA: If you feel like this — we'd *better* end it.

LEO: Ah, no, Tina — you were right: that's something we can't do.

TINA: If you think I could go on loving you, after —

LEO: Oh, we could end the love: such as it is. And the passion: about which, like dear Graham, I have no complaints. But for the rest — we're bound together for ever now, you and I.

TINA: Nothing binds us.

LEO: Fear binds us.

TINA: It doesn't bind me. As long as I stay with Graham —

LEO: And how long will that be? A man going downhill, half out of his mind already, no work, no money ...

TINA: That needn't trouble *you*.

LEO: It troubles me very much. The moment you leave Graham, then up, up out of his subconscious will crawl theses old, ugly suspicions that you say are there: and one breath of suspicion, and *I'm* blown sky high.

TINA: (*quoting herself*) That needn't trouble *me*.

LEO: I think it would.

TINA: Not at all. Why should it? Poor little widow — first husband died: accused of his murder, vindicated by the evidence of the doctor in charge of the case. And she marries another man. What does it matter to her — if they say that it was the doctor who killed her husband? As long as she stays married to this other man —?

LEO: But suppose the other man — once he suspects — won't stay married to her?

TINA: Oh, him! Well known to be going off his head. They often get strange fancies, poor deluded creatures — against their very nearest and dearest.

LEO: Poor deluded creature indeed — with you for his nearest and dearest.

TINA: How dare you!

LEO: And my God! — when I look at you — coldly and sanely — I'd as soon put my love and trust in a cobra.

TINA: I've finished with you! I've finished with you!

*Enter Bunny.*

TINA:      (*Irritably*) Oh, Bunny — don't come in bursting like that.
BUNNY:     He says it was sherry he was having all the time.
TINA:      Sherry?
BUNNY:     He took out his handkerchief. There's a damp patch on it. He
           says it's sherry — it is sherry — smell it! He says he must
           have spilt some and mopped it up ...

*Leo has drained his sherry glass and now surreptitiously throws the dregs on
Tina's skirt. She gives him a tiny glance of comprehension and complicity.*

BUNNY:     (*continued*) He thinks he remembers doing it. He wants me
           to look at the glass again.

*Leo sweeps one glass out of sight on the mantlepiece, behind a vase, and
hands her the other.*

LEO:       Here's the glass. But it's Dubonnet.
BUNNY:     Well! So it is!
LEO:       Tina — your skirt.
TINA:      My skirt! Of course. I split some sherry on it and I took his
           handkerchief to wipe it. Look — where's the place? — yes,
           here it is; still damp.
BUNNY:     Well — fancy him forgetting!
TINA:      I don't think he even noticed.
BUNNY:     He'll be so disappointed. But there it is — the patch on your
           skirt and all.
TINA:      Ought I to go up to him?
BUNNY:     I was going to take him some warm milk: we always use to
           have warm milk —
LEO:       Would you like me to push off, Tina?
TINA:      No, Leonard, don't go. Bunny, dear, you heat up the milk and
           I'll take it to him ...
BUNNY:     I'm afraid he'll be upset.

*Exit Bunny. Tina falls into Leonard's arms.*

LEO:       Darling — you're shaking!
TINA:      I was so frightened.
LEO:       You were wonderful. Catching on so quick.
TINA:      I couldn't think *what* you were doing — throwing sherry on my
           skirt!

LEO:          But you didn't bat an eyelid.
TINA:         Oh, Leo!
LEO:          I told you, darling — we can never end it. We're partners. We
              belong.
TINA:         The leopard and the cobra. Fancy calling me cobra!
LEO:          I guess I like cobras.
TINA:         And I like my leopard — my snarling, wicked, angry
              dangerous leopard. (*Embracing him*) My hungry leopard!
LEO:          Oh, Tina! Oh, God help me! Tina!
TINA:         Are you mad again, Leo? A little bit mad again?
LEO:          As mad as a hatter — damn and blast your eyes!
TINA:         Not all cold and horrible and sane?
LEO:          Mad as a hatter, Tina. Thank God for it!
TINA:         Thank God — to be mad!
LEO:          We mustn't think, Tina, we dare not be sane, we must just
              pray to God to keep us from giving our minds to it …

*A sound outside.*

TINA:         Oh, thank you, Bun. If you'll excuse me, Leonard, for a few
              minutes? Bunny, give Dr. Burge another drink.

*Exit Tina.*

LEO:          No, thank you, I won't. Don't rush off Bunny — I wanted to
              ask you —
BUNNY:        Ask *me*?
LEO:          Do *you* think he's —?
BUNNY:        He must be. I mean, if he wasn't … Have they told you
              about …? (*She gestures vaguely towards the chair where she
              saw the brief case, etc.*)
LEO:          These things aren't unusual.
BUNNY:        Oh, no, I know. That's the worst of sex.
LEO:          (*teasing*) You find that, do you?
BUNNY:        Me! — I don't have anything to do with it. I wouldn't. I mean,
              look at poor Graham.
LEO:          It started with the woman in the garden?
BUNNY:        It was horrible. I woke up and he was calling to Tina. She'd
              gone down to get a drink of water. He said there was a woman
              in the garden, all in black with a long black veil. But Aunt
              Tina was looking right out *on* the garden, and she'd said
              there'd been nobody there.
LEO:          Of course you all thought he'd been dreaming?

| | |
|---|---|
| BUNNY: | Yes, till the other things started. Forgetting things, imagining things, picks up a book and swears it isn't the book he put down ... 'I must be going dotty,' he used to say. But after a bit he didn't say it any more. He began to be afraid it was true. |
| LEO: | (*ashamed*) Yes. Poor Graham. |
| BUNNY: | Poor Aunt Tina, *I* say. |
| LEO: | The thing is — what to do about it. |
| BUNNY: | You're the doctor. |
| LEO: | But not a mind doctor. There's Dr. Brownlow ... |
| BUNNY: | Him! He's as batty as a crumpet himself. Do you know, he knits! A man — knitting! |
| LEO: | He's a psychiatrist. |
| BUNNY: | Well, Fritzie's a psychiatrist. |
| LEO: | No, he's a brain surgeon. |
| BUNNY: | Oh, well — we don't want any cutting. |
| LEO: | Now — odd that you should say that. There is an operation, that doesn't involve any 'cutting'; and Fritz is the one man in England who knows all about it. |
| BUNNY: | No cutting? |
| LEO: | They have a machine — like an X–ray machine. An Austrian is using it — Professor Mendlhum of Kultz. |
| BUNNY: | Fritz was in his clinic. |
| LEO: | That's the chap. |
| BUNNY: | How does it work? |
| LEO: | Well, I don't understand it myself — not the operation. They use this ray, it's really a tremendously high sound–ray. They put the thing against the frontal bone — here — and the ray passes through without damaging the flesh or the bone, and disrupts the tissue in behind the bone. |
| BUNNY: | Good lord — how peculiar. And is it a good thing? |
| LEO: | It seems to be — in cases like Graham's. It quietens them down, you know, makes them more manageable. |
| BUNNY: | He's *quiet* enough. |
| LEO: | So far. |
| BUNNY: | You don't mean ...? |
| LEO: | How can one tell? It's only just beginning. |
| BUNNY: | Whatever will happen to Aunt Tina ...? |
| LEO: | And Julie. And you? |
| BUNNY: | Oh, well, we're all right: Julie'll get married soon, she's so pretty and everything; and I expect I could get a job. But poor Auntie ... |
| LEO: | We must talk to Fritz. That's a good idea of yours Bunny, I'd never have thought of it ... |

*Enter Tina.*

TINA:        He now refuses to have the milk and says he's coming down to dinner. I can't do anything with him ...

*Bunny turns eyes of alarm upon Leo at this confirmation.*

TINA:        *(continued)* You go up, Bun, and see if you can manage him.
BUNNY:       Oh, dear. But if ...?
LEO:         It's all right, there's nothing to worry about; he's perfectly safe — so far — I promise you ...
TINA:        He's got a bottle of brandy; try and take it away. If he insists on coming down, just get on with dinner ...

*Exit Bunny.*

TINA:        What's all this?
LEO:         She's leapt to the conclusion that he's becoming violent!
TINA:        All the better. Any luck about Fritz?
LEO:         She suggested it herself. So I led her gently round to the Herr Professor. But I still think Graham will insist on a London man.
TINA:        You mean you still funk it.
LEO:         I mean just what I say.
TINA:        We can work up a line about keeping it all hush–hush. His work's in London. If it got about that he'd been consulting a mental specialist, no one would go to him.
LEO:         Well — all right.
TINA:        Now — this Mendlhum?
LEO:         I tell you — he's a phoney. He's invented this operation, using the ultra sonic ray, so that no one's afraid of it. With it, he's reduced a lot of light–hearted zombies to docile immediately. It does the lunatics no good but it's easier for their friends and relations; and they're the ones that pay.
TINA:        And if Fritz tells him Graham's mad —?
LEO:         That's the point. He's a phoney. He'll go ahead and no questions asked. But will Fritz play?
TINA:        You know quite well that anything you tell him, Fritz will believe. 'Dr. Burge is a great doctor!' — I've already had it today. And of course I can confirm things — not to mention make up a few that Graham never heard of. And here's Bunny all ready for him to start turning handsprings ...
LEO:         And Julie?

TINA:      I'll have to pack Julie off — abroad or somewhere.

LEO:       And then ...? When it's all done ...?

TINA:      (*impatiently*) Oh, Leo! Graham will be stupid, he'll be docile. I can make him do what I say — and go where I say. We'll move up to London, you'll be there already. In London, people won't talk, no one knows us — I can gradually shed him, park him somewhere, cook up a desertion, perhaps get a divorce ...

LEO:       That's only part of it, Tina. What really matters is Graham talking. One hint that we were lovers before George died —

TINA:      But he'll be an imbecile, Leo, you've said so. Who's going to listen to him talking? — away from here where people know us ...

LEO:       Well — I hope to God it works.

TINA:      It's got to work; there's nothing else to do.

LEO:       No. That's true. There's nothing else to do. We've killed one man. Now, through your folly, Tina — or your fear, or your greed, God knows! — we've got to get rid of another. We can't kill him too. As Oscar Wilde would say — to lose two husbands looks like carelessness.

TINA:      We couldn't kill him anyway. George — well, he was dying, Leo: we just hurried it on.

LEO:       We just murdered him.

TINA:      All right. So we can't just murder Graham. But alive and in his right mind, Graham is a danger to us. Alive, he's got to go on being: but in his right mind — we've got this chance now and we've got to take it. I mean, what a piece of luck — Fritz coming back, Mendlhum, all that ...

LEO:       Oh, splendid luck: for everyone but Graham.

TINA:      (*ignoring his bitterness*) It's all been our way, Leo. The woman in the garden! — I was terrified when I heard him calling, but it started this whole idea ...

LEO:       It was a crazy risk — for three minutes together.

TINA:      Ah — but what a three minutes!

LEO:       It was madness!

TINA:      For Graham! He fell for it so easily — that he must have imagined the woman. He was half tight, of course, when he went to bed.

LEO:       I suppose we're terrible people, Tina: sitting here just — discussing — such a thing.

TINA:      We're just people.

LEO:       No, we're not: not like other people. We have something that makes us not like ordinary people. It's the fact that we both have that something, that binds us together.

| | |
|---|---|
| TINA: | (*impatiently*) What something? |
| LEO: | Curiously enough — it's not so much a something, as a lack of something. I think it's a lack of what the Eastern religions call Compassion. |
| TINA: | I don't even know what it means. |
| LEO: | No, Tina: I don't believe you do. It's — well, it's just a feeling for other creatures. You see, we're not cruel, we're fond of animals and so forth ... |
| TINA: | I'm not. I detest them, smelly things. |
| LEO: | But you don't like to see them hurt or neglected. You don't like to see pain; and neither do I. We're not sadistic. But as long as we don't have to witness it — we can't feel anything about it. We lack compassion. |
| TINA: | How can you feel anything for something you don't see happening? You can't. It's just affectation. |
| LEO: | Not in other people. |
| TINA: | Yes, it is. They only pretend. We don't pretend, that's all. |
| LEO: | Not to ourselves. |
| TINA: | Or to each other. |
| LEO: | It wouldn't be much use, would it? But it does — set us apart, Tina. It's interesting, isn't it? We're set apart, you and I together, from all the people we know — by just this lack of one, single attribute. |
| TINA: | It's not interesting at all: it's horrid. I don't like being dissected. |
| LEO: | You'd rather dissect poor Graham. |
| TINA: | Poor Graham is a danger to us. He could get us both hanged. That old devil, Inspector Cockrill — |
| LEO: | I often wonder if he was really convinced. |
| TINA: | He sort of — looks through you. It was only because there was never a hint of anything between us ... |
| LEO: | Yes. If Graham ever tumbles to that ... |
| TINA: | And while his mind's clear, he may tumble to it at any moment. This is our chance now, our only chance. Leo! He's coming down. |

*Sounds of heavy feet coming in a hurry downstairs.*

| | |
|---|---|
| LEO: | Quick — sit over there. |
| TINA: | You talk to him. |
| LEO: | Not yet. |
| TINA: | Yes, Leo. Start now. |
| LEO: | What — Mendlhum? |

TINA:          No, no, not Mendlhum: just a vague idea about treatment, we
               daren't mention operation ... not for ages.

*Enter Graham: very shaky.*

GRAHAM:        Tina — what the hell's this — about some operation?
TINA:          Graham, what *is* the matter?
GRAHAM:        — some professor, some death ray or something ...?
TINA:          You've been drinking again.
GRAHAM:        I had some brandy. Tina, Bunny's been saying —

*He breaks off and stands stock still: he has seen on the mantlepiece the two
glasses.*

GRAHAM:        (*continued*)  What in God's name —?
TINA:          (*sharp with terror*)  Leo!
GRAHAM:        Two glasses.  Two spotted cat glasses.  A trick!

*He swings round upon Tina:  this enables Leo to snatch one glass from the
mantlepiece.*

GRAHAM:        (*continued*)  My God, Tina, you were playing a trick on me!
TINA:          You're drunk, Graham, let go of me, what do you *mean* — two
               glasses?
GRAHAM:        There are two —
LEO:           There's only one glass, old boy.
GRAHAM:        (*to Tina*)  You've moved the other one!
LEO:           She hasn't been near it.

*Tina holds up her empty hands.  It is dreadful, it is like a horrible children's
game: as Graham lunges between them, she deftly takes the glass from Leo.*

GRAHAM:        (*to Leo*)  Then you —
TINA:          Leave Leonard alone, Graham.  Why should *he* play such a
               trick on you?
GRAHAM:        This glass has had sherry in it.
TINA:          It can't have.  You had Dubonnet.
GRAHAM:        It's sherry.  Leonard — no, leave it alone, Tina — Leonard: is
               this sherry or is it Dubonnet?

*Leo takes the glass and sniffs at it.*

LEO:           Look, Graham — you aren't well, old boy ...

*Leo passes the glass to Tina who sniffs at it, meanwhile switching with the glass which she already holds.*

GRAHAM:     Is it sherry or Dubonnet?
LEO:          What does it matter what's in the damn glass?
GRAHAM:     She's playing a trick. I said I had sherry. There's sherry in that glass — there were two glasses.
TINA:          Oh, Graham, for heaven's sake! Why should I 'play a trick on you'? — what in God's name would be the point ...?
GRAHAM:     (*wearily*) *I* don't know; *I* don't know ...
TINA:          Just think about it, be reasonable ...
GRAHAM:     Yes. Why should you? But — there were two glasses there, I saw two glasses ...

*He suddenly thinks of something, rushes to the door and tearing it open calls:*

GRAHAM:     Bunny!

*There is no immediate reply; he goes out into the hall and roars up the stairs again for Bunny. Tina, seeing her chance, slips over to the book case, takes out two large books and hides the glass away behind them; the audience will have to recall, later, that this was done.*

LEO:          Graham, leave it, old boy, leave it ...
GRAHAM:     (*in the hall*) Bunny!
BUNNY:       (*upstairs*) Yes?
GRAHAM:     Bunny — come down here!

*Re–enter Graham, followed by Bunny.*

BUNNY:       Oh, dear — now what? (*To Tina*) I tried to make him not take all that brandy.
GRAHAM:     Bunny — when you came in here just now ...
TINA:          (*realising his intention*) Yes, Bunny! Yes, Graham! Bunny — when you came in just now: here, on this mantelpiece — one glass, or two?
BUNNY:       One glass or ...?
GRAHAM:     Did you see one glass on the mantelpiece, or two?
BUNNY:       Well — one.
TINA:          Of course.
GRAHAM:     You only saw one glass?
BUNNY:       Well — yes.
TINA:          Of course you only saw one glass. And in that glass, Bunny ...

GRAHAM:    All right, Tina: I'll ask her.  In that one glass, Bunny —
           sherry?  Or Dubonnet?

*Bunny stands miserable and indecisive.*

GRAHAM:    All right.  Don't look so solemn — it's not your fault.  Well,
           Tina — Bunny was saying:  about this operation ...

*The curtain falls.*

## Act 2

*A summer evening.*

*Tina and Graham are doing the Times crossword.  Graham appears to be
bearish and stupid but underlying is a sort of childish malice as though he
secretly enjoyed irritating Tina and may not really be as stupid as he seems.*

TINA:      (*reading out*)  Six, and three.  'It's particularly dense.'
GRAHAM:    Six–and–three, it's particularly dense?
TINA:      Not six–and–three, *six* and *three*: two words, 'It's particularly
           dense.'
GRAHAM:    Oh, I see, I thought you meant six and three, I couldn't see
           how six and threepence —
TINA:      No, well, never mind — it's 'London Fog.'
GRAHAM:    London fog?
TINA:      It's 'particularly' dense — well, London fog.
GRAHAM:    Is a London fog particularly dense?  In Manchester ...
TINA:      Oh, *Graham!*  A London Particular, a London fog.
GRAHAM:    *London Particular* was a book — that woman who wrote *Green
           for Danger.*
TINA:      I know it was, I couldn't read a word of it.  But it's also a
           quotation from Dickens.
GRAHAM:    So it is.  I'm afraid it's me that is particularly dense these
           days.  Ever since my operation ...
TINA:      Well, never mind that, Graham, we're doing the crossword.
           Now:  three words, three, four and four, 'the' something
           something, I think, and the third word begins with 'p'.
           'Protective colouring in dim–dappled grasses.'
GRAHAM:    (*reaching for dictionary*)  Quotation of sorts.  Under 'grasses'
           I should think.
TINA:      Never heard of it.  What are dim–dappled grasses, anyway?
GRAHAM:    Light and shade in the jungle, I suppose.  No — it's not here.

TINA:          Well, skip it, we'll go on to something else.

*Tina concentrates on a new clue and does not appreciate that he has moved behind her to a glass–fronted cupboard: we saw her in the first act hide the duplicate glass there.*

GRAHAM:        Where's the Maunders?
TINA:          The what?
GRAHAM:        That other old thing of quotations, it may be in that.
TINA:          I don't know, we haven't used it for years. Now. Six down, beginning with 'l'. That's the 'l' of London, 'You can go up or down to it': what on earth do they mean by that ...?

*Graham has found the book and pulled it out. His back is to the audience. He stands stock still for a moment: then swiftly moves together a couple of books to close the gap which revealed the glass. Standing there, he opens the dictionary.*

GRAHAM:        Grasses ... Dim–dappled grasses ... Ah — here we are: good for Maunders! Page 34 ...
TINA:          Loch Lomond. I don't call that very good.
GRAHAM:        Yes, here we are:     'Seeing,  yet  seeing not, the hunter passes.
                                     By the pied pard, in the dim–dappled grasses'.
TINA:          What on earth's a pied pard?
GRAHAM:        A pard's a leopard, 'freckled like the pard.' But this one appears to be piebald.
TINA:          Leopard's aren't piebald, they're — (*breaking off abruptly*)
GRAHAM:        They're spotted. The spotted leopard. That's a funny phrase: it has a sort of — ring to it. The spotted leopard. Like the ...
TINA:          (*hastily*) Only this one was pied.
GRAHAM:        Quite a conspiracy among the poets — freckled, pied, anything but poor old simple spotted.
TINA:          Anyway, that's the answer, is it? 'Protective colouring in dim–dappled grasses' — the pied pard. (*She writes it in*)
GRAHAM:        Protective colouring it certainly is. First he's pied or freckled or speckled — never plain spotted; and then he's a pard or a panther but never a leopard. It's a funny word, Leopard. I mean, one says leo–nine, and Leo–nid: why not ...?
TINA:          (*quickly and irritably, covering over his pronunciation of leo–pard*) Darling, are we doing the *Times* crossword, or are we not?

GRAHAM:     Yes, yes. I'm only saying — there's Leopold and Leonore and
            — no, of course, *Leon*ard. Leonard and leopard, they're the
            same.
TINA:       Graham — the crossword!
GRAHAM:     All right, my dear — don't snap at me.
TINA:       Well, you go meandering on, talking such nonsense.

*From now on, Graham sinks back into an apparently genuine apathy which
should deceive the audience as well as Tina.*

GRAHAM:     Yes. Nonsense. Was I? What was I — well, it's gone now.
            I'm afraid I do ramble on and then I forget what I've been
            rambling about. Poor Tina — you have a lot to put up with.
TINA:       Well — never mind me, Graham.
GRAHAM:     You're very good to stick it out like you do.
TINA:       You're muddled up still, that's all. Your mind's still woolly,
            you imagine things and you forget things.
GRAHAM:     Nothing stays in my mind for two minutes.
TINA:       You'll be better soon. It's early days.
GRAHAM:     It was five months ago.
TINA:       These things take time.
GRAHAM:     And meanwhile, Tina — it's so tough on you. Practice going
            to pott, no money coming in.
TINA:       Well, well — you can't help it.
GRAHAM:     It seems to come in waves. Now, two minutes ago, my mind
            was clear, at least I think it was clear — I could think, I had
            — I had some glimmering of an idea, if only I could remember
            it, that was clear or beginning to be clear in my mind. And
            then — a sort of cloud blows over: and the idea's gone.
TINA:       Don't worry about it: you'll get better.
GRAHAM:     Supposing I don't get better? I depend on my mind for my
            living — for our living.
TINA:       Well, Julie's married now and off our hands.
GRAHAM:     Yes. (*softly*) Poor little Julie!
TINA:       Poor Julie? *She's* all right.
GRAHAM:     Did I say ...? I expect I mean 'poor Tina.' Or poor old
            Graham. You know, Tina — there's one idea that doesn't
            vanish when the clouds blow across. 'I have been ... I have
            been ...'

*He slowly turns over the pages of the dictionary while Tina, with frayed
patience, waits for him.*

GRAHAM:   (*continues reading*) 'I have been half in love with easeful death ...' With easeful death! 'Now more than ever seems it rich to die, To cease upon the midnight with no pain ...' To cease upon the midnight. Would that perhaps be happiest for us all? For you, Tina — with such a burden on your lovely shoulders ...?

TINA:   (*Already the idea is dawning, of using this*) Suicide?! You're thinking of ... Oh, nonsense, Graham!

GRAHAM:   The operation hasn't worked, you see: has it? It was supposed to — to clear things up for me. Wasn't it?

TINA:   Yes, of course.

GRAHAM:   But it hasn't. I'm woollier than ever — as you're just said, yourself. So what have I got to lose? An addled head: a very weary heart.

TINA:   You're never said all this before.

GRAHAM:   I've often thought it. If only for your sake.

TINA:   (*delicately probing*) Me? What could *I* do? What would become of me?

GRAHAM:   You'd soon marry again.

TINA:   Me, marry again! Who, for example?

GRAHAM:   I've often thought that Leonard was a bit smitten.

TINA:   Leonard? My dear, Leonard is not a marrying man.

GRAHAM:   Well, no — he could have married you after George died.

TINA:   And he didn't — did he?

GRAHAM:   No. No, he didn't. Is he coming in tonight?

TINA:   He might drop round.

GRAHAM:   I thought you said we were going to be alone.

TINA:   I can't have — Julie and Fritz are coming, to collect the rest of Julie's things.

GRAHAM:   And Leonard 'might drop round.'

TINA:   In case he does, darling — had you better just put on a suit?

GRAHAM:   What, dress up — for Leonard?

TINA:   And the children — just back from their honeymoon! *Not* very respectful — in that tatty old dressing–gown.

GRAHAM:   Go upstairs and change?

TINA:   Darling, go *on!*

GRAHAM:   I never can find things, when Bunny's not here.

TINA:   Look in the wardrobe, Graham.

*Graham, who knows perfectly well that she is engineering him out of the room so as to ring up Leonard, takes a malicious delight in irritating her.*

GRAHAM:   (*at the door*) In the wardrobe? What is? Tina, I can't for the life of me remember what it is I'm going to do.

TINA: Your suit, Graham.

GRAHAM: I'm sorry, Tina, I know I must drive you crazy. I just can't ...

TINA: You were going to put on a suit — because of the children.

GRAHAM: Was I? It had utterly gone. Well, I'll go — before I forget again.

*Exit Graham. The door does not entirely close: his feet are heard going up the stairs; they stop — not over obviously — before he gets to the top of the stairs.*

*Tina rushes to the telephone.*

TINA: Leo? You must come round ... Yes, something's happened. ... No, I can't leave Graham, Bunny's not here. ... Yes, all right, and listen — we must give him a Morphon again, I've got to talk to you. ... Yes, but they'll be going. ... No, it's *not* dangerous, not in the least — it just makes him sleepy, he clears off to bed and then we can talk ... But Leo, he never suspects anything, why should he this time? ... Yes it is, it's terrifying, you *must* come: oh, don't be silly, how can I tell you on the telephone? Now, listen, Leo; I've used up what I had, bring some more and, listen — leave it on top of the things in your bag and leave your bag — unlocked — on the chair just inside the drawing room door. All right? And Leo — bring — don't just bring one phial, bring a lot of it. ... Nothing. ... No, nothing definite. ... Look, Leo, it's life and death, just do what I say, bring a lot of the stuff ...

*The door quietly opens. Enter Graham, still in his dressing gown.*

TINA: Oh, Graham! You made me jump.

GRAHAM: I've got my slippers on. That's why you didn't hear me.

TINA: I was just — ringing the children.

GRAHAM: Oh — that's what I was going to do! Change because of the children. I thought they were coming round?

TINA: So they are.

GRAHAM: Then why were you ringing?

TINA: Oh, I — suddenly wondered if it *was* tonight.

GRAHAM: Isn't that the Jag, now, coming up the hill?

*Enter Bunny into the sitting room, letting the door close. She is all lumping joy at seeing her dear Auntie Tina again, tripping over her metaphorical hockey stick as she advances to embrace her.*

BUNNY:     Hello, Auntie! Have you been all right ...
TINA:      Bunny, *mind!* Mind my makeup!
BUNNY:     Did the milkman come? I clean forgot to tell him to. There! —
           red roses!

*She unwraps a paper cone of rather droopy flowers; already a petal or two is loose.*

TINA:      Oh, Bun — for me?
BUNNY:     Fritz gave me a pound, fancy a pound, for helping Julie for two
           days. Here, they can fit in here ...

*She adds the flowers to a vase of roses also already past their prime.*

BUNNY:     (*continued*) He seems to be terribly rich, Tina, their *things!*

*Enter Julie and Fritz.*

JULIE:     Hallo, Mama.
FRITZ:     Bonsoir — bonsoir, ma *belle* belle–mere!
TINA:      Hallo, my pets.
JULIE:     We got you a lemon ice, just for a treat.
FRITZ:     Top shelf of the 'fridge, Bunny.
TINA:      Ugh! I've got that feeling that all this has happened before.
           Bunny arriving with flowers, you two putting ice–cream in the
           'fridge, Leonard coming round later ...
BUNNY:     Coming here? Tonight?
TINA:      Bunny objecting.
BUNNY:     Well — just when they've come back ... I'll go and start, Julie.

*Exit Bunny, sulkily.*

*Enter Graham, crossing with her. He now wears a lounge suit.*

GRAHAM:    Hallo, Bunny–rabbit! (*To the others*) What's the matter with
           her? ...

*Tina makes a gesture of bored irritation with Bunny's nonsense.*

FRITZ:     Hallo, sir.
JULIE:     Hallo, darling.

GRAHAM:     Hallo! Hallo! Hallo, my darling dovey — (*kissing her*) my
            darling dovey of a dear young married lady ...
JULIE:      Your darling what?
GRAHAM:     You don't know your Sairey Gamp. Well, Fritzie?
FRITZ:      You seem very well, sir?
GRAHAM:     I'm fine, I'm fine; only I get these clouds. How about a drink?
JULIE:      We mustn't start boozing. We've got at least two car loads.
TINA:       Two car loads?
JULIE:      May as well get it over ...

*Graham goes to the drinks table.*

TINA:       (*Not wanting the drinking to start till she has a chance to drug
            Graham's drink*) Wait till Leonard comes.
GRAHAM:     Oh, he *is* coming? I thought you only said he might?
TINA:       I said he might, and he might. I now say, wait a few minutes,
            this isn't a pub.
GRAHAM:     A pub, my dear?
TINA:       This isn't a pub that we've got to serve drinks the moment a
            customer demands it.
JULIE:      If I'm the customer referred to, I'm demanding nothing. I'm
            going up to pack.
FRITZ:      You'll call me, Julie, if you want things carried?
JULIE:      Yes, o.k., darling, I'll call you.

*Exit Julie.*

GRAHAM:     If Leonard's really coming round, I'd better go up and change.
TINA:       Change? What for?
GRAHAM:     I thought you told me to?
TINA:       But Graham — you've done it, you've changed, look at
            yourself, you've got a suit on.
GRAHAM:     Oh, lord — so I have.
TINA:       Graham — now we've got Fritz to ourselves, darling, you said
            there was something you wanted to tell him ...

*The doorbell rings.*

TINA:       (*continued*) That'll be Leonard.
FRITZ:      I'll go.

*Exit Fritz to hall: as he opens the door Julie's voice calls.*

JULIE:      Fritz!
FRITZ:      I come, darling. One moment.

*The door swings behind him. Graham pulls Tina over to him and gives her a quick, very sexy kiss, one hand rumpling her hair. (He is doing this for the malicious pleasure of putting one over on Leonard and hoping Leonard will observe the ruffled hair. Tina meanwhile is intent upon forcing him to mention his suicidal intentions).*

TINA:      Graham, don't. Graham, don't be naughty. Look, darling — tell Fritz and Leonard about it now, about you meaning to kill yourself.

*Fritz at the door, mock–butlering.*

FRITZ:      Dr. Burge.

*Exit Fritz to hall and stairs.*

*Leonard enters wearing a light overcoat and light gloves of a distinctive colour, carrying his medical bag in his left hand, and his hat in his right. He is not, in fact, carrying a glass with poison in it, concealed by his hat: but it should be so arranged that the audience could not say that he had not done this. He places his medical bag on a chair, with a tiny conspiratorial glance at Tina; puts the hat down on the drinks table, close to a large photograph — which could have concealed the glass — and throws his coat and gloves on top of the bag.*

LEO:      Hallo — you didn't mind my dropping round?
GRAHAM:      No, no indeed — pleasant surprise.
TINA:      More and more I get this feeling of 'I have been here before.' Bunny and flowers, the kids and ice cream, Fritz and Julie going off as Leonard arrives ...
LEO:      Leonard finding you with your hair rumpled.
TINA:      But — yes — it did happen. There *was* an evening like this: long ago in the winter. But they weren't red roses ...
GRAHAM:      No. That was another time. Red roses that changed into carnations. The day you mean — was the day you decided to have me operated on.
TINA:      I don't think we decided —
GRAHAM:      Didn't you, Tina? I think you did. Because of the sherry — in the spotted cat glass: it wasn't Dubonnet — remember?

*An uneasy silence. The sound of something bumping down the stairs. Julie, still looking upwards, backs into the room.*

JULIE:      We're taking the desk, Mother. (*Oh, sorry, Dr. Burge — Good evening*) It *is* mine.

TINA:       The regency desk?

JULIE:      It is mine.  Daddy always said it was — it belonged to his mother.

TINA:       Well then, of course you must have it.  It's the best thing in the house.

JULIE:      It's not a question of best or not — it's mine.

TINA:       All right, if you say so, Julie.

JULIE:      But Daddy always said ...

TINA:       All right, all right, for goodness sake — take the wretched desk.  Graham, go and help them, that'll ruin it, bumping it down like that.  Go on, Julie, look after it if you're so keen on the thing.

*Exit Julie, miserable but determined.*

*Tina is in a vile temper:  she loathes to part with anything — but her real object is to manoeuver them out of the room so that she can get the Morphon from Leonard's bag.*

*Enter Bunny.*

BUNNY:      Oh! — Julie's gone.  We've got the desk stuck at the turn —

TINA:       Graham, for God's sake go and cope with it. (*To Bunny*) Go on, go on ...

GRAHAM:     All right, my dear; we're going. (*As he passes the chair where the bag and coat and gloves are*) What's this here for?

LEO:        It's my coat —

GRAHAM:     I'll put it in the hall for you.

*He picks up the coat and gloves; Bunny is closely following him and she takes them from him, tucking the gloves into the pockets of the coat. Graham picks up the bag and the hat and they go out together. The door closes behind them but does not actually click to. Tina and Leonard talk in hurried whispers.*

TINA:       Oh, God!  Why on earth did you let him —?

LEO:        Couldn't you have stopped him —?

TINA:       *Now* what?  I'd manoeuvered them out of the room ...

LEO:        Never mind — I've got some here.

*Leo produces a tiny glass phial, containing a clear liquid, like water.*

TINA:       Oh, thank goodness. (*Holding out her hand for it*)
LEO:        I'll put it in. Ask me to do the Dubonnet.
TINA:       No, I don't trust you. Give it to me.
LEO:        You may still be able to get some from the hall. It gives us a
            double chance. Only, tip me the wink if you do — we don't
            want him getting two doses.
TINA:       How much did you bring?
LEO:        I got a new box, but ...
TINA:       Leo — listen. He's been talking of suicide.

*Leonard sees immediately the plan rapidly formed in Tina's mind.*

LEO:        Suicide? No, Tina — no!
TINA:       I'll make him tell Fritz. They'll just think that he —
LEO:        No, Tina. I won't do it.
TINA:       The stuff in your bag. Your bag unlocked. *He* took it out to
            the hall. Such a chance! — he's played right into our hands,
            we may never get a chance again. The children, here,
            witnesses, everything.
LEO:        I won't do it, I won't agree to it.
TINA:       Then I'll do it.
LEO:        If you do — I'll expose you. As God's my judge, Tina — if you
            do this, I'll give you away, I'll shout if from the rooftops —
TINA:       And get yourself hanged?
LEO:        All right — and get myself hanged. And you too. But I won't
            go on with any more of this.
TINA:       Hush, quiet, don't lose your head.
LEO:        Haven't we done enough to him — poor, blundering fool,
            drooling through life like a moth–eaten dancing bear? I won't
            go on any more.
TINA:       Your poor blundering fool has seen the significance of the
            spotted cat.
LEO:        Oh, no, Tina — you've cried wolf too often: I don't believe it.
TINA:       It's true, Leo.
LEO:        I don't believe it.
TINA:       Oh, God! — Leo, it's true, this time it's true. I told you lies
            before, I exaggerated, to try and make you do something, get
            on with it — but this time I swear, I swear it's true.
LEO:        It's true?
TINA:       The leo–pard, my dear. 'Such a funny word, one says leo–nine
            and leo–pold, so why not leo–pard?' And of course —

|        | Leo–nard? |
|--------|-----------|
| LEO:   | I don't believe it. |
| TINA:  | Look at tonight's crossword. And quite a conspiracy, he thinks, among the poets, the pied leopard and the speckled leopard and the freckled leopard — but never the spotted leopard. An odd phrase, anyway, 'the spotted leopard' — whatever does it remind him of? |
| LEO:   | He actually said that? |
| TINA:  | It seemed to ring a bell — that was it. 'A funny phrase — it seems to ring a bell.' |
| LEO:   | Well, let it ring. He knows about the Spotted Cat. |
| TINA:  | He has never before associated the Spotted Cat with *you*. |
| LEO:   | Yes, but … The whole thing really adds up to nothing. |
| TINA:  | The whole thing adds up to his having *seen* it, Leo. What we always dreaded. He's suddenly looked at it from a new angle … |
| LEO:   | I don't believe he's seen it. |
| TINA:  | He's seen half of it. I deflected his mind, but he's seen the first half of it. It's a matter of time. |
| LEO:   | He'll forget. He forgets everything. |
| TINA:  | He has forgotten — for the moment. Leo — quick! Make up your mind! Our chance is here, it may never come again … |
| LEO:   | No, Tina. |
| TINA:  | Make an excuse, get the stuff from your bag — the kids will think he must have taken it while they were busy with the desk. |
| LEO:   | I won't do it. |
| TINA:  | Who'll suspect *you*? |
| LEO:   | Two of your husbands — not one but two — die off opportunely from a dose of barbiturate: kindly supplied by me. Whereupon I settle down to console the widow. |
| TINA:  | But it all fits in. He knows about the stuff from defending me in court — he *would* choose something he knows about … |
| LEO:   | No, Tina, no. |
| TINA:  | If you don't, I will. |
| LEO:   | You're mad. You're mad. |
| TINA:  | I'm not mad — I'm frightened. |
| LEO:   | No — you're not mad, Tina. And you're not frightened, either. You're bored. Bored and fed up with this life, with having no money — |
| TINA:  | Money, money! — all you think of is money. Money is what it means — help in the house, a few clothes, decent cosmetics … |
| LEO:   | Ah! Here we have it! |

TINA:     Yes, all right, Leo — here you have it! A woman like me — working like a slavey in this house, dirtying my hands, ruining my skin with cheap paints and powders, wasting my life away, getting older, losing my looks — tied to this driveling buffoon, day after day, day after day; and you doing nothing to get me out of it!

LEO:     I daren't do anything. Not yet.

TINA:     You must. I can't stand it any longer. All this pretending ...

LEO:     What can we *do*?

TINA:     If you'd gone to London when you said —

LEO:     I'll be going in the Autumn.

TINA:     But we could begin now, laying the trail for divorce —

LEO:     We can't yet. One breath of something between you and me ...

TINA:     But this is why we started the whole thing.

LEO:     God knows exactly what we thought we'd get out of it. Whatever it was, it doesn't seem to have worked.

TINA:     Yes, it has worked. The chance was there — and we took it. We've muddled his mind, we've fuddled up his memory, and now out of it, a direct result of it, comes this suicide thing. It's our chance again, it'll solve everything ...

LEO:     I won't do it. I won't allow it.

TINA:     You're not going to try and back out now, Leo? You can't do that, you know, you're in it too deep. And I won't let you. It's not only you who can shout things from the housetops.

LEO:     'And get us both hanged?'

TINA:     I needn't shout all that much. *I've* got nothing to lose, my dear. But you ...

LEO:     You are not by any charming chance threatening me with the General Medical Council?

TINA:     I'm only saying that we can't go on like this. (*She sees she has now gone too far and turns on the tape of her charm again*) Oh, darling! The General Medical Council! What have we come to?

LEO:     God knows what we've come to. But we are not going to murder Graham.

TINA:     All right. Give him the single dose, and we can talk it over.

LEO:     And you can talk *me* over. No, Tina. We are not even going to talk things over tonight.

TINA:     I swear I won't try to persuade you ...

LEO:     Graham will get no sleeping drug while that new box of Morphon is in the house.

TINA:     What are you afraid of? The others will be in and out.

LEO:            Your 'witnesses.' No thank you. Not tonight. And after tonight, there'll be no lethal doses of anything in this house.

*There are sounds outside that the others are returning.*

TINA:           Leo! Give me the phial.
LEO:            No.

*He evades her, but she makes a pounce and thrusts her hand into his pocket where he has replaced the phial. As the others are entering, he is powerless to continue resistance.*

*Enter Fritz, Julie, Bunny.*

TINA:           Well — did you manage it?
FRITZ:          Splendid. It is like a stout lady, tied up on to the luggage rack wrapped round with a fat eiderdown, needing only a hat with roses —
TINA:           An eiderdown? Whose eiderdown?
BUNNY:          Only mine, Tina. The old one off my bed.
TINA:           How do you mean — *your* eiderdown?
BUNNY:          Well, the one off my bed. I didn't thin ...
TINA:           My dear Bunny — why stop at an eiderdown? Why not tear down the drawing room curtains and wrap the departing furniture in those ...
JULIE:          Oh, skip it, Mama. We'll buy you a new eiderdown and be done with it. Don't fuss, Bunny. Come and have a drink — you deserve one.
TINA:           I'm sure you all deserve one ... (*the implication is that they have carted out half the furniture in the house*)
FRITZ:          We brought along some sherry for Mr. Frere.
TINA:           Where is he, anyway?
JULIE:          He said he had to change.
TINA:           Oh, my God!
JULIE:          He seems very ... odd, tonight.
TINA:           Yes, very odd, worse than ever: and terribly depressed, Julie. Fritz, while he's not here, I wanted to tell you ...

*But Leonard is not going to have the path to a false suicide prepared. He cuts across, with a faintly triumphant look at Tina — which will later be repeated.*

LEO:            Have you a lot more to collect — oh, sorry, Tina, I interrupted — have you a lot more to collect, Julie? Can you do it all tonight?

JULIE:      If there's not an objection to every single object.

TINA:       I suppose I may be fond of my possessions?

JULIE:      These happen to be my possessions.

FRITZ:      Julie — now, Julie darling! I go now and get the sherry, eh?

*Enter Graham. He looks vague and foolish. He is carrying Leonard's hat in his right hand: under one arm is an evening paper, probably the local one brought in by Leonard; and he is wearing Leonard's light overcoat and driving gloves. They are all standing round the drinks table. Tina has his glass — the spotted cat glass — in her hand. She has just filled it with a tot of gin. (Having surreptitiously added a single dose of Morphon) — the audience need not see this happen, it is sufficient that it could have been done; but it is no secret from them that it has been done.)*

TINA:       (*exasperated*) Oh, Graham!

*Graham goes over to the drinks table. He puts the hat down, much where Leonard put his earlier; there is a large photograph or something else there, behind which it would be possible to conceal a glass. Graham in fact has carried in, under his hat, a spotted cat glass, about one–fifth filled with the colourless Morphon; once again, the audience need not — really should not — see this, but could be satisfied that it happened.*

GRAHAM:     You told me to put some more clothes on, my dear.

LEO:        But they're my clothes, old boy.

TINA:       He knows that. He's trying to be funny.

*Graham picks up the hat (leaving the glass concealed behind the picture or other object) and slamming it on his head, goes into an act — embarrassingly funny — dancing and singing.*

GRAHAM:     (*singing*) Poor Old Graham
            Can't even be funny,
            So no one pays to be defended by him in court
            and he hasn't any money!

*Julie and Bunny clap their hands and try to laugh.*

GRAHAM:     Encore! Encore! Success! Success!
            (*singing*) Clever Old Graham —
            Congratulate him on it!
            He's got a drop of gin

Now give him some Du–bonnet.

*He has shuffled over to the drinks table and now tries to take the glass to pass it between Tina and Leonard, who is dispensing Dubonnet. Tina irritably eludes his hand; and passes the glass direct to Leonard.*

GRAHAM:      The Queen is not amused! (*He suddenly appears to remember that he has his hat on*) Oh — pardon my Du–bonnet!

*He removes his hat and is then encumbered with the hat in one hand, the evening paper in the other. He chucks the evening paper across to a chair or the sofa; but it hits, or is in danger of hitting, the vase of red roses. Leonard puts down the glass with its tot of gin, which he has had in his hand only a moment, and rushes over to save the toppling glass vase; it may be that in his clumsy dash he actually overturns the vase. At any rate, it falls and breaks, or is trodden on or kicked.*

*The others stand looking on in exasperation: Bunny and Julie from the other side of the room, not having been near the drinks table, hurry forward and start cleaning up the mess, sweeping up the broken glass. Tina comes forward with the* Times *which has been lying on the sofa, and the roses, now hopelessly battered, are rolled up with the broken glass in the paper and stowed into a metal waste paper basket. None of this need be specifically observed by the audience, but could have happened.*

*Graham has remained, looking on and oafishly laughing, by the table. In fact he has — unobserved by the audience — been able to switch the glass from behind the picture, with the spotted cat glass just filled by Tina.*

*Over all this:*

TINA:        Oh, damn you, Graham — a good glass vase.
GRAHAM:      Sorry. Sorry!
BUNNY:       Come, I'll take the things ...
GRAHAM:      Things — what things?
LEO:         *My* things.
GRAHAM:      Your —? Good lord — this is your coat, Leonard. Why ...?
JULIE:       You were doing us a comic turn. Let Bun take them now.

*Bunny takes off the coat, he hands her the gloves, she puts them into a side pocket of the coat as she did earlier in the evening, and once more takes them out into the hall, with the hat.*

*They gather round the table, except for Julie. Graham has not left it since he threw the newspaper.*

FRITZ:          The sherry, darling?
JULIE:          I'll get it.

*Exit Julie.*

TINA:           You're not drinking sherry, Fritz?
FRITZ:          No, no always my dear gin and Dubonnet ...

*Graham passes across the spotted cat glass prepared for himself.*

GRAHAM:         Here you are then, Fritz.
TINA:           That's *your* glass, Graham.

*Leonard here see his chance to avenge himself a little on Tina by passing the drugged glass to Fritz. He insists, with some secret humour and a repetition of the triumphant glance with which he prevented her from preparing the way for Graham's suicide by talking to Fritz. He takes it from Graham's — apparently hesitant — hand and passes it on to Fritz.*

LEO:            Well — let Fritz have it this time.
TINA:           Leonard! It's Graham's glass.
LEO:            Graham won't mind — will you, Graham? Help yourself to
                Dubonnet, Fritz.
GRAHAM:         Yes, you have it, Fritzie.
TINA:           Fritz, no! Give it to Graham.
FRITZ:          Oh, dear — I have now put in Dubonnet.
LEONARD:        You stick to it, Fritz. After all — guests first!
TINA:           Graham — you know you hate that glass being used by anyone
                else.
GRAHAM:         Oh, nonsense — guests first, someone, drink up, Fritzie,
                compliment to you my dear boy; must compliment Fritzie,
                Tina after all, without Fritzie, I wouldn't be the man I am
                today ...

*He boisterously forces up Fritzie's arm and Fritz drinks. He is too well–mannered to comment on the taste of the drink – which in fact is Dubonnet and Morphon, but he does give a glance at the bottle, as though to say, what on earth brand is this?*

*Over his head and Graham's, Tina glares angrily at Leonard, who triumphantly smiles back.*

*Enter Julie, carrying a bottle of sherry in wrapping.*

*The others are meanwhile supplied with drinks. Graham, Fritz and Leo are grouped apart from Tina after Julie re–enters: there is a desultory conversation about Fritz's car, which may or need not be used.*

| | |
|---|---|
| GRAHAM: | How's the car? |
| FRITZ: | Oh, this car! A marvel! |
| LEO: | You haven't seen it since he painted it? |
| GRAHAM: | I hear it's bright yellow? |
| FRITZ: | A pale sandy colour with brown markings — enfin: a Jaguar … |

*Meanwhile:*

| | |
|---|---|
| JULIE: | There you are, Step. From the bride and bridegroom, with love. |
| TINA: | Quite the little Lady Bountiful! |
| JULIE: | We can't mop up his drink every time we come. |
| TINA: | Are you proposing to come so often? |
| JULIE: | I suppose we shall come and see you! |
| TINA: | Oh, I see. I thought you meant for more furniture removals. |
| JULIE: | I have taken exactly — one — small — desk. |
| TINA: | The one thing of any real value your father left me. |
| JULIE: | He didn't leave it to you, he left it to me. |
| FRITZ: | Julie! |
| JULIE: | You stay out of this Fritz. |
| FRITZ: | Then do not shout, please, at your mother. |
| JULIE: | My mother! You're very solicitous all of a sudden about my mother. |
| FRITZ: | I hope I — and you too, Julie — have respect for your mother. |
| JULIE: | Respect! You! You say yourself, she's the most insincere … |
| FRITZ: | Julie! |
| TINA: | Now, Julie, don't get into one of your tempers. |
| JULIE: | Oh, shut up, the whole lot of you. Nag, nag, nag, ever since I came here … |
| FRITZ: | Julie — Julie! Madam, I apologize … |
| JULIE: | 'Madam I apologize …' You're just as insincere as she is, 'Madam, I apologize …' |
| LEO: | Julie, Julie! |
| JULIE: | You shut up, it's no damn business of yours. |
| FRITZ: | Julie — you are speaking to Dr. Burge. |

JULIE:      Well, tell him to mind his own business!

FRITZ:      Dr. Burge, I beg you, excuse her, she is so ...

JULIE:      (*out of control*) Yes, yes, 'Dr. Burge, I beg you ...' Suck up to him, butter him up, he's another of them, 'Mrs. Frere, *ma belle belle–mere*'; 'Dr. Burge my hero' — that's not what you say about them at home, *is* it, at home you say they're as good as murderers, at home you say it was him that killed my father.

*Enter Bunny, looking scared at the uproar.*

BUNNY:      Oh, my goodness — Julie!

JULIE:      Come on, Bunny, let's pack and get out of this beastly house.

*Exit Julie and Bunny.*

*Fritz, meanwhile, is finding the effect of the drug and makes only an uncertain attempt to follow Julie.*

FRITZ:      Sir, Dr. Burge, you do not think ...

LEO:        No, no — I know Julie's tempers: she goes up like a rocket!

FRITZ:      But, sir, I am so sorry ... Madam, I am so sorry ... A moment, I shall speak with Julie ...

LEO:        (*putting a hand on his arm, so that he sits down on the sofa*) Leave her alone — she'll get over it.

TINA:       Oh, dear — what a storm in a teacup!

GRAHAM:     Are you all right, Fritz?

FRITZ:      I feel rather ... I should go to Julie.

TINA:       Leave her alone, she snaps out of it.

FRITZ:      But to say such things! Of course I did not say what she suggests. You understand: how Julie has repeated this, is all wrong.

LEO:        My dear boy, don't worry: you're free to say things in private to your wife.

TINA:       Such as — that you killed her father?

FRITZ:      Of course I did not —

LEO:        No, no. And after all — it's true in a way. I was careless — why shouldn't he say so to Julie?

GRAHAM:     Are you all right, old boy? He looks a bit odd.

FRITZ:      Yes, I feel — strange. My head swims round ...

GRAHAM:     You need another drink.

FRITZ:      No, no, no drink, thank you. I wonder — is there something wrong with me? Since that other drink ... I seem ... I feel ... (*He yawns violently*) I am tired.

TINA:       Yes — you're tired. Put your feet up and have a little snooze.
FRITZ:      Julie ... Ought to ... Where's Julie ...?
TINA:       (*laughing in spite of her annoyance with Leonard*) He's gone
            to sleep!
LEO:        (*to Tina*) So we can't have our little discussion after all!
GRAHAM:     Discussion?

*There has been an overlaying sound of things being bumped downstairs.*

TINA:       Nothing, Graham. See if she's all right.
GRAHAM:     (*at the door*) All right, Julie?
JULIE:      (*coldly, from the hall*) Yes, thank you.
GRAHAM:     Poor old Fritzie's gone to sleep.

*Julie appears in the doorway.*

JULIE:      Gone to *sleep*?
GRAHAM:     Let him have his sleep out. He'll be better.
JULIE:      He needn't disturb himself on my account.
GRAHAM:     I'll give you a hand.
JULIE:      I've finished. I'll take the car home and Bunny can help me.
GRAHAM:     What about Fritz?
JULIE:      He can find his own way home — or stay here, for all I care.
            Well, I'm going. Dr. Burge — I'm sorry I was rude to you; but
            you shouldn't have interfered. Goodnight.
TINA:       You can't manage all that heavy stuff, Julie.
JULIE:      There's no more heavy stuff, don't worry. I'm going to take the
            desk because it's mine ...
TINA:       Oh, darling!
JULIE:      (*continued*) ... and my father wanted me to have it. I've taken
            nothing else except my clothes; and I wouldn't take *them*, but
            you'd say I was laying claim to storage space. Good *night*. In
            fact, good*bye*.

*She flounces out. Fritz makes one last attempt to rouse himself but flops back
on the sofa: there is the sound of a car outside, driven off with an impatient
grinding of gears and over–rapid acceleration.*

TINA:       Oh, dear — that child's temper! One word, and off she goes
            like a sitting pheasant. Poor Leonard — you always seem to
            come in for our stormiest evenings.
GRAHAM:     Penalty of being *ami de la maison*.
LEO:        I prefer to say — privilege.

GRAHAM:      Oh, very smooth, dear boy, very smooth.  On that you must
             stay for dinner.
TINA:        Yes, do, Leonard.
LEO:         I mustn't be a nuisance.
GRAHAM:      You won't be a nuisance.
TINA:        We can rustle up some eggs.
LEO:         I make a smashing omelette.
GRAHAM:      Good idea!  You go off with Tina and make us an omelette.  Is
             Julie staying?
TINA:        Julie has just this moment flounced out of the house.
GRAHAM:      Has she?  Fritzie's still here.
LEO:         He's a bit off.  He wants to have a snig.
TINA:        So you stay and look after him, Graham, while we get the
             dinner?
GRAHAM:      I could help with the omelette.
TINA:        No, no, darling, you stay and look after Fritz.  M'm?  You'll
             look after Fritz?
GRAHAM:      Oh, yes, of course — poor Fritz.  After all — I owe Fritz a lot,
             Tina: don't I?  Without Fritz I wouldn't be the man I am
             today.  Would I, Tina?  Without Fritz, I wouldn't be the man
             I am today?
TINA:        No, Graham — you wouldn't.  So you look after Fritz?

*Exit Tina and Leo.*  As she passes the sofa she puts out a casual hand and
brushes back Fritz's hair.

TINA:        (*laughing, half–apologetically*) Poor old boy — what a shame!

*Graham waits, sitting quietly beside Fritz, till the sounds of footsteps in the
passage die away and the kitchen door slams.*

GRAHAM:      (*mockingly echoing Tina's words*)  Poor old boy! — what a
             shame!  But there it is — we must pay for our mistakes.  And
             you made a mistake — didn't you Fritzie? — didn't you, you
             poor little dupe, you poor little glib, self–satisfied jackan-
             apes ...? (*He produces from his pocket the spotted cat glass
             wrapped in a handkerchief.*)  The glass, Fritzie?  The spotted
             cat glass — the duplicate glass to make a fool of me, to trick
             me, to make me think I was going out of my mind ... (*He
             crushes it in the handkerchief*) Well — there it goes! —
             smashed into pieces like their filthy plot. (*He moves over to
             the waste paper basket*)  Well, now keep your eyes open, try
             and keep your eyes open, because you're going to see

something if you do: you're going to see the opening moves of the counter–plot. (*He takes out the flowers bundled up in paper which were thrown there when the vase was knocked over*) Ah — red roses! — what a charming touch. And — would you believe it? — the crossword page of *The Times*. What could be more appropriate — the spotted cat glass, hidden away in the heart of a bunch of red roses: wrapped in the crossword page of *The Times*.

It begins you see, Fritz: the counter–plot. You first: but then the first mistake was yours. You wanted to 'liberate' me, didn't you? — you wanted to liberate the dull Graham, the docile Graham, the easy, trusting, manageable — gullible — Graham; but you made a mistake, you see, dear boy, you and your filthy phoney operation, you opened the wrong door and out popped another Graham altogether. A Graham that none of us even knew was there: a Graham that could listen at doors and watch and scheme, a Graham that could plot and plan and bide his time, a Graham that'll make you pay, all pay — pay for your murders and pay for your lusts and pay for your tricks: and pay for your mistakes ...

*At the word 'mistakes' Fritz's hand slides off the sofa and falls to the floor with a little thud in the silence. He moans and begins to breathe stertorously again. Graham stands, silent and motionless watching him: as the curtain falls.*


# Act 3

*Scene: The drawing room.*

*Time: About eleven o'clock the next morning.*

*Inspector Cockrill is at the telephone and has evidently been there for some time. A couple of policemen are tidying up the room after the 'routine investigation'. There is a tray of possible clues and during the interrogation, policemen occasionally drift in and place notes before the Inspector at his table. These form quite a little heap before he is done.*

*Tina and Leonard will be dressed as last night — they will not have been to bed. Graham Frere is in his dressing–gown. Julie and Bunny will have been home and gone to bed and will have dressed hurriedly, in, or not in, the same clothes.*

*Inspector Cockrill is in plain clothes. He has been at the telephone for some time and is plainly exasperated, repeating himself all over again to someone hard of hearing, at the other end.*

COCKRILL:  ... in a coma, sir ...? I say, the boy was *in a coma*, sir. ...? They diagnosed barbiturate poisoning and rang me up. ...? No, not Dr. Burge — the hospital. I say, the *hospital* rang me. (*wearily*) Dr. Burge was here last night, the boy seemed sleepy, they left him on the sofa, they sat over dinner in the other room, so as not to disturb him. When they finally had a look at him, he was in a coma. They —? Yes, sir, that's right, into hospital ...? Yes, I've questioned them, I'm still at it, I've been here since four o'clock this morning ...? About seven ...? *Seven o'clock*, sir ... I say, it was seven — o'clock — this — morning — when — the — boy — *died.*

*Meanwhile, Bunny has entered with a cup of coffee. He motions to her to put it down and remain. On the last words, he slams down the receiver. (It is intended to some as a small shock to the audience that anything so final has happened.)*

COCKRILL:  Oh, sorry child! Chief Commissioner — Deaf as a bl... Deaf as a post.
BUNNY:  Nothing could make it any worse. Poor Julie! ...

*Enter Julie.*

BUNNY:  (*continued*) ... Oh, Julie, come and have some coffee, darling.
JULIE:  I don't want any.
BUNNY:  Oh, please, Julie.
JULIE:  All right, Bun. Thank you.
COCKRILL:  Let yourself go, Julie, don't fight it too hard.
JULIE:  We were angry, we were quarreling, I said beastly things to him ...
BUNNY:  He knew you didn't mean it, Julie, you always fly off the handle. (*Indicating the coffee pot*) Inspector?
COCKRILL:  Thank you, Bunny, I will. (*To the sergeant*) Ask the others to come in.

*Exit Sergeant Troot.*

JULIE:      Inspector — couldn't I go home now?
COCKRILL:  Very soon, Julie.
JULIE:      Surely you've asked me everything?
COCKRILL:  You want to find out what happened.
JULIE:      He's dead — that's all.
COCKRILL:  But why?  What went wrong?  Was there an accident?  Who
            was responsible?

*Enter Leonard and Graham.*

COCKRILL:  (*continued*)  I'm just saying to Julie — it's up to us all — the
            police and you too — to find out —
GRAHAM:    We've told you all we know.  Oh, thank you, Bunny.
LEO:        God knows what can have happened.

(*It will be appreciated that Leonard and Tina are genuinely horrified and
bewildered by what has happened.  They know or think they know, that Fritz
had one small dose of Morphon put into his glass by Tina.  Leo is secretly
terrified that Tina tried to give Graham a larger dose: though they have had
lots of time to consult, and Tina must have denied this.*)

COCKRILL:  We hoped he'd be able to help us.  But now — We must start
            all over again.  He took this overdose.  We know more or less
            when.  But where did he get it?
LEO:        He was a doctor.
JULIE:      And why?  Why take sleeping stuff at that hour of the
            evening?
COCKRILL:  He had no headache?
LEO:        He wouldn't take it for a headache.
JULIE:      And anyway, he had no headache.
COCKRILL:  Unless the quarrel brought one on.

*Enter Tina.*

(*Tina, knowing herself innocent, is still terrified lest the small dose she put
into Graham's glass — which was passed on to Fritz — must in some way
have contributed to his death.  She sees at once the possibilities in mention of
a quarrel.*)

JULIE:      The quarrel?
TINA:       Oh, darling!  Oh, my poor child!
JULIE:      What on earth do you mean, Mother?
TINA:       *We* know your temper, darling, but poor Fritzie ... Of course,

you *meant* nothing ...

JULIE:     Are you suggesting ...? What utter rot! Fritz, kill himself, because ... Cockie, it's utterly untrue. Dr. Burge — you know Fritz ...

LEO:       Of course, Julie, Fritz didn't kill himself.

TINA:      (*significantly*) It would explain a great deal, Leonard.

LEO:       It's not going to be explained this way.

JULIE:     Where could he get the stuff, anyway?

COCKRILL:  As Dr. Burge has said — he was a doctor.

JULIE:     He didn't go about with lethal doses of Morphon.

COCKRILL:  Dr. Burge does.

LEO:       I happened to have a new box of it.

COCKRILL:  And that box is still intact?

LEO:       I told you, I checked the minute we found he was ill.

COCKRILL:  You immediately checked your stock of Morphon?

LEO:       The symptoms were fishy — coma, cyanosis ...

COCKRILL:  But the box of phials is intact?

LEO:       Yes. Thank God!

COCKRILL:  'Thank God'?

LEO:       I'd have felt awful if —

COCKRILL:  You left your bag in the hall?

LEO:       Yes.

COCKRILL:  Unlocked?

LEO:       I mislaid the key. (*Improvising*) That's why I didn't leave it in the car.

BUNNY:     But the key was in the lock.

LEO:       Yes, I know, stupid of me, I didn't notice it.

COCKRILL:  (*to Bunny*) How do *you* know that?

BUNNY:     I saw it when I took out his coat and gloves and things.

COCKRILL:  And the Morphon was in the bag? At the top of the bag?

LEO:       Yes. But it's intact.

COCKRILL:  You bought this new box last night?

LEO:       Yes. On my — (*He breaks off; safer not to put it like that*) At about six o'clock.

COCKRILL:  On your way here? You were going to say?

LEO:       As it happened.

COCKRILL:  Where do you deal for your drugs?

LEO:       I get it at Stock and Halfords.

COCKRILL:  Don't you deal at Weatherby's?

LEO:       Yes, usually.

COCKRILL:  That's what I thought: most doctors do. But you got it at Stock and Halfords? That's *not* on your way here?

LEO:       I came that way last night.

COCKRILL:   I see.  Do you usually get this stuff in liquid form?
LEO:            I've been trying it.  Graham was having it in liquid form.
COCKRILL:   Oh?  You didn't tell me that before?
LEO:            There hasn't been time for everything.
COCKRILL:   *He's* been taking it?  In phials?  Is there any left?
TINA:          No.  None.  Really.
LEO:            You see — that's why I went out of my way to get some last
                   night.  Mrs. Frere rang me up: didn't you, Tina?
TINA:          Yes.  So you see there *was* none.
GRAHAM:     Oh, that's who you were ringing up?  You said it was Fritz and
                   Julie.
TINA:          I just didn't want to upset you —
COCKRILL:   (*to the sergeant*)  Let's see this box again.
TINA:          — I mean, talking about your health.

*Troot hands over the medical bag.  Cockrill removes a tall, white cardboard
box.*

COCKRILL:   You sleep badly, Mr. Frere?
TINA:          Yes, he does ...
GRAHAM:     Do I?  Sometimes after dinner, I can't keep awake!
TINA:          Well, I mean, off and on you do ...

*The box has half a dozen clear glass phials standing upright, their tapered
ends sticking up in the air.  Cockrill seems satisfied and is closing the box
when he notices something on it — this, in fact, is a stain on the white
cardboard.  He re–opens the box and takes out a phial: and then, each of the
phials, and looks at the bottom tip.*

LEO:            Oh, my God!
COCKRILL:   All empty.  Put back with the broken ends point–down.
LEO:            I never thought of lifting them out to see ...
COCKRILL:   No, it's very deceptive.  You didn't notice this stain?
LEO:            A stain?
COCKRILL:   The dye of the label has a run — a purple–ish dye.  When the
                   phials were emptied, some of the fluid ran down on to this
                   label.  There's a trace here inside, on the cotton wool.
LEO:            I was worried.  I was in a hurry.
TINA:          All of them empty?
JULIE:         Then that's what he died of.
BUNNY:        But who on earth would do such a thing?
COCKRILL:   Well — anyway now we know where we are.  And anyone
                   passing through the hall could have taken it.  Now: symptoms

came on —?
LEO:          About seven.
COCKRILL:  Last thing he took was this drink at half past six. Mrs. Frere ...
TINA:         *I* poured out the gin.

*Tina moves to the table. Cockrill reaches for an old glass from somewhere and hands it to her.*

COCKRILL:  Just walk through what happened — all of you. (*To Julie*) You and Bunny were over there?
JULIE:        Yes.
COCKRILL:  All right. Mrs. Frere ...
TINA:         I handed the glass to Leonard ...
GRAHAM:    I chucked the newspaper over to the chair and it hit the vase ...
COCKRILL:  (*to the rest, holding up action*) Just a minute.
GRAHAM:    ... and Leonard rushed over to save it.
COCKRILL:  All right. Run through that. Time it exactly.
TINA:         I handed the glass ...
LEONARD:   I took it ...
GRAHAM:    I chucked the paper ...
COCKRILL:  (*to Leonard*) All right, run for it ... Now: you all moved forward ...?

*They converge upon the vase–table, only Graham remaining near the drinks table; and stand about awkwardly.*

TINA:         We messed about with the vase and flowers. Then we went back ...
COCKRILL:  (*to Julie*) You and Bunny stayed where you were?
BUNNY:       Yes, we did but — I don't see why you ask.
JULIE:        (*worn out and irritable*) We couldn't have murdered Fritz, Bunny: that's all.
COCKRILL:  (*to the others*) Now — time it again.
LEO:          I picked up the glass and gave it to Fritz —
GRAHAM:    You passed it to me and *I* passed it on to Fritz.
COCKRILL:  How long did you hold it?
GRAHAM:    Oh, it was ... (*They pass the glass between them*) Like this.
COCKRILL:  Your memory's woken up, Mr. Frere?
GRAHAM:    It has fits and starts. Doesn't it, Tina?
LEO:          (*Watching Julie with compassion*) Julie ... Can't she go home now, Inspector? She and Bunny are out of it.
COCKRILL:  Not yet. But sit down, Julie.

TINA:         *(to Leo)* You seem very anxious to narrow down suspicion.
LEO:          Neither she nor Bunny touched his drink.  And he only had that *one*.
TINA:         Unless ... He didn't have a drink at home before he came ...?
COCKRILL:     No.  That's all accounted for.
JULIE:        What are you suggesting, Mother?  That *I* killed him?
TINA:         Darling, of course not ...
JULIE:        Because if so — may I point out that the only person who poured a drink for Fritz — was you.
COCKRILL:     Are you accusing your mother, Julie?
JULIE:        My mother has accused Fritz of suicide; now she accuses me of killing him.  I just wonder why?
TINA:         Julie —!
COCKRILL:     All right, all right.  Mrs. Frere — this glass has now been washed up?
TINA:         I *told* you.
COCKRILL:     You did, yes.  At one o'clock in the morning, he was taken to the hospital: and you then settled down to clear out the room and wash up the glasses.
TINA:         I knew people would be coming ...
COCKRILL:     They would be coming to examine the room; and especially the glasses.
TINA:         I just never thought —
COCKRILL:     Is that the only spotted cat glass in the house?

*For the first time, Tina remembers the duplicate glass still hidden, (long forgotten since the night when it was used to trick Graham) in the book case. (The audience have seen Graham find it there, more recently.) She exchanges a terrified glance with Leonard.  If the existence of the glass should become known, then Graham will understand the trick that was played on him: and putting two and two together — for he still has moments of appalling clarity — understand it all.*

TINA:         I think so.  Yes — only one.
GRAHAM:       Well, Tina — of course only one.  Part of a set, Inspector, with cats on them.  I got them at Bland's.

*Cockrill scribbles on a piece of paper and hands it to his sergeant.  Troot exits and can be seen in the hall, telephoning.  When he comes back, he places yet another piece of paper on the heap before the Inspector.*

COCKRILL:     I haven't seen any others.
GRAHAM:       We broke them.  Tina dropped the tray.  I only just saved my

spotted cat. *You* remember the spotted cat, Inspector?

COCKRILL: I do.

GRAHAM: *I* believe you dropped them on purpose, Tina, to get rid of my poor old spotted cat.

TINA: I thought this nonsense was in rather bad taste.

COCKRILL: No other such glass came into the house?

GRAHAM: Good lord, no. I mean ... You remember that time, Tina, when I thought I'd been drinking sherry ... If there'd been two glasses here then ... You remember the time, Tina?

TINA: Yes, yes, I remember.

GRAHAM: You remember I thought there *were* two glasses, then. And if there *had* been — it would meant you were playing some sort of trick on me ...

TINA: No, no, Graham, a trick — of course we weren't.

GRAHAM: We? Oh, yes — Leonard was here that night! I never thought of its being you and Leonard — playing this trick on me.

LEO: There was no trick, Graham, of course we weren't.

GRAHAM: I hope not. God help you, Tina — if it *was* a trick!

TINA: It wasn't a trick; there was no second glass — was there, Bunny, you'd know, wouldn't you?

BUNNY: Yes, of course, I do all the washing up.

COCKRILL: Only this one glass in the house?

BUNNY: Yes, only one: with the spotted cat.

COCKRILL: All right. Now, Mrs. Frere — let us get this matter straight.

TINA: Goodness me, Cockie — how fierce you sound!

COCKRILL: I am here on official business ...

TINA: I don't see why we need all be pompous about it.

JULIE: Your well–known charm is having no effect, Mother. You'd better keep quiet and listen for a change.

TINA: Very well — come on Inspector, with you 'official business'. Let's hear the speech for the prosecution.

GRAHAM: The case for the prosecution, my dear Tina, is beginning to look like no laughing matter. Is it, Inspector?

COCKRILL: No, sir — it is not.

*Graham begins, casually and lightly at first, to speak as though he were prosecuting counsel presenting a case in court: but seems soon to forget that he is not in fact in court.*

GRAHAM: The case for the prosecution, you see, is that poor little Fritzie — well, it was murder. The case for the prosecution, members of the jury, is that — the accused —

TINA: Accused! Me? Of murdering Fritzie?

*Graham's cutting in covers the word 'Fritz'.*

GRAHAM:     — that the accused had caused to be brought into this house,
            a lethal dose of poison. That she had access to this poison.
            That she had opportunity to administer this poison ...
TINA:       Cockie! Don't let him —
GRAHAM:     ... That later she washed the glass in which this poison was
            administered. The case for the prosecution is that besides the
            victim, she is the only person who put anything whatsoever
            into that fatal glass —
TINA:       (*terrified*) Why should I want to kill Fritz, why should I ...?
GRAHAM:     (*over–riding her, apparently miles away in a court of law*) The
            case for the prosecution is ... that here was a woman, still
            young and attractive, tied to a man sick in body and mind —
TINA:       (*In her turn, over–riding his words*) — I actually tried to
            *prevent* Fritz from getting that glass!

*A pause.*

GRAHAM:     She actually tried to prevent Fritz from getting that glass.
            *Why?*
TINA:       Why?
GRAHAM:     Why? Because she knew the glass was poisoned. After all —
            she poured it out — for *me*.
LEO:        Inspector — this is monstrous, he's building it all up out of
            nothing, all out of nonsense ...
GRAHAM:     Good lord! What's happening ...? I thought I was ... in court.
            What, Leonard?
LEO:        I say it's all utter nonsense ...
GRAHAM:     Oh, yes, nonsense, of course. And don't worry, Tina — not a
            shred of proof.
COCKRILL:   Do you think not?
LEO:        Proof? — what proof?
COCKRILL:   You yourself provide it. You say — and Mrs. Frere says —
            that there was no Morphon in this house: until you brought
            these six phials ...
LEO:        The six phials are intact.

*Cockrill signals to his sergeant who places before him the tray of broken glass
etc. The tray remains on the table.*

COCKRILL:   Yes. So what is this?
TINA:       What is —?

COCKRILL: This is broken glass from the vase. But this? — and this?

TINA: (*terrified*) The dustbin ...?

COCKRILL: Thrown away in the dustbin: the crushed up pieces of a single glass phial.

TINA: (*In utter terror*) Leo!

LEO: It's all right Tina ... we can explain it, we've only to tell the truth.

TINA: No! — No! — Leo ...

LEO: We've done nothing wrong ...

COCKRILL: Let us hear what you *have* done.

LEO: Tina, it's nothing, we can explain. Inspector ... Inspector, look — you know Graham Frere, you know he hasn't been well, we've done all we possibly could ...

GRAHAM: Oh yes! — all they possibly could.

LEO: ... but he hasn't made much improvement ...

GRAHAM: No, that's true, Leonard: not much improvement — not like you hoped, not at all ...

LEO: So — we thought we should have a discussion.

TINA: (*catching on: from now on she and Leonard are improvising*) Yes, because Fritz and Julie were coming ...

LEO: Fritz was his doctor.

TINA: You see, they'd been away, we hadn't seen them, so you see we had to talk to them and we couldn't talk in front of Graham ...

LEO: So we — we had this idea. Just one dose of the stuff in his drink: absolutely harmless. He'd just get sleepy a bit earlier in the evening: and clear off to bed.

GRAHAM: Good lord, old boy! — then all those other times ...

TINA: There've been no other times.

GRAHAM: When I've got sleepy early and gone up to bed ...

LEO: There've been no other times, Graham. Fritz and Julie were away ...

GRAHAM: Oh, I see. I thought you meant that you and Tina were always playing this — trick.

COCKRILL: Did Fritz Hart and Julie know of this arrangement?

JULIE: Of course not. As if we'd agree to such a thing!

TINA: I rang up to ask — I *told* you I was ringing them, Graham; but they'd just left.

GRAHAM: Oh, you did ring them? You said just now that that wasn't true; that you were ringing Leonard.

TINA: Well, I — I couldn't explain —

COCKRILL: Mrs. Frere — you put this — this single dose — in that glass of gin?

TINA: Yes, I did, I admit it.

COCKRILL:    And later, you crushed up the phial and threw it away?

TINA:    Only one phial, Cockie: you've only found one phial?

COCKRILL:    And washed up the glass? 'Not thinking'?

TINA:    Fritz dying like that — it would be so hard to explain ...

COCKRILL:    Much harder now to explain.

TINA:    What do you mean? You don't mean ...? You're mad, you're crazy, of course I didn't. Of course I wouldn't kill Fritz, of course I didn't mean to — kill anyone else, it's all some ghastly muddle, accident, suicide, God knows what ...

COCKRILL:    It was neither accident nor suicide.

TINA:    But why me? Why *me?*

COCKRILL:    *You* destroyed evidence, *you* washed the glass, you admit having put something into the glass: and nobody touched it but you.

TINA:    One does, I only had one dose ...

COCKRILL:    (*holding up the box*) The six phials in this box are empty: and *you* asked Dr. Burge to bring them into this house.

TINA:    Yes, but not to — (*she breaks off: for in fact she did want the phials for the very purpose of which she is now accused*)

GRAHAM:    Nemesis is overtaking you, Tina.

COCKRILL:    (*sharply*) What did you say?

GRAHAM:    I said you're never mistaking Tina for a murderer?

TINA:    (*terrified*) Of course I'm not a murderer, of course not, of course not; Leonard, for God's sake say something, get me out of this net, this net ...

GRAHAM:    Hush, Tina, hush, you're giving yourself — (*he is obviously going to say 'giving yourself away'*) You're creating a wrong impression. I *told* you — there is no proof.

COCKRILL:    No proof?

GRAHAM:    She wasn't the only person to handle the glass. *I* handled thte glass.

LEO:    So did I.

COCKRILL:    Only for a brief moment: you showed me, just now.

LEO:    I handled it twice: once when I took it from Tina, once when I handed it to Fritz.

COCKRILL:    For a brief moment, both times. Mr. Frere — you threw the folded paper —?

GRAHAM:    Very childish: but I get rather childish nowadays.

COCKRILL:    Not quite the desired result?

*Graham looks round with a sort of fatuous smile of enquiry at Leo and Tina, a sort of, 'Well — I wonder?' look.*

COCKRILL: Anyway — this created a diversion?

GRAHAM: Yes, Leonard rushed forward to save the vase, Tina rushed after him ...

COCKRILL: Leaving the glass unattended on the table?

TINA: Yes, that's true, that's true! So anyone, Cockie, anyone could have slipped something into the glass, it needn't be me, anyone could have done it ...

GRAHAM: The only thing is, Tina — no one did. *I* didn't leave the table; I was standing here all the time and no one put anything into the glass, no one came near the table ... I say, Inspector — could I go upstairs a minute?

COCKRILL: What for?

GRAHAM: I wish to go to the huh–ha.

COCKRILL: Oh, well, yes, sorry — all right.

*The moment he has gone — deliberately leaving the field clear — (the audience may even see his shadow hanging about in the hall, complacently listening to them saying just what he knew they would say) Leonard comes eagerly forward.*

LEO: Inspector — thank God he's gone out! — Look here, Inspector the whole thing solves itself ...

TINA: Graham! (*She and Leo are of course in fact innocent or murder and really believe that this is the solution. Their relief is enormous*)

LEO: It's true — he never left the table. He threw the paper — my God! — of course he threw the paper to create a diversion ...

COCKRILL: Why should *he* want to murder the boy?

LEO: (*working it out*) I don't think ... I don't think he did want to murder Fritz. I think ... He's been talking about suicide ...

TINA: Suicide! Yes. We told you, Julie, we told you ...

JULIE: You were always telling us things about him.

BUNNY: But this *would* explain.

LEO: And he's so — odd, he's so unstable, you couldn't be surprised if he went an odd way about it. Putting back the phials, doing it — or intending to do it — in front of us all.

TINA: He took Leonard's bag out from here (*indicating the chair*) to the hall. He'd see the stuff then. He took it then. He brings it in here, he diverts our attention, he tips it into his glass —

LEO: Into *his* glass, Inspector!

TINA: His special glass, the glass with the spotted cat. He put the stuff into that glass — *for himself.*

*A pause.*

COCKRILL: And then he calmly handed it to Dr. Hart?
LEO:       No, no, *I* made Fritz have it.
COCKRILL: You? Why *should* you?
LEO:       Well I did, I — I sort of forced it ... Graham was doing what I told him to.
COCKRILL: And you told him to give this doctored drink to Fritz Hart? Why?
LEO:       Well, because ... It was sort of — a joke, Inspector: against Mrs. Frere.
TINA:      Leo!

*(Tina does not know what Leonard can be going to say. The references here are, of course, to Tina's attempt to give a 'suicidal' dose to Graham — or, as a second resource, a small dose, to enable her to persuade Leo into the 'suicide' plan. Leo did in fact trick Tina, and took a mocking satisfaction in deflecting the drugged glass from Graham to Fritz. Obviously he can't explain the real reason to Cockrill.)*

LEO:       I was really against this drugging business. I didn't like to say this before but now ... It was Tina who insisted on it. That's true, Tina, isn't it?
TINA:      It is?
LEO:       *(dangerously)* Did I or did I not try to persuade you not to give Graham — a shot of Morphon? (Significantly) I mean, of course — this single dose.
TINA:      *(sullen, but afraid in face of this plain threat)* Yes.
LEO:       But you insisted?
TINA:      Yes.
LEO:       So you see — to pay her out, Inspector, I — well, I diverted the glass to Fritz. You saw what was happening, Tina, you understood?
TINA:      Oh, yes — I understood.
LEO:       I couldn't do Fritzie any harm. Of course I didn't know — God help me, I didn't know — that there was poison in the glass.
COCKRILL: But Mr. Frere did know? And — knowing it contained a lethal dose of Morphon — allowed it to be given to Fritz Hart?
LEO:       You see! He's not responsible for his actions! It's quite consistent — isn't it, Tina?
TINA:      You've seen him yourself — one moment quite rational, the next like a child.
JULIE:     But he's never unkind. He'd never be so cruel.

| | |
|---|---|
| TINA: | You're thinking of the old days, Julie.  He's changed since then. |
| JULIE: | He'd never have let Fritz die. |
| TINA: | *(feverishly anxious to prove what in fact she believes to have been the truth: for Tina, too, is innocent of this murder)* Oh, Julie, don't argue.  Don't you see, this explains everything ...? |
| JULIE: | As long as *you* don't suffer — |
| TINA: | Nobody will suffer.  This way, nobody suffers.  Graham won't — he can't be held responsible, he's mad, he didn't *mean* to murder Fritz ... |
| JULIE: | I don't believe it — I won't believe it.  He wouldn't have let Fritz suffer. |
| LEO: | Fritz didn't suffer, Julie.  Graham knew that:  he knew he wouldn't.  It was what he'd prepared for himself, to go to sleep, to cease — 'to cease upon the midnight —' |

*Enter Graham.  He recites: moving slowly past the Inspector, and stopping at last by his table, looking down at the tray of exhibits, including the broken glass.*

| | |
|---|---|
| GRAHAM: | 'To cease upon the midnight, with no pain.' <br> ... For 'many a time <br> I have been half in love with easeful death, <br> Called him soft names in many a mused rhyme						To <br> take into the air my quiet breath; <br> Now, more than ever seems it rich to die, <br> To cease upon the midnight with no pain ...' <br> Hallo you've broken my Spotted Cat glass after all! |
| COCKRILL: | *(sharply)* What do you mean? |
| GRAHAM: | *(pointing to the tray)* Here's a bit of it.  That's the broken vase ... But here's his tail — and here's his spotty shirt–front. |
| COCKRILL: | Sergeant? |
| TROOT: | The glass is here, sir.  Er — there's a note, sir. |

*He sorts out the pieces of written information which have been piling up before him as policemen came in and out ... Cockrill takes a long, long time to read it.*

| | |
|---|---|
| COCKRILL: | Dr. Burge. |
| LEO: | Who — me? |
| COCKRILL: | On November the fifteenth last, you bought, at Messrs. Bland's in the High Street, a cocktail set, price thirty shillings. Six glasses, each with a different cat painted on it: a black |

cat, a white cat, a ginger cat, a tabby cat, a striped cat — a spotted cat.

GRAHAM: My God! — then there *were two glasses.*

TINA: Graham! — no!

GRAHAM: But that was the day —

COCKRILL: Dr. Burge — please?

LEO: (*slowly*) You think that — last night — I brought a second glass in here ...?

TINA: (*terrified: watching Graham*) It wasn't here before.

COCKRILL: You asked the assistant to say nothing?

LEO: It was a present.

COCKRILL: Who for?

LEO: I didn't give it in the end.

COCKRILL: Where is the set now?

LEO: At home — put away.

COCKRILL: Intact?

LEO: I suppose so.

COCKRILL: I mean — is the glass with the spotted cat intact?

LEO: (*giving up*) The glass with the spotted cat — as you very well know — is there in front of you: broken, on that tray. How it got there, I don't know.

TINA: Leonard!

GRAHAM: November the fifteenth, Tina, that was the day —

TINA: There was no second glass here.

LEO: Tina — you don't see where this is leading. There *was* a second glass! Inspector, it's all quite simple, Tina, it's perfectly simple. Graham — well, he was so over–emotional those days, he set such store by this glass, we were afraid what would happen if it got broken. So I — got a replace-ment ...

GRAHAM: I see. Then that day, Tina, the day that finally convinced me I was going mad ...?

TINA: You've got it all wrong, Leonard: if you got a replacement you never brought it round here. Did he, Bunny?

BUNNY: *I* never saw it.

COCKRILL: If you brought one glass — why not the whole set?

LEO: They'd got a set.

COCKRILL: But the others were broken.

LEO: I didn't know that.

BUNNY: Ooh, Dr. Burge, you did. You were here when it happened.

LEO: Tina — you know what he's suggesting. If I brought a glass here last night it could only be for one reason.

GRAHAM: (*with terrible malice*) If you tricked me, Tina —!

TINA:   We only had one glass.
LEO:    That's a lie.
COCKRILL: Why should Mrs. Frere be lying?
TINA:   You see, Leonard — you can't answer that.
LEO:    No, I can't answer it. Whatever I say ... And so — if you won't
      stand by me ... Very well, Tina. There was no glass. Not till
      tonight. Tonight, I brought a second glass here — all prepared
      with a lethal dose of Morphon. I — let's see — I hid the glass
      here, behind this frame. I went through all that nonsense
      with the other glass, but that wasn't the glass that was used.
      That glass I broke when the vase was broken, I threw the
      pieces away with the pieces of the vase: and then I came back
      and handed the prepared glass to Graham.  That's the
      Inspector's case, Tina: look at him — he doesn't deny it. And
      unless you admit that there was a second glass in this house,
      all the time — hidden away in that bookcase over there ...
TINA:   I can't, Leo, you know I can't.
LEO:    My God — the bookcase!

*He brushes past Tina and across her protest and makes for the bookcase. He has forgotten for the moment that the glass is no longer there, but has appeared, mysteriously, broken, on the tray. Tina flies to the bookcase when she sees what he is doing: also forgetting. She flings open the bookcase doors. They stand silent, staring in.*

COCKRILL: The glass is here — broken, on this tray.
LEO:    (*defeated*) Yes. I'd forgotten. But ... The mark from the glass
      is here, a ring in the dust where it's stood all this time ...

*Tina swoops forward and with one sweep of her arm, obliterates the dust.*

TINA:   There's no mark there.
COCKRILL: Let me see.
LEO:    Don't bother. There's no mark there; not now. All right, Tina.
      You won't save me. So now — try and save yourself. Because
      — if I wanted to kill Graham — what motive could I possibly
      have? Only that we're lovers, you and I, and we've been lovers
      for years ...
TINA:   Leo — are you mad? It's a lie, Inspector, Graham, it's a lie ...
LEO:    If I'm going to be accused, you're in it with me, Tina. Come on
      over here and stand with your lover in the dock; we're accused
      of murder, dear, and not for the first time and this time
      there'll be no talking our way out ...

*He seizes her by the arm and, she resisting, pulls her over to stand beside him, as though there were in the dock together. The grouping of the room shifts and resolves itself into the grouping at a murder trial: Cockrill in the position of the judge, with attendant clerks and ushers, the police officers: Leo and Tina, apart, in the 'dock'; Graham again apart, soon to get up and cross-examine, as counsel for her defence; Julie and Bunny in the position of jury — possibly in such relation to the audience as to make the audience form part of an enormous jury too.*

TINA: Leo, for God's sake, what do you think you're doing?

COCKRILL: Are you making a statement, Dr. Burge, to this effect?

LEO: A statement! — yes, yes, I'm making a statement, come along, Sergeant, take it all down, scribble–scribble–scribble and it–may–be–used–as–evidence, I know, I know ...

TINA: Cockie, whatever he says, don't believe him: you were there at the trial, *you* know what happened ...

LEO: Oh, yes, he knows what happened, he's always known ... And now it's happening all over again, Inspector. A new method this time: drive the victim to threaten suicide, switch the glasses and — another sad incident in the life of this femme fatale! And another happy ending! — the poor little widow finds consolation with nice, rich, increasingly successful number three!

TINA: It isn't true.

LEO: Then tell them what *is* true. You can't you see. You're afraid of Graham if you do: and I don't know, Tina, that I blame you, because if — Graham — knew ... So you're letting me go to the gallows. But I won't go alone. And the day they hang you, Tina, they can hang me too, because I'll be glad to die, I'll be glad to die ...

*Graham once again takes up the lines from Keats. He rises and, grasping the lapels of his dressing gown as though he were in a barrister's gown, addresses the 'court'.*

GRAHAM: To die! 'To cease upon the midnight with no pain, While thou are pouring forth thy soul abroad ...' Well, well, Leonard — you certainly have ben pouring forth thy soul abroad ...

COCKRILL: Dr. Burge —

GRAHAM: Just a moment, Cockie. Just a moment, M'Lord! My Lord, you have heard, the jury has heard —

COCKRILL: Mr. Frere — please!

GRAHAM: My Lord — I represent the female prisoner at the bar ...

COCKRILL:    You want to defend Mrs. Frere? (*He thinks it over; after all this madman has been a clever barrister, something may emerge from his ravings*) Well — all right, Mr. Frere: go ahead.

GRAHAM:    (*instructing him in the judicial manner*) You may proceed with cross–examination, Mr. Frere.

COCKRILL:    All right, all right, proceed with cross–examination.

GRAHAM:    If your Lordship pleases. (*swooping suddenly upon Leo*) You and she were lovers — is that what you say?

LEO:    Yes.

GRAHAM:    And conspired together to murder the first husband?

LEO:    Yes.

GRAHAM:    Did you, in fact, marry?

LEO:    No; we did not.

GRAHAM:    No. Because, curiously enough — she married someone else! Whereupon — you conspired together to murder her second husband?

LEO:    Yes.

GRAHAM:    And did her second husband die?

LEO:    No. Her second husband didn't die.

GRAHAM:    This woman was so much in love with you that she killed her first husband to be with you — and then married someone else; and was still so much in love with you that she conspired with you to murder her second husband — and her second husband is very much alive?

*Leo is silent.*

GRAHAM:    (*continued*) It is your case that the glass was here all along?

LEO:    Yes.

GRAHAM:    And you ask her to bear you out?

LEO:    Yes, I do.

GRAHAM:    And if she won't bear you out — you threaten her, don't you? You'll tell this story and you'll drag her down with you?

LEO:    Yes — I'll drag her down.

GRAHAM:    But if, even now, she will bear you out — then you'll retract the story? And you *can* retract it — it's designed to be retracted, it's designed to be torn to shreds if necessary. And that's what I'm doing now — tearing it to shreds. This woman was never your lover at all.

*Leo is silent.*

| | |
|---|---|
| GRAHAM: | (*continued*)  You met her when her first husband was ill? |
| LEO: | Yes. |
| GRAHAM: | And fell in love with her? |
| LEO: | Yes. |
| GRAHAM: | There was an 'accident', a 'mix–up' — and the husband died? You had to go away on a job. But you come back —? |
| LEO: | I had to come back. My work was here. |
| GRAHAM: | — and sought her out again? |
| LEO: | We couldn't help meeting. |
| GRAHAM: | Her husband was doing well, everything was fine, she was happily married ...? |
| LEO: | (*ironically*)  Oh, of course — a perfect idyll! |
| GRAHAM: | But from the time of your return — there is a falling off? More drinks in the house now that the new boon–companion is always popping in and out! And a sort of — aura — grows up about the husband:  poor old Graham, tippling a bit again, going downhill again, getting depressed, getting morose, getting suicidal ... And one November day you go out and — in secrecy — you buy this glass? |
| LEO: | If I did — it was no secret from *her*. |
| GRAHAM: | And I say that it was a secret from her.  I say that she knew nothing, I say that this whole family has accepted you — |
| LEO: | (*ironically again*) What, poor little Tina — never even guessed my secret passion?? — |
| BUNNY: | There, Auntie Tina, I warned you. |
| LEO: | Never even dreamed that I was — for her dear sake — a murderer! |
| GRAHAM: | Twice over. |
| LEO: | A murderer — twice over!  Well, my dear Graham, we've listened.  The jury, as you yourself would say, have listened with exemplary patience to this rigmarole of yours and very clever and ingenious it has been.  But if your intention is to save Tina and leave me to be convicted of murder — I'm sorry, but that won't wash.  Because without my admission there's no proof whatsoever of murder number one: and as for murder number two — the intended victim is still alive. |
| GRAHAM: | Who says the intended victim is still alive? |

*A long pause.*

| | |
|---|---|
| LEO: | Fritz? |
| GRAHAM: | Ah — 'Fritz!?'  Fritz was there when George died — wasn't he, Leonard.  And Fritz was no bumbling, trusting Englishman, |

Fritz would see quick enough through your 'secret passion'. It was none of his business, you were useful to Fritz, Fritz would keep his trap shut ... Until — all of a sudden, it *is* his business, Fritz marries into the family and God knows what he'll blurt out to this young wife of his! And how right you are! — because last night ... What were the last words she spoke to him, what did she say to him, here in this room last night? — 'That's not what you say at home,' she said. 'At home you say — *that Dr. Burge killed my father*'.

JULIE:     (*weeping*) I didn't mean ... He only meant ...

GRAHAM:    (*storming on*) An accident! For God's sake — an accident! As if you couldn't have stopped him getting it — one sweep of your arm, and the glass goes over. (*To Cockrill*) He switched his plans, that's all. I was the first — oh, yes! — he would kill me as he'd killed her first husband, and get me out of the way. But he bided his time, and while he bided, this other peril blew up. So — the duplicate glass is all ready — to be used one day: against *me*. And last night he buys the poison, he transfers it to the duplicate glass, he brings it in here — remember him coming in here last night, carrying his hat in his hand? — he puts in down — here ...

*Graham comes in as Leonard came in last night: carrying in his hand an imaginary hat, with concealed beneath it, an imaginary glass; he places the glass on the table, behind the photograph frame.*

... And when the time comes, the glass is forced on the boy; he told you so himself, he told you he 'forced' the glass on Fritz like a conjurer forcing a card. An 'accident' — and the boy gets the glass — which I am then said to have prepared for myself, poor bloody, muddle–headed, would–be suicide. So that's the end of *us*: two of us with one glass — the in– convenient husband and a young man who knows too much.

*Tina has been standing all this time beside Leonard. Now Graham goes across and takes her by the arm and drags her away, leaving Leonard to stand by himself.*

COCKRILL: Well, Dr. Burge?

LEO:      All nonsense. Fritz knew nothing. He only meant that I had been careless over George.

COCKRILL: You bought this glass — secretly. You bought this drug — secretly. Dr. Burge — it will be best if I ask you no more

|  |  |
|---|---|
|  | questions at this stage ... |
| LEO: | You can ask me all the questions you like. Did I transfer the drug to a second glass, last night in my car? No, I did not. Did I then smuggle it in here? No, I did not. I did not, I tell you: I never so much as opened the box. |

*Cockrill holds out a hand to the sergeant who gives him Leo's driving gloves.*

|  |  |
|---|---|
| COCKRILL: | Dr. Burge — are these your gloves? |
| LEO: | My —? Yes — they're my gloves. |
| COCKRILL: | There were in the pocket of your overcoat. |
| LEO: | (*indicating Bunny*) She put them there when she took my things out to the hall last night. |
| COCKRILL: | You haven't worn them since? |
| LEO: | I haven't been out of the house. Fritz was taken ill ... |
| COCKRILL: | So you won't have observed that the fingers are slightly stained? |
| LEO: | Stained? Then — my God! — |
| COCKRILL: | Stained with the dye from this box — a purple–ish dye. |
| LEO: | But that means ...? |
| COCKRILL: | Who ever emptied the poison from these phials — wore these gloves. |

*A great light comes upon Tina and Leonard: and indeed upon Julie and Bunny.*

|  |  |
|---|---|
| LEO: | (*to Graham*) You! YOU! |
| TINA: | Graham! |

*Graham for the first time is utterly taken aback.*

|  |  |
|---|---|
| GRAHAM: | (*faltering*) I? Why should *I* be wearing your gloves? |
| LEO: | But he did wear my gloves. I haven't had them on since I got here last night. But he had them on ... |
| TINA: | You had them, Graham! My God — you! — you murdered Fritz, it was no accident, you murdered him ... |
| GRAHAM: | Why should I murder Fritz? |
| LEO: | Because you wanted me to hang for it. You devil, you cunning, filthy devil ... *He* wore those gloves last night, Inspector, it was he who emptied those phials, wearing my gloves. He came into this room last night, wearing my coat and my gloves — |
| COCKRILL: | Wearing your coat and gloves? |

TINA:        Yes, Inspector, yes, he did ...
COCKRILL:    Why?
GRAHAM:      Yes — why? Why? Come in here — wearing Leonard's coat?
             Why on earth should I do that? Julie! Julie, you'll bear me
             out —

*Julie starts to speak but stops; he can see that here may lie his salvation.*

GRAHAM:      (*continued*) — why should I come in here wearing Leonard's
             clothes? A charade, eh Tina? — eh, Leonard? — dressing up
             in his clothes, doing a dance, perhaps, ever so funny? Poor
             mad Graham, I suppose, doing a song and dance act, dressed
             up in Leonard's clothes.
LEO:         'Poor mad Graham'! You cunning, crafty, filthy devil ... So
             this was your revenge?
GRAHAM:      Revenge? What had I to avenge? You killed Tina's husband:
             but I married Tina — what had *I* to avenge? You killed Julie's
             father — but he was nothing to me —
LEO:         Julie, you were here, you saw him —
GRAHAM:      ... that's for Julie to avenge.
COCKRILL:    Well, Julie?
GRAHAM:      That's for you, Julie: that's for you to avenge.
COCKRILL:    Julie!
JULIE:       (*deliberately: indicating Graham*) Why should he be wearing
             Dr. Burge's coat and gloves?
TINA:        Julie! You know, you saw him wearing them —
COCKRILL:    This is a matter of life and death, Julie. If Dr. Burge was the
             last to wear those gloves — then he murdered Fritz, he
             murdered your husband.
JULIE:       Yes. I know.
COCKRILL:    Dr. Burge says that Mr. Frere had them last. So does your
             mother say so. And that you saw him.
JULIE:       Why should he wear Dr. Burge's coat and gloves?
TINA:        He's mad, Cockie, he does these childish things ...
JULIE:       You've heard him. Does he strike you as — childish?
COCKRILL:    Julie, you'll be on oath about this some day. Did you or did
             you not see your step–father with these gloves?
JULIE:       No. I did not.
COCKRILL:    You say he did not wear them?
JULIE:       No. He did not.
COCKRILL:    If your mother says he did ...
JULIE:       She's lying.
TINA:        Why should I lie ...?

JULIE:      To save Dr. Burge.

LEO:        Inspector, it's she who's lying, she thinks I killed her father, she's doing this for revenge, Bunny! Bunny, you saw him, here in this room …

GRAHAM:     Well, Bunny? Tina says yes: Julie says no. You have the casting vote.

TINA:       She'll tell the truth, *she* has no axe to grind …

LEO:        You saw him, Bunny, fooling about, it was you … Bunny! — it was you who took the coat from him, you put the gloves in the pocket, you took it out to the hall.

COCKRILL:   (*consulting his notes*) Yes. You said so just now. You said it was then you noticed the key in the lock of his bag.

BUNNY:      Well, yes — I did.

COCKRILL:   You actually took the gloves from Mr. Frere?

BUNNY:      Yes, I did. (*To Graham and Julie*) I can only say what's true.

*Cockrill makes a gesture of 'then that settles it.' Leonard puts his hands to his face sick with relief. Tina rushes across to Bunny and then to Leonard.*

TINA:       Oh, Bunny! — thank God! Thank God! You've saved him. Leo, she's saved you, thank God, Leo, she's saved you …

BUNNY:      (*slowly*) Why do you call him 'Leo', Aunt Tina? You never … (*called him that before*) Aunt Tina — you have a pet name for him — you have a private name for him. All this is true! He's been your — lover all this time! All this is *true!*

COCKRILL:   You're prepared to say later, on your oath, that —?

BUNNY:      (*deliberately*) But of course that was earlier, Inspector. Before the drink was poured out.

COCKRILL:   Before?

BUNNY:      That I took the gloves. That was when Dr. Burge arrived. He put his bag on the chair — there — and his overcoat and gloves. Mr. Frere picked them up. I took them from him — like you said and put them out in the hall.

TINA:       (*urgently*) Bunny — afterwards — Graham was out in the hall. He took the stuff then, he got the stain on the gloves; he came in here with the gloves, you took them from him then …

COCKRILL:   Did you see Mr. Frere with the gloves again?

BUNNY:      No.

COCKRILL:   Not wearing them?

BUNNY:      No.

COCKRILL:   You'll take your oath on this?

BUNNY:      Yes. I'll take my oath.

COCKRILL:   Dr. Burge — if you wouldn't mind …

*Two men close in upon Leo, not however touching him — he is not technically a prisoner, he is being 'asked to go to the police for further questioning'. There he will doubtless be arrested and later charged.*

*While this slight commotion is going on in the background, Graham makes a mocking little bow to Bunny.*

GRAHAM:   *Thank* you, Bun!
BUNNY:   Don't *speak* to me!
GRAHAM:   But ...?
BUNNY:   You're mad. But she isn't mad. And all this time ...

*Bunny breaks down, weeping. Julie puts her arm round her.*

JULIE:   Come along, Bun.

*Exit Bunny and Julie.*

TINA:   Leo! Inspector — you can't take him away like this, he's innocent, of course he never killed Fritz ...
GRAHAM:   You were not so concerned for your lover, Tina, when it meant saving yourself.
TINA:   You! You madman, you murderer! Leo! — don't leave me here, don't leave me here with *him*: Inspector, for God's sake, he's mad, *he* killed Fritz, you can't leave me here alone with him ... Yes — yes, there was a glass here all along, I'll confess it, Leo didn't bring one last night ...

*Cockrill ignores her, steadily continuing with his arrangements for the removal of Leonard.*

TINA:   ... Well, then, accuse me too, take me too, don't leave me here with him, take me too ... Leo, Leo, I'll come with you, I'll die with you ...
COCKRILL:   (*quietly*) Better stay here with your husband, Mrs. Frere. There's nothing else you can do.
LEO:   (*at the door: venomously, and with quite another intonation*) Yes. You stay here with Graham, Tina. There's nothing else you can *do*.

*Exit Leo and Cockrill, with policemen.*

*Tina and Graham are left alone. Tina looks with terror and revulsion at*

*Graham with whom she is now condemned to spend the rest of her life.*

TINA:          He's gone.
GRAHAM:    Yes. And you and I are left.
TINA:          They'll hang him.

*Graham shrugs non–commitally: they may – they may not.*

TINA:          They'll kill him! They'll kill him!
GRAHAM:    Keep your tears for yourself, Tina. They'll kill him — perhaps.
               But at least he'll know when it's coming. Not like you.

*He catches hold of her and puts his hands round her throat as though to strangle her; but immediately releases her and, thrusting her away from him — bursts out laughing.*

# A Checklist of the Cockrill Mysteries by Christianna Brand

## Novels

*Heads You Lose.* New York: Dodd, Mead & Co., 1942; London, The Bodley Head, 1942.

*Green for Danger.* New York: Dodd, Mead & Co., 1944; London, The Bodley Head, 1945.

*The Crooked Wreath.* New York: Dodd, Mead & Co., 1946; London, The Bodley Head, 1947, as *Suddenly at His Residence.*

*Death of Jezebel.* New York: Dodd, Mead & Co., 1948; London, Michael Joseph, 1949.

*Fog of Doubt.* New York: Charles Scribner's Sons, 1953; London, Michael Joseph, 1952, as *London Particular.*

*Tour de Force.* New York: Charles Scribner's Sons, 1955; London, Michael Joseph, 1955.

In 1963, Brand completed a seventh and final novel featuring Cockrill; the drafts are variously entitled *Jape de Chine* and *[The] Chinese Puzzle.* This novel, which has not been published, revolves around Arnold Dixon, a man whose first and second wife die in mysterious circumstances and who is himself murdered during a séance attended by Cockrill and Mr. Cecil, from *Death in High Heels.* On the evening of the first day of his investigation into Dixon's murder, at dinner with his sister Harriet and her husband, Major Dick Bull, Cockrill reflected that "a murder had been committed beneath his very nose, by one of six people in what amounted to a 'sealed room;' and that, in parlance of the young people nowadays, literally and figuratively, he hadn't a clue."

### Short Stories

"After the Event." *Ellery Queen's Mystery Magazine*, January 1958, as "Rabbit out of Hat."

"Blood Brothers." *Ellery Queen's Mystery Magazine*, September 1965.

"The Hornets' Nest." *Ellery Queen's Mystery Magazine*, May 1967, as "Twist for Twist."

"Poison in the Cup." *Ellery Queen's Mystery Magazine*, February 1969.

"The Telephone Call." *Ellery Queen's Mystery Magazine*, January 1973, as "The Last Short Story."

"The Kissing Cousin." *Woman*, 2 June 1973.

"The Rocking Chair." *The Saint Magazine*, August 1984.

"The Man on the Roof." *Ellery Queen's Mystery Magazine*, October 1984.

"Alleybi." This story, published in this volume for the first time, was probably written in the mid–1950s.

NB. Christianna Brand's original titles are used in this collection. While grateful to Fred Dannay who, in *Ellery Queen's Mystery Magazine*, provided a ready market for her short stories, she was incensed by his editorial "twitching hand." In a piece for the Japanese edition of the magazine, published in January 1983, she commented that "he had a compulsion to change the title, sending one quietly mad when one had written the whole thing round the title, only to find it replaced with something really quite pointless."

### Plays

*The Spotted Cat.* Previously unpublished; written in 1954-1955. Brand considered turning it into a novel but abandoned the idea.

### Miscellaneous

"Inspector Cockrill." *The Great Detectives*, ed. Otto Penzler. Boston: Little, Brown, 1978.

## Unfinished fiction

There are two unfinished stories featuring Cockrill. The first is a short story, "Musth," which takes place at a formal dinner in a hotel. Cockrill unravels the complicated truth behind the shooting of one man by another in Mysore, India, some years earlier — " 'I dare say you will claim,' said the gaunt lady in green, who sat on his right, 'that you've never known of a wrongful execution for murder.' She looked at him across her soup spoon with an odd sense of purpose. 'Well, *I* have.' "

The second is *Death on the Day*, a short story — or possibly, novel — on which Brand was working at the time of her death. Cockrill — "near retirement" and now a Chief Superintendent — has been invited to Oopt'il Castle by "his devoted admirer" the Dowager Duchess of Chaffinge to attend The Day, "held on the first Saturday of August, when everyone remotely connected with the family of Dukes of Chaffinge is entitled to come for lunch and tea, and a reunion with their curiously assorted relations." But a glorious afternoon is cut short by the discovery of a body, that of the Countess of Tregaron — "He looked at it closely, looked back again at the Countess with the dreadful orange lipstick streaked across the discoloured face, looked again at the white linen and lace of the tiny pillow. In the centre of a thin line of orange, an inch long or a tiny bit more ... Such a little murder. Such a very quiet, easy little murder. Anyone could have done it. A child could have done it."

Brand also completed the opening and closing 'chapters' of an incomplete and unpublished round–robin detective story, *The Greatest Mystery Round the World*. The story, planned by HRF Keating and Brand, was to have been produced as a recording to be broadcast on commercial radio with each of the chapters read by its author. Other than Brand and Keating, the eventual contributors were Len Deighton, Dick Francis, Patricia Highsmith, Ngaio Marsh and Helen McCloy. Records suggest that all seven completed their contributions but only the parts by Brand, Deighton, Highsmith, Keating and McCloy have survived. Other than Deighton, the authors used their best–known characters in their contribution i.e. Cockrill, Tom Ripley, Inspector Ghote and Dr. Basil Willing respectively.

# The Spotted Cat and Other Mysteries from Inspector Cockrill's Casebook

*The Spotted Cat and Other Mysteries from Inspector Cockrill's Casebook* by Christianna Brand, and edited by Tony Medawar, is set in 10–point Century Schoolbook font and printed on 60 pound natural shade opaque acid–free paper. The cover illustration is by Gail Cross, and the 'Lost Classics' series design is by Deborah Miller. *The Spotted Cat and Other Mysteries from Inspector Cockrill's Casebook* was published in October 2002 by Crippen & Landru, Publishers, Norfolk, Virginia.

# CRIPPEN & LANDRU, PUBLISHERS

P. O. Box 9315

Norfolk, VA 23505

USA

Crippen & Landru publishes first editions of short-story collections by important detective and mystery writers. Most books in the regular series are issued both in trade softcover and in signed, limited clothbound with either a typescript page from the author's files or an additional story in a separate pamphlet. Among the authors whose short-story collections have been published by Crippen & Landru are Doug Allyn, Lawrence Block, P.M. Carlson, Hugh B. Cave, Max Allan Collins, Michael Collins, Brendan DuBois, Susan Dunlap, Kathy Lynn Emerson, Michael Gilbert, Joe Gores, Ed Gorman, Jeremiah Healy, Edward D. Hoch, Wendy Hornsby, Clark Howard, H.R.F. Keating, Michael Z. Lewin, Peter Lovesey, Ross Macdonald, Margaret Maron, Patricia Moyes, Marcia Muller, Bill Pronzini, Ellery Queen, Peter Robinson, Georges Simenon, Raoul Whitfield, Carolyn Wheat, and James Yaffe.

☞This is the best edited, most attractively packaged line of mystery books introduced in this decade. The books are equally valuable to collectors and readers. [*Mystery Scene Magazine*]

☞The specialty publisher with the most star-studded list is Crippen & Landru, which has produced short story collections by some of the biggest names in contemporary crime fiction. [*Ellery Queen's Mystery Magazine*]

Crippen & Landru offers discounts to individuals and institutions who place Standing Order Subscriptions for all of its forthcoming publications, either all the Regular Series or all the Lost Classics or (preferably) both. Collectors can thereby guarantee receiving limited editions, and readers won't miss any favorite stories. Standing Order Subscribers receive a specially commissioned story in a deluxe edition as a gift at the end of the year. Please write or e-mail for more details.

E-mail: Info@CrippenLandru.com

www.crippenlandru.com

# CRIPPEN & LANDRU LOST CLASSICS

Crippen & Landru announces a series of *new* short-story collections by great authors who specialized in traditional mysteries. Each book collects stories from crumbling pages of old pulp, digest, and slick magazines, and most of the stories have been "lost" since their first publication. Each volume is published in cloth and trade softcover.

## THE FOLLOWING BOOKS ARE IN PRINT

Peter Godfrey, *The Newtonian Egg and Other Cases of Rolf le Roux*, introduction by Ronald Godfrey

Craig Rice, *Murder, Mystery and Malone*, edited by Jeffrey A. Marks

Charles B. Child, *The Sleuth of Baghdad: The Inspector Chafik Stories*

Stuart Palmer, *Hildegarde Withers: Uncollected Riddles*, introduction by Mrs. Stuart Palmer

Christianna Brand, *The Spotted Cat and Other Mysteries from the Casebook of Inspector Cockrill*, edited by Tony Medawar

William Campbell Gault, *Marksman and Other Stories*, edited by Bill Pronzini; afterword by Shelley Gault

Gerald Kersh, *Karmesin: The World's Greatest Crook — Or Most Outrageous Liar*, edited by Paul Duncan

C. Daly King, *The Complete Curious Mr. Tarrant*, introduction by Edward D. Hoch

Helen McCloy, *The Pleasant Assassin and Other Cases of Dr. Basil Willing*, introduction by B.S. Pike

William L. DeAndrea, *Murder – All Kinds*, introduction by Jane Haddam

Anthony Berkeley, *The Avenging Chance and Other Mysteries from Roger Sheringham's Casebook*, edited by Tony Medawar and Arthur Robinson

Joseph Commings, *Banner Deadlines: The Impossible Files of Seantor Brooks U. Banner*, edited by Robert Adey; memoir by Edward D. Hoch

Erle Stanley Gardner, *The Danger Zone and Other Stories*, edited by Bill Pronzini

## THE FOLLOWING BOOKS ARE IN PREPARATION

T.S. Stribling, *Dr. Poggioli: Criminologist*, edited by Arthur Vidro

Gladys Mitchell, *Sleuth's Alchemy: Cases of Mrs. Bradley and Others*, edited by Nicholas Fuller.

Margaret Millar, *The Couple Next Door: Collected Short Mysteries*, edited by Tom Nolan

Phillip S. Warne, *Who Was Guilty? Two Dime Novels*, edited by Marlena Bremseth

Rafael Sabatini, *The Evidence of the Sword*, edited by Jesse Knight

Michael Collins, *Slot-Machine Kelly*, introduction by Robert J. Randisi

Max Brand, *Masquerade: Nine Crime Stories*, edited by William F. Nolan

Julian Symons, *Francis Quarles: Detective*, edited by John Cooper; afterword by Kathleen Symons

Lloyd Biggle, Jr., *The Grandfather Rastin Mysteries*. Introduction by Kenneth Biggle

Hugh Pentecost, *The Battles of Jericho*, introduction by S.T. Karnick

Erle Stanley Gardner, *The Casebook of Sidney Zoom*, edited by Bill Pronzini

Mignon G. Eberhart, *The E-String Murder and Other Mysteries*, edited by Rick Cypert and Kirby McCauley

Lost Classics